Jane

Michelle N. Onuorah

Jane
Published by MNO Media, LLC
Printed in the U.S.A.

Printed Edition ISBN-13: 978-0692373262
Printed Edition ISBN-10: 0692373268

Please note there is occasional cursing, mild violence, and unapologetic references to sexuality and spirituality within this work of fiction. Reader discretion is advised.

Formatting by Polgarus Studio.

Scripture is taken from THE HOLY BIBLE, NEW INTERNATIONAL VERSION®, NIV® Copyright © 1973, 1978, 1984, 2011 by Biblica, Inc.® Used by permission. All rights reserved worldwide.

The fictional sermon given in chapter twenty is based on an actual sermon given by Dr. Timothy Keller entitled "Love and Lust." It can be found on the Redeemer Presbyterian Church website at www.redeemer.com.

Other Titles by Michelle N. Onuorah

Remember Me
Type N
Taking Names

Available online.

Jane

PROLOGUE

Morris Heights – Bronx, New York

Jane walked down the cracked, dirt-crusted sidewalk with sure steps and a confident stride. She'd learned early on that it was all about pretending. Pretending you were tough - that people didn't want to mess with you. If she walked tall and acted fearless, people were less likely to bother her. Being bothered could easily end up being dead. She walked quicker than usual this time because she held several conspicuous bags in her hands. She'd made a detour to the convenience store shortly after school. She hoped her surprise would work.

A mixture of relief and dread washed over the 15-year-old when she reached the depressing brick front town house. Like everything else around them, it was old, dirty, and reeked of weed mixed with fermented urine. Jane used her key, quietly entered the building and felt the heaviness settle. She just walked out of one war zone and into another. She played the part like a spy and tried to go by unseen.

She passed the living room and, no surprise, the woman was passed out on the couch, the TV on with molding pizza boxes surrounding her. She listened out for the man. If he found her with the bags, he would ruin the whole thing and probably punish her on top for coming up with it. He didn't appear to be home yet. Probably snorting another row with his supplier down the hall. Another wave of relief washed over Jane. She quickly and quietly hurried up the stairs, down the hall, and into their room.

It was the closest thing to an oasis they had.

"Jane!"

She immediately felt a pair of long, thin arms wrap around her waist. A head full of long, wavy dark hair tucked into her chest as the younger girl squeezed her tight. Jane dropped her bags and quickly returned the hug.

"Hey, little one," she whispered into the girl's rose-scented hair. As far as Jane was concerned, Alexa Channing was the only bright spot in that house. They held onto each other for a few moments, neither saying a word. It was their ritual, something consistent that they used to comfort themselves and each other. A fierce wave of love and loyalty rendered Jane's heart hostage as she looked down at the girl she considered her little sister. Which reminded her...

"I have a surprise for you," she said in a teasing tone.

The girl pulled out of her arms with a gasp. She looked up at Jane with wide hazel eyes that illuminated her already beautiful face.

"For me?"

"You are the birthday girl, aren't you?" Jane teased again. "Now turn around and close your eyes. I have to set it up properly."

Alexa immediately turned around in obedience, bouncing on the balls of her feet with a barely-contained anticipation. Jane crouched down, pulled the miniature single-person cake out of the bag and quickly opened the casing. She stuck twelve candles into the icing, pulled out the lighter and lit them up. She also retrieved the other bag, holding the younger girl's gift. Clearing the floor of other items, Jane walked to the door, turned off the room's light and whispered to Alexa.

"Okay. Now."

The girl slowly turned around and opened her eyes. She gasped again at the sight of the beautifully decorated strawberry shortcake, lit with candles that made the darkened room glow.

"Happy Birthday to you," Jane quietly sang. "Happy Birthday to you. Happy Birthday, dear Alexa. Happy Birthday to you."

Jane watched as her "little sister's" eyes filled with unshed tears. She smiled tremulously before the cake, closed her eyes and made a wish. She blew out the candles and the room filled with its swirling smoke. Jane turned the lights back on and soon found Alexa in her arms again.

"*Thank you, Jane. Thank you so much!*" Alexa whispered emotionally. Jane knew that if she could, the girl would express her joy a lot louder but in the two years since she'd arrived, Alexa had learned not to make noise. To be rarely seen and never heard. It was rule number one in this particular foster home.

"*Anytime, little one.*" Jane quietly replied. "*But I'm not done yet.*"

Alexa frowned in confusion. Her expression quickly turned to delight as Jane pulled the gift from behind her. Alexa squealed before clamping her hand over her mouth. She couldn't see what it was through the thick paper bag of the art supply store but the store logo gave part of the gift away. Jane didn't have enough money to properly wrap it but she knew Alexa didn't care. The girl pulled the multi-colored sketch pencils and sketch pad out of the bag and admired the different options.

"*Thank you!*" she said again, this time clearly captivated by the art supplies in her hands. She looked between the cake and the gift, as if unsure what to delve in first.

"*Food, then art,*" Jane quickly decided. She knew she had to get it cleaned and hidden before the man returned. And the last thing they wanted was another rat infestation from keeping food in their room too long.

Jane brought out a fork and napkin and handed Alexa her cake.

"*Aren't you having any?*" Alexa asked.

"*I can't.*" Jane shook her head, holding her stomach.

Alexa frowned. "*Not even a bite?*"

Jane looked at the cake anxiously. It looked good and smelled wonderful.

"*A bite won't do you over,*" Alexa added. She broke off a small piece with her fork and held it out to Jane. Jane hesitantly took the fork from her and felt the soft, moist strawberry delight practically melt onto her tongue. It was divine. She handed the fork back and smiled at Alexa.

"*Thanks.*"

"*No. Thank you,*" Alexa corrected and went back to scarfing down her cake. Jane watched her and smiled. The smile began to dim the more she reflected on Alexa's age.

Twelve. It was the magic number in this house. And for all the wrong reasons.

While the younger girl devoured her cake while somehow whispering incessantly about her day, her friends, and her gift, she didn't notice Jane's concern. She had no clue that, as much as Jane loved her, she hoped she would leave this house very soon. For the past two years, Jane had managed to protect her. If Alexa made a mistake or happened to be at the wrong place at the wrong time, Jane diverted the punishment, or mitigated it to the best of her ability. Sometimes she'd purposefully piss him off, just so she would distract him from hurting her dear friend. She'd kept her safe outside the house and protected her inside. But if age was a sign of things to come, Jane wasn't sure she could protect Alexa from the coming-of-age gift their foster father had given her when she had turned twelve.

Jane shuddered. Alexa needed to leave.

Alexa finished her cake and Jane immediately disposed of the leftovers at the building dumpster. Grateful she didn't run into a dealer or a pimp, her mood was light while she and Alexa sketched silly portraits of each other for the next two hours. They joked around and managed to pretend that they weren't where they were. That they lived in a normal house with normal people. They even pretended that they were adopted sisters. It was a multi-racial family, through and through with one black daughter, one white daughter, and maybe their parents could be an interracial Asian-Latino couple. In their heads, they were loved, well-cared for, and had no worries. In that moment, they had each other.

CRASH!!!

Both girls jolted awake at the noise. Downstairs, several things fell to the ground with an unmistakable shatter.

"Shit!" the male voice yelled. The tone was surprised but also angry. It was the anger that made Jane's stomach twist in apprehension.

Jane glanced at the clock. It was past eight. She and Alexa must have fallen asleep.

"What was that?" Alexa whispered. Her wide hazel eyes became even wider with fear, the dark tendrils of her long brown hair dangling near her cheeks. She pulled her skinny pale legs up to her chest and hugged herself, half in comfort, half in protection. Sometimes he was like a bear. If they curled up in

fetal positions, the attack wouldn't last as long. He'd get tired or distracted or bored. At least they hoped he would.

They soon heard heavy steps stomp up the staircase, the sound getting louder and louder…closer and closer to their room. Jane frowned. There was no trace of her surprise in the house. Minus the art supplies that they'd carefully stowed away, there was no trace of the cake or candles or lighter she'd brought home. It was all in the dumpster. She glanced at Alexa and noticed a look of understanding cross the girl's face.

"Why is he coming up here?" Jane asked. The girl remained mute, her body trembling in fear.

Jane tried again. "Alexa, why is he coming up here?"

She knew the girl knew but for some reason couldn't speak. Their time was up. The door flew open. He appeared at the threshold: tall, middle-aged, slightly overweight but still overbearing. His wife beater stained with beer and dirt; his eyes glinting with uncontained rage.

He held up a dark green raincoat.

"Whose is this?" The question came out in a quiet, menacing tone and in that moment both girls knew that whoever took the credit would have hell to pay.

He continued in the same eerily quiet tone, "Some dumbass left this on the floor and caused me to trip over the fucking kitchen table. Whose. Is. This?"

Jane didn't have to look at Alexa to know it was hers. And she didn't have to ask her to know the poor girl had merely left it on the coat rack. The same rack that coats often dropped off of for no reason. Jane kept her gaze on the man and quickly responded.

"It's mine." She knew Alexa couldn't handle what he'd have to dish. His dark brown eyes swung to Jane and she could see the slight shift in them: from rage to gladness. It was a sinister gladness because when he was done "punishing" her, he would take his time "comforting" her.

"Come here," he said quietly. Jane glanced at Alexa in time to see her eyes widen even further - this time in horror.

"Wait-"

"Don't," Jane quickly cut her off. If Alexa admitted to it, they would both be punished - one for the offensive jacket, the other for lying. Jane knew it was

too late to go back. She turned to follow the man but not before catching Alexa tearfully mouth the words, "I'm so sorry."

Five Months Later

The back of the hand swung heavy across her cheek.

Hard.

Fast.

She tried to anticipate when the blows would come but sometimes she couldn't. She felt the air escape her lungs as the pain burst through the right side of her face.

"Lousy, good-for-nothing bitch," the man grumbled.

Three more years *she thought to herself.* Three more years and I'm out.

Out to what?

It didn't matter. She tried to convince herself that it didn't matter that she had no job, no savings, and no prospects beyond her exceptional grades. She ignored the reality that she had no parents, no family, and no one to fall back on. In fact, one of the two people she had to her immediate assistance just struck her across the cheek. The other was passed out drunk on the couch. Had Alexa still been there, she would have helped her get some ice. She would have cried with her and reminded her that they would get out. But the girl was already out. She'd found a home and left Jane behind. It was the only comforting thought that came to Jane. Alexa was out and safe. She didn't have to worry if he'd go after her too. She smiled. She didn't have to worry anymore.

"What the hell are you smiling about?" he snapped. The smile immediately slid off her face. But it was too little too late. She stepped back as he stepped forward, mumbling in anger, dark intentions glinting in his eyes. He backed her up against the wall and reached up to her face again. Jane resisted the urge to flinch as his hand landed on her cheek - gentle this time, cupping it, caressing it. He pressed his heavy, sweaty body into hers and grinned menacingly.

"I'll give you something to smile about," he whispered.

She knew that he was far from done.

LUST

CHAPTER ONE

Nine Years Later – Manhattan, New York – University of New York

I hate my life.

The thought came out of nowhere. A random assault that hit her in the middle of the day. She wasn't even brooding over the miseries of life, far too busy actually doing her job. Jane shoved the errant thought aside and strode down the hallway of Burney West. UNY poured a few hundred thousand dollars into the renovation of the English department building. It was sleek, modern, and cool with beige tiled floors, gray counter tops, and clean white walls. Jane could hear the click of her heels as she made her way to room 163, Dr. Geissner's office.

The summer term over, she was now supposed to meet him with regards to some changes for the upcoming fall. The new semester started in less than a week and Jane was eager to get back in gear. She would normally knock on his door and let herself in but right as she was about to raise her fist to the wood, Jane paused. She heard voices inside and decided to wait in one of the seats positioned right beside the door. She could hear most of the conversation but didn't intentionally listen until she heard her name.

"How does Daugherty's file look?" Geissner asked.

"Same as always," a female voice replied. Jane recognized the voice. It belonged to Dr. Sarah Greenlay, one of the university psychiatrists on staff. Jane frowned. Odd that he would schedule her psych eval right before actually meeting with her. Jane leaned forward on her lap and listened intently, eyes fixed on her dark brown ankle boots before her.

"Jane Daugherty – 24 – single. One of the highest performing professors on staff – the youngest, too. In spite of her age and lack of tenure, she scores as one of the most preferred instructors in the department."

"Her…background…hasn't affected her work?"

"Not as far as I can tell. No outbursts, no records of impropriety, not a single disciplinary issue on file - from her or her students. She's clean."

She's clean. What a strange use of words. As if her background somehow made her more prone to unprofessionalism. Jane could feel the surge of resentment rise in her chest at their conversation. She understood the need to assess the staff for their mental stability, especially when responsible for an entire student body. She had willingly granted the department permission to obtain a background check and went through every psychological hoop they made her jump through. She even granted them the optional permission to discuss her evaluation results with her supervisor. But she still didn't like it. She didn't like what she heard, the tactless way they talked about her past as if it was her fault.

So wrapped up in her irritation was she, that Jane barely composed herself in time to see Dr. Greenlay leave the office. The middle-aged blond woman paused in her tracks at the sight of Jane, clearly concerned about what she may have overheard. Jane purposefully guarded her expression and stood to her full height, immediately dwarfing the other woman. Geissner appeared at the door, equally surprised.

"Hello, Jane." he said cautiously. "I hope you weren't waiting too long."

You wish, Jane thought.

"Patience is a virtue, right?"

After an awkward farewell to the therapist, Jane followed the older gentleman into his office. He was a tall man on the thin side with a balding crown but confident air. As he sat down at his desk, Geissner glanced at his calendar and frowned. Clearly he hadn't expected the two appointments to be so close together. His secretary probably did it.

Too little too late.

Geissner clasped his hands in front of him and leaned forward on his desk. Jane leaned back in her seat, her nonchalant demeanor the guise of confidence.

"Well, Jane. I'm not sure how much of our conversation you might have heard but I'll go ahead and tell you the reason for it."

Jane raised her eyebrows in surprise. It was one of the things she liked about Geissner - his honesty. He didn't beat around the bush or pretend something didn't happen when it did. Any other department chair would have pretended they weren't talking about her just moments ago. And even if they didn't pretend, they wouldn't have felt the need or consideration to clue her in on the situation.

Geissner continued, "I asked Sarah Greenlay to do a psyche eval on you not because of your history but because of an opportunity I hope you'll accept."

Jane frowned, not sure if she should be excited or concerned.

"Up until this point, you have only taught introductory English courses for incoming freshmen. President Rachel Schneider will be inaugurated this fall and is determined to usher in a plethora of changes, including the improvement of diversity at UNY. As a part of the university's diversity initiative, we want to open a new course called Race and Ethnicity in American Lit. It's a level 200 course and will be open to students of all majors and all years. Depending on how many students enroll, we may even open it up to auditors or graduate students not taking it for credit. You wouldn't have to worry about the curriculum. We've already developed one subject to your amendment and input."

Race and Ethnicity in American Lit. Wonder why they chose me, Jane thought sarcastically. But when she put her smarmy thought aside, she couldn't deny the trickle of excitement that coursed through her at the sound of the class. UNY was diverse to some degree because of its standing and reputation as one of the finest universities in New York; but it still had much progress to make in its outreach to minority students and its cross-cultural educational opportunities for students in general. At just over 200-

years-old, the majority of its students were still white upper to upper-middle class students from very affluent New York families.

Geissner continued, "You're currently on the tenure track. It would improve your profile to have courses outside of just English 101."

Jane couldn't agree more. It was a small miracle for her to be hired as an assistant professor in the first place. Rarely did entry-level professionals her age land full-time, salaried faculty positions right out of their master's program but Jane had impressed her mentors at UNY so much that they eagerly referred her to their innovative department chair for an undergraduate teaching spot. Geissner saw past her age, focused on her credentials, and gave her a shot teaching courses that would give her the least flak. It appeared his confidence in her ability was confirmed.

The course was much needed, it would look good on her resume if successful, and was bound to be interesting when teaching slightly older students.

"Would you like the course?" Geissner finally asked.

Jane did not hesitate to say yes.

Shortly after the meeting, she packed her own bags and walked briskly out of the building. She smiled and waved at the few people who greeted her, some of them students. But when she reached the subway, swiped her card, and caught her train, the smile disappeared. There was no one to pretend to. And she felt a mixture of relief and grief. She sat in the middle of the silver tube and pulled out her Kindle as the train jerked and swayed. Some days the sound of the grinding metal grated on her nerves. Other days, like today, the sound was soothing.

She took the long ride uptown and made her way to her East Harlem apartment as though on autopilot. She didn't know anyone close by, didn't even know her neighbors' names. And that suited her just fine. She was grateful to have a place of her own in one of the safer parts of the rough city. It was a far cry from her days in the Bronx. She punched the entrance code and walked up two flights of stairs to her landing, reached her door mid-way and turned the key. Her apartment was a small studio, about the same size as the Milstein dorm at UNY. The size surpassed "homey" and bordered on "claustrophobic." But the tiny place, rented to her by a kind elderly Jamaican man, saved her thousands of dollars a month and she was a firm believer in scraping and saving early so she could live like no one else later. This night would be like all the others. A creature of habit, Jane locked her door, shook off her purse, and stowed away her shoes at the closet nearest the door. She went straight to her bathroom and emerged an hour later, clean and comfy. Dressed in her warm pink sweatpants and soft black cami, Jane curled herself onto her couch, pulled out her Kindle and started reading. She enjoyed *Gone with the Wind* for two solid hours before taking her medicine, grabbing some dinner and popping in an old movie. She kept her own company for the remainder of the evening.

I hate my life.

The thought flew out at her again. This time, she rebutted it.

No, I don't. I have a good life. I may not love it, but it sure as hell beats what I came from.

And it was true. She'd built a new life for herself. Built it from the ground up. Although Jane knew it was boring at times, she wasn't thirsty for an adventure. After a lifetime of instability and no control over her life, she wanted nothing more than predictable routines, accented by changes only *she* would initiate. She couldn't survive the alternative.

Not again.

UNY – New York, New York – First Day of Class

"Welcome to Race and Ethnicity in American Lit. I am Professor Daugherty and I will be your instructor for the duration of the course."

Several eyebrows shot up in surprise and Jane knew it was because of her age. In the past, her students had all been wide-eyed freshmen looking to get in good with the scary new specimen called the "professor" but many of these students were sophomores, juniors, and even seniors. They knew the typical age of full-time professors at UNY and she did not fit the bill. To her pleasant surprise, the class was very full. She knew that numbers would fluctuate in the first two weeks of the semester but she was happy to see such a surge of numbers for a class that was very much an elective.

She walked to the edge of the classroom and handed out her syllabus row by row.

"Take one, pass it down."

Surveying the room, Jane went into her customary first-day-of-class speech.

"If you are not officially registered for the course, you are welcome to check back with me in three days to see if there is room for you to add it. Adding and dropping ends next Friday. Keep that in mind if you change your mind about taking this class. For those of you committing to stay, please note that our first reading out of The Norton Anthology is due next class for discussion. If you have not ordered your books, now is the time to do so. If buying is too expensive for you, you can always rent your copies online."

Jane didn't know why she felt the need to throw that out there. The majority of these students could afford to buy half the textbooks in the bookstore for one semester. But she couldn't help remembering the years when she struggled to get by on her scholarship and part time jobs. Instructors often made the assumption that she could afford whatever textbook they wanted her to buy. She mentioned it on the off chance that *someone*, anyone, wasn't rich in the classroom.

Jane turned and walked back to the front of the room. As she reached her table, she heard the door to the room suddenly swing open. She glanced up, fully expecting to see a flushed-face student, embarrassed to be late. She got the flushed-face student. But she also got the surprise of her life.

A pair of striking hazel eyes met hers and it was as if no time had passed at all. She was taller than average, about 5'8" with long dark brown hair, healthy glowing skin, and a pretty, feminine face. The face was flushed but very familiar - featuring the same marks of that 12-year-old girl curled up in a fetal position all those years ago. Alexa's expression flickered in instant recognition. She opened her mouth as if to say something but quickly remembered herself, glanced around the room, and quietly walked to one of the two open seats left in the classroom.

Jane also remembered herself and forced herself to move forward with the section. She did class-wide icebreakers and tried to pay equal attention to every student but one in particular. She couldn't help but pay closer attention when Alexa spoke.

"Hi, I'm Alexa Masterson. I'm a senior majoring in Art with an emphasis in graphic design. I'm taking this class because I just learned that I need an English elective and this course sounds like the most interesting one."

Jane appreciated that she didn't make their history known. She was sure the young woman recognized her but she appreciated her discretion. The encounter was jarring - sending back a flood of unwanted memories of that house and the monster she'd tried to protect the younger girl from. Jane went through the motions for the remainder of class, dismissing the students thirty minutes early since they had nothing from the course material to discuss yet. She began packing her things when she heard a hesitant voice call out behind her.

"Jane?"

Jane turned and smiled. "Hi, Alexa."

To her surprise, the young woman threw her arms around her unreservedly and gave her a strong hug. Jane could smell the whiff of her sweet perfume and hesitantly hugged her back.

"Oh my God! I can't believe this. It really is you! How are you? It's been so long." The words flew out of the girl's mouth at a pace that could barely match her visible exuberance. Jane took her in once more: her long, wavy dark hair, her hazel eyes, which were more brown than green. Her straight white teeth that showed off her beautiful, genuine smile. This was definitely the same girl Jane knew all those years ago. Her kind, cheerful personality hadn't changed one bit.

Jane was glad.

Alexa was still talking. "How did you become a professor here? Are you a TA or is this really your class?"

Jane was used to the question and smiled wryly. "It's my class. I'm on staff here."

"Since when? How have I not run into you before?"

"Your major is Art, right?"

"Yeah."

"Did you take English 101?"

"No, I AP'd out of it."

Jane shrugged. "Well, there you have it. I only teach English courses and prior to this year, I only taught introductory English courses. You never took one. It's a pretty large school…"

She shrugged again. Alexa continued shaking her head in wonder.

"We need to catch up," she said decisively. "Are you free now? I'd love to take you to the café. My treat."

It wasn't the first time a student had invited Jane to coffee. Normally, she would decline unless it had anything to do with her class. And if it did, she would simply invite them to her office during her office hours. But she was genuinely happy to see Alexa again and curiosity got the better of her. She wanted to know how Alexa was doing. What happened after she left the house? Did she adjust to her new family? The curiosity was a foreign sensation to Jane. One she hadn't felt in years. One she couldn't ignore.

"Okay."

CHAPTER TWO

"They're awesome," Alexa answered. "Mom and Dad took me in and loved all the fear out of me. I don't know if they took classes ahead of time or something but it's like they were prepared for everything I put them through. When I shut down, they gently brought me out of my shell. When I threw a tantrum, they patiently walked me through it but also kept their rules. When I cried for no apparent reason, they just held me and were there. They're amazing. So is Aiden."

"Aiden?" Jane asked.

"My big brother. He was twenty-one when Mom and Dad got me, already a junior in college but he came home often to help me adjust. If I couldn't talk to Mom or Dad about something, I could always talk to him. I don't know. Maybe I would have done well as an only child again but there was something about having *three* adults look out for me. I think I subconsciously knew that even if Mom and Dad passed, I'd still have a big brother to be my family. He reminds me all the time that he'll always be there for me. And he has been." Alexa smiled tremulously. It was that smile that shattered every feeling of potential jealousy in Jane and replaced it with an overwhelming sense of gratitude. One of them really did make it out okay.

Jane wagged her foot back and forth as she sat on the chair in the campus café. They'd been there for more than half an hour, talking mostly about Alexa and what happened after the social worker took her from their Bronx townhouse to her new family in Manhattan more than nine years ago. So far the conversation was comfortable - as long as they kept the focus on Alexa. That was how Jane liked it. She learned that Alexa's adoption was everything she had hoped for and more. Her parents helped her heal and fostered her interest in art, so much so that she had already done several gallery shows and sold various pieces.

The conversation shifted and placed the spotlight on Jane.

"Enough about me," Alexa spoke the dreaded words. "What about you? What happened after I left?"

Immediately, a barrage of images flooded Jane's mind: her curled on the ground, him kicking at her torso, slaps across the face, vile names spewed at her, spit flying in the air right into her face...

"Jane?"

Jane looked up and saw an almost-stricken look on Alexa. Whatever she saw in Jane's eyes disturbed her enough to snap her out of her happy disposition. Jane straightened in her seat and shielded her eyes from Alexa's probing ones.

"I got transferred six months after you left. Left the system when I turned eighteen, went to SUNY on a partial scholarship and graduated in three years. I earned my master's in one and started working here two years ago. I'm looking into starting my PhD in American Literature next year."

Alexa looked over her admiringly.

"What?" Jane asked. She shrugged.

"Nothing, it's just...you're amazing. You did so well for yourself and..." Alexa cocked her head to the side.

Jane frowned, waiting to hear the rest.

"Don't take this the wrong way," Alexa began, her eyes still perusing Jane's face. "I'm totally straight, but you are stunning."

Jane rolled her eyes and waved the compliment away with her hand.

"No, don't do that!" Alexa exclaimed. "I mean it. I was trying to put my finger on who you look like - Lauryn Hill! That's it! A young Lauryn Hill."

Jane smiled reservedly and gave the obligatory, "Thanks."

She'd heard the comparison before but couldn't see the resemblance herself. In her mind, the legendary singer was much more beautiful. Especially since she didn't have her scars...

The thought bothered her. So much so that Jane quickly stood up and glanced at her watch.

"I'm sorry. I have to go," she lied. She picked up her satchel from where she'd slung it on her chair.

"Oh!" Alexa exclaimed in surprise. She pouted her pretty lips. "So soon? That's okay - I understand. Thanks for having coffee with me."

"Thanks for treating me," Jane said, while adjusting the bag on her shoulder. She looked up at Alexa's open, happy face. "I'm glad things worked out for you. You look really happy."

Something flickered in the younger woman's eyes and for a brief moment, Jane wanted to know what it was. But the girl's carefree expression quickly returned.

She stood up, pulled Jane into a warm embrace, and quickly told her, "Obviously, you're Professor Daugherty in class, but you're Jane outside of it. I've missed you so much. I really want us to be friends again. Sisters. I mean it, Jane."

The sentiment stirred something deep within Jane, something that hadn't been stirred in years. It made her uncomfortable and slightly sad. She mustered up a stiff smile and tried to reassure her old friend.

"Well, if you're in my class, we're bound to keep in touch." She tried to ignore the slight disappointment that flashed on Alexa's face. "Thanks again for the coffee. See you around."

She then did what she did best. She fled.

"The question up for debate today: are stereotypes true?"

It was the first "real" day of class and Jane started with a bang. She looked around the full room and was happy to see that most students had decided to stay and the ones who left were promptly replaced by other students eager to take the class. For the second day, she had the new students quickly get acquainted with the old ones and jumped right into the material. The class would be broken up into units, following much of American History to trace the literature it produced.

The students stared back at her as if she'd asked a rhetorical question. She quickly dispelled that notion.

"I want to know your honest opinion." Jane repeated, "Are stereotypes true?"

"Doesn't it depend on the stereotype?" a young blond woman asked. Jane glanced at her class sheet - she would do this with every student who responded to learn their names better. Vanessa Rogalski was her name.

"Does it?" a male student with wavy brown hair responded. Vincent Johanson. "Aren't all stereotypes offensive?"

"Not necessarily," Kayley Price answered. "What about the stereotype that all Asians are smart or all black people dance really well? There are some positive stereotypes."

"But that doesn't make them true."

"Well, it never does whenever you say *all* people of a particular race or group is good or bad at something or does something in general."

Jane observed the debate unfold with watchful eyes. She loved these moments - when students felt the freedom to say what was on their minds and engage in an invigorating and intelligent conversation. Because the topic was touchy, she'd have to carefully monitor the discussion for any micro-aggressive comments or offensive implications, but so far it looked like she had a mature batch of students.

"Well, is there a difference between stereotypes or trends within people groups?" Vincent asked. "In many African cultures, beat-driven dance is very prevalent. Hip-hop was pretty much founded amongst black people. So wouldn't it be fair to say that black people dance really well because it is a part of their culture?"

"But not all black people dance well," Vanessa replied. "Isn't that where we get into trouble?"

"Is it?" Kayley jumped in again. Jane could see she liked playing Devil's Advocate. "Just because there are a few exceptions to a general trend, doesn't make the trend irrelevant."

To Jane's surprise, a mostly-quiet Alexa spoke up.

"I think there is a difference between a trend and a stereotype. A statistical trend may state that the highest concentration of serial killers are profiled in white men but a stereotype would conclude that all white men are crazy or dangerous serial killers and that's not right. Same goes for black people and crime. An overwhelmingly large percentage of black men are imprisoned but the stereotype that all black men are dangerous criminals is ignorant and hurtful."

"Okay," a new student named Matthew Holver spoke up. "It's a fallacy to say *all* black men are dangerous criminals but would it be a stereotype to say that many are, given the high imprisonment rate?"

"I don't think stereotypes are that big of a deal," Carter Jacobs threw out.

The room quieted as the students turned to look at him. Jane saw Alexa frown in disgust.

"Care to elaborate, Carter?" Jane asked.

"What's the big deal?" he shrugged. "If you make an assumption about me or my character because of my race, that's your problem, not mine."

"But you're white," Alexa pointed out.

"So?" he replied. "You are too."

"I know, but unlike you, I get it." The room quieted further.

Alexa continued, "I understand the concept of white privilege. When people see me - or you, for that matter - they don't assume that I'm a criminal up to no good. They don't assume that I'm easy because other girls of my race dance like sluts on music videos. I don't get followed around in stores or pulled over because of my race."

Jane watched as two red circles surfaced on Carter's face during Alexa's calm speech.

"If anything, people assume I'm trustworthy and capable and give me a fair shot until I prove otherwise. However, even as a woman, I face the stereotype that I'm overemotional and not as capable of rational thought as a man. When you say that stereotypes are no big deal, you invalidate the negative experiences people have suffered - and even died for - *because* of the stereotypes projected onto them. Trayvon Martin? Michael Brown? Eric Garner, anyone?"

The class was silent as the weight of her words sunk in. It only took one glance at Carter's blanched face to know that he was not about to put forth a rebuttal. Jane took back the reigns.

"Along that vein, let's discuss today's reading. We're in our Native American unit and you were assigned Red Jacket's letter to Reverend Cram..."

The remainder of the class went very smoothly. More students gradually participated in the conversation and Carter, though humbled, rejoined the discussion and contributed decent insight to the readings. Like clockwork, the students began packing their bags five minutes before the end of class. Jane reminded them of their assignment for the next meeting and then dismissed them. She appreciated that the class was only twice a week and every other day at that. It was good to space out potentially heated conversations.

Jane was busy packing her own satchel when Carter approached her.

"Professor Daugherty?" he said timidly.

"Hi, Carter." She looked up at him and waited. She noticed Alexa hanging back over his shoulder but refocused her attention to the student before her. He looked down at his fidgeting hands before meeting her eyes again.

"I...I just wanted to apologize for earlier."

She frowned. "You mean about the stereotype conversation?"

He nodded.

"Don't," she replied. His eyebrows shot up in surprise.

"But I was wrong, wasn't I?"

She nodded. "I disagree with your initial comment, yes, but you have every right to express your opinion like everyone else. As long as it's done respectfully. In your case, you could have said it with more tact and less arrogance but I think you've learned your lesson, don't you?"

He nodded quickly. She glanced at Alexa briefly.

"You understand what your classmate was saying then?"

He nodded. "I don't know why but I didn't think it was an issue because it wasn't an issue *for me*. I definitely have a lot of food for thought and this is just my first day." He smiled sheepishly and Jane knew in that moment that she liked him. Anyone who was humble enough to apologize and realize they were wrong that quickly had her respect.

"See you next class, Carter."

He waved and ambled off. Jane slung her satchel over her shoulder and turned towards Alexa, curious as to why she was still there.

"You ready, Shark Bait?" a deep baritone voice called out. The pitch of it was powerful. Jane could almost feel it vibrate down her spine. She looked up and saw who it belonged to.

A tall man, probably 6'4," dressed in a tailored gray suit that fit his body immaculately. He hugged Alexa and gave Jane a brief moment to observe him from top to bottom. He had the body of a runner - with strong lean muscles, perfectly proportioned for his tall frame. He had thick dark blond hair, tossed about in a stylish 'do and a face that was perfectly symmetrical. It had all the marks of a handsome mug: strong square jaw line, sharp high cheekbones, straight nose, perfectly spaced, well-shaped eyes. Even his thick dark blond eyebrows complimented his face. Though white, his skin had a healthy bronze tan. But the winning feature was his eyes.

They were amber. Not brown, not green, not hazel. But amber gold. Like God took a bottle of whiskey, liked the color, and decided to infuse his irises with the same color. They were arresting.

And piercing.

He pulled out of Alexa's arms and when his eyes landed on her, Jane felt an involuntary ripple course through her stomach. For the first time *ever*, it was a pleasant sensation. It became unpleasant when Jane considered who it was. Alexa had a beautiful boyfriend who, from the looks of it, was already a working professional.

Figures.

His whiskey colored gaze swept over her frame in five seconds flat but didn't leave a detail to spare. He took her in from the crown of her head to the soles of her feet as if he had x-ray capabilities. By the time his eyes clashed with her own again, Jane could almost feel his touch on her body. She needed to leave.

"Hello," he said in a cultured, educated tone. He extended his hand, his eyes never leaving her own.

"Hi," she replied. She pulled her sleeve to the edge of her wrist before reaching out to shake his hand. He had a strong, masculine grip and his large hand nearly enveloped her own. The warmth from it radiated up her arm. She gave it a brief, strong shake before pulling back.

"Jane, this is my brother, Aiden." Alexa said.

The shock that washed over Jane felt like a bucket of water being poured over her body. The feeling was soon followed by the sensation of what felt like warm syrup filling her insides at the realization that this man didn't belong to Alexa - well, not in the sense that Jane had thought.

"Aiden," Alexa continued. "This is *Professor* Jane Daugherty. She's teaching my Race and Ethnicity in American Lit course. She and I were also in the same foster home when Mom and Dad got me. Can you believe she's been a professor here for two years? I had no idea!"

His dark blond eye brows shot up in surprise.

"This is Jane? Well, it's a pleasure to meet you. Alexa has said so much about you." He looked between the two of them. "Forgive me for asking, but how old are you? Alexa's still a student and you're already a professor...?"

Jane waved the question with her hand. She was used to it by now.

"I'm twenty-four. Sped through my degrees and was lucky enough to land a decent job."

His eyebrows rose again, but not in surprise. As he perused her face, Jane had no idea what he was thinking but felt glad to be the object of his attention, no matter how fleeting.

What is wrong with me? she thought. *I'm acting like a school girl.*

Alexa turned to Jane. "Hey, would you like to come over for dinner tonight?"

Jane blinked. "Sorry?"

"Yes, my parents would love to meet you! Like Aiden said, I told them all about you growing up."

Jane must have looked like a deer caught in headlights. Alexa hadn't mentioned telling her adopted family about her before. She opened her mouth, immediately ready to decline but to her surprise, Aiden spoke before she could.

"Yes, we'd love to have you over." His eyes were dancing with amusement, as if he *knew* she was trying to decline. Something shifted in his gaze as he continued to speak; a new determination in them. "If only to thank you for what you did for Alexa all those years ago."

She frowned. *What did she tell you I did?*

"I can't tonight," she said, already racking her brain for an excuse.

"Tomorrow night?" Alexa asked.

Aiden added, "I'm sure you'll want to learn more about Alexa's life since you last lived together. Maybe even see some of her art?"

Jane was surprised. She had been ready to point out that she and Alexa had caught up pretty well over coffee but she still had not seen the girl's art - something Alexa was very eager to show her.

"Yes! Mom and Dad are my best patrons so far. My art is literally all over the apartment." Alexa grabbed both of Jane's hands and looked at her beseechingly. "Tomorrow night. Please tell me you'll come?"

With a plea like that, what else could she say? She looked between the two of them and smiled nervously.

"I'd love to."

CHAPTER THREE

She was beautiful.

It was a refrain that kept playing in Aiden's mind and he kept changing the variations to describe the woman he had just seen minutes before.

She was....

Beautiful?

Stunning?

Gorgeous?

Perfection to behold?

She was all that and above, no question mark required. But none of those words or phrases were good enough as far as Aiden was concerned. He quickly realized there was no word in the English language adequate enough to describe just how beautiful Jane Daugherty was to him. Her features were already permanently tattooed in his mind and he had no desire to remove them. The scenery of the busy city was completely invisible to him as he thought about every inch of that woman's person. He'd purposefully memorized her face, figure, and clothing long before Alexa opened her mouth to introduce the two of them. Dark molasses skin, sharp high cheek bones, a straight nose, full lips, perfectly spaced dark eyes, and hair that was arranged in what looked like tiny balls strategically and stylishly placed around the circumference of her pretty head. It wasn't that one particular feature stood out to him, though each part of her could stand out as attractive on its own. It was the fact that she possessed the combination of all of those features and they were arranged with such precision and perfection on her face, no cosmetic surgeon could *ever* craft such an allure.

The woman was an aesthetic goddess and the crazy thing was, Aiden knew she didn't even realize it.

She was tall, at least 5'10". And even through her oversized sweater, Aiden could see that she had a very slender physique. He had no complaints. Not only was she thin, which he was not ashamed of being attracted to, she still had curves in all the right places. Slender curves, but curves nonetheless.

She is all woman, Aiden thought.

And he wanted her.

"Aiden?" Alexa said. "Aiden?"

Aiden felt his sister's tiny fist pummel into his muscular bicep with an unspectacular thump. If she was trying to hurt him, she'd failed miserably, but she did manage to snap him out of his all-consuming thoughts.

"Huh?" He looked away from the taxi window and over to her quizzical frown. He shook himself to and quickly focused.

"I'm sorry, Lex. I didn't mean to tune you out."

She narrowed her eyes suspiciously before breaking out into a bright smile and stuffing her iPhone back into her pocket.

"I just got off the phone with Mom. She can't wait to meet Jane tomorrow."

It was the last sentence Alexa should have said if she wanted to keep her brother's attention. His mind immediately went back to the tall, slender, young black woman standing at the front of the classroom. She had a confident air about her and was soft-spoken, albeit highly educated. Alexa had mentioned that she'd been teaching at UNY for two years. If she was a professor, that probably meant she had her PhD. Or at *least* her master's when she started two years ago. Her master's at *twenty-two*?

How did she accomplish that *at such a young age?* he wondered.

"Hello? Earth to Aiden!" Aiden snapped out of it again, only to find his sister standing outside of the taxi, in front of the restaurant. He felt a rush of heat flood his cheeks as he quickly pulled out his wallet, handed the driver several bills and told him to keep the change.

He scooted out of the cab, closed the door, and avoided his sister's probing gaze as he escorted her into the chic diner and grill. The host took them straight to their reserved table and they settled in for the meal.

"Are you okay?" Alexa asked. He saw the concern in her pretty face and felt his never-ending affection for her swell up once more. She was always looking out for him, even though he was the older one.

"I'm okay. I'm sorry I've been so out of it."

"Is it work? Did something happen at the office?" Aiden shook his head. If something *was* wrong with work, it wouldn't be an office issue but a client issue. Not that he could explain the intricacies of Wall Street to his artsy, free-spirited sister.

"Everything at work is fine."

Better than fine, actually. At only thirty, Aiden was the fastest rising stock broker in his firm. He had a client roster that would take most brokers twenty years to acquire. Studying to be a broker, taking the Series 7, and getting his foot in the door had been the hard parts of his career. He was now flying high on the roster he'd earned and the good advice he dispensed.

"Then what is it?" Alexa asked. "You've been distracted ever since we left the campus."

He shook his head.

"I promise you, it's nothing. I'm sorry," he apologized again. He leaned forward and put on his most charming smile. "Tell me all about your first week of your last year of college. How are classes?"

She fell hook, line and sinker and dove right in.

"It's great! I got all the classes I wanted. I was able to squeeze in Ceramics IV even though it's the most coveted class. I shouldn't have been able to get it because my emphasis has nothing to do with classical art..."

Focus on sister. Focus on sister. Focus on sister...

Normally it wasn't difficult to focus on what she was saying at all. Aiden loved Alexa. She was the most kind, considerate, and generous person he had ever known. He loved hearing about her interests and was rooting for her art because the kid was incredibly talented. But in this moment, he couldn't help but see dark brown eyes instead of hazel ones. He saw small twisted knots instead of free-flowing wavy hair. He saw dark chocolate syrup for skin and wanted nothing more than to taste it.

"Aiden!"

Aiden snapped back into focus and this time, he met a very irritated baby sister. Their food was already on the table and Alexa had long since dug in. He wiped a hand over his eyes and squeezed the bridge of his nose. He was able to concentrate this time, only because a hot surge of guilt was flooding his stomach.

"I'm so sorry," was all he could say.

Alexa shook her head.

"Not good enough," she answered. "Seriously. What is with you?"

She leaned back and looked at his contrite expression carefully. She frowned, as though trying to figure out a puzzle, when suddenly, her eyes widened in shock.

"Oh my God," she said.

Aiden frowned. "What?"

"Oh my God," she repeated.

He frowned in confusion and waited.

"You like her."

Aiden suddenly felt trapped under the pin of Alexa's mischievous gaze. He felt another surge of heat rush, this time to his collar, and he opened his mouth to deny it but she swiftly cut him off.

"Uh-uh. I won't buy anything you have to say unless it's the truth. *You like Jane.* You haven't been able to concentrate since the minute we left her. She's all you're thinking about."

"Alexa-"

"Oh, this is awesome!" she suddenly screeched in excitement, making Aiden jump. Several patrons' heads turned to their table.

"Alexa!" he admonished. She waved away his embarrassment and leaned forward in her seat.

"Are you going to ask her out? Maybe you can do it at dinner tomorrow."

He immediately held up a hand. "Wait just a minute. Who said anything about asking anyone out? I admit it. I find her very attractive." That was the understatement of the millennium. "But I don't even know this woman. I don't know anything about her other than a two-second introduction from you and the fact that she helped you as a kid."

Aiden watched as Alexa shook her head and grew very somber. "She didn't just help me, Aiden. She saved me. Over and over and over again. She put herself at risk to keep me safe. She stuck her neck out in order to save mine. If it wasn't for her, I don't know if I would be alive today."

Her words chilled him and rocked him to his core. He looked at his sister's grave expression and a rush of emotions raged against his heart like waves crashing into the shore. He knew about the abuse. The way that animal wouldn't hesitate to pull out his belt and beat his foster children into submission. He could still remember the vacant look of terror in her eyes when she first arrived at their home. So traumatized, she couldn't string two sentences together, much less speak about her foster "family" for eight months. And by the time she did…by the time she'd had the courage to speak about what she'd endured, the man responsible for her terror was already imprisoned, locked away by the voice of another child he'd abused.

He wondered about Jane and what exactly she had done to protect his little sister. Alexa spoke of her whenever she spoke of those years in the system, but she never went into specifics. He didn't know if this was because Alexa didn't know everything Jane had done to keep her safe or if what she knew was too traumatizing to recall. Maybe he didn't need to know all the details. What he knew about Jane already earned her his undying respect and gratitude. Jane had looked after and protected his little sister long before he'd even known Alexa existed. He owed her a debt he could never repay. Aiden focused his attention on his beloved "Shark Bait." He reached out and grabbed her hand lying on the table.

"I love you," he whispered.

She smiled tearfully. "I love you, too. Always."

She'd made a mistake. In the twenty-four plus hours that had passed since Alexa's invitation, Jane had time to seriously regret ever accepting the offer. She paced left and right in her tiny excuse of a living room, vacillating between trying to figure out what to wear and trying to figure out how to cancel her appearance at a dinner that was scheduled to start in less than two hours.

What the hell was I thinking? she admonished herself.

The nerves were wreaking havoc on her already messed-up stomach. How was she supposed to eat dinner when her belly was doing nothing but tossing and turning and making her even more nauseous than usual? Jane stopped pacing and covered her face with her hands.

What is it? she asked herself. *Why are you so damn nervous?*

Almost as soon as she asked herself the question, Aiden Masterson's face appeared in her mind's eye. His tousled blond hair, piercing gold eyes, and perfect straight teeth. She could even recall the scent of his fresh, masculine cologne. He smelled like fresh mountains and wide open air. It was refreshing. Clean. Addicting.

This wasn't good. Feelings that she hadn't felt for the opposite sex since seventh grade were suddenly flooding her senses. Sure, she'd gone on dates. She'd felt lust before. But this was different. She wanted to *know* him. What did he do for a living? Was he always as charming and polite as he appeared yesterday? What made him smile? What made him tick? As much as she enjoyed looking at him physically, he'd managed to gain her curiosity about the thoughts inside that pretty head of his.

And that was unacceptable.

Jane thought of Alexa. How the girl she once considered her little sister was sweet and gentle and still very innocent, even after what she'd endured. She was stronger now, too, if her class monologue the previous day was any indication of her conviction and confidence. She'd grown into a fantastic young woman and it truly made Jane glad. But Alexa obviously wanted to re-build their friendship and Jane wasn't sure if they could. She hadn't had a close friend since Alexa's departure from her life nine years ago. Going to dinners and having coffee after class was just inviting something into her life that she wasn't sure she could invest in, especially if it included further contact with a man around whom she couldn't control her thoughts.

Her cell phone suddenly rang. Jane jumped at the sound and quickly retrieved the phone.

"Hello?"

"Hey, Jane! It's Alexa. How are you?"

"Um, I'm okay. Listen, Alexa-"

"We are *so* excited to see you tonight." Alexa's bubbly voice exclaimed. "It truly made my day when you said yes yesterday."

"Really?" Jane asked in surprise.

"Of course! When I told Mom I'd found you, she squealed into my phone like a banshee. She's been planning this dinner since yesterday afternoon."

If the previous words hadn't cemented Jane's resolve to go, that statement just sealed her fate. There was absolutely no way she could back out of the dinner now.

"You got my text for the address, right?" Alexa asked.

"Yep, I have it."

"Perfect. Give me a call if you have any trouble getting here. We'll see you soon!"

Great.

CHAPTER FOUR

What the hell?

Alexa had said nothing about being rich.

Jane gathered that her family might have a little money given the address Alexa texted her earlier but nothing prepared her for this. Alexa had told her "casual smart" for the attire that night. But as Jane walked up to the mammoth-sized Upper East Side apartment on Fifth Avenue, she quickly wished that she had dressed more formally. The building screamed upper class wealth in a subtle New York fashion. The 19th century architecture rippled with symbolic emblems, crests, moldings, and delicate designs in the white-washed stone. The lights cast an intentional gold hue across the front of the building. The sidewalks were immaculately clean and beautifully trimmed bushes lined the front gate. It was the sort of building Jane had sped past several times on her way to a meeting or a museum. The sort of building that was understated but spelled r-i-c-h without any effort. It was the sort of building one would be hesitant to walk into unless they had a clearly written invitation or a very large wallet.

Jane had the invitation but was still very nervous.

To her surprise, as she crossed the street and made her way to the tented entrance of the building, she saw Alexa standing on the sidewalk, cheerfully chatting with the doorman. When she saw Jane approaching, she quickly excused herself and met Jane halfway to the entrance, pulling her into one of her patented bear hugs.

"Jane! You made it!" She pulled back and gave a sweeping look over her friend. She saw Jane's hair and gasped in delight. "Oh my God, you hair is *beautiful!*"

Jane had almost forgotten that she'd released her Bantu knots into a full afro. She didn't know why she chose to let her hair out but she supposed Alexa's parents may have seen an afro before as opposed to the knots she often wore in class. Either way, Alexa's reaction, while flattering, reminded her that she would most likely receive questions about her hair, regardless of what style she chose. The girl instinctively reached up as if to touch her hair before quickly yanking her hand back down and blushing.

"I'm so sorry. I literally almost stuck my hand in your hair."

"You can touch it," Jane replied. She felt a small pang of sadness as she said it. Nine years ago, Alexa wouldn't have hesitated to touch her hair. Now, they were re-learning each other. Nothing was as easy as it was before, regardless of how they wanted to pretend. Alexa reached up again and gently touched the ends of her hair.

"It's so soft." She pulled her hand back. "Really, you're stunning."

She grabbed her arm and escorted her to the building. She paused at the doorman. "Sam, this is my friend Jane Daugherty. Jane, this Samuel Richards. He's been manning the door here for more than ten years."

Jane waved at the middle-aged gentleman who gave her a friendly wave in return.

Alexa continued into the building. "See you later, Sam."

"Goodnight, Miss Masterson."

She rolled her eyes and glanced at Jane. "I've been telling him to call me Alexa for years but he never listens." She continued talking about something but Jane wasn't paying attention.

The minute they entered the lobby, Jane's heart nearly stopped.

The 19th century architecture carried on into the interior of the building, reaching up into high arches that towered over the two women. Tall, thick columns reminiscent of Rome held the historical structure intact. Luscious chandeliers hung in perfect tiered procession and illuminated the marble tiled floor in gold. The layout of the common entrance was the modern version of the Beverly Wilshire featured in *Pretty Woman*. Jane could completely empathize with Julia Roberts' character. It took everything in her to keep her mouth closed at the obscenely opulent wealth displayed before her. Beautiful floral arrangements adorned every tabletop along the floor. Elegant seating areas were perfectly arranged at focal corners of the space. The walls featured large classical paintings of stunning landscapes, encased in golden frames that had to have cost a fortune. It was decadent, warm, modern, and tasteful, all the while boasting the best that money could afford.

In the center of the lobby stood what looked like a concierge desk. The employees there clearly recognized Alexa as she waved to them and escorted Jane past the desk and the security officers flanking the elevators. Jane heard her $20 Payless heels click along the marble flooring that probably cost more to procure than what she earned in an entire year. She knew that Alexa had been adopted into a kind, loving family that could clearly afford to send her to UNY. Never in a million years did she think her old friend had landed the jackpot of adoptive families. Whatever her parents did, they were clearly worth millions. She couldn't even imagine the cost to buy an apartment there.

As she followed the still-chatting Alexa into the gold-encrusted elevator, Jane glanced down at her outfit and frowned. She hadn't felt this self-conscious about what she was wearing since the days she'd been forced to wear high-water jeans at school. For dinner, she was wearing a sleek pair of black slacks, a black fitted cotton shirt, and a gray flowing cardigan on top. She pulled at the sleeves of her sweater, wishing she'd added bangles to her look instead of a plain silver locket and fake pearl studs. She felt terribly under-dressed in such a setting and even more conspicuously covered in comparison to Alexa's pretty lace summer dress. Though modest, the dress showed off Alexa's sleek long legs and graceful lithe arms. Jane watched her insert a plastic card into a slot just above the elevator menu before pressing the button to the 25th floor.

They're that *rich?* Jane thought in amazement.

She nearly crossed her arms across her chest in a protective posture before realizing what she was doing. She was making herself even more uncomfortable than she had to be.

Snap out of it, she told herself.

She decided then and there that what she was wearing was fine. It was what *she* could afford, it looked good on her, and it wasn't unreasonable considering that fall was only a few weeks away and the weather had already cooled down at night. If they gave her strange looks for wearing cotton instead of silk, she could comfort herself with the thought that she'd never have to see them again. Jane straightened her back, stiffened her spine, took a deep breath, and forced herself to relax.

She looked at Alexa, *still talking,* completely oblivious to her anxiety, and realized in amazement that her old friend was nervous too. Not about how she would fit in but whether or not she would actually *like* the dinner at their palatial abode. To Alexa, this place was home, not some fixture out of a movie. It was clear that whatever culture shock she experienced being transplanted from a Bronx foster home to an Upper East Side penthouse was long gone. It had been nearly a decade since her adoption and she was clearly comfortable with her new surroundings. That didn't keep her from nervous chatter, though.

"Mom made the meal from scratch. She loves to cook if it's not for a large group of people. I told her how much you loved Thanksgiving-style meals minus the turkey so she decided to make her famous stuffing, greens, and mac and cheese. She cooked a glazed ham instead of the turkey. Is that okay?" Alexa asked, her hazel eyes nervous.

Jane smiled. "It sounds delicious."

She saw the younger woman's shoulders fall at least an inch. "Oh, good. I didn't know if you still liked those foods."

"I do and I'm sure I'll like whatever your Mom serves."

"I hope so," she replied. "I asked Mom to keep it basic so it would agree with your…" She gestured to her belly.

Jane nodded, grateful that she remembered. "Yeah, it should be fine."

"Oh! I'm so excited you could be here!" Alexa squealed unreservedly. She started bouncing on the balls of her feet and Jane's smile widened. It was night and day from the last time she'd seen her do that. She no longer had to whisper or keep her excitement contained. Fearless looked good on Alexa.

The elevator chimed their arrival.

"Here we are." Alexa pulled the key out of the slot and walked into the well-lit, beautifully decorated hall. It looked like the hall of a luxury hotel, minus the numerous suite doors. In fact, only one door stood at the hall, two yards away from the elevator. Alexa used the same card key to open it. Jane quickly realized that her family *owned* the entire floor. It dawned on her that the farther they went inside, the more extravagant the decorations became. Despite the beauty of the exterior and the breathtaking layout of the lobby, nothing could prepare her for the masterpiece that was the Masterson penthouse interior.

The minute Jane's foot crossed the threshold, her nose was caressed with the intoxicating scent of peaches and peony. She could barely dwell on the scent because her ears were preoccupied with the soothing sound of jazz music filling the well-lit, modern chic home. She almost found it hard to believe that people actually lived there. It looked like a model home that had barely been touched. Polished hardwood floors covered every inch of landing, accented by heavy, Persian rugs. It was incredibly spacious, yet warm and inviting at the same time. The gold-encrusted wall paper, plush beige furniture, and honey-colored wooden tables made the large home bright and welcoming. A grand staircase with a beautifully decorated wrought iron railing, wound its way to the second floor in a grand arch.

"Jane." The sound of her name snapped her out of her trance-like observations. She turned her head to the direction of the call and found herself quickly arrested by a pair of amber gold eyes. Aiden Masterson quickly descended the stairs and extended his hand to her.

"Good to see you again," he said with a friendly smile. His eyes once again devoured her from the crown of her head to the soles of her feet; though, this time, they took their time observing her new hair style. She couldn't exactly read the look on his face but it was dancing with a sort of curiosity or excitement.

"Likewise," she replied. "Thank you for having me."

He was dressed in a pair of black slacks and a crisp white dress shirt, the top two buttons undone. She didn't know if she was glad he was dressed less formally or bothered by the slight peek of his tan well-formed collar bone. Jane chided herself. She *was not* about to develop some stupid crush on her friend's older brother. She needed to focus on Alexa, the dinner, and getting through the night without embarrassing herself. After that night, she would never see Alexa's family again. She turned to the girl and asked, "Are your parents here?"

Alexa gasped. "Oh! Of course. I didn't even think to announce us. Come on."

She grabbed one of Jane's hands and pulled her further into the house. Jane gave herself a wide berth around Aiden as she followed Alexa closely. She could feel his gaze on her back and wondered what he was thinking. They walked down a short hallway, up a small set of steps and into the informal living space. It too was spacious, with a stunning backdrop of the city skyline in floor to ceiling windows. Just to the right was the chef-graded kitchen where they were met with the mouth-watering smells of well-seasoned meat, vegetables, and whatever else the family matriarch was cooking.

The lady of the house was a beautiful brunette woman in her mid-fifties, busy bouncing around the kitchen island with a red apron covering her dark green dress and stunning emerald necklace. Her husband, a tall handsome man with graying blond hair sat at the kitchen bar, studying *The New York Times* with a pair of professorial reading glasses. He was dressed even more casually than his son, wearing simple khakis and a dark gray sweater.

"Hey guys!" Alexa said, leading the pack.

"Oh!" the woman exclaimed. "Here she is!" She dropped her hand towel, removed her apron, and immediately approached Jane with open arms. Pulling her into a warm hug very similar to Alexa's greeting of choice,

Mrs. Masterson immediately set Jane at ease. She pulled back slightly and met her eyes. She'd aged gracefully, her wrinkles adding to her beauty rather than detracting from it. The most beautiful part about her, Jane decided, was the genuine kindness in her light blue eyes.

"Hello, dear. I'm Dr. Ava Masterson." Jane was surprised by the title. Alexa hadn't mentioned her mother's profession. "I'm Lexi and Aiden's mom. You can call me Ava."

She pulled back and turned to her husband, who approached the pair. "This is my husband, Michael Masterson."

The man was an older replica of his son. The only difference, besides age, was his eyes. Instead of whiskey gold, they were a grayish blue - still striking but in a different way. He gave Jane a warm smile but she could already tell he was more reserved than his exuberant wife.

He shook her hand and simply said, "It's a pleasure to meet you, Professor Daugherty."

"Please, call me Jane. The pleasure is all mine," Jane replied. "Thank you for having me." She gestured at her empty person and quickly added, "I'm so sorry I didn't think to bring anything."

"Oh, nonsense!" Ava quickly cut her off. "You're our guest. We didn't expect anything but your lovely company tonight. Please, please have a seat. The food will be ready in just a moment."

Alexa joined her mother in the kitchen and Michael quietly asked his wife how he could help. Jane made her way further into the living space but instead of sitting, found herself drawn to a large and impressive portrait of a handsome man with jet black hair in a formal black suit. He wore a fierce expression that almost marred his handsome features. He looked like a man not to be trifled with. She stepped closer and realized what it was about the portrait that drew her in. His eyes.

They were amber gold.

"My grandfather."

Jane slightly jumped at the voice beside her. She glanced up in time to see Aiden smile.

"Sorry," he said. "Didn't mean to startle you."

She brushed off her embarrassment. "Don't worry about it. This is your father's father?"

Aiden nodded. "When he was a lot younger. He's rather friendly but growing up, he used to scare the crap out of me."

She looked surprised at his admission. "Why?"

"Oh, I don't know." He smiled. "Something about the way his eyes clashed with his hair. It was startling. Catlike. He had this…presence. And he almost always wore black suits so it made his eyes even more intimidating."

"You got them from him, obviously," she pointed out.

He shrugged. "I know. But I think blond hair is less disarming than raven black."

She smiled and nodded. "Does he scare you now?"

Aiden scoffed. "Of course not. His hair is gray, now."

She laughed.

"Okay," Ava called. "Dinner is served!"

The group moved over to the extravagantly decorated dining table. Everything, from the surface of the table to the arms of the candle holders to the tines of the fork, shined with an expert polish. She followed Alexa's lead and sat down next to her, acutely aware of Aiden's movement as he took the seat opposite her.

Great. Now how was she supposed to concentrate during the meal?

She watched Ava Masterson put the last dish on the table and sure enough, it was a meal that might as well have been served during Thanksgiving. Mashed potatoes, corn on the cob, ham, sweet potatoes, stuffing, green beans, cranberry sauce, and steaming gravy all managed to make her stomach growl. Michael Masterson sat at the head of the table, next to Alexa and Ava took the remaining seat between her husband and her son.

To Jane's surprise, the family linked hands and looked at Alexa expectantly. Jane hesitantly joined hands with Alexa and Aiden, trying to ignore the warmth that radiated from the latter's strong grip. Alexa bowed her head and gently said, "Dear Lord, thank you for this food and this time of fellowship. Thank you for Jane's company. Please let her feel at ease and let us all enjoy each other's company. Please bless this food and let it add to the nourishment of our bodies. In Jesus' name, amen."

"Amen," Ava politely replied.

Jane opened her eyes to see Michael Masterson grinning at her. He seemed to have picked up her surprise.

"Alexa's the holy roller among us so she always blesses the food." He winked at his daughter while Ava and Aiden laughed. Alexa rolled her eyes at the quip but Jane could see her visibly stiffen at the remark. She wondered about this new information. When they were kids, Alexa had never expressed an interest in a higher power or any spiritual matters. Then again, she was only twelve. Jane wondered what it was she believed and how she came to her conclusions. She also wondered why she was the only one in her family to believe.

They passed the food around and dug in.

"So Jane, I understand that you've been teaching at UNY for two years now?" Ava asked.

"Yes," Jane replied. "I joined the fall after I earned my master's there."

"How old are you?" Michael asked.

"I'm twenty-four."

"So you earned your master's degree at twenty-two." Ava concluded.

Jane nodded.

"Wow - that is very impressive! How on earth did you manage to do that?"

Jane shrugged. "Summer, winter, and spring break courses. I also took the maximum number of units during the regular terms."

Aiden glanced up from his plate. "It sounds like you were doing everything in your power to finish early."

She nodded, feeling a strange stirring when she met his eyes. "I guess I was. The longer I stayed, the more debt I'd have to accrue."

"You paid your whole way through?" Aiden asked.

Jane held his gaze and silently nodded.

"How did you do it?" Alexa asked in awe.

Jane glanced at her and shrugged again. "I worked. I got scholarships and grants, jobs to make ends meet, and loans for whatever I absolutely couldn't cover."

"'Jobs?'" Ava repeated. "As in multiple?"

She nodded.

"How many jobs did you have to work?" Alexa asked.

Jane looked around the table at their dumbfounded expressions. Like the concept of working multiple jobs was a foreign theory to be analyzed and studied. Maybe it was: to rich people.

"It depended on the semester," Jane answered. "I typically worked three jobs a semester."

"*Three?*" Ava asked, horrified.

"Well, they were all part time." Jane reminded her.

Michael whistled and cut into his ham. "Regardless, that had to be very taxing on you. Three jobs plus a full load at school."

"Not to mention the pressure of funding your own education in one of the most expensive cities in the world," Ava added. "I really admire your work ethic. Good for you."

"Thank you," Jane quietly replied. She shifted in her seat. Though she knew the gravity of her accomplishments and how far she'd come, it felt strange to have privileged individuals acknowledge it. It felt strange to have *anyone* acknowledge her struggle and how she overcame. She was so used to glossing over her credentials; people often focused on her age as the most remarkable factor of her achievements - rarely on the backdrop that should have prevented it.

The conversation shifted to Alexa and her art classes.

Jane turned to her plate and carefully forked two well-cooked green beans. She bit into the delicious vegetable, which practically melted in her mouth, and carefully chewed the small morsels. She dipped the edge of her fork into her tiny portion of sweet potatoes and again ate the smallest serving possible. The food was delicious and she wished she could eat in larger proportions. She cut a small corner of her ham and briefly closed her eyes, savoring the tasty meat. When she opened them, she noticed Aiden watching her across the table. He looked down at her plate and back up at her, a frown of concern somehow making his face even more handsome.

He gestured at the tiny portions on her plate. "Is the food not to your liking?"

Alexa's conversation with her parents came to a halt as all three looked at Jane and her plate. A wave of heat quickly washed over Jane in poker-hot embarrassment and she looked at them apologetically.

"The food is delicious." Jane assured…she wasn't exactly sure who she was trying to assure. "I just-"

"You don't have to explain," Alexa stepped in. She frowned at her brother. "Leave her alone, Aiden."

A look of regret crossed his face. It seemed that he hadn't meant to embarrass her.

"I'm sorry," he apologized sincerely.

Jane gave him a brief tight smile and went back to her plate. *Not forgiven.* Up until that moment, Jane hadn't been able to find a fault in him and was liking him more and more by the minute. His unexpectedly rude question gave her all the ammo she needed to guard against any potential crush.

Jerk, she thought. Even if he wasn't, she was going to conclude that he was so that he would no longer have an effect on her. She summarily dismissed him from her mind, shifted in her seat, and focused on Alexa, Ava and Michael before her.

Ava smiled at her and said, "Alexa has told us so much about you growing up. It feels like we're meeting with an old friend."

"Oh really?" Jane asked, "What did she tell you about me?"

Alexa answered, her cheeks growing rosy. "Just that you always had my back at the home. You always looked out for me. Made sure I got to school safely, that I got my homework done, had dinner, took my baths." She frowned in embarrassment and her parents laughed. Alexa suddenly perked up in her seat and turned to Jane.

"Do you remember when we used to play *Xena: Warrior Princess* on the weekends?" She turned to her parents as Jane rolled her eyes. "Oh my gosh, we had the best time. We were obsessed with the re-runs of that show and we would pretend to be Xena and Gabrielle on some quest to stop the gods from destroying the world."

"How did you do that?" Michael asked, his eyes dancing in amusement.

Alexa recalled how they would carefully re-arrange their beds into forts and castles, using sheets as makeshift ceilings and walls.

"Jane saved up a bunch of toilet rolls and paper towel rolls and taped them together to make a staff for me. I'd use it on our day-long treks through the country and it could also double as a weapon." She flailed her arms as if carrying the staff and fighting the bad guys. Her parents continued laughing. Jane smiled fondly at the memory. They'd had a great time of the imagined adventure until Alexa accidentally broke a lamp with her staff. The noise had caught the man's attention and all hell broke loose.

Something must have shifted in Jane's expression because by the time she'd re-focused her attention on the Mastersons, they were looking at her with curious, concerned expressions. She glanced at Alexa and knew the girl remembered the incident just as vividly. Alexa grabbed her hand and squeezed it in comfort. Jane leaned back in her seat. Her meager appetite was now completely gone.

Ava lowered her fork to her plate and carefully met Jane's eyes. "Jane, I hope you don't mind my asking… Alexa ended up in the system when her parents passed in a car accident. What about you? Did you know your parents at all?"

Jane stiffened, reluctant to share such information with strangers, particularly one across from her. She felt his eyes on the side of her face but still chose to ignore him. Rather than overreact and make a fool out of herself, Jane decided to answer the question directly.

"I don't know the identity of my biological father and I am unaware of the whereabouts of my biological mother. I was given to my grandmother when her daughter proved unfit to be a parent and stayed with her until her death. I entered the system when I was ten and remained in it until I was eighteen."

The tone and cadence of her voice brokered no further questions and Ava and Michael's gentle smiles assured her they would ask no more.

After dinner, the family congregated into the impressive living room. The well-lit space showed off two of Alexa's canvas paintings. Though studying to be a graphic designer, Jane could tell from the pieces alone that Alexa had a flair for abstract art. Her paintings had heavy brush strokes and vivid red hues. Jane took in one of the pieces admiringly.

"It's beautiful, Alexa."

Her friend smiled. "Thanks."

Then she frowned.

"What?" Jane asked.

"It feels weird hearing you call me Alexa. I'm so used to you calling me 'little one.'"

Jane laughed. "Well, you're not little anymore. Hell, you're almost my height."

Alexa looked up at her and grinned. Her stare shifted past Jane's shoulder and Jane saw that she was looking at her brother. Aiden, though speaking with his father, was clearly watching the two of them converse.

"He likes you," Alexa said quietly.

Jane frowned. Where did that come from? Alexa read the look on her face and sighed.

"Sorry. I don't know why I said that. I promised him and myself that I wouldn't interfere. But…" she paused and grinned mischievously. "He likes you."

Ava reached in a nearby cabinet and pulled out a board game.

"Anyone up for monopoly?"

Ten seconds earlier, Jane would have been happy to play but now all she could think about were Alexa's disconcerting words and the prospect of sitting in close proximity to the man she was doing her best to dislike.

"I want to play!" Alexa exclaimed. She turned to Jane and grinned. "I never win. Aiden always ends up with the most property and money. He can even beat Dad."

"That's because he learned some new tricks in the Series 7." Michael quipped.

"You're a stockbroker." Jane said. It was the first time she'd spoken to him since his comment during dinner. He looked as surprised to hear her speak to him as she was that she'd done it.

He nodded and said, "Yes, I am."

There was an awkward silence as the two looked at each other with inscrutable expressions. She couldn't decipher what he was thinking and she would be damned if she'd let him see her thoughts. At that point, *she* couldn't even pinpoint what she thought of him.

"Okay then," Ava's gentle voice broke through. "Let's play."

For the next hour, the Masterson family reacquainted Jane with the art of monopoly and Aiden, as Alexa predicted, trumped every single one of them. Jane wasn't caught up so much in the game or the rules of it, but found herself observing the family dynamic as a whole. It was a happy family. She watched them tease each other and laugh, encourage one another and give unsolicited advice about each other's moves. She noticed the little things, consistent eye contact between husband and wife, father and daughter, mother and son. Gentle touches on the shoulder or playful punches along the arm. She felt as if she was watching a heartwarming family movie and they were the stars. There was an ease in their interaction with each other. Clearly they'd done this game and several other family activities with each other on a regular basis. There weren't any verbal jabs, name calling, outbursts, or threatening glances. There was respect and love. A love so tender, so strong, it almost moved Jane to tears. And in that moment, Jane wanted to get away from them.

Maybe I'll have a family of my own like that someday.

But she didn't have it now. And it stung. Alexa's cell phone rang, pulling Jane out of her self-contained misery. She looked up from the property cards in her hand and met Aiden's observant gold eyes. They were kind and compassionate, as if he could see the pain and frustration on her face. She didn't like anyone looking inside. She looked away and watched Alexa stand up.

"Oh! It's the agency I'm using for my year abroad. Excuse me."

Year abroad? Ava read Jane's expression and explained.

"Alexa's planning on spending a year in Europe after she graduates."

"Oh."

How nice Jane thought sarcastically. Inwardly, she frowned at her smarmy reaction. What was wrong with her? Growing up, Alexa was her best friend. She'd always wanted the best for her back then and she still felt the same now. Jane knew that she didn't resent Alexa for her trip to Europe in and of itself. It was that she resented the girl's freedom to go where she wanted and when without debt, lack of resources, or a full-time job to hold her back. She began to notice that the more time she spent with Alexa, the more she resented the years of hard work, struggle, and careful planning she'd had to rely on to make it through life.

Just once, she wanted to be able to forget about money or have enough budgeted to do something just for the fun of it. As grateful as she was for her apartment, there were times when she really felt trapped living in Harlem, the roughest part of Manhattan even though she'd clawed her way into a full time academic profession. Becoming reacquainted with Alexa made Jane ask the irritating question that she tried to avoid whenever she was around privileged people: why them and not her? Why did she get what looked like the short end of the stick and Alexa got the lottery? Why was she still clawing her way up when the girl she'd looked after was traipsing around Europe on her parents' dime?

Why did she get good parents and not me?

Jane stood up and set her cards on the table. Ava, Michael and Aiden looked up at her in surprise.

"Thank you for having me," she said. "But I need to get going."

"Oh," Ava said, disappointment marring her handsome face. "Already? I feel like you just got here."

It had been a couple of hours but the time had flown.

Jane smiled and nodded. "I'm sorry but I have class tomorrow and I'd like to make it back at a decent hour. My line takes me about thirty minutes to get home."

Michael frowned before understanding dawned on his face. "Oh, you don't have to worry about that. We've ordered a car for you to take you back home. Tipped and everything."

Jane's jaw dropped in astonishment. These people thought of *everything*. All the same, she was ready to leave. Private car or not, she did need to get back at a decent hour and she also needed to get away from them. She wasn't about to tell them that she was so overwhelmed with jealousy and self-pity she might burst into tears right in front of them.

"Thank you for having me," she repeated. "Will you please tell Alexa I said goodbye?"

Ava stood up and so did the men. "Of course we will," she said, pulling Jane into another warm hug. The gesture, though lovely, only increased Jane's desire to leave. "I hope you'll come back. It was a pleasure getting to know you and I would love to get to know you more. You're welcome back anytime, okay? We mean it."

Jane nodded at the pleasantry. "Thank you."

She gave a friendly wave to Michael Masterson, nodded at Aiden, and began to walk to the exit.

"Wait," Aiden called out to her. She turned to find him approaching her. He gently cupped her elbow and answered her frown of confusion.

"I'll walk you out," he said.

They remained silent on the walk down the hallway and into the elevator. Halfway down the ride, Aiden spoke, gaze focused on the descending numbers.

"Did you enjoy dinner tonight?"

"I did. Thank you for having me."

"It was our pleasure. You know, my mom is serious about what she said."

Jane frowned, not following.

"About coming back?" he said. "She doesn't say that to everyone who comes for dinner. In fact, she rarely says it at all."

Jane didn't know what to say to that, or what to think for that matter.

"I appreciate that," was all she could think of.

Silence. The elevator chimed floor by floor. It hadn't stopped at a floor yet.

"I'm sorry again about what I said. I shouldn't have put you on the spot like that."

Jane looked at him in surprise. He was looking at her, his expression very sincere with regret.

"I accept your apology," she said but even to her, it sounded like a robotic reply.

Something flickered in his eyes but she couldn't read what it was. Finally, the numbers descended to the first floor. The elevator opened and the two of them got out. Aiden led her to the entrance where a sleek black car was waiting.

"This is Professor Daugherty," Aiden said to the driver. "Please take her wherever she wants to go."

The driver opened the door and nodded agreeably.

"Thank you, Aiden." Jane glanced at him and nearly gasped. His eyes had darkened from amber to a more copper tone. Something else was brewing in them but he glanced at the car, then back at her before nodding and stepping back.

"Good night, Jane." he said, then quickly strode into the building.

Jane quickly strode through the entrance of her apartment, reluctant to be out and about in the often crime-riddled town. The driver had been kind enough to wait until she was inside but Jane wouldn't feel completely safe until the dead bolt was locked with her securely inside her studio apartment. She practically ran up the two flights of stairs and felt her heart stop at the sight of someone at her door. She barely managed to hold back a scream when she realized that the short, portly man standing at the door was her landlord, Mr. Rankine. He was posting something on her door but paused at the sight of her.

"Oh, hello Prof. How are you tonight?" he said in his kind, thick accent.

Jane nodded, relief still flooding her senses. "Fine, Mr. Rankine. And you?"

"I am well, thank you." He pulled the tape off the corner of the notice and held it hesitantly in his hands. "Em, listen, I am terribly sorry to do this but I'll cut right to the chase."

Jane felt a sense of foreboding.

"My youngest daughter, Janet, just got married and she and her husband will be coming in from Kingston next month. I'm sorry to have to do this but I'll be needing this apartment back for her and her husband. There's no space in our own unit."

Jane felt her heart stop once more. This time, it was slow in starting back up. Blood rushed to her ears as the news sank in. The short, balding man gently handed her the termination of lease notice with a regretful expression.

"I'm terribly sorry for this, Miss Jane. You've been a wonderful tenant - the best I've had in years. But she is my child and blood comes first. I'll be returning the last two month's rent to you along with your full deposit tomorrow morning. You'll have three weeks to find a new place."

He pointed to the back of the notice. "I also included a list of apartments nearby with reasonable prices. Sorry, eh?"

Jane didn't say anything. Shell shocked she slowly nodded and barely registered the sight of Mr. Rankine walking around her to his own apartment several floors down. She turned the key to what was once her apartment and tried to wrap her mind around her life's latest survival challenge.

CHAPTER FIVE

Jane arrived at the classroom early. As the first professor to teach there on Wednesday mornings, she had the advantage of setting things up early or simply going to a large room to enjoy the silence by herself. She reviewed her lecture notes and established a list of topics she needed to cover to stay on track.

With ten minutes remaining until the start of class - which meant five if any of her early bird students decided to show up - Jane reviewed her apartment options so far. She had looked over the listings Mr. Rankine had given her but they were either out of her budget or in areas of the city too dangerous for her to consider as a young single woman. She had no legal recourse to take against her landlord because the lease had allowed for him to break it so long as he paid the penalties, which he had that morning. She'd taken an assessment of her finances. Because she'd saved so much money by living in that tiny studio for two years, Jane had managed to save enough to pay off her student loans. She could either pay off her debts with her savings or use her savings to support the renting of a more expensive apartment in a safer area of town.

Safety or financial freedom.

What lovely options she had.

She sighed, yanking at the ends of her sleeves, shifting the bangles to a more comfortable position. There had to be another way. What she needed was a miracle because at this rate, she was not willing to take the money she'd saved for her loans and blow it on housing that was overpriced anyway.

But she was running out of time.

She leaned back in her seat, took a long stretch, and switched to her email. Whatever the solution was to her living situation, she wasn't going to find it in the five minutes she had left before class. She scanned through the dozen emails waiting for her and clicked on the one most prominent - an email from the newly inaugurated university president - sent exclusively to faculty.

Dear Faculty,

I want to thank you all for the warm welcome you have bestowed upon me as your new president. I am exceedingly grateful to be a part of such a supportive and accomplished team. I said it amongst students and I will say it again here: I am determined to forge a brighter, intellectually stimulating path for all students who choose to join the UNY family.

With this in mind, I want to make you aware of a shift in policy I have proposed to the board of trustees regarding the current tenure track of faculty. The majority of our tenured professors currently come from in-house faculty. I am proposing a shift to the lateral recruitment of tenured staff. It is my firm belief that with experience comes wisdom and the lateral recruitment of distinguished and experienced professors will enrich the academic fiber of our university.

Tenured faculty would not be affected by this change but if passed, non-tenured faculty will have to undergo a careful review to determine where their talents would best be served...

Meaning at UNY or another university altogether. Jane's stomach dropped as she glazed over the last paragraph of the letter. President Schneider mentioned the vote that would take place as well as welcomed feedback over her proposal. Her hands shook at the sinking realization that she was not only facing the loss of a home but the potential loss of her livelihood.

Early bird number one, Vanessa Rogalski, strode into class, her wavy blond hair bouncing carelessly on her shoulders.

"Good morning, Professor Daugherty." she said cheerfully.

"Good morning, Vanessa." Jane replied, her voice hollow. She turned to the projector and attached her laptop to it before the student could observe her sullen expression. In the next five minutes, more students flooded the classroom, aware that, unlike some professors, Jane did keep a tally of who was tardy or not. Alexa walked in right before the clock struck 10:00 and Jane started class.

She couldn't tell how she did it or what she said. She led the class as if on autopilot but the students didn't seem to notice. Between discussions about the Trail of Tears and Native American attempts to assimilate, Jane could really only think about her job at risk, her tenure unsure, and her impending state of homelessness unless something changed fast. She hated feeling like this. She hated feeling like everything was out of her control - and only in the span of twenty-four hours! The last time she stood in front of this class, she'd had a year-long lease, was set to pay off her student loans, and was enjoying a job that held a promising future for decades to come as long as she did her part.

Had she not done enough?

She thought about her decision to delay her PhD. She could have applied to and entered a program fresh off her master's degree but her mentor at the time had advised her to get some experience. And Jane, eager to beef up her resume and pay off *some* of her debts, at least, took her mentor's advice and jumped on the position offered her. The whole thing was horrible timing. If she was losing her apartment and her job *next* summer, and had a program to look forward to entering, she wouldn't be so worried. But she didn't know how long she could stretch her savings even if she delayed paying off her loans. With no job to supplement her living, she was screwed. New York City was one of the most expensive places to live in the world - unless you took residence in places where it wasn't worth living. She remembered her days in the Bronx.

I'll be damned if I go back there.

"Professor Daugherty? Professor Daugherty?" Carter called to her. She shook herself to and looked at him expectantly. They were in the middle of reading an article to themselves. "Are you collecting the index card assignment today?"

Jane shook her head. "Those are due next class."

"Okay, thanks."

She turned to head back to her desk and noticed Alexa watching her. The girl gave her a friendly smile and Jane smiled back, aware that her own smile was tense and forced.

She reached her desk, disconnected the projector and pulled up her email. Forwarding President Schneider's email in the body of the text, Jane addressed the letter to Dr. Geissner, the man who told her just weeks ago that she was on the tenure track.

She chose a simple line for the subject: "Should I be worried?"

Mercifully, class wrapped up thirty minutes later without any major blunders on Jane's part. The students left the class, just as oblivious to her issues as when they first arrived. Jane stuffed her papers and laptop into her satchel, preparing to leave. She saw two familiar feet approach her.

"Hey Alexa," she said. She reached into her satchel and pulled out a small envelope. She looked up and saw a hesitant expression cross the younger woman's face.

"Hey," Alexa replied. "I'm sorry I missed you leaving last night. The travel agent picked a horrible time to call."

Jane shook her head and waved it off. She couldn't believe she'd felt irritation or even jealousy at the prospect of Alexa getting to travel through Europe carefree. At this point, she'd be grateful for the stresses of a job and the inconveniences of a tiny apartment - she appreciated them now more than ever. Now that they were at risk.

"Don't worry about it," she replied. She handed Alexa the envelope. "Can you please give this to your parents? It's just a thank you card for last night."

Alexa smiled, pleasantly surprised. "Oh, of course! Thank you. We're all so glad you could come. I hope you'll join us again soon."

Jane sighed, the weight of her problems taking a toll on her ability to pretend.

"I appreciate the invitation Alexa, but right now I'm a bit preoccupied with some things."

Alexa nodded, her expression sobering once more. "Yeah, I noticed you seemed a bit…off today. Can I ask what's wrong?"

Jane stiffened at the question. She never told people her business. Ever. A part of her felt grateful that Alexa noticed her mood and even cared to ask. Another part of her felt annoyed at the intrusion. Then she reminded herself who this was. Alexa wasn't some random student or even peer. She was the only other girl who'd lived in that house with her.

Jane took a deep breath and spilled, "I received a notice from my landlord last night. His daughter is immigrating to the States with her husband and he's decided to give her my apartment."

Alexa's mouth dropped.

"I know. He says I have three weeks to find a new place but that's proved difficult."

"Where do you live now?" Alexa asked.

Jane stiffened again.

"If you don't mind my asking." Alexa added.

"Harlem," Jane answered, not sure why she felt defensive about it. They'd both lived in the Bronx at one time. But only one of them was living on the Upper East Side now.

Alexa nodded, completely unfazed by her revelation. Not only did she look unfazed, she looked *happy*. Jane frowned again. How could she look *happy* at her dilemma? She didn't expect Alexa to help but she sure didn't expect her to be so insensitive.

"This is great," Alexa said. "This is such a God-thing."

"Excuse me?" Jane asked, irritated.

"I know a place where you can stay."

That got her attention. Alexa pulled out her phone, texted Jane an address and told her, "Meet me at Sixth Avenue between Lispenard Street and Canal Street tomorrow afternoon. We'll figure this out."

"Morning, Masterson."

"Morning, Jones."

Aiden strode through the office hallway, coffee in one hand, briefcase in the other as he beelined his way to his own private abode. His co-workers were typing away, running numbers, making offers, cajoling clients…he knew it because he'd done it all. He still was doing it - just better than everyone else. It had been eight years since Aiden joined Weinstein Trade as an intern right out of college. He'd been fresh-faced, openly ambitious, and sharp as a tack, eager to climb the corporate ladder. He quickly discovered that while all of those qualities were to his advantage, the best asset he could bring was his charm.

So he'd used it.

Aiden charmed his way into the good graces of his supervisor, charmed his way into the hearts of the partners, and charmed the signatures out of a slew of coveted clients the minute he'd passed his exam. If he thought about it, aside from the headache inducing hours in school and studying for his exams, most of Aiden's success could be attributed to his charming personality. He did great work, he was thorough and gave sound advice. He'd made his clients and his firm a ton of money; but he also knew his clients and his firm would not have given him the time of day if he didn't have such a pleasant personality.

So why couldn't he charm her?

"Morning, Lisa." he greeted his assistant.

"Morning, boss."

She briefly gave him the rundown of messages, meetings, and pressing client concerns. He walked into his office, closed the door, sat at his desk, and flipped open his laptop. It then occurred to him that he'd barely registered anything Lisa said. He swiveled away from his desk and faced his floor to ceiling windows, overlooking the financial district. The view was spectacular and all he could see was *her*. Her brown eyes. Her full lips. Her brief smiles. Her tight frown.

She'd been overwhelmed last night. Alexa was too nervous to notice but he had. It hadn't taken a rocket scientist to deduce that Alexa had failed to mention their family's enormous wealth to her old friend prior to their dinner. Aiden had stood at the top of the stairs, watching Jane Daugherty try to wrap her mind around everything she was seeing. He remembered how her beautiful dark eyes had rounded to saucers. Her dark brown hands kept pulling at the ends of her sleeves and her head kept turning left and right, picking up more details that only increased her already-visible anxiety. *His* eyes had widened at the sight of her hair. Once stylish little knots, she had transformed them into a fiery full afro that perfectly framed her face and made his heart slam against his rib cage.

Does her beauty ever end?

He frowned at the thought. He didn't even sound normal to *himself*. He'd heard of men breaking into poetry at the sight of a beautiful woman but he wasn't planning on being one of them. His thoughts shifted to her behavior. The minute he'd made his presence known, she'd shielded her nervousness with a mask of confidence so convincing, he'd almost questioned if he'd seen her nerves in the first place. She managed to keep up the facade the majority of the night until his comment about the food. It was more a question at her small serving sizes. He knew it was inappropriate the minute he'd voiced the question but he couldn't help but wonder why she was barely eating anything that night. Maybe she was nervous.

Maybe she's anorexic.

He shook his head. She was slender but not dangerously thin and the little food she did eat, she seemed to savor. It really wasn't his business why she ate the way she ate or ate the little that she ate. And apparently, she felt the same. He could still remember her embarrassment at his question. How mortified she'd looked when trying to assure his mother she enjoyed her food. If she were white, her cheeks would have been red and on fire. Once the embarrassment had passed, something had taken its place because even when he'd apologized, she ignored him the remainder of the evening. She wouldn't meet his eyes or glance his way, even for a second. Several times, he'd felt as if he weren't even in the room as far as she was concerned. Normally, he would have shrugged it off. But this time, it had really bothered him. He spent the remainder of the evening vacillating between feeling guilty for his comment and angry at her snubbing.

Why was she so oversensitive?

But was she? When he'd apologized a second time that night, she verbally accepted it.

That didn't mean she wanted to be friends, though.

His phone rang, snapping him out of his spiraling thoughts.

"Hello?" he answered.

"Aiden, how you doing?" Richard Weinstein greeted. The man had a booming voice to match his booming brokerage firm. "Listen, did you get the email on the Wellington contract?"

Aiden frowned. "Yes, I did. His team finished drafting it around nine last night."

"Have you read it?"

"Yes. It looks good to me. I made a couple notes that legal might want to look at."

"Fantastic," Weinstein replied, clearly pleased. "I knew you would get it done."

Aiden held back a sigh of irritation at the unspoken expectation. He was the fastest rising broker in his firm because he was also the fastest working broker. If a client wanted to sign, he signed them immediately. If a client wanted to invest, he set up the deal within the hour. If a contract came through well past quitting time, Aiden had the document reviewed and notated by the next morning. It was an eager beaver attitude that his partners thrived on but were reluctant to implement themselves. He'd been happy to do it in his early twenties but now the "do it now" attitude of the firm rubbed him the wrong way. Not because he resented efficiency but because he resented impatience. Charles B. Wellington had made it clear that he was more than comfortable with having the contract settled by the end of the following week. Money-hungry Weinstein wanted it settled by the end of the following day.

Aiden wrapped up his call with Weinstein, gave his notes to Lisa and had her deliver them to legal for further review.

Aren't you tired of this? a weary voice asked him. He knew it was his thought but Aiden had never had the courage to ask it before.

There has to be more than this, the same voice whispered. He knew what "this" was: money-grabbing, fortune-chasing, fibbing and charming to get the deal done. As much money as his career had earned him, Aiden sometimes felt like a prisoner of it. He was lucky nothing big came up during his dinner last night. If it had, he would have had to leave early or canceled altogether. Even after an exhausting day of work and a confusing dinner with family, Aiden had spent several hours later that night reviewing a contract that he'd been given more than a week to follow up on.

His phone rang again.

"This is Masterson," he said in a snappish tone.

"Whew! Honey, are you alright?" Ava said, half-amused, half-surprised.

"Oh! Sorry, Mom." Aiden apologized, sweeping a hand over his face. His voice softened considerably. "Hi. How are you?"

She laughed lightheartedly.

"Clearly doing better than you. Are you okay?" she asked, concern evident in her voice.

He sighed and shook his head. "I'm fine. I'm fine. What's going on?"

"Not much. Your Dad and I wanted to know if you're coming for dinner."

Aiden felt heat rise at the back of his collar. He was thirty-years-old and spending regular evenings with his fifty-something-year-old parents.

"No, thanks." he said. He couldn't spend *all* his evenings with his folks.

"Oh, are you going out with friends?"

It was an innocent question but one that irritated him nonetheless. He was partially to blame but so were the circumstances of life. All of his friends were either settled down with kids, out of state in new jobs, or too busy in their own professions to hang out with him. As charming as he was in making connections, Aiden noticed that he had a difficult time in keeping them. Unless they were clients or family, he did not invest the time needed to keep relationships going. Moves and marriages and kids were a natural part of life. It was his own fault for turning to work instead of building newer or stronger friendships. He didn't answer the question. His mother must have picked up on his irritation because she moved on to something else.

"How do you think dinner went last night?"

"Great," he replied. "You made a wonderful meal, as usual. I think Alexa's friend really enjoyed it."

"I hope so," she said, her voice softening. "She didn't eat much despite her answer to your rude question."

Ouch. Of course, leave it to mother to notice.

"Mom-"

"I know you didn't mean to embarrass her, but sometimes you really need to think before you speak, Aiden."

"I know," he said. "I'm sorry."

"What do you think of her?" she asked.

Aiden frowned. "What do you mean?"

His mother chuckled. "Well, she's very beautiful."

Oh no, not you too!

"Mom…"

"What? I'm not the one who had my eyes on her the *entire* evening. Even your father noticed."

Aiden didn't believe it. His father would never gossip about him to his mother.

"I'm married to him, Aiden. We talk about you all the time."

Ugh! How did she do that mother mind reading thing?

"What did you think about her?" he asked, trying to take the heat off himself.

"Oh, I love her." his mother said easily. "I hope you told her I was serious about my invitation. She's such a wonderful girl - even better than

Alexa could have described. To think of all that she's overcome at her age - and how she protected Lexi when she was just a child herself..." He could just see his mother shaking her head in awe.

"Yeah, she's pretty remarkable," he agreed absentmindedly, her stunning face in his mind's eye again. A question came to him that he hadn't thought to ask before. "How soon did Alexa mention Jane after she first started talking?"

A pause over the line. "Immediately. After eight months, it was like a watershed of information. The adoption agent hadn't mentioned any other girls in the foster home. We'd assumed Alexa was the only one. By the time she started speaking, by the time she mentioned Jane, Jane had already been transferred to another home."

"No forwarding info?"

"None that we could access. If we could, we would have adopted her too."

Aiden almost asked why the adoption agency hadn't mentioned Jane in the beginning but he thought he already knew. Between the two of them, the agent probably figured that his parents would prefer the pretty white girl over the older black teenager. They probably hadn't realized that his parents were willing to adopt them both. If they had known, Jane would have been his little sister. He shuddered. Though the alternative could have happened he had no desire to imagine it – especially when he felt the way he felt about her now.

"Mom...did Alexa tell you exactly *how* Jane protected her in that foster home?"

"She mentioned that he verbally and physically abused the children there. She and Jane were the only girls housed there but he treated them just as harshly as he did the boys. Thankfully, Jane was already there when Alexa arrived. You know how sensitive she is. I'm not sure she could've handled that."

How did Jane?

The question rang in his mind long after he hung up with his mother. He managed to get work done that day, and stayed ahead of the game, but he didn't know how. All he really cared to think about revolved around a stunning black professor who'd had more than her fair share of hard knocks. He remembered the look that flashed in her eyes during the monopoly game. He'd watched her observe their family and he saw an almost tangible look of longing. Little did she know he felt the same type of longing.

For what exactly? He didn't know. For something more meaningful than chasing after money and climbing the corporate ladder. For a deep connection that ran outside of his immediate family. He loved his parents. He loved Alexa. But maybe it was an almost carnal need in him to follow his friends' example and start a family of his own.

The thought scared him. He'd never had it before. Sure, he'd always known he wanted to get married and have kids *someday* but that prospect had always been in the future. Now, it was something he was seriously inclined to consider. Did Jane want the same? And even if she did, what did her desires have to do with his?

She's your sister's friend, he reminded himself.

He had no business thinking of her as anything else.

CHAPTER SIX

"What do you think?" Alexa asked.

Jane was in love. She was absolutely, positively, madly in love.

The apartment was breathtaking. Located in the heart of Tribeca, it was a modern, glass-encased high rise, overlooking the sparkling water of the Hudson River. It was in the perfect location - peaceful, safe and quiet. The Hudson River Park was a five minute walk away and the ACE metro line was right around the block. She could get to UNY in ten minutes flat if she took the express line. But it wasn't the location of the building that rendered her breathless. It was the apartment itself.

It somehow looked even more spacious than the Masterson's Upper East Side penthouse. The ceilings were incredibly tall with individually framed windows running from the top of the walls to the bottom, spilling in a refreshing pool of natural light, which reflected off the white interior. Everything was sleek, modern, and chic. The walls were stark white, matching the furniture, the floors were a rich dark chocolate oak. The kitchen, though smaller than the penthouse, held polished white marble countertops and a solid kitchen island that doubled as a bar. Sleek loft staircases carried the women up to two bedrooms and two full baths, continuing the white-brown, modern-chic interior design. It was a luxury hotel parading as an apartment.

There was no way in hell she could afford it.

She looked at Alexa in confusion. "Why are you showing this to me?"

"You need a place to stay, don't you?" Alexa replied. Jane peered into her hazel eyes and saw her shift on her feet. She frowned, her confusion growing.

"Yes, I need a place to stay," she said. "But this is completely out of my budget." She looked around the place. "How did you get a key? Who lives here?"

Alexa sighed, walked over to the kitchen and perched herself on the wooden kitchen bar stool. "I do," she admitted. "This is my apartment. I live here with a junior from Columbia and I'm in need of a new roomie since she'll be leaving soon."

"You guys got this apartment together?" Jane asked, still trying to fit the pieces together.

Alexa shook her head, her wavy tresses swishing. "My parents own the apartment. They used to use it as a rental property but allow me to stay here under the condition that I have a respectable roommate to offset some of the cost. They did the same thing for Aiden when he was a student. Anyway, Alana's leaving in one week. This might be perfect for you."

Jane shook her head, already seeing the problems in the arrangement.

"Why is she leaving?" she asked.

Alexa's expression darkened at the question. She leaped off her stool and walked back up the stairs. Jane followed, nervous about what she was about to see. On the second floor, Alexa walked down the short hallway, past her room to the firmly closed door at the end of the hall. She opened the door and gestured with her head at the room.

Jane gasped.

It was a mess.

No.

A mess would be a few clothes thrown around and some homework unorganized.

It was a catastrophe.

Clothes strewn across the bed, on the headboard, on the desk. Food on *several* plates lying opened, mugs with coffee residue stacked about precariously. Papers, books, magazines, and more clothes, piled at every corner of the massive room. Jane coughed at the moldy, pungent smell in the room. It was stale coffee mixed with takeout gone bad.

It was hideous.

The bones of the room revealed what used to be a stunning oasis with another window overlooking the river but the content of it was a horror show.

Who could live like that?

"Did you say a *girl* lives with you?" Jane asked.

Alexa nodded emphatically. "Yes. She's from Russia. Her father is a shipping magnate."

She closed the door and led them back down to the living room.

"Apparently she was raised with a diamond spoon in her mouth because the prospect of picking up her own clothes or throwing away her own food was too much to bear. She never used the common areas so I didn't know about the severity of the problem until I went to borrow a book from her. I thought I'd have a heart attack."

Alexa explained how she told her parents and they in turn had a long talk with the girl's parents. They all agreed to part ways amicably with the father apologetically offering to pay for any cleaning, renovations, and repairs that needed to be made.

"I promise you, it will not look like that in two weeks. The room will be stripped of all the furniture, thoroughly washed and re-decorated. It will be a brand new space."

Jane shook her head. "I can't."

Alexa frowned, her pretty lips protruding into a pout. "Why not?"

"Conflict of interest."

"Oh," Alexa said. "Don't worry about it."

"I have to worry about it if I want to keep my job," Jane replied. Thought, at this point, she didn't even know if she *had* a job. She still hadn't heard back from Dr. Geissner regarding the tenure policy change. In an "up or out" climate like academia, Jane needed to know if she had a chance of moving up at UNY or if she needed to find a place to move on to.

Alexa sighed. "Do you want the apartment or not?"

"I wouldn't be able to afford it."

"How much is it in Harlem?"

Jane scoffed. "A lot less. This has to be at least $6,000 a month."

"How much is it in Harlem?" Alexa repeated calmly.

Jane cocked her head and looked at her friend's steady expression. "$1,600."

"You can have this place for $1,500."

Jane's jaw dropped. The price was unheard of. She could barely find an apartment that low in the safer areas of *Harlem* much less in Tribeca! Clearly Alexa would be paying more. Or her parents would be earning less.

"Is that how much your roommate pays now?" Jane asked.

Alexa shrugged nonchalantly.

"Is it?" Jane insisted.

Alexa rolled her eyes. "No, but who cares? *She* didn't pay anything anyway. Her daddy did. You'll pay less and have a great place to stay. Contrary to what you may think, I haven't changed much since the last time we lived together." Jane felt a slight pang at the though of that house. "I'm quiet, I'm chill. I'll always respect your space…"

"I appreciate the offer, Alexa, I really do. But I'm still your professor-"

Alexa held up a hand, silencing Jane mid-explanation. She pulled out her iPhone, punched a few buttons and handed Jane the phone, saying, "Not anymore, you're not."

Jane looked at the Alexa's personal UNY student account. She just dropped the class online.

Jane opened her mouth then closed it, speechless. Finally, she handed the phone back to Alexa and asked her in a quiet voice, "Why are you doing this?"

Alexa's face softened.

"Do you really have to ask?" She paused, looking around her apartment as if dumbfounded. "Jane, I don't know what happened to you since the day I left that hellhole. I'll never forgive myself for not speaking up about it sooner."

Jane frowned. "What do you mean?"

"I mean...when I first arrived I was shell-shocked. I was still that frightened little kid who could barely get a word out unless I was alone with you. I didn't talk to my parents for eight months. All of my communication with them was through gestures and nonverbals."

Jane nodded, not following. She stayed quiet, hoping she would understand.

"By the time I talked to my parents, I trusted them enough to tell them everything. And a huge part of everything was you." Alexa smiled. "And how you protected me. My parents were shocked that there was another girl in the house. They had no idea that you were there. And when they learned about how violent *he* was, they reported him immediately. That's when they learned that he'd already been reported. He was serving time and you were in another home, one that couldn't be traced. Had they known, they would have adopted us together."

Jane frowned in surprise. She never would have guessed all of that had transpired shortly after Alexa had left. Part of her was happy that Alexa cared enough about her to mention her to her parents. But another part of her wished she didn't know. Who wanted to hear that they were just eight months short of being rescued and adopted into an über wealthy family? Who wanted to hear that they didn't *have* to give up the only friend they'd ever had - one they regarded as their little sister? Who wanted to learn that they *just* missed the mark of a completely different, infinitely easier life? Jane wasn't one of those people.

Let it go, she told herself. *What happened, happened and you can't change it now. Change what you* do *have control over.*

"Anyway," Alexa continued on the same vein. "You're here now. And I know a lot of years have passed and we're both different people now but..." She met Jane's eyes and to Jane's surprise, tears started to gather in her hazel eyes. "I've missed you. And I never got the chance to properly thank you. I'm not just grateful to you. I'm grateful to have you back in my life. I hope you are too."

A foreign sensation gripped Jane's chest. It was a burning that started behind her rib cage and traveled to the back of her eyes. To her horror, she realized she was starting to tear up too. She looked away and stared at the grand piano sitting on the elevated footing of the living space. In that moment, she felt an unspeakable shame for every jealous thought, feeling and attitude she'd harbored since seeing Alexa's childhood home. There was a time when she had been selfless and only cared to protect the girl in front of her. But somewhere along the line, maybe when Alexa finally made it out into a good home, the caring side of Jane had died. A harder shell emerged, encasing her heart and all of her hurts inside of it. She didn't do vulnerable. She didn't do tears. And she didn't do reminiscing over nostalgic memories. Her tears dried.

"I'm not the same, anymore, little one."

Alexa gasped. Jane turned back to her. A bright smile lit up her friend's face as her tears fell.

"You called me 'little one.' That's the first time I've heard you say it in years."

Jane smiled sadly and shook her head again. "You're not listening."

Alexa immediately sobered. "I am."

The shift in her expression was so sudden, it almost alarmed Jane. Alexa squeezed her hand and held her steady gaze.

"I know you're not the same, Jane. I know you've changed. Even with me, you're not as warm and welcoming as you once were - and I don't say that to guilt you or make you feel bad. I just mean... I get it. You're not fifteen anymore. A lot has happened and I can't expect you to revert to the girl I used to know. What I'm trying to say is that I want to be your friend again - not based on our past alone but based on who you are now. I mean it."

I mean it. Those were the same words Ava Masterson had used. Jane could see the sincerity in her eyes. She could feel the shell around her heart crack just a little. It was enough to welcome warmth, hope, and a desire for the friendship Alexa offered her. She squeezed Alexa's hand back and smiled.

"I think I'd like that."

CHAPTER SEVEN

Jane lugged the heavy cardboard box into the living room and carefully rested it on the white marble counter, pausing to look around at her new home.

It was a new life.

That was the only way she could summarize her move to Tribeca. It had been nearly a month since Jane and Alexa had their conversation in the grand living room of Alexa's apartment. Alana Yegorov moved later that week, professional cleaners finished a week after that and the movers positioned the new furniture, paintings, and finishes to Ava Masterson's exact specifications two days later.

According to Alexa, her mother had pitched the best kind of fit at the news that Jane would be her daughter's new roommate. She and her husband insisted on supplying Jane with the same moving company they used for the furniture at no cost to her. They signed her to an unheard of "at will" year-long lease; essentially a lease that could be broken by her at any time for any reason, so long as she gave two weeks' notice.

When she'd stepped into her new room days after signing the lease, Jane nearly dropped the box in her hands at the sight of her new space. The cleaners, movers, and Ava had all done their magic - transforming the room from the pigpen it once was to the masterpiece it was meant to be.

Like everything else in the apartment, the room was huge. It more than doubled the size of her old studio. The walls were stark white with accented art pieces complimenting the silver-gray chaise and artfully distressed wooden tables. Jane had a full-sized desk and chair, a small white sofa, and a long gray foot stool positioned at the foot of her perfectly-made, massive queen sized bed. Long soft white curtains draped the tall windows positioned at the side of her room, overlooking the city streets below, the river just beyond the park. The attached bathroom was marble white with swirls of gray mixed in. It had a free-standing shower and a separate full-length tub that could comfortably hold her 5'10" frame.

All of this, for $100 less than what she'd paid for her rinky-dink excuse of an apartment in Harlem. Not only did Jane gladly kiss that shady place goodbye, she also submitted her very last payment to the federal government for her loans. No more student debt. It was the greatest victory she'd gained since earning her degrees in the first place. So far she had no complaints about the place. It was stunning, safe, had a magnificent view, allowed her more than enough space of her own, and was much closer to UNY's campus. She and Alexa often took the subway into Greenwich Village together and she enjoyed their renewed friendship.

Jane reached into the box on the counter and pulled out her most prized possession: her Canon 5D DSLR. Outdated by several years, it was still the best camera she'd ever owned. She'd saved up for three years to purchase it. She pulled out her 2009 PC and fired it up. As she downloaded the latest footage from her Canon, she thought more about the Masterson family. They had been nothing but generous, welcoming, and openly kind to her since she first met them four weeks ago. She'd dined with them a couple of times since then but typically turned down their frequent invitations for dinner. She knew it was unfounded, but a large part of her felt very suspicious of people's kindness. She was waiting for the other shoe to drop when they'd ask something of her or reveal themselves to be less than gracious. Not only that, but she was wary of spending too much time in the company of Alexa's brother. Every time she joined them for the evening, *he* was there with his piercing amber eyes and smirking full lips.

She quickly discovered that Aiden Masterson was a very confident man. Outspoken, blunt, and all-too-charming. While he refrained from saying anything else about her eating habits - though she noticed his frequent glances at her plate - he didn't refrain from saying much of anything else. He spoke about business and trade with his father, who Jane learned was a prominent investor; he discussed Alexa's art classes with her and had a rich knowledge of the Baroque movement along with several other artistic eras. He could even engage in lively debates with his mother about the efficacy of modern child psychiatry in the face of rising mental illness cases. She admired his intellect and his brass but she shied away from his presence and his conversation altogether. If he asked her a question or tried to engage, she kept her responses brief, often leaving him with a puzzled expression on his handsome face.

Someone knocked on the door.

In Harlem, a knock on the door would have sent a current of fear through her chest. This time, she only felt curiosity as she strode to open it.

Speak of the devil.

"Hello, Jane." Aiden greeted.

"Hi," she said.

As usual, his piercing eyes looked her over before shifting to look over her head into the apartment.

"Is Alexa home? I'm taking her out to dinner tonight."

She shook her head. "She's not back yet."

Alexa had a busy life of her own and gave Jane plenty of space, reading her as well as she did when they were kids. She noticed that she and her brother spent an inordinate amount of time with their parents or with each other on a day-to-day basis for a family with two adult kids. They seemed especially close.

Must be nice, she thought.

She waited a beat before realizing common courtesy would require her to step back and let him in. She moved out of the way, wordlessly allowing him to enter. He hesitated at the threshold.

"You don't mind if I wait for her?" he asked, a blond eyebrow raised.

"Not at all," she lied. She turned on her heel and headed back to the kitchen while he closed the door. She pretended that he wasn't there. According to Alexa, he'd been over enough times to know where everything in the house was. He could pour himself a drink if he wanted to. She retrieved the box from the counter and took it back to her room, ignoring the heat of his gaze on her frame.

When she returned, he was stationed in front of her computer, looking at the images she downloaded. He gestured at the laptop.

"You're a photographer?"

"It's a hobby."

"You're really good," he said. She knew he wasn't flattering her.

"I know."

He looked up from the screen and grinned. She smiled back and added, "Thank you."

"You don't teach photography?" he asked.

"No. Just English."

"Why?"

She frowned slightly at his curiosity. Did he really want to know or was he just making small talk? She looked him over and knew the answer. He had a tendency to tilt his head and smirk when he was trying to charm someone. This time, he was asking the question directly, no smirk or grin, or tilt of his head. He really wanted to know about her interests. What she didn't know was why.

"Why don't you do photography for a living?" he asked.

Why do you care? she thought.

"Photography is a hobby," she answered. "Literature is a passion."

He nodded and to her surprise, a look of regret soured his handsome features.

"That must be nice," he said absentmindedly. "To know what you're passionate about."

"Don't you?" she asked. Her question was so blunt, he looked at her sharply, clearly startled. Something flickered in his golden eyes but he didn't get the chance to answer.

"Hey, I'm home." Alexa called as she walked through the door. She looked between the two of them and smiled. "Hey, what's up?"

"Not much, Shark Bait." Aiden answered. Jane looked at his easy grin. He'd clearly recovered from whatever it was that bothered him. "You gonna be ready soon? I'm hungry."

Alexa dropped her backpack and pulled out her wallet.

"Why do you have that? You know you don't need it." Aiden waved at it in annoyance. Alexa smiled and put the wallet back in her bag.

"Okay, I'm ready then." She smiled. She glanced at Jane. "We're having dinner at *Le Rouge*. Do you want to come?"

Jane wondered if the Mastersons made a habit of inviting people to all their meals and gatherings. As many times as she declined, they always extended an invitation. She didn't want to offend them and she always had fun the few times she did say yes but she also noticed her tendency to capitulate to Alexa's wishes. She was an introvert and her extroverted friend seemed determined to change that. She glanced at Aiden and couldn't discern his expression. Did he want her to go?

"No, thanks." she replied.

Aiden frowned. "Why-"

"Aiden," Alexa interrupted. He looked at his sister who shook her head slightly. The nonverbal cue was so obvious, Jane couldn't have missed it. It clearly said, *If she doesn't want to go, she doesn't want to go. Leave her alone.* Jane smiled at Alexa appreciatively. She glanced at Aiden who still wore a confused frown. He picked up his sister's cue and let the subject drop. Perusing her face once more with his impenetrable eyes, Aiden nodded at her—

"Have a goodnight."

—and escorted his sister out of the apartment.

"Why didn't Jane come with us?"

Alexa shrugged her shoulders, busily eating her pasta.

"If it was just you going to dinner, she would have said yes, wouldn't she?"

His sister shrugged again. He frowned at her evasiveness.

"I still can't believe she's a professor at only 24-years-old. She said she earned her master's at twenty-two. Who does that?"

Alexa smiled affectionately. "Jane does. She was always a hard worker. When we were kids, she would collect plastic bottles and scrunched up cans along the street and turn them in for money. At Children's Aid, she would look for designer clothes in the donations so she could turn around and sell them for profit. She was always hustling to make a dime."

He nodded, admiring her childhood business acumen. He looked at his sister.

"What did you do to make ends meet?"

Alexa shrugged, color rushing to her face. "That's the point. I didn't *have* to do anything. If I needed something, Jane got it. If there was a field trip that cost money, Jane filled out the form, explaining why I couldn't afford it. She was the foster parent in that house for all intents and purposes."

"How long had she been a resident there when you arrived?"

Alexa frowned at him, slowly chewing her food. She put her fork down and carefully contemplated the question.

"I think she'd been there for three years...? Yeah." Alex nodded, more sure. "Since she was ten."

"She had no family to claim her? Not even distant relatives?" he asked.

"Two of her aunts kept her for a couple of years after her grandmother died. I think they shuffled her back and forth between them for a while but they eventually turned her over to the state. Said they couldn't afford her." She frowned in clear disgust. Who did that to their family?

"Why was she taken away from her mom?" he asked.

Alexa sighed. "Aiden..."

He frowned at her. "What? I'm just asking a question."

She met his eyes and he saw a quiet determination in them. "I know you're curious but I can't answer those questions. Jane wouldn't appreciate me telling all of her business to you-"

"I wouldn't tell-"

"I know you wouldn't but all the same, I'm going to respect her privacy. If it was just about me, then you know I would tell you everything. But it's not. It's her story and I want to respect that. She deserves it after everything she did for me."

He nodded, putting a hand up. He could already feel the bud of guilt blooming in the pit of his stomach. They ate their food in silence for the next few minutes, both of them deep in thought. Finally, Alexa looked at her brother and let out a frustrated sigh. He frowned at the noise.

"Will you just ask her out already? She can tell you everything you want to know and I know she likes you too."

"Listen, Lex. I appreciate your need to respect her privacy. Do me a favor and respect mine."

He wasn't surprised when she rolled her eyes in response and scooped a forkful of pasta into her pretty little mouth.

She'd made a mistake.

Jane sat at the kitchen barstool, lights on as the New York City skyline became brighter and brighter and the night became darker and darker. It was Friday night and she was home, alone, grading papers. It was her least favorite part of being a professor. So much so that she looked forward to the day when she'd have a TA to do it. Unless she came across a well-written paper - usually drafted by an upper class English major - Jane did not enjoy reading the rambling thoughts of supposed college students who shouldn't have been allowed to pass their high school Lit and Composition courses.

She finished paper number forty-two before leaning back on the stool and staring out the window.

What is the matter with me? she wondered. She should be happy. Just hours ago, she'd received an email from Geissner telling her that he and his department chair colleagues didn't think President Schneider's proposal would pass. He initially told her to sit tight while he looked into it. After a month of waiting and wringing her hands, she'd received the news she'd hoped for when he essentially told her not to worry.

So why wasn't she happy?

You're lonely.

She frowned at the words. She frowned at the voice. She looked around, briefly wondering if she'd had a hallucination. She'd heard the words but they weren't her own thoughts.

Great. You're sad and confused and now you're hearing shit.

She sank her head into her hands and pressed the heel of her palms into her closed eyes. She used to do that all the time as a kid. If she pressed hard enough and long enough, she'd see stars behind her eyelids and it made her forget about her troubles if only for a moment. She opened her eyes and felt unexpected tears rush to them.

She *was* lonely. She'd made a mistake. She should have said yes to the dinner invitation but she was too proud to rectify it now. Besides, she thought as she glanced at her watch, Aiden and Alexa were probably starting on their dessert. It would be foolish to give Lex a call.

Someone knocked on the door. Jane frowned at it and walked over, wondering who it could be because Alexa never forgot her keys. She opened the door and felt a jolt of surprise.

"Oh! Hello, Dr. Masterson."

"Ava. Ava! How many times do I have to tell you, young lady?" the older woman reprimanded her, smiling. She walked inside, carrying three trays covered in aluminum foil. "Michael told me to tell you hi."

She headed straight to the kitchen, opened the fridge, and started re-arranging its contents.

"I brought you girls some lasagna and vegetables. I also made a strawberry pie."

Jane folded her arms over her stomach. The meal sounded delicious to her ears but did nothing for her stomach. She knew Alexa would have to eat most, if not all, of it.

"Thank you," she said quietly. She went back to her stool and watched Ava organize their fridge then their freezer as she chatted about Alexa's classes and asked Jane about hers. Jane realized this was natural for her. She was doing her "Mom thing." It was nice but odd and for some reason, it made her feel sad. She'd never had a mother to ask how she was doing in school or bring her home cooked meals. She looked down at her papers, her mood sinking even further than it did before.

"Jane?"

She looked back up to see Ava's concerned face. Alexa's mother glanced at the papers on the kitchen bar.

"I'm sorry - I must have interrupted your work." She then looked at the fridge and freezer she'd just re-arranged. "And I can't believe I just upended your food without asking," she groaned. "Oh, I'm sorry. You must think me the most pushy, intrusive-"

"No, I don't." Jane said. "You're just being a mom. Alexa's very lucky. Aiden, too." she added.

Ava's eyes softened. She looked at Jane for a moment, her gray streaked eyebrows turning down. "Are you all right, sweetheart?"

The endearment surprised her. She didn't know how to answer.

Ava peered at her closely, her analytical mind clearly at work. "You seem sad. Did something happen today?"

Jane shook her head. She began to squirm under the psychiatrist's perceptive blue eyes. She looked down at her papers again, shook her head and tried to shrug off the sadness like a coat.

"Sorry," she said, smiling in embarrassment. "I'll be fine. I don't want to hold you up."

"You're not holding me up," Ava said immediately. Jane was surprised at the almost fierce assurance in her voice. Ava waited, watching Jane squirm even further under her keen stare.

"Where's Lexi?" she finally asked.

"Out at dinner with Aiden."

"And they didn't invite you?" she asked in surprise.

"I declined."

"I see."

Ava waited. Jane realized she was expecting some sort of explanation.

"I'm not…" she began. "I'm not used to this."

"To what?" Ava asked gently. Patiently.

"To people acting like they care."

There. She'd said it.

"I care," Ava replied. Jane finally met her eyes and saw the warmest, most open expression. "All of us do, dear."

Jane didn't say anything but looked back down at her papers.

"You're worried that this is too good to be true, aren't you? That we'll end up being bad people or the friendship will end."

Jane gasped in surprise. She looked back up in time to see Ava nodding with a smile

"It might," Jane finally answered.

"It doesn't have to," Ava replied.

It doesn't have to. It was a prospect that both thrilled and terrified Jane. Could a long term friendship with Alexa and her family actually happen? She never got adopted. Never connected with anyone in school or at work for that matter. But could this be the connection she'd always longed for as a child?

Ava glanced at the papers strewn across the bar counter.

"Do you *want* to be left alone?"

Jane shook her head. "But I have to get these graded."

Ava nodded, went to her purse, and pulled out what looked like a Kindle. She sat on a barstool two seats away from Jane and began to read. Jane watched her for a few moments, confused, before Ava glanced up and quickly said, "I'll be quiet," before going back to reading her book.

It was that moment that sealed it for Jane. As they sat in companionable silence, she decided she *would* give the friendship a chance. Not just with Lexi but with Ava and Michael as well.

CHAPTER EIGHT

"That was *awesome*!" Alexa announced as they walked in their apartment, hands filled with bags. She dropped them on the kitchen bar and immediately went to the fridge. They'd eaten a couple hours earlier but Alexa had an insatiable appetite that never seemed to show on her trim figure. Jane wasn't hungry but knew she'd have to take her medicine and eat in a few hours. She took a seat and watched Alexa pile her mother's lasagna onto her plate.

"I *love* the Statue of Liberty. It never gets old for me. To think of all the immigrants who came to America and saw that Statue on their first day here." She shook her head in awe.

"It was a great day." Jane agreed. The best day she'd ever had. They had kidnapped her: Alexa and her mother; surprising Jane with a day in the city, playing tourists and just having "girl time." They'd seen all the famous sites: The Empire State Building, Times Square, the Statue of Liberty, and Central Park. They topped the day off with a shopping spree on Madison Avenue. Jane couldn't erase her smile as she recalled the way Ava surprised her with an expensive Ralph Lauren sweater and black leather tote bag – items she had silently admired but had no intention of ever getting. Alexa's mom had observed her silently and made the purchase behind her back, instructing the sales associate to give it to her when they were on their way out. Jane had initially refused but stopped her protest when Ava said it would only make her feel bad about her kind gesture.

No one's ever done that for me before.

The thought sank into her bones. It was like something out of a fairytale or a movie. She'd never spent so many uninterrupted hours with female friends, laughing it up and just having a good time. So much of her life had been consumed with work, especially during college - a time that should have been her most sociable years.

She looked up from the counter and notice Alexa watching her.

"Are you sure you had a good time?" she asked gently.

Jane smiled. "It was wonderful. Thank you so much for inviting me."

A strange expression crossed Alexa's face.

"What?" Jane asked.

"Jane, we didn't 'invite' you. We hung out with you. This wasn't like a dinner party or some event we asked you to tag along to. If you'd said no, we probably wouldn't have gone out."

Jane's chin practically hit her chest.

"Are you serious?"

"Yes," Alexa nodded. "Mom told me a little bit about last night. I know it's been hard for you to open up. At first it stung a little given our past but then we talked about it and I understood. I just…I want us to find our new footing as friends. And not just friends, but sisters. If it wasn't for you, I would probably be on the streets somewhere strung out on drugs."

Jane shook her head. "Your parents rescued you, not me."

Alexa disagreed. "They changed my life, of course. But they didn't stand in the gap between me and that monster. They didn't give me medicine when I ran a fever. They didn't do everything in their power to give me a normal childhood until a placement could be found. *You* did that, Jane. *You*. You always had my back, even at the expense of yours. I'll never forget that. I want you to know that I have your back too. I love you."

It was the first time those words were spoken since they'd reunited more than a month ago. Alexa didn't wait for Jane to say it back. She walked around the island-bar and pulled Jane into a long warm hug. By the time they pulled back, both women were teary.

"Look what you did," Jane murmured.

"What *I* did? Girl, please."

Jane was surprised to hear the phrase come out of her very white girlfriend. You could take the girl out of the Bronx but you couldn't take the Bronx out of the girl.

Jane sighed and wiped her eyes. "Want to watch a movie?"

Alexa squealed in delight. "Yes! What do you have?"

An hour later, both girls were curled up on the couch, watching the most recent version of *Pride and Prejudice*. Curious as ever, Jane looked at Alexa's longing gaze fixed on the TV and asked, "What's going on in your love life?"

Alexa kept her gaze on the screen and replied, "It's nonexistent." She turned to Jane. "Yours?"

"Ditto," she said.

They stared at each other for a few seconds then burst out laughing.

For some reason, Aiden's face came to mind mid-laugh, causing Jane to sober. Alexa glanced at her, wiped her eyes, and said, "I'm waiting for God to send me the right one but I wish He'd hurry up."

Jane glanced at the pretty silver ring on Alexa's commitment hand. She pointed at it.

"Is that a promise ring?"

"Close," Alexa replied. "It's a purity ring. I'm waiting 'till I'm married."

Jane was surprised. She loved how matter-of-fact Alexa said it but she had to know how rare it was to wait for sex these days. She was about to ask her if it had anything to do with her religion when someone knocked on the door. Alexa looked at it and frowned.

"I hope Mom didn't put any of her stuff in my bag," she said, moving to answer it.

"If she did, she can stay and watch the movie." Jane called after her. She was in an unusually cheerful mood and thought the more, the merrier.

"Aiden!" Alexa exclaimed cheerfully. Jane's heart stuttered. She craned her neck towards the door and saw a very tall, very sexy Aiden Masterson walk through the door. He had two large paper bags in his hands as he leaned down and kissed his sister's forehead.

"You hungry, Shark Bait?"

"I just had lasagna but I'm sure Jane would like some food."

His amber eyes landed on hers, sending a strange ripple through her stomach.

He smiled politely and greeted her. "Hello, Jane."

She nodded. "Hi."

He was dressed in all black: black trench coat, black sweater underneath, and a pair of black slacks. She never knew such a morbid outfit could look so sexy on a man. It made his dark blond hair and unusual gold eyes stand out all the more. He strode over to the kitchen and laid the bags on the counter.

He glanced at the TV, saying, "I'm sorry I interrupted your movie."

Alexa waved him off and pressed pause. "Don't worry about it. We can just pick up where we left off after we eat. You don't mind, do you, Jane?"

Jane shook her head silently. She followed Alexa into the kitchen and watched Aiden busily unpack the food at the dining room table just a few feet away from the hub of the kitchen. Like the kitchen bar, the dining table was high seated with several elevated chairs circling it but it made for a much more feasible place to eat and socialize than the one-sided island.

Jane grabbed some napkins and passed Aiden to place them on the table. He surprised her when he looked at her and said, "That's a lovely sweater on you."

"Thank you," she smiled. He looked surprised at her response and she wondered why. Did she come off as an ornery person? *Probably*, she thought, holding his stare.

"Doesn't it, though?" Alexa joined in, oblivious to their looks. Jane turned to the table, away from his probing eyes. "Mom surprised her with it on our last stop home."

"Oh! That's nice," he said.

Again, she wondered what he was really thinking. As Alexa recounted their shopping trip, she wondered if he thought her to be some sort of gold digger, setting her sights on his kind-hearted mother and sister.

"It sounds like you guys had a great time," Aiden said, smiling. "I'm glad."

Jane met his eyes once more and could see the candor in them. There was nothing suspicious in his gaze and she once again rebuked herself for being so wary of others.

Stop making something out of nothing! she told herself.

They sat down to eat and joined hands as Alexa briefly said grace. Jane noticed that Aiden didn't echo "Amen" even out of polite appeasement of his sister's beliefs. Alexa didn't seem to mind, though.

"I thought you just had a sandwich," Aiden said as he watched his sister chow down on the pork-stuffed dumplings he brought.

Alexa shrugged. "My stomach made room."

If only mine would, Jane thought. She carefully dished two spoonfuls of steamed rice, some broccoli, and a small piece of Teriyaki chicken. Of all the foods, the chicken might give her stomach the most trouble. She told herself to tread carefully.

She cut off a tiny piece of the already-small chicken and tasted to see if it was spicy. When she realized it was sweet, she took a larger piece and enjoyed the savory taste in her mouth. But she also balanced the flavorful bites with several bites of rice and plain broccoli. She didn't want her stomach to react. She glanced up to find Aiden staring at her plate once again. He met her eyes and this time, didn't hold back.

"You're welcome to have some more," he said, something burning beneath his golden gaze.

Jane swallowed and shook her head, suddenly nervous. "I'm good, thanks."

He frowned at her response but she didn't elaborate.

Let it go, she thought. *Please just let it go.* She could tell he wanted to say something but hoped he would show restraint once more. Out of the corner of her eye, she could see that Alexa had paused, her dumpling poised over the sauce, her hazel eyes darting between the two.

Aiden sighed irritably and finally said, "You're not good. You barely ever eat from what I see. Clearly, you like the chicken - much more than you like the rice and broccoli. If you like it and it's to your taste, why not have more?"

"Aiden." Alexa said in warning. He ignored her this time.

He looked past Jane's plate and over her figure. "If you're on some anorexic diet, you should stop before you hurt yourself. You're thin enough as it is."

"Aiden!" Alexa exclaimed, horrified.

Jane was speechless. It took her a couple of seconds to realize that her jaw had indeed dropped and she was staring at Aiden with her mouth wide open. She'd never had someone speak so bluntly about something so personal to her. She was used to receiving stares whenever she ate but no one had ever commented on her eating habits so forcefully and so tactlessly. In her opinion it was rude even if it was well-intentioned.

Who does he think he is? she thought.

"You're thin enough as it is," he'd said. He clearly assumed she was anorexic. A hot wave of embarrassment washed over her. She wore over-sized, layered clothes so that people wouldn't pay attention to her slender figure. She often ate in private to avoid this very scenario. She closed her mouth and looked down at her sparsely-covered plate. A hollowness covered every corner of joy she'd just had minutes before.

She was no longer hungry.

She stood up, took her plate, and threw it in the trash can. "I'm going to bed."

"Jane?" Alexa asked, worried. Aiden frowned in surprise.

"Wait," he said. She turned from the trash and met his concerned look. His eyes darted between her and Alexa, slightly alarmed at their reactions. "I'm sorry. I-"

She didn't want to hear it. Wasn't this his second apology for the same thing?

"Have a good night," she said. "See you tomorrow, Lex." She walked up the stairs, ignoring the guilt-ridden, worry-driven stares of the brother and sister behind her.

The minute the sentence came out of his mouth, Aiden knew this woman would never want to be around him again. It only took one look between his sister and her roommate to realize he'd crossed the line. He wasn't sure if it was because he'd broached the obviously-touchy subject again or if it was because of the *way* in which he'd warned her to eat more. But he'd not only embarrassed Jane this time around, he'd hurt her.

He watched every ounce of the day's happiness drain from her face in the span of two seconds. In its place, a cold vacant look took over, causing her to throw away her food robotically, ignore his apology and disregard Alexa's concerned voice. But it was the look that flickered in her eyes right *before* she'd shut down. It was a look of deep pain and incredible vulnerability.

He turned from staring at the stairs and met his sister's very angry hazel eyes.

"What is *wrong* with you?" she asked, her voice trembling.

He frowned. "Alexa, I didn't mean to-"

"You put her on the spot *again* - this time, even worse than the last."

"She was hardly eating!" he said, his defenses rising. "She hardly *ever* eats! I was just trying to-"

"What?" Alexa exclaimed, her cheeks flaming red. "Diagnose her as an anorexic when you have no idea what hell she's been through?"

Silence.

Aiden watched as Alexa pinched the bridge of her nose, lowered her voice, and met his eyes again, the redness starting to fade. She spoke again, this time more controlled.

"I'm only telling you this so that you know not to *ever* bring it up around her again. Jane is not an anorexic, nor is she purposefully denying herself food. She has a condition called gastroparesis and she's had it since she was a child."

Aiden frowned. "Gastro…?"

"Gastroparesis," she repeated quietly. Her voice was almost a whisper and Aiden figured she didn't want Jane to overhear. "It's a partial paralysis of the stomach, which means the food she eats stays in her intestines for an abnormally long amount of time. She has to take medicines to help regulate it, eat basic foods instead of spicy ones, and eat in very small amounts over the course of the day."

Aiden felt a plethora of feelings compete for his attention. Understanding washed over him but so did confusion, both of those followed by a harrowing amount of guilt. He'd unintentionally humiliated her about something over which she had no control and was trying to manage the best she could.

"How on earth did she get it?" he asked. "Is it genetic?"

Alexa shrugged. "I don't know if it is in others but I know Jane's case isn't. She developed it as a child. One of the reasons she was taken away from her birth mother was because the woman wouldn't feed her for days on end - chronically. By the time she was transferred to her grandmother, her stomach was ruined. She's lucky she didn't develop rickets."

Aiden's jaw dropped. He couldn't wrap his mind around such abuse. He'd seen pictures and footage of starving children in Africa, India, and other under developed regions - but the adults there often had little or nothing to give those children. They didn't intentionally starve them. He couldn't fathom a human being, much less a mother, blatantly refusing to give her child food - especially in an affluent country like the States, where government programs and aid were plentiful for mothers with young children. What kind of monster gave birth to Jane? What kind of woman was entrusted with her as a child?

No wonder I hit a nerve. Not only did I point out something embarrassing and physically painful, I reminded her of something unspeakably traumatic from her childhood.

The more he understood, the more he wanted to know. Something told Aiden that her mother's early abuse of her was just a snapshot into the many abuses Jane faced growing up. Up until that point, he'd thought the foster home was the main reason for her tough exterior. But apparently, she'd been experiencing hell from the minute she was born. Aiden stood up slowly, the shock of what he'd learned rendering his legs a little shaky. He took a deep breath and met Alexa's eyes.

"I'm sorry," he said. He shook his head. "Thanks for trusting me with this."

She gave him a stern look. "Don't bring it up to her."

He immediately shook his head. "I won't."

He kissed his sister on the forehead, grabbed his coat, and got out of dodge. He grabbed a taxi and zoned out as the driver honked and sped all the way to his high rise apartment downtown. No matter how far the car carried him away from his sister's apartment, Aiden could not escape the feeling of guilt and regret for how he treated Jane that night. Especially now that he knew.

He also couldn't escape the curiosity. About her past, her present. How she'd risen out of her circumstances into the successful woman she was today. He marveled at her resilience...and her reluctance to share her experiences.

She's your sister's friend, he thought once more. It was the thought that reminded him he had no business thinking of her as anything else.

Too bad, he thought.

Because he no longer cared.

CHAPTER NINE

"If you're on some anorexic diet, you should stop before you hurt yourself. You're thin enough as it is."

Jane could hear the words vividly as she scooped a spoonful of oatmeal into her mouth. She stepped out onto the terrace, adjoining the kitchen and tried to remove the memories from her mind. He was gone now, probably scolded by his sister, and regardless of how often she'd have to encounter him in the future, Jane was certain she would never have to break bread with him again.

It was brisk outside, the fall weather quickly turning into the chilly winters New York was notorious for. But that morning, the sun was enough to warm Jane's face as she closed her eyes and enjoyed the rarely quiet street outside. She could even hear the water of the Hudson lapping against the shore.

The moment was short lived.

Someone knocked on the door and Jane stepped back into the apartment to answer it.

Aiden stood at the threshold, a nervous expression on his handsome face.

Jane frowned. Alexa was at church. Why wasn't he with her? Then she remembered that Alexa was the only Christian in her family. Apparently, she converted when she was eighteen and hadn't looked back since. She had yet to convert her family, though.

Aiden saw her frown and misunderstood the reason behind it. "I know I'm the last person you want to see this morning - especially after what happened last night - but please. Can I please come in?"

She wordlessly stepped back and allowed him in. She closed the door, walked past him, and perched herself against the kitchen island. His eyes swept over the entirety of her. He noticed that she wore long sleeves and long pants despite the warmth of the apartment.

Why does she always cover herself up? He had a sneaking suspicion it wasn't just a personal style choice.

"I don't know when Alexa's service ends..." she trailed off. His sister was the only reason he was there, right?

"I'm not here to see Alexa," he confirmed. "I'm here to see you."

A look of surprise crossed her face. Jane crossed her arms over her chest and waited, a formidable expression taking over. He shoved his hands in his pocket and looked around the room before meeting her gaze again. He'd had an entire speech prepared from last night and that morning on his way over. But as he watched her unwelcoming stance and angry frown, the speech flew out of his head and he decided to just go for it. He didn't waste time with small talk.

"I clearly owe you an apology for what I said last night," he began. The deep timbre of his voice rolled down her spine. "It was foolish of me to say anything about your eating habits the first time I did it and pretty much unforgivable the second time I did. That being said, I truly am sorry for what I said, how I said it..." he trailed off and sighed. "It was rude and insensitive of me and it will not happen again. I promise you that. Please forgive me."

"I accept your apology," Jane said coldly.

Aiden frowned. "No, you don't."

He almost smacked himself in the head for blurting that out. But he couldn't take it back now and he knew it.

She raised an eyebrow at his nerve. "I don't?"

"No," he said. He met her eyes and didn't seem deterred by her fierce expression. "You don't. You accepted my apology too quickly and I can tell you're still pissed."

"Don't I have a right to be?"

"Absolutely," he conceded. "But don't lie and say you forgive me when you don't."

"I didn't say I forgive you," Jane corrected. "I said I accept your apology."

He smirked. So she wanted to play semantics?

Okay, Professor.

"Like you did the last time?" he asked. "You accepted my apology but didn't forgive me then and my actions last night just stacked my offenses against you like a miser stacks his coins."

She smirked at the irony of his words. A stock broker talking about stacking coins.

How cute.

"What do you want from me, Aiden?" she finally asked. She looked into his eyes and saw something shift in them. They somehow became more intense. He took a step forward, his heart suddenly pounding. He could barely hear his own voice as he spoke.

"I want you to forgive me," he said.

"I will. It just takes time."

"How much time?"

She frowned at him. "Why do you care?"

"Because I don't just want your forgiveness," he answered.

She waited.

"I want you to go out with me."

Her jaw dropped. Did he really just say what she thought he said? His eyes remained steady as she folded her arms and said, "I'm sorry, I must not have heard you-"

"You heard me perfectly well," he interrupted. "Will you go out with me?"

She narrowed her eyes at him, dumbfounded. He didn't know if that was good or bad.

"Why?"

Why what? he thought. *Why do I want to go out with you? Or why should you let me take you out?*

He took a risk and wagered it was the former. He looked down at his jeans then back up at her. "Why else do people ask other people out?" he replied. "I like you. I want to get to know you. I want to take you on a date."

But why *do you like me?* she thought. She didn't voice the question but it was written on her face so he answered.

"You're smart, you're selfless, well educated and accomplished. You had the bravery to protect my sister when no one else could - when you yourself were a kid, and you've overcome your challenges with remarkable strength. Those are the non-vapid reasons why I want to know you. The truth is..." he closed the space between them with careful, marked steps and pinned her eyes with his. "You are also the most breathtaking woman I have ever laid eyes on. I want to go out with you."

His words rendered her legs unstable and Jane took advantage of the kitchen stool right beside her hip. She replayed the words that would forever be seared in her mind.

"The most breathtaking woman I have ever laid eyes on."

She had to look away from his piercing regard to think straight. Her heart was racing and her stomach turned.

"I thought I was too thin," she blurted out. His words contradicted what he'd said last night and even though they excited her, Jane was not about to ignore the discrepancy.

She met his eyes again and saw something flicker in his amber gaze. She wasn't sure if it was confusion, curiosity, or even annoyance that his words didn't render the response from her he'd hoped for.

They did, she thought. *I'm just not going to let you see it.*

He took a deep breath and said, "I never said you were too thin."

His eyes grazed over her slender frame, admiring the lean curves of her chest, waist, and hips. "You *are* thin," he acknowledged. "You're also tall. You have the body of a model. But you also have curves. And in all the right places." She blinked at his frank admiration. "As far as I'm concerned, you have the perfect shape. You. Are. Beautiful."

He said the last statement with such conviction, Jane believed him. She didn't have that many self-esteem issues. She was too annoyed by insecure women to become one of them. She also liked what she saw in the mirror. Her face was one of the few things *he* hadn't damaged growing up. Though picked on in school for looking "too African," Jane knew there were women who were lauded for the exotic look she possessed. She appreciated the work of Iman, Naomi Campbell and other models of African descent. She knew that beauty was in the eye of the beholder. She was just surprised that Aiden's eye seemed to behold *her* type of beauty.

He won't admire all of it, the thought crept into her head. *When the clothes come off, will he like what he sees then?*

Some of her thoughts must have traveled to her face because he tilted his head and peered into her eyes, his eyebrows drawn in a frown.

"You okay?" he asked. An almost haunted look had crossed her face and he wished he could read her mind that very moment.

"I'm fine," she said, looking away. To her surprise, he touched her chin with the tip of his finger and made her face him.

"Will you go out with me?" he asked again.

"No," she swiftly said.

"Why?" he asked, the frown deepening. He wasn't going without a good reason.

She needed an excuse and searched for the most plausible one.

"You're my roommate's brother. I don't want complications."

Not good enough.

"Life is full of complications," he answered. "Why not indulge in the good ones?"

She took for granted how determined he would be. She could see it in his crystal gold eyes and wondered where the resolve came from. His hand traveled to the side of her face and he cupped her left cheek. She watched his eyes travel over the planes and angles of her face, openly admiring her makeup-less features. She was drawn to his boldness.

It was sexy.

He repeated once more, "Will you go out with me?"

"Alexa won't be upset?" she asked, already knowing the answer.

"Quite the contrary," he smiled slightly. "She'll be relieved that I'm finally doing what I wanted to do the first day I met you at UNY."

Jane took a sharp inhale of surprise. His sister *was* right.

"Will you go out with me?" he asked a fourth time. He was ready to ask all morning if she kept this up. But she'd run out of reasons to protest and the truth was, she really didn't want to. She paused, looked around the room, and finally gave him an answer.

"When?" she whispered, relenting.

Victory flashed in his eyes.

"Tonight?" he asked.

She raised an eyebrow.

"I know it's short notice but I'm really eager to know you. I don't want to waste time."

It was the patented candor in his voice and eyes that had Jane nodding to his unexpected request. By the time Alexa came back late that afternoon, Jane was busy looking through her clothes. Alexa knocked on the door. Her muffled voice called out, "Are you getting ready for your date?"

Jane rolled her eyes. Was nothing sacred in that family?

"Yes!" she yelled back. "You can come in if you want."

Alexa burst through the door like a fireball of energy, her wavy hair bouncing as she jumped up and down excitedly. "Oh my God! He finally asked you out!" she squealed. "It's about freakin' time!"

"How did he tell you?" Jane asked.

"Text," she replied with an expression that said *duh*.

"Did he tell you anything about where he's taking me?"

Alexa grinned mischievously and nodded. She walked around Jane and into her massive walk-in closet. Jane felt the size to be a bit ridiculous because her clothes only occupied one-fourth of the entire closet space. She could probably sleep in it if she wanted to. Within seconds, Alexa pulled out the only short black dress Jane owned and laid it on the bed. Jane walked to her dresser and retrieved a pair of black panty hose to complement the look.

"Tights?" Alexa frowned. "Really?"

"Yes," Jane stated firmly. She never exposed her legs. Ever.

Her friend shrugged and proceeded to pull out a sexy pair of black stilettos. They had to be at least four inches tall. It was a good thing Aiden was taller than average. Jane felt her heart rate quicken at the thought of him. She still replayed their conversation from that morning in her mind and the memory of his words made her shiver.

"You okay?" Alexa asked.

Jane nodded. "Are you really okay with this?" she asked her friend. Alexa's hazel eyes softened. She grabbed both of Jane's hands and nodded once more, emphatically.

"I'm more than okay with this," she said. "Jane, I'm thrilled!"

Aiden arrived at Jane's door at seven on the dot. When she answered it, he lost track of whether he was coming or going, sitting or standing. He took a thorough sweep of her from the crown of her full afro to the soles of her stilettoed heels. He paid particular attention to the figure-hugging cocktail dress that both covered and showed off her body in the best way possible. They were well matched: she wore all black and so did he, except for a white dress shirt to go with his suit. His eyes lingered on the slight swell of her breast and the curve of her hips. She had a slender hourglass figure and his hands itched to rest at the slope of her waist.

He looked back up at her face. He couldn't decide if she was more stunning with makeup or without. Her dark brown skin glowed when she wore nothing on it but she also knew how to make her exotic features stand out when she elected to use makeup. He decided she was flawless both ways: a rarity he admired. She had an expectant look in her eyes and he realized she was waiting for him to say something.

"Beautiful," was all he could utter at the moment.

She smiled shyly, secretly appreciating his obvious approval. "Thanks."

"You ready?" he asked.

She nodded, her coat slung over her arm.

He glanced over her shoulder and for the first time, noticed his sister watching them with a knowing grin.

"See you later, Shark Bait." he called, before offering his hand to Jane. She took it and he immediately felt a warmth travel up his arm. She must have felt it too because she started to pull her hand out of his but he tightened his grip, met her dark brown eyes, and smiled. She gave a slight smile in return. He led her to the apartment elevator, thrilled to see she could keep up with his long strides. He loved her height.

"I'm surprised you didn't cancel on me," he finally broke the ice.

"Why would I cancel?" she asked.

He shrugged. "I don't know. It was a hard-won 'yes' getting you to go out with me."

"Well, hopefully you'll make it worth my while."

He laughed in surprise. "Wow! Aren't you humble!"

She grinned and said nothing in reply. They exited the apartment and took the private car he had reserved for the evening. The ride was silent at first as Aiden watched Jane watch the pedestrians outside. She fidgeted with her hands and pulled at the ends of her sleeves. He noticed it was a nervous habit of hers.

To his surprise, she turned to him and finally broke the ice herself.

"Where are you taking me?" she asked.

He smiled. "It's a new spot on Madison Avenue called Icing. Not a club but not as stiff as most upscale restaurants."

She nodded and started to look outside the window again.

"What did you do after I left?" he asked. She turned back to him and thought for a moment.

"Nothing, really. I got some sleep, finished a book I've been reading, and started getting ready for tonight."

"Did my sister help you?"

She rolled her eyes. "Yes. She came into my room like a bat out of hell. Why did you text her about this?"

He laughed and shrugged. "We're really close. I share almost everything with her and vice versa."

"So the age difference doesn't matter?"

"Not at all," he replied.

It used to, he thought. But they were both adults now.

"You're really close to your parents, too." she observed.

He nodded. "Yeah. There's something about having a psychiatrist for a mom and an unusually patient man for a dad. They're both super easy to talk to."

"Why do you think that is?" she asked, turning more towards him. He could see the tension leave her body as she relaxed into her seat. He kept talking, glad to see it.

"I have a theory. I was a hard-won baby." She raised an eyebrow and he explained. "My parents had tried for years to conceive but after a slew of miscarriages and stillbirths, they had me. By the time I was born, they had a full library of books on parenting and I think patience and communication were two of the predominant themes."

Jane nodded. "Your parents seem like great people. You and Alexa are lucky."

He agreed with her and nodded but he couldn't help but notice the slight resignation in her voice. There was a quiet sadness in her eyes and it reminded him of the look she had right before leaving his parents' place the first night she came over.

What is it that's bothering you? he wondered. *And how can I make it go away?*

By the time they arrived at Icing, he was burning with questions to ask her. They took their seats at the candle-lit, beautifully decorated table and placed their orders. The minute the waiter left, Aiden dove in.

"It's weird. I feel like I know a lot about you because you're Lexi's friend but I know next to nothing about you at the same time."

She smiled and wondered what he wanted to know.

He continued, "Do you enjoy being a professor?"

She felt herself relax. She could talk about work.

She nodded. "Yes. If there is such a thing as a dream job, I think I'm working mine right now."

His eyes lit up at her response. "That's great! Why do you enjoy it so much?"

She glanced down at the table then looked back up into his amber eyes. The candle light from the table seemed to make them glow even more.

"I like seeing the light bulbs come on," she explained. "I love that moment when a student gets what I'm teaching. And I enjoy watching them figure it out. I also really love literature and it comes alive the most when people are discussing it."

He nodded, fully tracking with her. The service was incredibly fast - their waiter arrived with their food - a large steak with vegetables for Aiden and a small salad for Jane - and they began to eat without pausing the conversation.

"Who are your favorite authors?" he asked.

She smiled, as though pleased with the question. "Leo Tolstoy, Zora Neale Hurston, Jane Austen. I also enjoy what I call 'one-hit-wonders' like Margaret Mitchell and Harper Lee."

He nodded. "I always wonder about authors like them. They write the great American novel and never write again. Or never release their writing again. It almost makes their one piece more valuable."

She grinned at him, appreciating his insight. "Yeah. It also makes them fascinating as people. I heard that Lee chose not to write again because she couldn't handle the pressure of living up to *To Kill a Mockingbird*."

"That's sad."

"I agree. But then you have Margaret Mitchell who didn't write another one because she didn't want to. Some novelettes and early writings of hers were published long after her death, but during her lifetime, she only released one book. Why not capitalize on the success?"

"Like Grisham?" He grinned.

"You like his work?" she asked.

He nodded. "I like his early stuff. It was fresh, original, and kept you on the edge of your seat. Now his writing feels a little more sedate. Comforting, almost."

She cocked her head. "I think it depends on the book. *The Associate* kept me on my toes."

"Ah, I almost forgot about that one. And he released that in 2009, I think. Okay, maybe he's still got it."

She laughed. So he could talk literature and actually keep up with her. He was the first man able to do so and she appreciated that. She didn't know why she was surprised. It was Aiden after all. He could talk to anybody about any topic and seem well-versed enough to navigate the finer details.

"Where did you go to school, Aiden?"

He smiled, pleased that she finally asked *him* a question.

"Columbia '06."

"For both degrees?"

He cocked his head. "How did you know about my MBA?"

She shrugged. "Alexa or your mom told me. Besides, I figured you had to have a masters for your line of work."

He smiled and nodded, noting that nothing could escape her sharp mind. Her power of deduction was a turn on.

"I went to Harvard for my MBA."

Jane whistled.

He chuckled. "It's not *that* big of a deal."

"Please don't. You know you're talking to a professor here, right?"

"Now *that's* a big deal. Teaching at university level at twenty-four. *And* you earned your masters at a time when most, myself included, are just getting their bachelors."

He watched as she grew silent, slowly picking at the remains of her tiny chicken Caesar salad.

"What is it?" he asked.

She looked up and frowned. "Huh?"

"What are you thinking?" he amended.

She shrugged, his probing gaze piercing her. "It's nothing. It's just…"

He waited.

"People talk about my education and age like it's some huge accomplishment and I guess it is but the process of getting those degrees was extremely challenging."

He nodded soberly and she continued.

"If I could have done it differently - like enjoy four years of college and the full time allotted for my masters, I would have done it that way. As it was, I was operating like a maniac to rush my way through school. I did what I had to do but I wouldn't wish it for anybody."

He waited for her to meet his eyes again before he asked, "You didn't have anyone to help you?"

She knew what he was asking. *You didn't have family or friends to assist you with school? With a place to live? With pocket change?*

She shook her head. "I've been on my own since I was eighteen."

"When you left the system?"

She visibly stiffened but nodded all the same.

"How long were you in it?"

"Since I was a kid," she answered a little too quickly.

"How old?"

"I don't know," she lied. "Young." Her tone was sharp, her eyes cold. She clearly didn't want to talk about it and he knew better than to push her. He pointed at her plate.

"Are you done?" he asked.

She nodded, a feeling of worry starting to creep up her spine. She regretted shutting down so quickly, responding to his questions so harshly. He was only curious and she reacted like he pissed her off. Was he ready to take her home because of it? Had she ruined the date already?

Why do you even care? she asked herself. *He was the one pursuing you, not the other way around.*

And yet she did care. As he paid the bill and helped her slip on her jacket, Jane realized that she really liked Aiden. She enjoyed getting to know him and being in his company. She realized with startling clarity that if he decided not to ask her out again, she would be very disappointed.

Aiden looked down at Jane and saw the apprehension in her eyes.

"Hey," he said. She looked up at him. "Are you alright?"

She nodded, but it was unconvincing. Did she already want to go home?

"Listen," he said. "I was hoping this would be the first part of our date. I'd like to take you to the Met now if you're up for it."

To his surprise, and delight, a bright smile immediately lit her face.

Jane felt a wave of relief and nodded unreservedly. "I love the Met."

It was true. She loved the Metropolitan Museum of Art. But she wasn't grinning because of her excitement to see the place. She was happy to know that he wanted to take her there, that she hadn't ruined their evening.

Fifteen minutes later, they were strolling through the classic art gallery of the famous museum. They walked into a room reserved for the famous Leutze painting, *Washington Crossing the Delaware*. Aiden watched her admire the gigantic artwork but grinned when she quirked an eyebrow at the piece.

"What?" he asked her.

She glanced at him and shrugged. "It's beautiful. But totally inaccurate."

He glanced at the painting and grinned as well. "I know, right? They crossed when it was still dark with fog everywhere and he definitely wouldn't have stood up like that for fear of being spotted by red coats."

Jane was shocked. He could converse 18th century American history *too?*

"Is there anything you *don't* know?" she blurted.

He blushed. Was he coming off as a know-it-all? He tried to explain himself.

"I really like history. Especially early American history."

"So do I," Jane replied. He looked down at her and realized she wasn't chiding him for being pretentious but was genuinely pleased to know someone else who appreciated history. He relaxed, glad to have found something else in common with her.

"What about it do you like?" he asked.

"Oh, I don't know. I think there's something almost romantic about colonial history. Everything from the clothing to the manner of speech to the values they had. The exciting time of new opportunities while supporting one another in community. I would love to go back in time. Just not as a black person."

He laughed uproariously at her remark. "I love that you just said that!"

She smiled, pleased to see that he appreciated her humor.

"Why do you like history?" she asked when he finally calmed down.

"Oh, I don't know," he said, mimicking her response. She giggled and he winked at her. "I think I like it because it tells a story."

She nodded in agreement.

"I also like it because of the lessons that can be learned when people make note of past mistakes and resolve not to repeat it." He paused in thought. "History holds a lot of pain but it also holds a lot of triumph."

"Kind of like life," Jane observed.

"Exactly! There's a comfort to knowing that people have gone through this challenging thing called life for thousands of years before our very conception."

She shook her head in wonder.

"What?" he asked.

"Nothing, it's just...I never met someone who appreciates history as much as you seem to. Not from a scholarly perspective per se, but just in general. For the story and the simple lessons it holds."

"Ditto." He smiled down at her. "If a girl can enjoy a decent history channel documentary as much as she enjoys a *Pride and Prejudice* chick flick, she must be a keeper."

Jane laughed. "I like historical romances. Some don't have enough historical value but they can be very enjoyable."

"Oh, I know," Aiden said in a wry tone. "I have *Persuasion* on repeat every time I want to watch an Austen film."

They laughed and chatted effortlessly, barely taking in the art but fully taking in one another. By the time they left the museum, it was chilly enough for Aiden to purchase two hot chocolates for them.

"Put that away," he ordered lightly when Jane pulled out her wallet.

"You already paid for dinner-"

"Like any man should," he said.

She raised her eyebrows in surprise. "You never go dutch?"

It was his turn to look at her in surprise. "Never. What kind of man allows his date to pay her way?"

She couldn't put her finger on it, but she felt her respect and admiration for him climb several notches higher at those words. She didn't care if it was old fashioned of her but to her, he sounded like a provider and it was comforting to know. She allowed the sweet hot chocolate to warm her insides as she silently sipped and strolled alongside him. Within minutes, he led them to their final destination.

"Central Park?" she asked.

He smiled at her and took her free hand into his. His large hand immediately warmed her slender one. He frowned at the ice cold feeling of it.

"You must be freezing," he said. Without another word, he tossed his empty cup in a nearby trash, pulled off his wool trench coat, and wrapped it around her shoulders, flooding her with a much-needed warmth her own jacket couldn't supply.

"Aiden-" she tried to protest but he wouldn't hear it.

"I'm fine," he said. "I want you to fully enjoy this."

She frowned questioningly. "Enjoy what?"

Her question was soon answered as he led them to a waiting carriage on one of the park pathways. Jane blinked in surprise as Aiden greeted the coachman and paid for his reservation of the ride. She climbed into the carriage with his help and leaned into his side as the coachman took off, horses trotting along the scenic route of New York City's most famous park.

No one had ever put such thought into a date with her before.

Aiden watched her take it all in. The grass and trees around them, the people still milling about the place. He enjoyed the feel of her leaning into his side, her body relaxed against his. It was a complete turnaround from the beginning of the date, when she'd fidgeted uncomfortably.

"I don't come here enough," she said quietly.

"Sometimes you forget there's more to the city than concrete."

"Hmm," she murmured. The sound did something to his extremities. "Growing up, I used to hate living in the city."

He perked up at that change of conversation. She was actually mentioning something about her past of her own volition. He treaded carefully.

"Why did you hate it?"

She shrugged. "I don't know. I kind of felt the whole setting was depressing. And it was - probably because I was in the Bronx. I used to think the happy places were the places in picture books - where there was a lot of grass and space and fresh open air."

He nodded. "When you want to escape, you probably think of the opposite of your current environment as the perfect ideal."

She nodded wordlessly and shifted beside him.

"How do you feel about the city now?" he asked.

She smiled. "I don't hate it anymore. But I can't say I love it. There are nights, like this, when I remember I couldn't get this experience anywhere else. The restaurant, the Met, and Central Park all in the same night?" She lifted her smile up to him and it warmed him better than his coat ever could. "Thank you for this, Aiden. I really had a great time."

His hand reached up and caressed her soft cheek. The silk of her skin was intoxicating against his warm fingers. They held each other's gaze for a long, silent moment. Like magnets drawn to metal, their heads began to draw closer. Aiden's eyes shifted to her full lips as he lowered his head to meet her tilting face. Their lips met and they kissed. Pure ecstasy washed over Jane like a wave crashing against the shore. Eyes closed, she gave into the delicious sensation of his full soft lips expertly caressing her own. She felt his nose press against the side of hers as she molded her mouth to his.

Aiden could barely hear anything as the blood rushed to his ears. He tasted the hot chocolate on her smooth, warm lips. The taste became richer as he probed her mouth with his tongue. She opened for him and his tongue collided with hers. He'd never kissed someone with such soft, full lips and he reveled in the sensation. Heart pounding, he felt the blood in his body surge to a particular place that he could not control in that moment. He pulled back from her, panting in a desperate attempt to regain control. He hoped she couldn't see the cause of his sudden discomfort.

Thankfully, she only had eyes for him. She admired the color in his golden skin as she too fought to catch her breath. His eyes collided with hers and pierced her with a look so fierce, so intense, she almost started hyperventilating. If looks could remove clothing, hers would be scattered across the park. They didn't talk the rest of the carriage ride. Aiden politely tipped the coachman and quietly escorted her home. The trip cleared his head enough for him to walk straight again.

By the time they reached her door, he leaned in for another kiss. This one was chaste, and quick. At least it would have been had she not cupped her hand around the back of his neck. He groaned against her mouth and felt her shiver in his arms.

"When will I see you again?" he asked huskily. He could barely think straight, enraptured by her soft brown gaze.

"You tell me."

"Tomorrow night," he immediately answered.

She laughed, her beautiful dark eyes sparkling.

"Okay," she simply replied. She handed him his coat and he was pleased to catch a whiff of her perfume on it. She unlocked the door and started to turn the handle when she felt his hand at her waist, turning her back around.

"Just one more," he whispered, leaning in to steal yet another kiss. His gold eyes were all she could see when he finally pulled away.

"Good night, Jane." he said and turned to take his leave.

CHAPTER TEN

He was in trouble.

It became more and more apparent to Aiden that Jane was taking up permanent residence in his mind. He couldn't think of anything but their date last night. It was six in the morning and he was halfway done with his morning run. If he wasn't careful, he was going to get hit by a car. Stop lights and bustling cars were the last thing on his mind when he remembered her soft full lips.

It was the best date he'd ever had. It was also the most planned out date he'd ever had. He'd never put so much energy and thought into an outing in his entire life but it paid off huge dividends. The more he got to know Jane, the more he really liked her. "Like" was too weak of a word. He admired her, respected her, and was all the more intrigued by her. She carried a mysterious element to her even though she was very kind. He was pleasantly surprised to learn how social she *could* be when she loosened up and felt comfortable. He felt privileged to see that side of her. The only time she really held back was when he mentioned her past. He knew much of her mystique had to do with that part of her story.

Though the date had gone well, he would not forget how quickly she shut down when he started asking about her childhood. Clearly, her time in the system was a sensitive subject for her, one that she was not willing to discuss or disclose. Would she ever be ready to disclose it? What exactly had she protected Alexa from?

As if aware that his thoughts had wandered to her, Aiden's phone rang and he paused in his run to answer it.

"What's up, Shark Bait? You're normally not up this early."

"Whatever," she replied. He could almost see her rolling her eyes. "I'm calling to see how things went last night."

Oh, my nosy lovable sister.

"Why don't you ask Jane? You saw her last night, didn't you?"

"Yeah, but I want to hear it from *your* point of view. When she wasn't telling me about the night, she was grinning like an idiot so clearly you did something right."

He could feel an involuntary smile overtake his face. So, she *had* enjoyed the night. He was glad to hear it confirmed.

"It went well," he said. "We're going out again tonight."

He held the phone away from his ear while she squealed on the other end. She calmed down and spoke again, this time, her voice was serious.

"I'm really glad you guys have hit it off. I love you and I love her and I hope it works out. Just…"

He frowned at the pause and waited.

"Just be gentle with her, Aiden. Treat her well."

His frown deepened. "You know I will, Alexa."

"I don't mean it like that. Of course you'll treat her well. What I mean is…be patient. And gentle. Delicacy isn't exactly your strong suit."

He ignored the observation and focused on the general idea.

"Is there something you want to tell me, Alexa?" Why was she warning him to be gentle with Jane? What did she know that she wasn't sharing?

"It's not for me to say," she replied. "Just promise me you'll treat her well."

He was getting annoyed. "Yes, Alexa." he said curtly.

"Okay," she backed off. "I'll let you get back to your run. I love you."

"Love you, too."

He took off for his run again but it wasn't with the cheerful bounce it started with; his mind was occupied once more but with more questions than answers. He perceived Jane to be a strong, overcoming woman. But his sister clearly had a different perspective. Now, more than ever, he wanted to know the reason why.

Jane opened the door with a smile and it only grew bigger at the sight of him. Aiden leaned against the door frame with an easy grin and the hint of a beard growing in. He would probably shave it off soon but she found the dark blond five o'clock shadow sexy on him.

"Hey you," he greeted. He leaned in and gave her a soft peck on the lips.

"Hey yourself," she said. She walked through the door and pulled it shut behind her, tucking her hand into his proffered arm.

The date was much more relaxed than the previous night. Aiden had called her ahead of time to dress casually. They took a cab to Times Square and caught an action movie. Afterwards, they walked along the busy street. He got them both hot dogs, chips, and hot chocolate and decided to people watch for their entertainment. He noticed that she didn't open her chips, only took a couple bites of her hot dog, and tucked the food in her small purse, choosing to consume only her drink. He didn't say anything. She was probably still full from the popcorn earlier. If she wasn't going to eat, he was sure it was best for her stomach.

"It's crazy the number of people who mill about this area," she shouted over the noise of the street.

He leaned down and replied into her ear. "Tell me about it. I wonder if they've done a statistic on how many people frequent this area on a day-to-day basis."

"How many tourists," she said.

"Americans versus internationals."

"The country breakdown of foreigners."

He looked down at her and smiled. She spoke his language and he loved their banter. They crossed a busy street and walked down another block. Aiden had the craziest urge for Cold Stone ice cream and laughed at her expression when he voiced it.

"Hot cocoa followed by ice cream?"

"I know, it's weird. But I get the strangest cravings," he explained.

"How do you keep the physique you have if you listen to whatever your stomach wants?" she asked. She wondered the same thing about Alexa.

He shook his head. "I don't listen to it most of the time. I'm actually pretty good about my eating during the week and very rarely splurge. Besides, most of my cravings are for healthy foods. Caesar salads, organic cheese, fresh salmon…"

She smiled at his list and shook her head. It sounded weird to her but clearly the man was in top shape.

"Attention! One-hundred sex positions! Spice up your love life for a dollar!"

They both turned to the voice and saw a man with a large sign held over his head. It read: "100 Different Sex Positions: $1.00 Sheets." Aiden couldn't help where his mind went that moment. Immediately, he pictured himself wrapped around her in nothing but silk sheets. He shook the thought from his mind but was shocked when she started to lead them over to the man. He watched as she reached into her pocket, pulled out a dollar and thanked the street hustler for the single purple sheet.

Jane saw the shocked expression on his face and shrugged. "What? Don't you want to know what positions you've missed out on?"

I do want to know, he thought. *I want to know with you.*

She unfolded the sheet and held it out before them. Though he immediately began to blush, she was too curious to be embarrassed. He wondered at this new side of her. Very rarely did he meet a woman who wasn't afraid of her sexuality but didn't flaunt it like a common harlot. They perused the sheet together and quickly realized that many of the positions were repeats - just rotated on the page to look different.

"How many original positions do you think are actually on there?" he asked.

She peered at the sheet again. "Hmmm, maybe forty."

He nodded in agreement, though he realized he was probably only up to try ten of them. The majority of the other ones looked uncomfortable or downright dangerous.

She tucked the sheet into her pocket.

"You're gonna keep it?" he asked in disbelief.

"I paid a dollar for it! I don't want to waste my money."

He reached into his pocket, handed her a bill and took the sheet out of her hand. Crumpling it up in his fist, he tossed it in the nearest trashcan and led her into Cold Stone.

"Hmm, I've never tried this flavor before," she said around a mouthful of cake batter ice cream.

"It's my favorite," Aiden admitted, licking his lips. "Have I converted you to the family?"

She laughed. The way he said it made it sound like some sort of cult.

"Not quite," she answered. "This taste good but butter pecan will always have my heart."

"Ouch!" He clutched his chest like she'd stabbed it with a dagger. She giggled at his melodramatic display. He wrapped an arm around her shoulder and pulled her closer into his side. They walked into the elevator of her apartment. Though tired, Jane was not happy to see her home so soon. She wanted to spend more time with him. Just the thought of him brightened her day.

She tucked her face in his chest and inhaled his clean, masculine scent.

"I wish I didn't have work tomorrow." she whined.

"Hmm, that makes the two of us."

He looked down at her in his arms and couldn't believe the change two days could make. While he enjoyed their first date the previous night, he loved their time together this night. There were no awkward moments - it was completely night and day. There was an ease in their conversation and she clearly felt comfortable around him. He wouldn't trade that feeling for anything in the world. If anything, he only wanted it to grow.

Once again the image of her wrapped in his arms in a much different setting captured his mind. He pushed it to the background and focused on the moment. Walking her to the door, he stopped her hand from turning the key.

"I want to see you again," he said.

She smiled. "Of course."

He shook his head. He wasn't being specific enough. "I don't mean like just another date. I want to keep seeing you. Indefinitely."

She blinked at his blunt declaration. It was only the second date in and they were already having a define the relationship moment. He watched as she tried to process his words.

"What exactly are you saying?" she asked.

"Are you dating anybody else?" he countered.

She blinked again. "Not at the moment-"

"Good. That's what I mean. I don't want you to."

She cocked her head. "Are you trying to lay some sort of claim to me?"

"Yes," he answered confidently. She blinked again. "I don't want to waste time with ambiguity and I don't want to date a girl who is dating other guys at the same time." He stepped closer to her, the sweet scent of his ice cream still fresh on his lips. "I'm saying I don't want you to see anyone else but me."

"And are you willing to adhere to this exclusivity yourself?"

"Absolutely," he replied without hesitation.

She looked into his amber eyes and saw no hint of deception or doubt. She felt a rush of anxiety hit her at the idea of committing to anything with another man. But it battled with the candor and clear desire in his eyes. No one had ever looked at her the way Aiden did. No one had ever treated her the way he did. No one had ever claimed her the way he was trying to. She wanted to know what it would feel like to be the sole object of his affection. And she was willing to ignore all others to find out.

He could see the minute she decided to acquiesce to his request. Her dark brown eyes softened before she slowly nodded. "Okay. I won't see anyone else for now."

He didn't like the "for now" caveat but he decided to ignore it. He'd gotten what he wanted and that was worth celebrating. He leaned down once more, tipped her chin with the edge of his finger, and captured her lips with his own in a slow, thorough, toe-curling kiss. She tasted the cake batter ice cream and it added to the pleasure of having his tongue dance with hers. He pulled her fully into his embrace and held her so tightly she could feel the definition in his strong towering arms. She didn't know if she was sitting or standing, if she was carrying her weight or if he was. It didn't matter as she lost herself in his mind-numbing kiss.

A sharp whistle broke through their endorphin-soaked minds and the couple broke apart, startled by the sound. Alexa walked up to them with a wide grin and shook her head at the two. Jane glanced at Aiden and saw a clear blush rush to his cheeks. She didn't know why but she found it endearing: that he could be sexy alpha male one minute and the sweet bashful brother the next.

They scooted out of Alexa's way as she turned the key Jane had already inserted in the door. "Don't mind me," she teased. "Clearly you guys have mastered the art of necking. Far be it from me to interrupt this cute little love fest."

"Lexi!" Aiden groaned while Jane laughed.

CHAPTER ELEVEN

Three Weeks Later

"All right, everyone. Let's begin."

The room quieted down as Dr. Geissner started the meeting. They had them every month to keep each other abreast of what was going on. And in this meeting there was a frenetic energy associated with President Schneider's new proposal.

"Listen, I know many of you have been a little rattled by President Schneider's email last month. I've corresponded with several of you." Geissner's eyes briefly met Jane's and she smiled slightly. "I firmly believe that this isn't something to worry about. New presidents occupy universities all the time and try to usher in changes *they* feel are necessary."

Really, it was a stupid move on her part. Schneider had been there all of five minutes and was already alienating herself from her faculty. Unless, of course, she managed to get the proposal passed and bring in a passel of older, amenable staff.

"Off the record," Geissner lowered his voice. "I think she's just flexing her muscle." The faculty chuckled at that. "But I repeat, I am not concerned. The minute I have reason to be - and I don't think I will - I'll let you know."

Nothing to worry about, Jane thought. Once again, she was relieved. And not only was she relieved, she was happy. They continued the meeting with other notes of address but Jane couldn't concentrate. She was on cloud nine and nothing they said could bring her back to earth.

Immediately his face flashed in her mind.

Strong sharp cheek bones, chiseled jaw, perfect straight nose, full pink lips, and stunning amber eyes. The image followed her wherever she went. She would think that after three weeks of dating him, she'd get used to his masculine beauty; but her fixation with it only got worse. The only time she could fully concentrate on something besides his appearance was when he was actually in front of her, speaking to her. He never had anything meaningless to say. His intellect and rare confidence always kept her on her toes. She smiled a goofy smile but wiped it off her face as soon as she realized it was there. She had to at least *try* to look professional.

When the meeting was adjourned, she grabbed her belongings and headed straight home. Everything was on autopilot. She relied on route memory to take her on the correct metro line to her apartment. As she walked the familiar streets lining the Hudson River she reflected on the numerous outings she'd been on with Aiden since he first asked her to date him exclusively. They'd frequented the Met, gone on runs in Central Park, seen shows on Broadway, and hung out at her place when neither felt like going out. Alexa teased that she would have to start charging her brother rent for his almost-constant presence at their place.

As much fun as she had going out on the town with him, Jane found that the quiet moments in her apartment, were her favorite. She got to learn more about his job, how hard he'd worked to not only get his degrees but get his foot in the door at his firm. She'd felt a swell of pride when he told her he'd refused his father's offer to get him an internship. He landed the job on his own and made his own connections on Wall Street. Even with the recession of 2008, when graduates were running away from the field, he took the plunge and entered it, going above and beyond the call of duty to stand out to his agitated, worry-ridden bosses. With the long hours, high stress levels, and financial pressures his job entailed, it was a wonder he looked so good. No one could ever call her a gold digger but Jane found it absolutely sexy to see a man successful in his business, whose hard work paid off. That said, she could tell there was a hint of discontentment in what he was doing. She hadn't asked yet but she wanted to know if he was planning on leaving the industry or moving to another firm. She didn't care about the financial ramifications of his decision. She wanted him to be happy.

Hmmm, she thought. Next to Alexa, she'd never really cared for someone else's unequivocal happiness. Alexa was her best friend. But Aiden was her boyfriend. She smiled at the thought. She still felt a slight thrill from referring to him as such. She could still remember the first time he'd referred to her as his girlfriend at a restaurant. It had been so unexpected she'd looked at him in surprise. He in turn shrugged and gave her a look as if to say *so what? You are my girlfriend.*

Jane finally snapped out of her thoughts long enough to turn the key and enter her apartment. She enjoyed a couple hours of downtime - i.e. daydreaming about him - and started to get ready for the evening. After showering and changing into something more comfortable, she was in the middle of spritzing her body splash when her phone rang.

"Hello?"

"Hey, sweetie." Aiden greeted lightly. She immediately smiled.

"Hi."

"I wanted to know if I'm taking you to my parents or if we're meeting there?"

"Pick me up," she ordered jokingly.

He laughed on the other end, the deep rumble of his voice soothing her.

"Okay, then. I'll be there in twenty."

He was there in fifteen. She opened the door and found him already smiling.

"What's that goofy grin for?" she teased.

"The same reason you're wearing one," he retorted and leaned in for a slow kiss.

She moaned against his mouth and sent a ripple of pleasure down his spine.

Not now, not now, he thought. Three weeks and he could still stand to attention if he wasn't careful around her. He took her hand. "Let's go."

"You know, anytime you want to help, Aiden, you can!" Alexa called jokingly from the kitchen. Aiden rolled his eyes and leaned deeper into his seat. They were sitting on his parents' sofa while the rest of his family congregated around his mother in the kitchen, eager for her to finish and serve them. Jane was reclining with her head at the arm of the couch and he sat at the other end, her legs folded over his lap. She began to get up, clearly ready to assist but Aiden laid a heavy hand on her hip and kept her stationary on the couch.

"I should be helping," she told him guiltily.

He shook his head. "You should be staying here with me. Besides, she was joking."

"I was joking, Jane." Alexa called out. "Don't you dare get up. My parents want to see more lovey-dovey affection between you two."

"Wait, there's *more?*" Michael asked sarcastically.

Aiden knew Jane would blush if she could. He saw a wave of embarrassment wash over her but he laughed right along with his parents. Leaning in, he wrapped a hand around the nape of her neck and pulled her to him for a kiss. Jane gave him a receptive peck and pulled back, thinking that would be the extent of their PDA; but he kept his strong hand secure at her neck and pulled her back in for a longer, sweeter kiss.

She moaned against his mouth. "Aiden," she rasped.

Opening her eyes, she saw the amusement in his and quickly kicked his thigh with her foot. He immediately caught it in his hand.

"Hey now," he warned. "A few inches higher and you would've wrecked the family jewels."

"Then the jewels must not be that strong to begin with."

"Oh! I cannot *believe* you just said that!"

She tried to pull her foot out of his hands, worried he was going to tickle her in retaliation. He held firm and rolled her sock off her foot. She pulled harder but he resisted.

"Aiden, what are you doing?"

To her surprise, he began to kneed his fingers and thumbs into the soft flesh of her foot like a baker would knead dough. She stared at him in wonder as he continued his spontaneous massage like it was an everyday occurrence. She watched the laser-like focus in his golden eyes as he caressed and rubbed every inch of her foot, flexing the arch and stretching the toes, listening to the slight sounds she made in response to his soothing hands. How could hands so strong perform an act so tender? Selfless was the real word. He continued to massage her foot for ten minutes before switching to the other one.

"Aiden, this feels amazing."

He smiled as if to say *I know it does.*

"Thank you," she whispered.

He met her eyes and gave her a very serious look. "It's nothing," he said. "I'd do anything for you."

They silently watched each other for several long moments while he continued to rub and massage her other foot.

"Okay, dinner's ready!" Ava announced as she walked into the room. Jane yanked her foot out of Aiden's hand and started to peel her socks back on. She glanced up and found his mother beaming at what she just witnessed.

The dinner was a blast. Aiden was observant as his family and now girlfriend ate yet another meal together. He couldn't help but think it was night and day from the first time Jane came over to eat. For one thing, their obvious wealth had shocked and overwhelmed her back then. And though she wasn't completely acclimated to the environment, she was mostly relaxed whenever she came to his parents' place now days.

"Sooo…" Alexa began, drawing the word out. "I have a request of you all."

"What is it?" her mother asked.

"I have a performance on the fifth and I wanted to invite you all to come."

"You still sing?" Jane asked with a smile.

Alexa grinned and nodded her pretty head. "I do. It's really cathartic and a few people say I'm good at it."

"You're excellent at it," her father praised her. "Where are you performing?"

"At Redeemer. Their morning service."

There were no awkward pauses, no long silences.

"We'll be happy to go," Ava immediately replied.

Her husband nodded. "Absolutely."

"You're gonna do great, Shark Bait."

Jane could see the surprise and relief on her friend's face and wondered just how often her family judged or criticized her for her beliefs. They didn't just then but it seemed like either that was a rare moment of acceptance or her friend was just oversensitive about her faith. Jane wagered it was the former.

The rest of the dinner went smoothly. They genuinely enjoyed each other's company and meshed. Aiden noted that his mother and sister didn't have to carry the conversation. Jane could start and carry one herself without any hesitation or discomfort. It made him happy to see her fully relax.

After dinner, they all loaded their dishes into the sink.

"Are you sure you don't need help?" Jane asked once more. She felt horrible about the prospect of leaving those dirty dishes to the same person who cooked all night. Ava smiled and hugged her tightly.

"Don't even think about it," she said, releasing her.

Alexa touched her arm and assured her. "I've got them covered. Enjoy the night with Aiden."

Jane smiled appreciatively and hugged her as well. They said goodbye to the family and took their leave. Minutes later, they arrived at a hole-in-the-wall establishment called *Tunnel's Funnels*. Jane looked at her boyfriend questioningly.

"Funnel cakes," he said, as if it was obvious.

"Don't tell me this is another one of your cravings. Didn't we just have ice cream?"

"*You* had ice cream. If you recall correctly, I didn't eat any."

"And why didn't you?"

"It's too cold for ice cream. I want something warm."

Jane howled with laughter at the irony. He looked at her in surprise as she doubled over right in front of him, right in front of everyone, and indulged herself with the humor of the moment.

"What?" he asked in amazement. She continued to chortle and he pushed himself to wait.

Still fighting through the remnants of her infectious giggles, she finally said, "Three weeks ago, you took us to Cold Stone to have ice cream after walking in the freezing streets of New York for nearly half an hour. You didn't care that it was already cold. You had a craving for ice cream and just had to have it. Now, when you've been offered ice cream - your favorite flavor by the way - in the warmth of your mother's home, you turn it down so you can go somewhere to get funnel cake because ice cream right now is 'too cold.' Do you not *see* the lunacy of your logic?" She started to laugh again, leaning heavily on his arm for support. He supposed it was funny and the more she laughed, the more stares she drew, the more he found himself starting to loosen up and join her. He chuckled at his idiosyncrasy and her response to it. As she calmed down once more, he admired her face. She was flushed with laughter and though her skin color didn't change, her eyes were bright with happy tears and her skin glowed from something other than makeup.

She looked ravishing.

Before she could think or say anything else, Aiden pulled her into his arms and captured her mouth once more. The pleasure was like an electric current running down her body from the base of her skull to the end of her heels. He pulled her flush against him and lazily explored her mouth. By the time he released her, she was relying on him to support her weight once more, but not because of laughter.

"Funnel cake?" he asked again.

She nodded quietly and followed him in.

Minutes later, they took a seat at one of the tiny tables squeezed in the tiny establishment. The cake was a masterpiece - fried sweet batter topped with maple syrup, fresh strawberries, and doused in powdered sugar. The smells radiating from it were heavenly and she could see why he craved the sugary confection.

Aiden saw his girl eyeing the cake and quietly cut off a small piece. He held it out to her wordlessly. She smiled, took the piece and broke off an even tinier piece before trying it. He scooped whopping forkfuls into his mouth while she slowly but surely nibbled on her tiny piece until it was gone. He cut off another small piece and offered it to her. She silently accepted it but cut it in half and once again started nibbling. He watched her do it silently.

"I'm not anorexic," she said. It didn't sound defensive, just matter-of-factly.

"I know you're not," he answered calmly. But his heart was pounding at her unexpected decision to speak about it.

"I have a condition called gastroparesis. It means my stomach doesn't digest food normally and I have to eat very small amounts and be careful with my diet."

He nodded. Though he knew all this already, there was no way in hell he was about to admit it to her.

She frowned. "You're not going to ask how I got it?"

He almost laughed. Whenever he tried to dig deep and ask her about her past, she brushed him off or shut down. He had an insatiable appetite to know her more but asking her uncomfortable questions was like trying to do surgery without the anesthetic and he'd realized early on that he was doing more harm than good trying to siphon information out of her that she wasn't ready to give. Now she was mad at him for choosing to respect her privacy?

He didn't mention the irony but simply said, "Do you want to tell me how you got it?"

"My biological mother," she answered quickly. "She consistently denied me food when I was an infant and toddler so my stomach got messed up. I don't have rickets but that would have been next had they not removed me from her in time."

Though he already knew about the cause of her condition, it hurt Aiden to hear it repeated. He felt such a foreign rush of rage and helplessness at the thought of a miniature Jane crying to sleep because her empty belly was in pain. Starvation was a torturous affair and no child should have to experience it, especially if food was available to be eaten.

"She never starved, did she?" he asked, already knowing the answer.

Jane saw the look of outrage in his eyes and smiled. She liked that he was concerned, angry on her behalf. He couldn't do anything but it reminded her that he cared.

"No, she didn't. Sometimes she would dangle the food right in front of me and taunt me because I couldn't have it."

What kind of demented woman does that? he thought in horror.

Jane continued, "If I snuck into one of the cookies or had a bite of fruit, she would beat me. One time, she hit me so hard, I fell and hit my head on the edge of a table. I was the source of her social security checks and government benefits so while she hated me, she didn't exactly want me dead. She took me to the hospital and claimed I tripped and fell while playing with my non-existent Barbie. They gave me eight stitches." She reached up and parted her afro to show him the faint scar lining her scalp. He never would have guessed, never would have known that those scars were there unless she showed him. He never would have known what she'd endured unless she told him. Aiden stood up, circled around the table and pulled her into his arms. He felt her tremble slightly and he knew it was from sharing something so profound.

Jane looked up at him and could almost see the question mark forming in his mind.

"Go ahead," she said.

"Hmmm?"

"Go ahead and ask. What are you thinking?"

"I…" he hesitated. She looked at him expectantly. "I was just wondering about your biological father."

She stiffened in his arms but only slightly.

"What about him?"

"You have no idea who he is?"

She shook her head. "Or was. I don't even know if he's alive anymore."

"But Daugherty isn't that common of a name. Is it your mother's maiden name?"

She chuckled derisively. The complete absence of mirth in her eyes startled him.

"Daugherty wasn't my birth name."

He peered at her questioningly and she met his eyes.

"My full legal name is Jane *Doe* Daugherty. When I was born, my birth mother put 'Jane Doe' on the birth certificate because I 'could be dead' for all she cared."

Jane watched as Aiden blinked, horrified at the new revelation. A fresh sheen of tears surfaced in his eyes but she looked away for fear of crying herself. She'd never told anyone that before - not even Alexa. Most people didn't know her full name and while she could have removed the "Doe" from it when she adopted her new last name at eighteen, she kept it to remind her of people's cruelty and their ability to always hurt her if they wanted to. She decided she would never forget.

Aiden tried his best to regulate his breathing but the more he tried, the worse it got. How could someone be so cruel? How could someone be so *evil?* And to their own flesh and blood. He wondered in passing if her birth mother had been raped. That was the only feasible explanation he could think of to call for such hatred and even then, it was no excuse. If she didn't want Jane, why not just give her up for adoption? He could only imagine the confusion and repeated waves of pain she experienced as a child. It was natural for a child to trust and love their parent. It was a brutal, heinous reality to realize their parent didn't love them.

He wasn't hungry anymore. He tossed the remnants of his funnel cake into the trash and guided her out of the diner, his arm wrapped around her shoulder.

"Thank you for sharing that with me," he whispered into her hair.

She nodded and tightened her arms around him. "It wasn't much."

He knew what she meant. The story she told him was probably just the tip of the iceberg in a long line of traumatic memories and events she survived. But he knew it *was* much. It took a lot of courage for her to share that - first about her stomach and then about her mother. And all of that had happened before her nightmarish years in the foster system.

How much can one take? he thought, amazed at her resilience.

They were silent for a few moments, Aiden unsure of what to say.

"You don't have to use kiddie gloves," she said suddenly.

"What do you mean?" he asked, surprised at her sudden remark. He watched as she surveyed the street, keeping her eyes - and her thoughts - hidden.

"I mean I'm not made of glass."

"I know that," he said defensively.

"Do you?" She quickly turned, her expression challenging him. "Prior to knowing the details, you didn't act so hesitant around me. Like I might break."

"Have you ever?"

Her expression changed to startled surprise.

"Well?" he asked. "Have you? Did you ever get a chance to really cry?"

He watched as a coldness swept over her eyes, shielding her heart, and cloaking herself from him. Her next words chilled him.

"Why cry over spilt milk?"

He didn't know what to say to that so he folded her back under his arm and kept walking.

"I don't want to go home yet," she said.

He nodded. "Okay, we don't have to."

He hailed a cab and gave the driver an address.

"The financial district?" she asked, turning to him. He looked at her and nodded.

"That's where I live."

She didn't say anything else. When they got to his place, Jane followed his lead as he escorted her through the secure, classically modern lobby and up the elevator to his floor. He didn't own the entire floor but his door was one of only two on that landing. They entered the door on the right and Jane got to see his place for the first time.

It was all male.

Dark oak wood floors, black leather couches, chairs, and tables. Gray fixtures and artwork along the dark gray walls. Anything that wasn't dark in tone was glass by structure. It was distinctly masculine but the array of golden lights warmed the place up. She was almost surprised to see that his apartment was about half the size of her and Alexa's place but it made sense since he was a bachelor. Despite the dark, overtly masculine decorations, it was really a beautiful apartment, tastefully decorated with a huge floor to ceiling window displaying the skyline of the city's financial district on the west, and the Hudson River on the east.

Aiden watched his girlfriend observe his place but couldn't decipher a single thought under her passive expression. She was very good at concealing her thoughts. It probably came from years of practice.

Self-preservation.

"Come here." He took her hand and led her to a couch. They sat down and he pulled her into his side, wrapping both arms around her. She reciprocated and tucked her nose into his chest.

"Thanks for bringing me here," she said. "You have a nice place."

He chuckled. "You don't have to lie. It's probably too Batman cave-ish for you."

She giggled into his side; he could feel the warmth of her breath on his shirt.

"I'll take anything over being home alone. Sometimes it takes me a while to get the thoughts out of my mind."

"I can only imagine."

He squeezed her to him until there could be no space left between the two of them.

"I'm sorry if it came off like I was treating you differently," he said.

She shook her head. "I was just being paranoid. I've never told anyone what I told you. Alexa doesn't even know about my name."

He looked down at her and tilted her chin up to meet his eyes. "Then I'm honored that you trusted me enough to share."

She smiled slightly and lowered her eyes to his lips. He bent his head and gave her a gentle, tender kiss. It started off with gentle pecks, sweet reminders that they were in each other's arms. Then it grew, and slowed down, and transformed into a languorous expression of desire.

"Jane…" Aiden began to pull back, reluctant to take advantage of her.

She ignored his withdrawal and pulled him back to her.

He pulled away again and raised an eyebrow at her agitated grunt.

"Jane," he said seriously, searching her hazy brown eyes. "You're upset. This isn't the right time."

"I'm not upset," she replied with eerie calm. "I want you. I'm ready. Kiss me again, please."

His last thread of resistance snapped and Aiden claimed her lips once more. His hands began to travel from her cheeks, down her neck, and further below. He acquainted himself with the delicate swell of her breasts, her hips, her thighs and made himself at home with her body. Lifting her off the couch effortlessly, he carried her into his room.

Like the rest of the house, it was a dark gray mass of minimalist chic. Jane only had eyes for his massive queen sized bed. He laid her gently over the silk comforter and reached to turn on the light. She stopped his hand.

"Don't," she said.

"I want to see you."

"Not this time."

"Jane-"

"Do you really want to argue about this *now*?"

A part of him wanted to say yes but he followed her logic and tried to see her the best he could in the nearly pitch black room. It was only illuminated by the New York skyline visible through the floor to ceiling windows. It really was romantic. Perhaps that's why she wanted the lights to stay off. They explored each other once more, this time without the barrier of clothes. It was just as he had imagined three weeks earlier - nothing between them but silk sheets, heavy breaths, and skilled hands.

He felt her nails dig into his shoulders as she hissed into his ear. "Stop teasing me. Please!"

He knew what she wanted, what she was ready for, and he took what she freely offered.

"Oh, Jane!"

Jane closed her eyes at the sensation and heard him groan in her ear. He was all around her, literally, but this was different than anything she'd experienced before. A deeper level of intimacy than she knew could exist. Something bottomed out in her heart and it scared her. Her fingers tensed at the rippling muscles in his arms and she turned her head away from his probing mouth.

Aiden felt her withdrawal immediately. Despite the euphoria of being joined to her, *feeling* her completely around him, he couldn't ignore the sudden change. She wasn't pushing him off of her but he could tell she wasn't "there" even as she moved beneath him. He wanted her to enjoy it as much as he did.

"Hey," he panted out. She didn't answer. "Hey."

To her surprise, he paused, refusing to match her thrusts.

"What are you doing?" she rasped out.

"Where did you go just now?" he asked her.

"What are you talking about? I'm right here."

"You are but you're not. How are you feeling? Am I hurting you?"

She couldn't believe him. He was asking her how she was feeling mid-stroke!

"I'm fine," she said hastily. She began to undulate beneath him once more. "Don't stop. Please."

He started up again and expertly worked his way around her body. Her moans filled his ear as he continued in a relentless rhythm, teasing her to within an inch of her life. He plucked her like the strum of a guitar until she finally released, crashing against the earth, tuning everything out. She was undone.

I want more, Aiden thought. He not only hadn't released yet, he wanted more from *her*, from her response. This wasn't what he expected their first time to be. There was no tenderness, no affection, just rutting hips and racing endorphins. This couldn't be *it*. There had to be more. So he kept moving; in spite of her whimpers, her utterances to give her a break.

"Aiden, what are you doing?" she finally asked, fingers clutching his biceps.

"I'm going to take you there again," he answered with steel determination.

"What?" she exclaimed. "You can't. I'm not multi-orgasmic."

"Watch."

She had no idea.

It was all the challenge he needed. His eyes adjusted to the dark as he wracked her body again and again with earth shattering convulsions. Her mind began to drift into a constant state of euphoria as her body gave in time and again to the ecstasy he commanded. No one had ever put her body to the test like that. His skill, attention, and stamina were unprecedented.

"Aiden!"

As he watched and felt her reach yet another release, Aiden sighed in defeat and confusion. She didn't get it. And neither did he. The more he made love to her, the more she withdrew into herself and at that point, he didn't know if he could blame her. Maybe it was the only way to handle the paces he was putting her through.

Enjoy it, he told himself. *Let it go.* Finally, after nearly an hour of intimacy, he allowed his well-disciplined body the release it was demanding.

Jane felt her body fall back to the bed, his on top of hers as he sought her lips fervently. He kissed her slowly, expertly exploring every crevice of her mouth with his tongue. She felt his groan vibrate down her throat as he shifted his body in the afterglow. Jane tore her mouth from his and, gasping, turned onto her side, her back facing him. He frowned at her withdrawal and spoke when he saw her sit up on the edge of the bed. Though his eyes had adjusted, he could still only make out her outline in the darkness.

"Are you okay?" he asked.

"I'm fine," she calmly replied. She was slightly out of breath but her breathing was coming under control. He watched her quietly pick up her clothes from the floor.

"What are you doing?"

"Getting dressed."

"Why?" he asked.

"I'm going home."

"Why are you going home?" he asked, a feeling of foreboding washing over him.

She looked at him, confused. "We're done."

He sat up and looked at her steadily, processing her bemused tone. He realized what she was *really* saying was: "We had sex. We just finished. There's no reason for me to stay."

As in wham, bam, thank you, ma'am.

And he was the ma'am!

Aiden was shocked. He'd never had a woman walk out of his bed right after sex. He'd done it to women a couple of times but always felt guilty afterward so he usually tried to stay the night even if it was a one night stand. But he'd never had a girl voluntarily take the initiative to leave his side. She hadn't even caught her breath and she was bailing!

She's acting like a guy, Aiden thought.

This guy didn't like it.

"Stay," he said quietly. She turned to him and frowned.

"Stay," he repeated. "Stay the night. There's no reason for you to leave."

She continued dressing, as if he hadn't said anything.

"Jane, I want you to stay." He couldn't believe this was happening. He couldn't believe that she was leaving and that *he* was the one suddenly begging her not to. In fact, it looked as if she'd doubled her determination to go. She pulled on her pants quicker than she'd pulled on her shirt. Finally, completely dressed, Jane turned to him and said almost robotically:

"It's easier this way. See you around."

She turned on her heel and saw herself out.

CHAPTER ELEVEN

Jane stretched in her bed and yawned away the last bit of sleep from her body. Her body was sore. Muscles ached along her back, arms, but mostly between her legs. She stared at the ceiling and felt more than saw the memories of last night rush back at her.

We did it. We did it. *We had sex. Did the deed. Sealed the deal. Made lov- can I even call it that?* she asked herself and frowned. Sure, they'd had sex but could it be considered making love? No. She didn't know what that was like. She'd had sex, just like all the other times. But this time was different - he was better than anyone she'd ever been with - and a hell of a lot more tender. But making love was for people in love. She and Aiden did not qualify. She thought back to the minutes they were together. How it felt to be with him…with him in the most intimate way a human can be with another person. She thought of his eyes and how they were hooded in desire. How they would briefly close whenever he felt a particular strike of pleasure. She could still feel his breath, hear his groans, his gasps of ecstasy.

If she thought Aiden was attentive in general, he was downright studious in bed. It was as if he watched her every cue to increase her pleasure. At the slightest expression, whimper, or movement, he would change pace, position or stroke to suit her needs. And now she could think of nothing else. It was bad enough he'd branded her body with his; but he'd also branded her mind. She'd woken up thinking about him and their night together. She tried to ignore the strange twist in her gut when she recalled how she'd left. She had seen the shocked look on his face when she first started getting dressed but she had ignored it.

He was a man. Didn't most men want the girl to leave as soon as they'd had their fun? She'd been in more than enough situations where the guy got dressed almost as soon as he caught his breath. She figured she'd spare him the trouble of hinting for her to leave. Still, her mind was restless from the moment she'd woken up. Jane stretched once more and got out of bed. She trudged her way to the spacious kitchen and made herself a cup of tea. Alexa was already in class, having signed up for some God-forsaken 8:00 AM art class. Jane didn't have class until the afternoon and none of her appointments were in the morning. After the workout Aiden put her through, she was grateful to have some moments to just think things through.

Someone knocked on the door.

So much for thinking time.

The person knocked on the door again, this time quicker and harder. Thinking Alexa had forgotten her keys or a book, Jane rushed to the door and yanked it open. At the threshold stood a very flushed, very agitated, and all-too-sexy Aiden. Jane nearly gasped at the sight of him. He was dressed in a tailored navy suit and starched white dress shirt. His hair was tousled and still wet from the shower. The scent of soap and shampoo radiated off of him in tantalizing waves. Jane felt her stomach twist again - this time in acute desire.

"Stop it," he said.

She frowned. "Stop what?"

"Stop looking at me like you want me to repeat last night."

She blinked at his blunt response. "Don't you?"

He walked past her into the apartment and Jane could almost outline the tense muscles in his shoulders. She closed the door and turned to face him. The redness in his cheeks resurfaced.

"No, quite frankly. Not if you insist on treating me like a male prostitute."

She inhaled sharply. So he *was* offended that she left.

"What happened?" he continued. "We were getting so close. You trusted me enough to share some really painful memories with me and just when we're about to get even closer, you shut down."

"What are you talking about?" Jane replied. "I didn't shut down. I didn't lead you on. We started to do it and we *did it*."

"I'm not talking about the sex." He let out a frustrated sigh, ran his fingers through his hair and met her eyes again. "Do you want to know why I kept going last night? Why we did it over and over again?"

She shrugged. "Because it felt good?"

"Because I wanted to get through to you. It's like your mind was a million miles away."

"Forgive me for losing focus while you made me com-"

"Can you not be so vulgar?"

Jane felt heat rush to her face. She looked down at her feet and nodded. "I'm sorry."

"Thank you. My point is you shut down. And then you took it further by leaving. *I* don't even do that to girls. I've never had someone do that to me."

"There's a first time for everything," she quipped.

He gave her a severe frown that made her heart drop. He wasn't in the mood for jokes.

"Sorry," she repeated, then sighed. "I didn't mean to offend you last night. I didn't mean to make you feel cheap or make it seem like what we did was cheap. I guess I treated it like a one night stand because that's what I'm used to."

His heart plummeted when he heard that. Was that really all she was used to? She shrugged again and looked at him, watching the tension leave his shoulders and his fierce scowl soften into a tender look. He closed the distance between them and pulled her into his arms. She wasn't prepared to feel the rush of relief at his forgiveness, at the two of them making up. She wrapped her arms around his waist and dug her nose into the lapel of his suit, deeply inhaling his cologne. He cupped her cheek and lifted her head to meet his probing gaze.

"What?" she asked.

"Do you regret telling me about your mother?"

The look in his eyes was so sad, so tender, she almost felt tears rush to her own. She held them back and said with candor, "Not at all. I'm glad you listened." She smiled slightly. "Thank you."

He bent his head and claimed her lips. She sank her hands into the silky soft hair at the nape of his neck and deepened the kiss. She felt his arms tighten around her waist as his tongue demanded, and received, entry. After a few moments, she pulled back, leaned her forehead against his and worked to catch her breath. She felt his fresh breath tickle her nose. She leaned back slightly and met his amber eyes again. They were calm but she sensed a longing behind them...like he wanted more. So she made her position known.

"I won't do what I did last night. But I want us to take it easy."

He frowned. "What do you mean?"

"I mean, I don't want us to rush into something deep. I like dating you. I like getting to know you. I like having sex with you. I like the status quo. Let's just keep it that way for now. Okay?"

His frown didn't leave his face. She saw the muscles work in his tight jaw as he processed her words. For a moment, it looked like he wanted to protest what she said.

But he finally nodded and said, "Status quo. For now."

He bent to re-claim her lips and she enjoyed the fresh scent radiating out of his pores. For all the soap, shampoo, cologne, and toothpaste scents she was enjoying, he sure didn't seem to mind her morning breath. He nibbled and worked his way around her mouth like a sculptor working his way around a block of marble. His hands stroked and caressed the muscles along her back so expertly, she felt a shiver ripple down her spine. His hands peeked their way under her tank top. She grabbed his hand and pulled back slightly.

"Not here," she panted.

"I know," he groaned in reply. He pecked her lips again. "Tonight?"

She nodded and smiled up at him. He rested his forehead against hers again, closing his eyes for a few brief moments. He opened them, smiled, and kissed her one last time.

"See you tonight," he repeated.

"See you tonight," she replied.

He grabbed his briefcase and headed for the door. It opened right before he reached it, Alexa spilling through with a bag of art supplies.

"Oh, hey!" she greeted them.

"Hi, Shark Bait. Bye, Shark Bait." Aiden kissed her forehead affectionately and quickly strode out of the apartment, throwing Jane one last grin over his shoulder. She smiled back and waved. He was so sexy, it was ridiculously distracting. It turned out she hadn't needed to think things over after all. The man at the center of her turbulent thoughts swept right in and cleared things up. She smiled. He had a way of doing that all the time.

By the time she focused her attention back on Alexa, her roommate was standing there with a smirk and perfectly raised eyebrow. There was no denying she'd been in la la land.

"My bad," Jane said. "Did you say anything? 'Cause clearly I wasn't listening."

Alexa laughed. "No worries. I didn't say anything. I just watched you stare after him like an idiot."

"Hey!" Jane cried. She moved back to the stove and re-lit the cooling kettle. She watched Alexa silently climb the kitchen bar stool, rest her chin on her hands like a little girl, and wait expectantly for Jane.

"What?" Jane asked.

"You tell me," she replied. "What happened last night?"

"Alexa…"

"Jane…"

Jane sighed. "You're his sister. I can't-"

"I'm also your best friend. If you can't tell me, who can you tell?"

"No one."

"You did it last night, didn't you?"

"Alexa!" she exclaimed. She was shocked that Alexa could be so blunt about the matter. Maybe Aiden wasn't the only straight shooter in his family.

"Well? Did you?"

Jane met her candid, open look and slowly nodded. Alexa nodded in return, clearly unsurprised. She wasn't thrilled but she didn't look at Jane with condemning eyes and for that, Jane was grateful. She pulled the screeching kettle off the fire and poured the piping hot water over her tea bag.

"Do you want one?" she asked Alexa.

"Sure."

She set to the task of making another cup, all the while wondering what her friend was really thinking. Was it awkward for her? She'd seemed really excited about the two of them getting together but it probably just became a whole bag of strange to think of her best friend sleeping with her big brother. She handed Alexa the cup of tea and leaned against the counter, slowly sipping away. Alexa ran her nails down the side of the cup and looked out at the city skyline.

"I'm sure you can guess my stance on premarital sex," Alexa said, her gaze still averted.

Jane glanced at the purity ring prominently displayed on her commitment hand.

"Yeah. Your religion teaches against it."

Alexa turned and met her eyes. "I believe it's a sacred act meant for marriage, yes. That being said, I know that you're not a Christian. And neither is Aiden. It's not my place to judge what you two do. I love you both and that will never change."

Jane frowned, waiting for the "but" in her statement. It never came. Alexa blew at the steam rising from her tea and took a sip. She smiled in contentment.

"Ooh, I can feel it in my belly. Don't you love it when you can feel the liquid go all the way down?"

Jane smiled and then frowned. "You're not going to say anything else?"

Alexa frowned. "Like what?"

"Like 'don't do it'?"

"I just told you my stance on it. I mean…you're not planning on doing it *here*, are you?" A look of horror crossed her face at the prospect of seeing or hearing her brother have sex anywhere near her vicinity.

"Oh, God no!" Jane exclaimed, equally horrified. "No, we would never disrespect you like that."

Alexa nodded. "Yeah, I thought so. We're cool."

They continued to sip at their tea. The silence was comfortable but Jane's mind continued to run a thousand miles. She didn't know why but she wanted to ask Alexa more about her views. She said sex was a sacred act meant for marriage. Why marriage exclusively? And how could it be "sacred"? She also noticed the slight reaction her roommate had to her use of the word "religion." Did it offend her? Wasn't she in fact religious? She wanted to delve through those things but knew that the topic of sex and religion would open a Pandora's box that she wasn't quite sure she was prepared to face. So she sipped her tea and looked at the skyline. The magnificent view never got old.

Jane reviewed the checklist one last time before hovering her cursor over the "Submit" button. Her application to the University of Cambridge's PhD program was complete. In five months time, she would find out if it was an option for her to earn her doctorate in American Literature there. It was a shot in the dark, applying to the school. She was surprised that they'd even invited her to apply. Jane hadn't considered earning her degree abroad before, especially in a topic that was so entrenched in American culture. She was curious to know how the British would teach the subject. She could also admit, in the deepest corner of her heart, that the idea of moving to England filled her with excitement. Hope. The possibility of a different life in a brand new country. She'd filled out the application, guided by her imagination. Trips to London, walking historical shores, visiting Wales, starting a brand new life for herself with a clean slate.

What about Aiden?

Her finger paused over the mouse. It dawned on her that her hesitation came from him and him alone - her relationship with him. Just that morning, he'd made it clear that he took them more seriously than casual sex partners. He wanted to be with her. She was his girlfriend. How could they be together if she left for a three year program in England?

Don't think about that now, she told herself. It was a sad thought, but Jane knew that nothing was guaranteed, including the longevity of her current relationship. She didn't want to be the stupid girl who gave up the chance of a lifetime because she was infatuated with a man. Infatuated with a relationship that might not work in the long run. She clicked the button and leaned back in her seat. Her life couldn't revolve around Aiden.

She wouldn't let it.

The phone rang on her desk, jolting her out of her thoughts.

"Hello?" she answered. She normally didn't receive calls during her office hours. And so far, she hadn't received students either.

"Hi Jane, it's Robert." Dr. Geissner's voice carried across the line. She frowned in surprise. He never called her office. Almost all of his correspondence was through email or in person.

"Hello," she said cautiously. "What can I do for you?"

"I was wondering if you were busy at the moment. If not, could you come down to my office for a few minutes?"

"Right now?" she asked.

"Yes, please."

She hung up and made her way to his office. His secretary smiled at her kindly and allowed her to go right in.

"Hi, there." Geissner stood behind his desk. He gestured for her to take a seat and sat back down as well.

"I know this is a bit unorthodox," he began. "But I wanted to see you in person and noticed that you have open hours right now."

She nodded silently, glad she had completed her Cambridge application before his call.

"How is Race and Ethnicity in American Lit going for you?" he asked.

She frowned, sensing that he didn't call her in to talk about that class. Nevertheless, she answered. "It's going well. The students have been very receptive to the material and all seem to respect each other."

He nodded thoughtfully as he surveyed her face. "I'm glad I placed you with that class. Not only are you the best instructor for it, it has now diversified your portfolio to a degree."

She nodded. That was the same thing he'd told her months ago.

"Is something wrong, Dr. Geissner?"

He took a deep breath and when he didn't deny it immediately, Jane's stomach turned. She waited.

"I'm afraid I was too hasty in my assurances both in email and during the department meeting. There are only a handful of non-tenured professors in our department and I thought you all were safe. I thought the board would throw her proposal out." She knew he was referring to Schneider. "I have it on good authority that the board is seriously considering her proposal after all." He took one look at her face and rushed ahead with, "I still wouldn't worry yet but it might not be a simple show of muscle after all."

Jane took a deep breath and tried to steady her racing mind. "What do I do?" she asked. "How can I prove myself?"

He shook his head. "You already are. Just keep up the good work and-"

"Is this even *legal*?" she blurted out. "She's targeting younger professors. I'm only twenty-four. I know where the axe will swing."

He didn't deny the ageist proposal or who it would hurt the most.

"It is legal," he said. "Because it's not a ban on young professors but a shift in policy that happens to favor those older. Of the non-tenured professors on staff, only two are under forty. Only one is under thirty."

He gave her a pointed stare.

"I'll keep you posted on any changes. I'm sorry I didn't have brighter news but I wanted to admit my error as soon as I learned it. I'm still hopeful we can beat this but I don't want you to be caught off guard."

She nodded and stood up. As she left his office, a brand new weight settled on her shoulders. The same weight that comes when a new problem introduces itself and makes it clear that it cannot be easily dismissed. She was shocked. He'd assured her that she was safe. He'd promised her weeks ago and then repeated the same sentiment just yesterday! She felt a surge of white hot anger at Geissner for his false assurances. But she also felt a generous helping of anger at *herself* for her complacency. The Jane she knew wouldn't have settled for the department chair's opinion. She would have dug around some more to see if the proposal had a chance.

She would have pleaded her case to the president or looked into the legality of the situation or done *something* to get ahead of the problem before it could bite her in the ass like it was doing now.

Why didn't I see it before?

The answer immediately came to mind: Aiden. She hadn't focused on solving her problems because she couldn't see reality. She'd allowed her relationship and infatuation with Aiden to supersede her better judgment, putting her livelihood and career at risk.

Just then, her phone buzzed. She unlocked the screen and saw a text from him.

What time should I pick you up? it read. Her anger, worry, and frustration boiled over. Jane typed a hurried reply and hit the send button. At the moment, he was the last person she wanted to see.

"Hey, hey, hey!" Alexa greeted her as she walked through the door. The girl was bouncing around the kitchen making something for an early dinner. Any other time, Jane would have asked what she was doing, smiling at the sight of her bubbly friend.

But right then, all she could muster was a limp, "Hey."

Alexa glanced at her and immediately laid the spatula down.

"Hey," she repeated gently, walking up to Jane and pulling her into a hug. "What happened? You look like you've been run over by something."

Jane inwardly rolled her eyes at the girl's tactless statement. She took the love behind it and told her, "Just a really bad day at work."

Alexa rushed back into the kitchen and turned off all the burners on the stove. Turning back to Jane, she pulled her into the living room, sat on the sofa beside her and said, "Spill."

Jane spent the next thirty minutes recounting everything that happened. Repeating it only made her feel worse.

"What does Aiden think about this?" Alexa finally asked.

"Nothing. I didn't tell him."

Alexa frowned. "When will you? Aren't you seeing him tonight?"

"No, I canceled." Her face began to burn with the way she replied to his text. Alexa watched her closely.

"What? Did you say something else to him?"

Jane met her eyes and admitted, "I told him to leave me alone for a while."

"*What?*" Alexa exclaimed. "Why would you do such a thing?"

"I was angry, all right? I've been so distracted with him and what's going on between us, I allowed myself to get complacent at work. And now I might not *have* a job soon. I need to come up with a plan to get ahead of this and fast." Alexa was shaking her head before Jane even finished her sentence.

"You're making a mistake, Jane. Blaming Aiden is not going to solve your problems at work."

"I'm not blaming him," Jane said defensively.

"Yes, you are." she replied firmly. "It's not his fault you guys fell for each other at the time you did. You've been nothing but happy since you first started going out so instead of blaming this situation on him and the relationship you've built, you better turn to him and seek his support to help get you through this."

Jane blinked at the bold words coming out of Alexa's mouth. Her friend was so forthright and unwavering. She also brought up some very valid points. What was the point of having a man in her life if she couldn't share some of her trials with him? Alexa peered at her friend and softened her voice.

"What's the real problem here, Jane? Why did you really choose not to tell Aiden?"

Jane looked around the apartment, feeling trapped under the fix of her friend's gaze. She finally met her eyes and told her the truth. "I don't want to become reliant on him. I've always been independent."

Alexa nodded like she wasn't surprised in the slightest. She smiled and squeezed her friend's hand. "There's a difference between support and reliance. Swallow your pride and let him in. He wants to be there for you in the good times and the bad."

Jane nodded and gave her friend a grateful hug. She pulled out her phone as Alexa returned to the kitchen. No surprise - she'd missed at least a dozen calls from her blunt, lay-it-on-the-table boyfriend. Keeping it brief, she sent Aiden another text.

I'm sorry for what I said earlier. Can you please come over after work?

CHAPTER TWELVE

Aiden knocked on her door, unsure of what to expect on the other side. He could still remember her first text. It had been short, acerbic, and very unlike her.

I don't want to hang out tonight. Please leave me alone for a while.

When she refused to answer his calls, the panic had really settled in. Had he done something wrong? Was she mad at him for some reason? Was their talk that morning bothering her? But his anxiety was abated with her last text, apologizing and asking him to stop by. Now he was determined to get to the bottom of things. She couldn't just yo-yo him around with her unpredictable actions. If something happened at work, she'd better tell him right away because that was about the only excuse she could give for treating him like that.

She opened the door and the sight of her knocked the breath out of him.

"Hi," she said softly. She crossed the threshold and reached up to give him a soft kiss. "I'm sorry," she said immediately. "Please, come in."

Whatever anger had been building up in him died a quick death at that greeting. He followed her inside and looked around for his sister.

"She's in her room. She wanted to give us some time alone."

And probably eavesdrop, he thought.

He watched her fidget before him and waited for her to meet his eyes.

"What happened?" he asked when she finally did.

"It was work," she said. He felt a huge rush of relief that it was exactly what he suspected. She continued, "The new president of the university has submitted a proposal to the board of trustees which, if approved, would pretty much take me off the tenure track at UNY."

He frowned. "What? Why would she do such a thing?"

Jane rolled her eyes. "Something about there being 'wisdom with experience.' Her new policy would basically only make older professors eligible for tenure."

"That's ageist," he spat out in disgust.

She nodded.

"Is that even legal?" he asked, clearly upset. His anger with her was long forgotten. He was furious with his sister's institution.

She nodded again. "It's not a specific ban on young professors but it's-"

"An institutional loophole to shrink that pool of faculty," he finished for her.

She sighed with a slight smile. She loved how quickly he caught on to things. He focused on her and pulled her into his arms. "I'm so sorry, honey. You don't deserve that."

She smiled into the lapel of his suit. "Thanks," she whispered. His fresh cologne enveloped her senses in a comforting embrace. She felt his chest rumble with the vibration of his voice as he spoke again.

"Would you like me to get you an attorney? Maybe we can find out what your options are."

She shook her head and smiled up at him appreciatively.

"I don't want to be *that* professor - who turns to litigation to solve her problems. Besides, we don't know yet if the board will pass her proposal."

"So just sit tight until we know more?" he asked. She noticed that he once again used the word "we," referring to her problem as his as well. *This was what Alexa meant.*

She looked at him in wonder and nodded. It felt wonderful to feel like she wasn't on her own. He bent down and gave her a soft kiss.

"Want to go for a walk with me?" he asked. She nodded.

Ten minutes later, they were strolling down the bend of a relatively empty Central Park. Jane smiled, realizing it had sort of become their special place. It suddenly occurred to her that they were so wrapped up in *her* work situation, she'd never asked him about his.

"Aiden?"

"Hmm?"

She looked up at his thoughtful face and wondered if he'd be open.

"Do you *like* being a stock broker?"

She saw a muscle twitch in his jaw. Aiden was surprised. Despite her own stressful situation, she was taking the time to ask him about his. He was also surprised that she could discern his dissatisfaction with work. So many others assumed it was a high profile, glamorous job.

Jane could see that he was measuring his words carefully.

"I used to," he admitted. "Lately, though…something's been missing. Either that or I've changed."

"Maybe it's both," she said quietly. He glanced at her and gave a smile that didn't quite reach his eyes. "What do you think is missing?" she asked.

He sighed. "I don't know. Every time I walk into the office, I see another money-obsessed person. It's all they can think about and what's worse, it's all their *supposed* to think about."

"Is there a lot of corruption?" she asked bluntly.

"No. Thankfully, my firm still has a great deal of integrity and is known for it. But that doesn't mean the hunger is less real. I guess I would understand it in interns or new associates but when the partner of your firm texts you at one in the morning because they want to discuss a deal, something's wrong."

She nodded in complete agreement. She had no idea things were that bad.

"It sounds like an obsession," she agreed. "As well as a boundary issue."

"What do you mean?"

"I mean there is no other profession outside of medicine that can really make a demand at such an ungodly hour. But it seems that your supervisors and co-workers make a life and death situation out of something not nearly as important: money."

He stared at her in amazement. In just three seconds flat, she had summarized everything Aiden found wrong with his job and his career at the moment. He squeezed her hand and continued to walk.

Jane sighed. "Then again, who am I to judge?"

He frowned. "What do you mean?"

She glanced at him. "If I'm being honest, I have to admit I have my own hang ups and issues with money. To me, it's always meant independence and freedom."

He nodded, seeing a whole new dimension of her open up right before him.

"The thought of losing my job scares me. I'm trying to get this PhD half because the subject interests me and half because it makes me more competitive in my field."

"I got my MBA for the same reason," he told her. "People who say money doesn't matter are kidding themselves. Or never have to work for anything they have."

She quirked an eyebrow at him. She never thought *he*, a Masterson heir, would get it.

He read her look. "My family may have money, Jane, but we *all* work really, really hard."

She nodded silently. He was about to ask her what she was thinking when she sighed again. "Why can't things be simple?"

"They probably could," he replied. "If we bought a farm in the Midwest or something."

She laughed. "No, we'd probably have issues there, too. Like crops failing or big businesses running us out of the market."

"It's inevitable, isn't it? Problems."

They smiled at each other in heartfelt commiseration and continued to walk along the park. By the time they got back to her apartment, both of them knew without saying it, that making love that night was not an option. They were too drained mentally to do anything physically.

They heard multiple voices when they stepped into Jane's apartment. To their surprise, Alexa was seated in the living room with Ava and Michael, busily chatting away. Ava saw them first and rose to greet them.

"Hey, kids! So glad you finally got back." She pulled Jane into a warm hug and kissed Aiden's cheek.

"You were waiting for us?" he asked.

Michael stood and greeted the pair as well.

"Yes," he answered his son. He looked down at his grinning wife. "We have a proposition for you two. Alexa has already said yes so she seconds us."

Jane looked between the three of them.

"What is it?" Aiden asked.

"What do you say to a trip to Edgartown this weekend?"

"Edgartown?" Aiden asked, frowning. "What's the occasion?"

Alexa jumped in, "Grandpa. He's getting an award from the historical society at Oaks Bluff and has invited everyone." She turned to Jane. "You love history. It would give you the chance to check out Martha's Vineyard."

Martha's Vineyard? Jane thought. When she heard the name of the famous island, she often associated it with the Kennedys, politicians, and celebrities trying to get away from busy lives. Then, there were families like the Mastersons who had second, third, or fourth residences there at their disposal.

Aiden looked down at her with raised eyebrows. "Wanna go?"

She shrugged. "Why not?"

The minute she spoke the words, Jane couldn't decide if she was excited or nervous. Nervous, because she just agreed to meet Aiden's extended family; excited because she'd never been to Martha's Vineyard and it was a once in a lifetime opportunity. She needed the escape and was eager to get away from her problems.

She decided to be excited.

CHAPTER THIRTEEN

"You're not calling shotgun, Aiden?" Alexa asked in surprise. She frowned as their mother took the front seat next to her husband. They were renting a large Lexus SUV for the journey. Ava and Michael had already picked up their son. Jane and Alexa's apartment was their last stop before they hit the road. It was almost comical how they stood on the curb as Alexa tried to figure out why her 6'4" brother was surrendering the front seat. Jane was surprised that they'd elected to go on a road trip in the first place. They were also driving themselves instead of using a driver. Alexa said it was a family-bonding thing. They'd even traveled cross-country together before.

Aiden shook his head as he loaded the last of the girls' luggage. He looked between his sister and his girlfriend and shrugged. "I'll be fine in the back."

Jane tilted her head in suspicion. His golden eyes looked innocent enough but she wondered...

Alexa voiced what she was thinking. "You just want to sit next to Jane." She broke out into a huge smile. "*Aww!* That is *so sweet.*"

Aiden rolled his eyes and nodded. "Now that, that's established, can we please go?"

He met Jane's eyes and saw her smile in appreciation. She held his thick wrist lightly and asked, "Which side will be better for your legs?"

He peeked in the backseat. It was spacious for an SUV and would accommodate most heights but he knew his large frame was asking for trouble.

146

"Probably a window seat. I could angle my legs and make it work...somehow."

His mother turned in her seat and smiled at him. "We can pull over and switch anytime," she reminded him.

He grinned at her appreciatively. But as the three of them sat in the back and Jane leaned into his side, he knew he wasn't going to take his mother up on the offer. He kissed Jane's forehead as the city streets and tall skyscrapers transformed into flat freeway and grassy plains.

Jane felt the solid muscle of his shoulder against her cheek. She curved her hand around the firm column of his bicep and admired the static strength in his powerful frame. She glanced up at his face and followed the line of his gaze. He was looking at the front consul, where his father quietly held his mother's hand. Aiden silently opened his hand and found Jane's free one. He looked down and met her calm eyes. They smiled and briefly kissed.

The ride was a quiet one at first, with everyone but Michael allowing themselves to fall asleep as the car cruised along. Though tall, Alexa managed to curl her limber legs into a fetal position as she leaned against the other car door and napped peacefully. The journey from the city to Woods Hole, Massachusetts was a little more than four hours - chump change for champion road trippers like the Mastersons - but Aiden offered to switch driver duty halfway to give his father a break. Michael pulled into a service station for gas. Jane, Alexa and Ava retrieved food for everyone while Michael and Aiden checked the car and re-fueled it. The guys clapped and cheered when the ladies re-emerged with the food.

"Photo op!" Alexa yelled before they climbed back in. She ran off and flagged down a gracious traveler, handing him her phone for the photo.

"Wait, wait, wait!" Michael protested. "If we're going to do a family photo, we're going to do it right."

He reached in the car and to Jane's surprise, pulled out a Canon EOS 5D Mark III. It retailed at about $4,000 and was one of her dream cameras. Only a serious photographer would invest in it. She had no idea Michael was one of them. She watched them gather together, the men standing in the back, Ava and Alexa standing in front of them. They looked at her and frowned.

"Jane," Aiden said. "What are you doing?"

"Yeah, silly. Get over here!" Ava exclaimed.

She smiled, a feeling of relief and belonging flooding through her as she came to Aiden's side. He wrapped his arm around her shoulder and Alexa reached behind to grab her hand. They scrunched in and grinned for the camera.

Back on the road and wedged between Ava and Alexa, Jane watched her man drive. She once again admired one of her favorite parts of his body. His strong arms unconsciously flexed as he manned the steering wheel. His sleeves were slightly rolled up, showing a light dusting of dark blond hair across his forearms. He wasn't doing anything particularly sexy. Just driving. And yet the sight of him doing it turned her on.

Get a grip, Jane. His mother is right next to you.

She observed the side of his face and knew that he was relaxed by the lack of tension in his strong, sharp jaw. She forced herself to lean back in her seat. Without him beside her, she didn't feel like nodding off to sleep. She looked back up and glanced at the rear view mirror. Her eyes widened when they clashed with his amber ones. He'd been staring at her through the mirror the entire time!

He smiled at her look of surprise. When was she going to get it?

I'm always *aware of you,* he thought, looking back at the road. It was a small miracle that they made it to the Steamship Authority Dock without any incident. Woods Hole, Massachusetts was a small ferry town with narrow winding roads and an influx of residents that required the most attentive drivers to navigate the tenuous traffic. And attentive was the last word Aiden would use to describe himself when Jane was in the car with him. He managed to steer them all safely to the dock and line their vehicle in lane eight as they and several other families waited for the boat to arrive.

Michael looked at his watch and turned to his family. "Okay, we board at 6:00 PM. That gives us about thirty minutes to use the bathroom, get food, stretch your legs."

Alexa smiled. "Okay…break!"

They all got out and went their separate ways. Michael, Ava, and Alexa went to the on-site restaurant and bathroom. Jane looked around the dock and admired the beautiful homes perched along the shore. Aiden kissed her cheek and grinned at her.

"Tired?" he asked.

She yawned. "Only a little. How are your legs?"

He shook them out and bounced a little. "Good. I'm glad it wasn't that long of a drive." He glanced at the on-site restaurant. "I'm gonna grab something. You want anything?"

She shook her head and, to his amusement, yawned again. "No, thanks."

"Okay. Don't get into trouble."

She rolled her eyes. "Yes, Dad."

He laughed as he walked away. She looked around and tried to decide what to do. She didn't want to join the Mastersons at the restaurant. It was filled with people and crowds weren't her thing. She walked to a railing near the quietest part of the dock and watched the boats on the waters of the Vineyard Sound. She turned her gaze to the people milling in and around the various vehicles parked at the dock. Elderly couples walked hand-in-hand. Young families carried bags of takeout. New families held small infants in chest-carriers. The only things that tipped off their wealth, besides their very presence there, were the quality of their clothes, the emblems on their vehicles, and the enormous rocks on some of the women's fingers. Jane's eyes zeroed in on a young woman in particular. She had wavy blond hair and wore a long cashmere cardigan. Her husband, tall and handsome beside her, held their sleeping baby daughter in his arms while she walked hand-in-hand with their toddling son. Jane wondered what it would be like to live in her shoes. What did it feel like to make a purchase and not worry about your general finances? What did it feel like to be able to get *both* items instead of having to choose one?

What is it like to be married? With children?

She suddenly saw an alternative picture form in her mind: with her holding a young boy's butterscotch hand and Aiden carrying a baby girl with a head full of tawny curls. She gasped at the image and felt a yearning so sharp, so tender swell in the center of her chest. It wasn't envy but a deep awareness of the lack of fullness in her own life. So much of her thoughts and attempts at happiness had been centered around her work and financial stability. She'd made a huge stride in paying off her debt. But on days like this, she wondered if she'd ever reach the level of stability she longed for. The level of security. And she certainly wondered if she'd ever be able to share it with a family of her own one day.

Suddenly, the child leaned his entire body back with all of his might and attempted to yank his tiny hand out of his mother's firm grasp. She paused in her stride and looked down at him, a look of exhaustion and impatience coloring her pretty face. Jane couldn't hear what she was saying over the noise of people and steamships but she gathered that the young mother was telling her son to get up and he was too busy throwing a temper tantrum to listen. Her husband frowned at his son's outburst and also began to reprimand him. The baby, jolted awake by the exchange started to cry and all hell broke loose for the once picture perfect family.

Jane started to laugh. Not at their misfortune but at the irony of the moment. Sure, they probably had a life she would love to lead but even in obscene wealth, their lives were not perfect. No life ever could be.

Aiden watched Jane throw her head back and laugh freely at whatever she was looking at. He was too enthralled at the sight of *her* to see the source of her private outburst. He reached into his pocket, pulled out his phone, and quickly captured the moment on his cell. Then he continued to watch her. He loved every curve of her face, the trace of her full lips as they stretched back to reveal perfectly-lined, bright white teeth. The setting sun created a glowing rim around her afro and her eyes lit up her entire countenance as she laughed carelessly near the water.

"What's so funny?" Jane heard as her laughter died down. She turned to the sound of Aiden's voice and felt her breath catch in her throat. The sun hit him at the perfect angle as he approached her, illuminating the natural highlights in his dark blond hair and reflecting the specks of gold in his bright amber eyes. It even added a warm glow to his naturally tan skin. He was the image of perfect male health. She could smell his masculine cologne as he closed the space between them and handed her a cup of coffee. She smiled her thanks, knowing it would be useless to protest his getting her something despite her earlier refusal.

They both turned towards the water and Jane enjoyed the sensation of him wrapping his arms around her from behind. She smiled and leaned into his embrace. He tucked his face into the side of her neck and planted a warm wet kiss.

"What were you thinking?" he asked, his deep voice reverberating down her spine.

"Not much," she replied. "It's really pretty out here."

She felt his body tense around her. She was lying and it bothered him.

He sighed. "Why do you do that?" he asked.

She turned and was surprised to find a severe frown on his face. "Do what?"

"Hide from me," he answered. His golden gaze bore into her. "You saw something that made you laugh and your whole face lit up."

She gasped in surprise. How long had he been watching her?

"You were so beautiful," he continued. "I just wanted to know what it was that made you laugh like that."

I want to know how I can make you laugh like that.

She looked down at the collar of his trench coat, guilt rising in her chest. She'd held back from him and he'd caught her red-handed. Even after the progress they'd made last night, she didn't know how she could share it all. What would he think if she told him she was thinking about having a family of her own? How would he react if she shared with him her financial frustrations? Could she even do it? She'd spent her whole life working to never rely on others ever again. She didn't know what would happen if she changed that resolution. It was so deeply entrenched in her.

She raised her eyes to his and said, "I'm sorry."

His eyes immediately softened, like they always did when she apologized.

"I didn't mean to shut you out." She took a deep breath and fessed up. "I was looking at a family and this kid threw a temper tantrum. It was cute and funny but it also made me think about some things."

"Like what?" he asked quietly.

Could she tell him what she was really thinking? She looked back down. Aiden watched her hesitate to share.

She sighed, looking at the water. "I don't know what I'm doing, Aiden."

He frowned, trying to understand. "What do you mean?"

He tipped her chin and forced her to meet his eyes. What he found there surprised him. It was the most vulnerable look he'd ever seen on her.

"Aiden, I've never had this before," she gestured between them. "A serious relationship." She looked back down, realizing how presumptuous it sounded. "I mean-"

"No, I know what you mean," he interrupted her. "This *is* a serious relationship. I am serious about you."

She looked up again and saw the sincerity in his eyes.

"Have you had one before?" she asked. He knew what she meant and shook his head.

"Nothing like this. I had girlfriends. It's weird - I was more serious about the girls I dated in high school than in college or afterward. Work kind of took over." He smiled. "You came at the perfect time."

He saw the fear creep up in her eyes. He now recognized it for what it was. Every time he got closer to her or revealed more of his intentions, that look would surface on her face. He was determined to see the day when it didn't appear. In the meantime, he enjoyed watching her purposefully push it away. When she mentally combated every last trace of fear, he leaned down and met her lips, enjoying the soft plush feel of her mouth on his. He parted her lips with his tongue and entered her warm mouth, dancing with her tongue, tightening his arms around her waist. He felt desire rise in his center. She moaned against his mouth, communicating her desire too.

"Hey! Hey!"

They pulled apart at the sound. The lined up cars were slowly rolling out to board the ferry. Ava and Michael were grinning at them while Alexa stood at the open door of the back seat, waving them over.

"Quit necking and get in the car! It's time to board."

The boat was nothing special. A large ferry that could fit a couple dozen cars at the base and numerous people a couple floors up. Aiden's father carefully guided the Lexus into the spot the ferry crew designated for them. They once again left the vehicle and found more comfortable seating on the next level up. Within minutes, Jane realized that the ride was completely uninteresting to the Mastersons. Alexa fell asleep again while Michael and Ava read from thick novels.

Aiden could see Jane craning her neck to get a better view of the water and shore through the thick windows of the old boat. He nudged her leg with the end of his knee and gestured for her to get up. He saw his mother smile as they held hands and stepped out onto the deck of the ferry.

He escorted her to the front of the boat and circled his arms around her again.

"Thank you." She smiled up at him, knowing he was only doing this for her.

"Anytime," he replied with a calm grin. He watched her soak in the sight of the dark blue water, the bleached beach shores, and the beautifully constructed homes that lined the edge of Vineyard Sound. Within minutes, the shores disappeared as they got closer to the other end of their journey: Martha's Vineyard.

"Did you come here often growing up?" she asked over the sounds of the boat.

"Hmm-hmmm. Every summer and almost every Christmas. My great-great grandfather bought a chunk of the land in the mid-nineteenth century. His son developed it right before the Great Depression and managed to hold on to it. My grandfather has used it as the family compound and reunion site since."

"Did you enjoy it?" she asked.

He nodded. "It was nice. One of the first ways I could see the impact of my family's wealth. During the summers, it's notoriously crowded but we have so much land, I was never affected by the swell in tourists."

He told her about the adventures he and his cousins would embark on as kids. The small boats they used to get from one private marsh to another.

"I never told my parents, of course."

"Of course," she replied, smiling. She could only imagine the fit his mother would have at her only child going off unattended.

"Just when I got tired of the place, Alexa arrived. And we had our own adventures all over again. I can still remember the look on her face the first time we came here. It was much like your own."

She smiled at the clear tone of affection in his voice. He really loved his sister.

"Was it hard at all? Going from being an only child to an older sibling?"

He blinked in surprise. She asked some of the most insightful, thoughtful questions of him and he loved that about her. He kissed her forehead and shook his head.

"Not at all. By the time Alexa arrived, I had my own life at Columbia. I came back to help her adjust as much as I could but I didn't need my parents' attention the way I did as a kid. It was a joy to make it about her."

She looked at him admiringly.

He smiled, confused at her look. "What?"

She shook her head. "You're just…you're really selfless, you know that?"

He laughed. "*I'm* selfless? What about you, Miss Guardian Angel? You're all my sister could talk about when she finally opened up to us."

He watched the light dim in her eyes and regretted bringing it up.

"Hey," he touched her chin with the tip of his finger. "Someday you're gonna open up to me. And someday you're gonna move past it. And I'll be there to help you."

She gave him a slight smile, the light returning to her eyes.

CHAPTER FOURTEEN

They arrived at Vineyard Haven twenty minutes later. Aiden explained that they were looking at another thirty minute drive into Edgartown to reach the family compound. Alexa pointed out several shops and markets to Jane as Michael drove them further into rural land but Aiden knew what she was thinking about. It was a historical city on a historical island. He watched her soak in the colonial homes and the cobbled sidewalks along the narrow roads. He could see her picturing the town during the 17th century. He too wondered what it looked like back then.

Jane leaned her head against Aiden's shoulder as the scenery became more and more remote. They were all quiet, clearly tired by the journey. The sun was going down and her thoughts shifted to what lay ahead. How many people were they about to encounter? Did they have some sort of activity planned or would they allow them to rest? The car began to jump on its suspensions as the road got rockier and rockier. They were surrounded by trees, the road so narrow, a car could only pass if the other one pulled over. Five minutes later, Michael pulled off into a long, gravel driveway which opened up into a spacious compound.

Aiden watched Jane gape at the family estate. He looked back at it and frowned. When he really thought about it, it was more like a luxury hotel. It was a little over an acre of land and the house continued to expand as his grandfather added wings to the building. It looked like an over-sized wooden cabin with surrounding windows where wealthy families could go "glamping" - or camping without the roughing it. The property was beautifully landscaped with flower paths and trees carefully lining the perimeter of the estate. He felt her stiffen at his side and he looked down at her. She was no longer gaping at the estate but had a thoughtful look on her face.

He nudged her with his arm. "You okay?" he asked gently.

She barely glanced up at him when she nodded.

"It's much homier on the inside," he said. He frowned in concern. She was still staring at the place. Was it intimidating to her? Did she feel uncomfortable? He usually didn't feel embarrassed by his family's wealth but for the first time, he felt discomfort and he didn't know why. Was the house too showy? His grandfather extended it as more grandkids and great-grandkids joined the family but he knew there was a slightly ostentatious element to the grand estate.

He shoved the thoughts from his mind and climbed out with the rest of the family. He and his father quickly unloaded the trunk and passed the ladies their rolling bags. He grabbed Jane's free hand and followed his parents and sister as they met his Aunt Lizzie at the front porch.

"Mike, Ava! Good to see you. Hi, Lexi! How was the trip?"

Jane watched Michael tower over a woman whom she guessed was his older sister. She was short and slightly plump with dark black hair and the same grayish blue eyes as his. Though pretty and feminine, she had the same cheekbones, nose, and lips that Aiden and his father possessed. She hugged and greeted Michael, Ava and Alexa before turning to Aiden and Jane.

"Aiden!" she greeted warmly, her nephew dwarfing her small frame in a hug. Aiden turned to Jane and smiled.

"Aunt Lizzie, this is my girlfriend, Jane. Jane, this is Elizabeth, Dad's older sister."

Elizabeth gave Jane a welcoming smile and extended her hand. "Welcome to Longbourne, dear."

Jane shot Aiden a questioning look as his aunt turned away and escorted the group inside.

He whispered, "Longbourne is the official name for the estate. We don't really call it that."

Except around strangers, Jane thought.

The exterior had prepared Jane for the interior. Like the outside, the grand living room doubled as a lobby and reeked of old money wealth. It was huge, with towering wood-beamed ceilings, several ceiling fans, and a spacious family room center stage of the entrance. The sight of it made Jane wonder just how many people were staying in the house. Why would they need that much space?

Apparently Elizabeth was the estate organizer for all intents and purposes because she briefed the group on their room assignments, the planned itinerary, and what would happen that night. Jane didn't pay much attention to the briefing. She was tired and ready to take a nap. The minute she learned they would have time to rest before dinner, she zoned out. They began to migrate up the stairs. They'd all been given their own rooms and Jane assumed she'd have hers until Ava turned to her and Aiden.

"I had Aunt Lizzie reassign you to the same room," she said.

Aiden raised surprised eyebrows. "Oh. Thanks, Mom."

Jane saw Alexa briefly raise an eyebrow but to her credit, she kept silent.

Jane didn't even know how *she* felt about the arrangement. She knew Ava was trying to be helpful but why have them sleep in the same room together? Did she assume that they were already sleeping together or was it something Aiden shared with his already open-book family? She wasn't sure she liked the prospect of either question. What she *did* know was that this would be the first time she and Aiden spent the night together. Stayed in the same bed overnight.

She didn't realize it, but Aiden was watching her closely. He tried to read the expression on her pensive face but as usual, couldn't discern what his girlfriend was thinking. Did she want a different sleeping arrangement? Was she uncomfortable at the thought of spending the night with him? Did she feel like his mother was unintentionally fast-tracking their relationship?

So wrapped up were the two in their thoughts that they barely noticed the beautifully decorated bedroom they were assigned to. It had a large queen-sized bed with white satin sheets. A small window roof was perched above their bed and it had an en-suite master bath. Jane sat on the bed and watched Aiden unpack. His dark blond eyebrows were drawn together as he moved his clothes from suitcase to closet.

"You okay?" she asked him. He paused in his movements, the slight frown clearing.

"Yeah." He nodded. The frown returned. "Are you?"

She nodded silently. He approached her and perched himself on the bed next to her. Scanning her face, he focused on her eyes.

"You don't mind the sleeping arrangement?"

"What? Sharing the room with you?" He smiled at her bluntness.

"Yeah," he nodded. "You weren't too keen on staying after we-"

"I thought you'd forgiven me for that."

"I have," he quickly said. "I just want to make sure this isn't rushing it for you."

She smiled at his visible concern. She loved that he was always looking out for her, trying to make her comfortable.

"It's not," she said. Her gaze lowered to his full lips. She leaned in and kissed them, nibbling on his bottom lip until he groaned.

He looked down at her sleepy eyes and gave her one last peck. "I'm going to take a shower."

Jane couldn't remember what she said in reply, if in fact she did say anything. Her eyes were closed before her head hit the pillow.

"Wake up, sleepy head."

Jane roused from her sleep and felt his large strong hand stroke her back in soothing circles. She turned to her side and saw him perched on the bed, an affectionate smile on his face. His hair was wet and looked dark brown instead of blond. Fresh smells of soap and shampoo radiated from him.

"How much time do I have?" she asked, her throat scratchy. She wondered if she should take a shower too or if she was okay to go down to dinner. She cleared the cobwebs out of her throat as he answered.

"About five minutes." Aiden smiled as she yawned once more and stretched, her lean body extending like a feline. He could see the outline of her curves under the blanket and it turned him on. He forced himself not to think down that road. If she wanted to be intimate with him during the trip, she would be. But he refused to initiate something she might be uncomfortable with.

Jane watched him as he stood up abruptly and turned his back to her, the gray sweater he'd changed into stretching across his tightly muscled back. She loved it when he wore sweaters like that. It wasn't too tight or too loose and reminded her of his athletic physique. She got out of bed and shrugged off the blanket she couldn't remember covering herself with.

He must have done it, she thought with a smile. She reached into her suitcase and pulled out a black v-neck sweater, a pair of skinny jeans, and a checkered scarf. She closed the bathroom and changed into her new outfit, wondering if Aiden was puzzled by that move. They'd had sex and she was changing in the bathroom like she was trying to preserve her modesty.

Aiden *was* puzzled but didn't bother to ask. He was spraying his cologne when she emerged from the bathroom and discretely pulled out a bottle of pills. He watched her dry swallow two different colored tablets. She turned to him, expecting him to say something but he didn't. He simply smiled, held out his hand and they walked down to the massive dining room together.

Most of the family was assembled in the room. Name placards were distributed throughout the table, giving each member placement for the evening. Jane suspected she was reading Elizabeth's delicate penmanship. While they waited for dinner to be served, Aiden introduced Jane to his extended family: all twenty-one members of them. She learned that Michael was the second-youngest of six children. His oldest brother, James Masterson IV was married with two kids and two grandchildren; one daughter was married, the other engaged. The next brother was Titus Masterson, who was married to Darlene and had two teenage boys. Elizabeth was one of the middle children and the eldest daughter, married with two daughters of her own: Carly and Laura. They were busily chatting with Alexa and looked to be around her age. Jacob Masterson was next and, as Aiden quietly whispered, was divorced with two boys: Jake Jr., known as "JJ" and Riley. Michael's only younger sibling was his sister, Celia Masterson who was also divorced but had no children. There was no way Jane was going to memorize all of their names but she tried to pay attention to the adults, especially Aiden's grandparents when he brought her to them.

"*Ciao, Nonna.*" Aiden greeted the elderly woman in Italian. He leaned in and kissed her wrinkled olive skin and it all clicked for Jane. Though he worked long hours in an office, he managed to keep his golden complexion because it was in his genes. He was a quarter Italian!

"Aiden! *Il mio bambino!*" the woman pulled her towering grandson into a warm hug. She was petite and very beautiful. Her wrinkles added to her dignified look and a streak of gray accented her mostly-black hair. Her grayish blue eyes shifted to Jane with keen interest. Aiden introduced the two.

"*Nonna*, this is my girlfriend, Jane. Jane, this is my grandmother, Mrs. Contessa Masterson." A strong leathery hand clapped him on the shoulder and an older replica of Michael Masterson suddenly appeared next to Aiden. "And *this* is my grandfather, Mr. James Masterson III."

Jane leaned into Mrs. Masterson's outstretched arms, which gave her a firm, warm hug. She pulled back and met her friendly blue eyes. They sparkled like she knew a secret.

"Welcome to the family, dear."

Jane gave her a surprised look and the old woman's smile widened.

She sputtered. "It's nice to meet you, Mrs. Masterson."

The family matriarch shook her head. "Call me *Nonna*."

She turned to her husband and rattled off something in Italian. A look of surprise quickly brushed his face before he turned to Jane and gave her a polite kiss on the cheek.

"Oh, so *you're* Jane. Welcome. My granddaughter tells me you're a professor?"

Jane almost missed the question while looking into Mr. Masterson's vivid gold eyes. She initially thought he looked like an older replica of his son, Michael. But the more she thought about it, the more she realized she was looking at a senior version of Aiden. With the exception of gray hair that was once black, James Masterson III had Aiden's amber eyes, sharp high cheek bones, and charming smile. It was hard to believe this was the same man featured in the imposing portrait hanging in the Masterson home in New York.

"Yes," Jane replied. "I teach at UNY."

He nodded. "Fine school. How old are you, though? You look very young to be a professor."

"She's twenty-four." Aiden answered, a hint of pride in his tone. Jane smiled up at him. Out of the corner of her eye, she noticed his grandmother smiling at the two of them. She wanted to know what was going through the old woman's mind but quietly listened to Aiden and his grandfather talk.

Within a few minutes, everyone was called to dinner and they took their places at the enormous, twelve foot table. Aiden sat to her right, one of Elizabeth's daughters, to her left. Alexa sat across from Aiden and Elizabeth's other daughter sat next to her. To her surprise, they joined hands at the table and *Nonna* Masterson led them all in prayer.

After a resounding "Amen!" they began to eat. Though a large party, the family broke off into clusters and had their conversations with the people closest to them.

Jane felt Aiden's eyes on her profile. He often observed her and she wondered why. She turned and met his gaze.

"Loud, huh?" he asked with a small smile.

Aww, she thought. He was worried for her.

She nodded. "A little, yeah."

Sometimes it amazed her how well he could read her. Clearly, he could see that she was overwhelmed by the size of the dinner party and the noise it produced.

He leaned into her ear and whispered. "Don't worry. It won't be like this every night."

She gave a slight nod and he kissed her temple before returning to his plate.

"So Jane," one of the girls said across from her. "Lexi tells me you grew up with her?"

Jane looked at the stranger across from her. She didn't look a lot like Aiden or his father but she had her mother's gray-blue eyes and straight nose. It complimented her strawberry blond hair.

Where is all the blond hair coming from? Jane wondered. There was a mix of it in the family but neither *Nonna* nor her husband had blond hair. *Probably from generations past.*

She returned Alexa's smile and answered her cousin's question. "Yeah, we were close as kids."

"Was this in a foster home?" the girl next to her asked. Jane felt the hair stand at the back of her neck. She didn't like this line of questioning.

She met the girl's eyes. She had the same blue eyes, blond hair and straight nose but upon closer examination, Jane noticed her face was slightly more angular than her sister's. They could easily pass for twins.

"Yes," she answered quietly.

"What was it like?" the girl continued.

Aiden frowned. "What is this? Twenty-one questions, Laura?"

Jane felt a surge of relief and comfort as her boyfriend intercepted the line of questioning. She met his eyes and smiled at him appreciatively. He nodded slightly, as if to tell her *I have your back.*

"I was just asking," Laura said defensively.

"Think before you ask," Carly reprimanded her. She had a deeper resonance to her voice and Jane wondered if they were twins or if there was a difference in age. So she asked.

"Are you two twins?"

Aiden, Alexa and Laura chuckled while Carly rolled her eyes in good humor.

"Nope." she replied. "I'm twenty-four. Laura's twenty-one."

Jane nodded. Though they looked almost identical, Carly carried herself like a full-fledged adult. Laura acted, and sounded, like someone just emerging from adolescence.

"They're not twins, but everyone refers to them as 'the twins.'" Alexa explained.

"Yes, much to my sister's disdain," Laura added.

"Did you guys grow up here too?" Jane asked.

The question launched the girls into various childhood stories about life on Martha's Vineyard during school vacations. They even threw in a couple featuring Aiden. The girls' laughter resounded around the table as Aiden shook his head vehemently.

"I *never* went streaking. Riley and JJ made the whole story up. That doesn't even *sound* like something I would do."

His voice was light but Jane could see the faint trace of red under his bronze cheeks.

Laura ignored him. "I've never seen Uncle Mike so irate. I thought he was going to spank you at that point."

"Did he?" Carly asked.

Aiden shook his head. "Of course not. He knew better than to just take JJ's word for it."

Jane looked past his profile at the other cluster of cousins further down the table. To her surprise her eyes immediately clashed with a pair of bright green eyes. She didn't need a reminder to know that they belonged to JJ himself. He had jet black hair and all the features of the trademark Masterson face. With the exception of his eyes, he probably resembled a younger version of his grandfather the closest.

Jane realized that he'd either heard their conversation, which was impossible at the pitch and general noise of the table, or he'd been watching her for several moments before she even looked in his direction. When her eyes did catch his, he tilted his head slightly and gave her a smile she wished he hadn't. Because unlike everyone else in the family, his smile sent a repulsive shiver down her spine. It made her uncomfortable with a sort of discomfort she hadn't felt in nearly ten years. The last time someone had looked at her that way, she'd been living in a dilapidated foster home in the Bronx. She quickly looked away.

She saw Ava chatting very intently with a man beside her. It was one of Aiden's uncles but she couldn't remember his name. He glanced at her for a fraction of a second before turning his attention back to his sister-in-law.

"Aiden," she leaned into his ear. "What's your uncle's name again?"

He followed her line of sight and answered. "Uncle Titus. He's married to Darlene and they have Cameron and Joey."

Right, she remembered. The teenage boys.

She frowned, wondering what they could be talking about so intensely. Jane noticed that Michael wasn't even in on the conversation. He was busily chatting with his other siblings beside him.

"Is he a psychiatrist too?" she asked, still watching them.

Aiden shook his head. "No. He and his wife are social workers. They referred us to the agency that arranged Lexi's adoption."

Well *that* was interesting. Maybe they were discussing child psychology research or something. But as Jane watched the two, she couldn't help but wonder in the corner of her mind: were they talking about her?

"Jane, do you have any siblings?" Laura asked beside her.

Jane tore her eyes from them and quickly shook her head. "No."

"Oh, that must've been nice, being an only child. What do your parents do?"

Jane felt a surge of panic rise in her chest. She glanced up in time to see Alexa's look of surprise and Carly's frown of disapproval, aimed at her oblivious sister.

"Laura, that's enough." Aiden quietly said.

Laura looked around at all of them: her sister and cousins' chiding expression, Jane's tense demeanor, and immediately dropped the subject. The conversation picked up on a different track but Jane couldn't concentrate anymore. She tried to focus on her food and eat little bites when she suddenly felt a pang of pain in her stomach. It was sharp and unexpected. She paused, her fork mid-way to her mouth.

She felt Aiden's hand on her knee.

"Are you okay?" he asked quietly.

The pain was subsiding. She nodded but put her fork down. She chalked it up to something she ate. Maybe the salad didn't agree with her stomach. But if she ate more, she might feel worse. She noticed Laura eyeing her small portions.

"Geez, no wonder you're so thin!" she said admiringly.

Some things never changed.

CHAPTER FIFTEEN

After dinner, the family gathered outside to the spacious backyard, overlooking a private lake. There was a beautifully landscaped fire pit and in no time, the fire was lit, illuminating the various family members, circled up, talking in groups. Aiden approached Jane from behind and laid a kiss at the curve of her neck.

"Hey, you."

"Hey yourself." She smiled. She watched him look over her shoulder at the paper she was writing on. He laughed.

"A family map? Really?"

"Don't make fun of me!" she cried. "There are so many people here. I'm just trying to get the names down."

He picked it up, still chuckling and looked over the detailed tree.

"They like you," he said. He looked at her and saw the doubt rise up.

"Really?"

He nodded. "Aunt Lizzie told me I picked a good one. The twins like you too."

Jane smiled. She liked them as well. They were the friendliest of all his extended family and made her feel welcome instantly. She could see why Alexa liked their company so much.

"What's the deal with JJ?" she suddenly asked.

She glanced up in time to see his eyes darken. "He's one of the less tolerable cousins in the family. Uncle Jake divorced Aunt Kathy when JJ was a kid and his father has a tendency to spoil his kids as a result. Overcompensation. Guilt."

She could see the traces of his psychiatrist mother in him and smiled.

He continued, "Riley wasn't that affected by it. He's pretty down to earth. But JJ...let's just say he needs to get knocked a few pegs."

She nodded, remembering the slimy way she felt after catching him look at her. She looked around and saw him chatting with one of his uncles, too distracted to eye her. She was surprised to see Titus still talking to Ava. He glanced at her and smiled but Jane felt a sense of unease rise in her gut. She almost thought to ask Aiden but shrugged it off.

She was being paranoid again.

"Are you okay?" Aiden asked her. She looked at him, frowning in confusion. He couldn't read her that well, could he?

"I mean..." he added. "We went from a very diverse New York City to a very homogeneous environment."

Relief washed over her as she laughed at his way of pointing out his all-white family reunion. His eyes leveled with hers seriously.

"I want to make sure you're comfortable," he said.

She smiled and felt her heart melt at his concern. She also loved that he wasn't ignoring the elephant in the room. The fact that he noticed the racial disparity and pointed it out before she did showed her how much he had her back. He probably never thought of his race on a day-to-day basis but he was putting himself in her shoes to make sure *she* was comfortable.

"I'm okay," she assured him. "This isn't the first time I've been the only black person somewhere. And I'm more comfortable because I'm here with you." She kissed his full lips. "Thank you, baby."

He groaned at the endearment, then winced in pain. She frowned.

"Are *you* okay?"

He nodded. "It's just my stomach. It hurts a little."

Hmm. Maybe it is the food, she thought.

"Did it just start now?"

He nodded. "But I probably had it coming. All that candy and crap I ate on the road. My healthy eating habits go out the window whenever I travel."

She stood up. "Okay, come on."

She led him back into the house and made him sit on the large living room couch. When she returned with her purse, she found him practically sprawled out on the sofa - his long limbs stretched from top to bottom with his large hand cupping the base of his rigid abs. He moved his leg aside as she perched herself beside him.

"Take these," she said, emptying three Tums into the palm of his hand. He chewed them while she ran into the kitchen and brought back a cup of milk. He sat up and accepted another small pill she handed him.

"What is it?"

"A probiotic," she answered. "It helps regulate the bacteria in your stomach."

He downed it with the milk and slowly drank the rest of it. She reached into her purse and pulled out another item.

"A heating pad?" he asked in disbelief.

She nodded. "It will help the muscles in your stomach relax."

She plugged the pad into a nearby socket. While waiting for it to heat up, she reached down and began massaging his rock hard abs. He watched her with a look of mingled curiosity and amusement. She read the question in his eyes.

"It'll help the food move through your digestive tract, which should bring relief."

She was right.

Within minutes, he began to burp. He covered his mouth with his fist.

"Excuse me," he said, clearly embarrassed. "Glad it didn't come out the other way."

She smiled. "It might. If it does, just let it out. Don't hold it on account of me."

His hand covered hers, stopping her soothing movement. He looked around at all her tricks and digestive paraphernalia before meeting her eyes again, a sobering expression on his handsome face.

"Is this how you feel all the time?"

Her smile saddened as she nodded. "A lot of the time. Especially if I'm not careful."

He nodded seriously, another burp erupting behind his closed lips. She reached for the heating pad and made him lift his shirt so that she could place it directly on his skin. Even in something as unsexy as treating her boyfriend's indigestion, she found herself turned on at the sight of his tight torso. He laid back against the couch and smiled sweetly at her as she stroked his brow. He almost looked like a little boy being cared for by his mom. A few minutes passed before he sat up again. He removed the heating pad, leaned in and kissed her.

"All better," he whispered. "Thank you."

They broke apart right in time as the rest of the family poured into the house, each member herding into one area or another. Aiden's dad and uncles called out to him.

"We're playing pool. You coming?"

He glanced at Jane who smiled and nodded discretely.

"You sure?" he asked.

"Jane, come to Lexi's room." Laura called out, walking up the stairs. "We're having a girl's night."

Jane smiled and quirked her eyebrow at Aiden. "I'll be fine."

He grinned and kissed her once more, ignoring the catcalls of his cousins as they separated into guys and girls for the night.

"That's a scratch," Michael said.

"No, it wasn't!" JJ snapped back.

The men paused at his disrespectful tone and Aiden frowned at his older cousin. He watched as heat poured into the man's face, clearly embarrassed at his own outburst.

Michael leaned back on his heels and crossed his arms, glaring at the younger man. "What were you saying?"

JJ glanced at the scowling faces of his uncles and cousin. Even his younger brother Riley frowned in distaste.

"I'm sorry for my tone, Uncle Mike" he mumbled. "But that wasn't a scratch."

"It looked like a scratch to me," James declared.

"I agree," Titus added.

"Sorry, Jay." Jake Sr. shrugged, clearly trying to pacify his grown son. Aiden kept silent. If his jerk cousin said one more disrespectful thing to his father, he'd end up with a shiner by the end of the night. It was his turn. He lined his cue against the ball and took his shot. The ball went in the hole with perfect precision. He took two more shots before scratching.

By the time it was JJ's turn again, he had calmed down and even managed to chat while taking his shots.

"So, Aiden," he began. "How long have you been dating Jane?"

Aiden immediately felt his hand stiffen around his cue.

"A few weeks," he answered. "Why?"

He felt his father's eyes on him but focused his own on JJ. His cousin grinned as he lined up his cue.

"You always did get the pretty girls," was all he said before taking his shot.

"Yeah, well don't you worry about this one," Aiden barked. JJ's eyes snapped up to his then back to the table. He'd missed. He backed away with his hands slightly raised, a mocking smirk marring his handsome face.

"So territorial," he teased.

Aiden took his shot and missed immediately, his mind preoccupied with JJ's comments. Was that why Jane mentioned him earlier? Had he said something to her without his knowing? His eyes were on the game but his mind was a million miles away. He no longer even noticed his father watching him.

"Aiden," Titus approached him. "Can I talk to you for a minute?"

His uncle pulled him off to the side and began without preamble.

"Your mother wants my help on getting some information about Jane. She asked me to pull up her social work file to learn more about her history."

"Uncle Titus…" Aiden frowned, immediately shaking his head. Why were they doing this? He knew his mother wanted to help but this was crossing the line and could backfire on them majorly if Jane found out.

Titus grabbed his nephew's arm and quickly said, "Just hear me out. Your mom knows how to handle cases like hers. She only wants to help but she can't do it if she doesn't know the specifics of Jane's history. I thought about asking Lexi, but I didn't want to bring up uncomfortable memories for her. You don't have to betray her trust. Just tell me one or two facts, that's all."

Aiden still shook his head. *Technically* he wouldn't be betraying Jane's trust but he knew she would consider it a betrayal if he shared *anything* about her history with his uncle, especially so that he could gather more information about her.

"Don't you want to know about her past?" his uncle asked him. Aiden looked at his uncle and saw the concern. He knew the man meant well. The question began to work its desired effect on him. He *did* want to know about her past. Maybe if he did, he could navigate the waters of their relationship better. Maybe he could avoid some of the emotional land mines he kept stepping on.

He sighed. "What do you need to know?"

Girl time.

It was quickly becoming an activity Jane enjoyed almost as much as her time with Aiden. She had changed into her pajamas - a long pair of yoga pants, a tight-fitting cami, and her UNY sweatshirt on top - and was sprawled out on Lexi's queen sized bed between the twins and her best friend. They were in the middle of watching *The Devil Wears Prada* and laughed uproariously over Meryl Streep's smart aleck remark to Anne Hathaway.

"She is such a brilliant actress," Carly commented.

"Tell me about it," Alexa replied. "She can play any role convincingly."

The movie switched to a scene with Anne Hathaway and Adrian Grenier. The girls gave the customary groans and commentary on how sexy he was. Laura was the exception.

She rolled her eyes and said, "He has a nice face and pretty eyes but have you seen him topless? He could use a few rounds at the gym."

Alexa pouted. "Very rarely will a guy have a pretty face and an equally gorgeous body."

Jane raised an eyebrow and Carly saw the look. "Clearly Aiden doesn't have that issue. Jane's a lucky girl!"

The twins squealed in laughter as Alexa clamped her hands over her ears and groaned. "Please don't! He's my brother and you guys are his cousins."

"We are," Carly replied. "But we still have eyes!"

She turned to Jane. "What's it like dating Aiden?"

Jane looked at their expectant faces. Even Lexi had lowered her hands to hear her speak. She shrugged.

"He's…" she began, trying to think of a word to describe him. His face came to mind and she couldn't find the words. Her heart began to thunder in the cavity of her chest at the memory of his voice, his laughter, his strong arms around her waist. The way he brought her blinding, sometimes violent, pleasure.

She shivered and heard Laura groan into the comforter of the bed.

"You don't even have to say anything," she lamented, gesturing at Jane.

"It's written all over your face. I want that!" she cried.

"Me too," Carly echoed.

"And we'll get it," Alexa, the ever-optimistic one, said. "We just have to wait and see."

Jane smiled at her and punched her arm playfully. By the time, they finished the movie, Laura and Carly were passed out on Lexi's bed. Jane bid her a quiet goodnight and crept back to her room. She stepped into the darkened room and found Aiden fast asleep on his stomach, stretched across the bed. He would never know. He would never see how Jane admired his face and the peaceful look of him sleeping, his breath moving in and out of his lungs at an even, steady pace. She leaned forward and gently kissed his forehead. Climbing into bed, she quickly fell asleep.

CHAPTER SIXTEEN

Jane woke up in complete peace. She felt the sun on her skin before she opened her eyes to see it. Soft white sheets surrounded her and the plush feathered pillows enveloped her head. Heavy, muscled arms were tight around her waist. She could smell his fresh deodorant and feel the warmth of his breath on her neck. She turned and there he was.

A beautiful sight to behold.

His short blond hair lay against the white pillow like a halo around his head. His five o'clock shadow brushed the sharp lines of his chiseled jaw. She heard the steady rhythm of his breathing, his eyes closed to the world, his full lips closed without a trace of drool.

Only you could look put together in your sleep, she thought, wryly.

He also looked focused; like he was going to get the best quality of rest during his time in la-la-land. Everything was an investment and he would invest wisely in his slumber. She admired the planes and valleys of his sculpted face and began to think she'd never grow tired of looking at him.

She felt an emotion surge within her. Affection?

No.

She knew it was something much deeper than that. One could feel affection for a stray cat. She was staring at the man who made her heart stop with his very look. A man whose voice and laughter she could hear audibly even when he wasn't in the room. And as instantly as lightning could strike a tower, Jane *knew*. She *knew* in the pit of her soul that he was the one. If there *was* such a thing as a match. A soul mate. A destined partner for life. She was looking at him right beside her. Whether she loved him or not was irrelevant. Whether she spoke it aloud or not was a moot point. She was looking at a man who'd changed her so deeply, no other would ever be able to suffice. The thought filled her with elation and dread. And she couldn't figure out which feeling to camp on. He shifted in his sleep, his arms tightening even further around her waist. He was so strong. Even in his sleep, she could feel the strength radiate from his long arms. The feel of them around her both aroused and comforted Jane.

He made her feel safe.

He shifted some more before finally opening his eyes. Though he looked focused in his sleep, he looked perfectly at peace when awake. His gold eyes stared into hers like he'd been expecting her to wait for him all along. Neither said anything. They basked in the moment. The sun. The soft sheets. The feel of each other wrapped in their arms. There was an unspoken agreement to keep silent.

He reached up and caressed the edge of her cheek with his large thumb. His eyes raked over her face, soaking in the sight of her the way a desert ground would soak up water. She was his oasis. He stroked the side of her face, admiring the golden glow in her brown skin at morning's light. He glanced at the head wrap she wore and smiled at the irony. They were in bed, an intimate setting for any couple, and she was completely covered - from her pajama pants to her long sleeved sweatshirt. But the clothes didn't create a barrier to their eyes. Her skin felt silky under the pad of his thumb.

He scanned her face, once again focusing on her glowing brown skin. It was young, tight and soft. Some parts were darker than others but there was a uniformity to her skin tone that made her breathtaking. He wondered what it would look like when she grew old.

Will I be here to see that day? Will she still be mine? His heart ached at that question and in that moment, he knew. *I love her.* The words, though only spoken in his mind, slammed his heart against his rib cage with breathtaking clarity. He loved her.

He loved her.

Her hand covered his. She turned and kissed the thumb caressing her cheek and his eyes softened. She smiled at him and he smiled in return. They couldn't speak what they felt. But they could say it with their eyes. It was the most intimate thing they'd done in their relationship and it felt so right. Natural. Unforced. No miscommunication.

I could do this all day, he thought.

A knock at the door. It jolted both of them out of the moment. Jane's gaze flickered to the door. She sat up in bed as the door opened and Ava came in, carrying a breakfast tray with two mugs.

"Good morning," she said softly. "I come bearing gifts."

She smiled at the two of them in bed, completely unfazed by the sight. She went to Jane's side and laid the tray down, handing her, then her son, piping hot mugs.

"Thanks, Ava." Jane said.

"Thanks, Mom." Aiden echoed, his cheeks red with embarrassment. Ava noticed the blush and called him out on it.

"Come now, Aiden. There's nothing to be embarrassed about. I asked Alexa to bring you these but she refused. I didn't catch you two in the middle of something, did I?"

Aiden coughed into his mug, coffee sputtering from his lips. Jane smiled at Ava and shook her head. She *had* interrupted something but Jane didn't think she nor Aiden could articulate what it was.

They went into town and split up in groups. Alexa and the twins took off for the shops while Aiden and Jane focused on history. Jane marveled at the town structure. Everything was smaller and closer together. It felt like a picturesque colonial town out of the popular *American Girl* books. Cobblestone streets, perfectly swept sidewalks, the small stone buildings for the courthouse, library, and town museum. Various stone placards denoted famous homes or locations of historical events. Aiden pointed out his favorite sites and Jane took photos of them all.

Her favorite spot was the tall, white chapel that housed The Federated Church. Aiden smiled at the building. "It was established in the mid-seventeenth century. People still worship there today."

"Wow," Jane murmured in awe. They tested the doors to see if they could go in. To their surprise, the locked door opened from the inside and Alexa's pretty face poked out.

"Hey, guys!" she said. "Want to come in?"

"How did you get in?" Aiden asked as they crossed the threshold. Inside, his *Nonna* stood in one of the sanctuary pews, head bowed as she said a prayer.

Alexa whispered, "*Nonna* got the keys from Grandpa and wanted to visit."

Jane was about to ask how their grandfather got the key before remembering what they were on the island for: his celebration as a history conservationist. Alexa excused herself to join her grandmother in the sanctuary. Jane and Aiden looked around the lobby for a few minutes. They landed on two large marble slabs, engraved with the names of various men.

"Every pastor that's served this church," Aiden explained. He pointed to one man's name near the top. There wasn't an end date next to his 17th century tenure. "Thomas Mayhew, Jr. He went missing during a voyage to England to secure more funds for his missionary efforts to Native Americans. His aging father took over, walking miles to minister to them himself."

"His only son?" Jane asked. Aiden nodded. Though the tragedy had occurred centuries before her birth, Jane still felt a strange sense of sadness for the man's loss. They were both long dead but the thought of an elderly man losing his only son...it was still sad.

"What do you think about religion?" she asked him. He looked at her in surprise, immediately wanting to know *her* thoughts on the issue.

"I don't know," he admitted. "*Nonna* and Lexi take it very seriously. Grandpa goes to church with *Nonna* every Sunday. My own parents aren't that religious. I don't know what I think, really."

He was embarrassed to say he didn't think about it. Only when Alexa or his grandmother prayed, did the thought of God ever really cross his mind. He was turned off by people who shoved their religion down other people's throat. But he was also offended by the militant atheists who tried to tear people down for having a belief system.

Jane nodded and looked at the names of men who devoted their entire lives to their religion. She wondered what it was like to have a conviction that strong that they would be willing to commit their whole being to it.

"I believe in God," she said. "I think it makes sense that He made everything and everyone in it. I also think that Jesus was real."

"You think he rose from the dead?" Aiden asked. He wasn't being sarcastic or mocking her. He genuinely wanted to know.

"Yeah," she said. "I do. People say it's impossible but they weren't there. I think miracles happen all the time, even if we don't see them today. I've never had a problem believing what Christianity teaches about Christ."

Aiden cocked his head and peered down at her in curiosity. She met his eyes and shrugged her shoulders defensively.

"What?"

"Nothing," he said. "I'm just looking at you. I wouldn't have guessed you were-"

"What?"

"Religious."

"I'm *not* religious," she corrected. She pointed at *Nonna* and Alexa in the sanctuary. "*That* is religious. I just have an open mind."

He nodded and kept silent, not wanting to start a debate. They went into the sanctuary and looked around the church a little more. *Nonna* kept praying while Alexa shared her experience having attended the church before.

"The services are very short," she said. "Most of the attendees are old. You usually see grandparents and grandkids but rarely do you see young adults."

"How do they stay afloat?" Aiden asked. They knew he meant financially.

"The historical society patronizes the church but while their members are old, many are very well-off. It's sad though," she murmured, looking around. "This was once the hub of society centuries, or even decades, ago. Now, most of the townspeople are *outside* of the church, not in it."

Aiden remained silent but Jane nodded in agreement. Religion aside, it was sad to see what was once the epicenter of a community become irrelevant. The couple waited until *Nonna* finished her prayers. The old woman kissed them both on the cheek, happy to see them inside. She showed them her favorite nooks and crannies of the old building before it was time to take their leave.

They arrived at the estate to find much of the family hustling and bustling to get ready for the ceremony that night. Aiden quickly changed into a smart navy suit that complimented the golden glint of his eyes. He glanced at his watch as Jane made her way to the bathroom.

"We have about thirty minutes before we got to go," he warned.

She gave him a quizzical frown. "I'm not showering. Just changing."

He frowned in return. "In the bathroom?"

It was the question that had finally reared its ugly head. Why was she changing outside of the view of her boyfriend, one with whom she'd already been intimate?

She ignored the question and closed the door, once again propelling the onslaught of confusion in his mind. Was she self-conscious? Did his presence make her uncomfortable? It couldn't - not after the moment they'd had in bed that morning. He shook his head, bemused. When would he ever be able to figure her out?

Minutes later, Jane emerged from the bathroom, dressed to the nines in a form-fitting dark blue cocktail dress. Her dark tights complimented the outfit in a vintage sort of way. Aiden made note of the long sleeves. Rarely did he see a short dress with long sleeves. The front of it, at her chest, was also fully covered. He didn't say anything but he had the distinct impression that she was hiding from him under that dress. Covering herself up was clearly her preference and while he didn't want a hooker for a girlfriend, he couldn't help but wonder *why* she was so modest. Alexa was modest - and still showed more skin than Jane.

Jane began to fidget under the focus of his piercing gold gaze.

"Is this okay for the occasion?"

His heart dropped at the nervous tone in her voice. He met her eyes and immediately felt guilty for putting her on edge. He was curious about her constant desire to cover up but he still found her breathtaking to behold. She could wear a burlap sack and he'd still find her irresistible.

"It's perfect," he assured her. "You have no idea how beautiful you are to me."

She smiled shyly. "Thank you."

He closed the space between them and pulled her into his arms. She enjoyed the concentrated rush of his cologne as he gave her a slow, sensuous kiss. He groaned against her mouth when someone knocked on the door. She winked at him and moved to answer it.

"Hey, Jane!" Laura exclaimed. Her eyes admired Jane's outfit. "Geez, how are you so stunning? Sorry to interrupt but Carly and I wanted to give you this." She handed her a medium-sized silver box with a pretty white ribbon over it.

"Oh!" Jane said in surprise. "Thank you. You didn't have to-"

"Of course we didn't," Laura interrupted her. "We wanted to. Open it! Open it!"

Aiden watched as Jane undid the ribbon and pulled the top off. Inside sat a simple yet beautiful gold bangle. It was the perfect gift for someone fond of bracelets. He met his cousin's eyes over her shoulder and smiled in appreciation. Jane began to tear up at the unexpected gesture. She fingered the beautiful golden piece and accepted it for what it was: a token of friendship. To her surprise, and probably Aiden's, she fit the bangle onto her wrist before enfolding Laura into a strong, tight hug.

"Thank you," she said. "That was really, really kind of you."

Laura hugged her in return and promised to pass Jane's gratitude to Carly, who was still getting ready. Turning back into the room, Jane gave Aiden a slight smile as he watched her with steady eyes. He was proud of her; for getting along with his cousins, fitting in with his family. They had some issues to tackle still, but at least this wasn't one.

It took them less than half an hour to get to Oaks Bluff. It was a completely different culture and feel than that of Edgartown. A city of historical little cottages, Jane took in the colorful and ornate decorations of the distinguished vacation homes. Though the houses lined the streets in an almost crowded, circular fashion, the town wasn't nearly as full as it would be in the summer. It appeared that most of the owners were on the mainland during the fall. She saw cottages ranging from all-blue to all-pink to all-American in design. Aiden explained to her that most of the island's affluent African Americans lived in Oaks Bluff.

The ceremony was being held at the Martha's Vineyard Campground Tabernacle. The site couldn't be missed because it sat in the very heart of the town on a large round patch of grass. Alexa explained the spiritual significance of it.

"Just after the Civil War, this site was used for open air Christian revivals and Christian camps under the Methodist denomination."

Jane tried to imagine dozens, if not hundreds, of people sitting in that very spot, worshiping. She, Aiden, and Alexa walked across the lawn with the family to a large open air building that read, "Martha's Vineyard Camp Meeting and Association Tabernacle." There was a stage erected on the inside and several rows of benches along the lit interior. Jane looked around at the people who did attend. Though the town was nearly empty, the ceremony was very lively and full with island residents from other towns or even guests who flew in, congregating around the benches. There were at least two-hundred people in attendance. Aiden led Jane to the third row of seats and sat down. Within minutes, the conversation died down and the ceremony began.

Jane tried her best to concentrate but continuously found herself observing others. Sometimes her people watching habit got out of hand and this was one of those nights. As the president of the historical society spoke, introduced Mr. Masterson, and then Mr. Masterson himself went up to speak, all Jane could focus on were the people around her. And all she could see were the tailored suits, silk blouses, diamond rings, sapphire necklaces, and designer bags. It was a formal occasion, no doubt, but the luxury of the event only made the wealth of those in attendance more prominent.

And for the first time since meeting the Mastersons so many moons ago, Jane felt uncomfortable. Like she didn't belong. She glanced at Aiden and remembered they were from two completely different worlds: economically and socially. Mr. Masterson kept his speech brief and when he finished, Jane barely had time to process her new thoughts about her, Aiden, and her role in his circle. The after party was in full swing and everyone was mingling - the very activity Jane despised in social settings. Aiden peered down at her and lifted her chin so he could meet her eyes.

"You okay?" he asked in concern.

She shrugged. "I hate mingling."

He nodded. "I can tell. You have this look of perpetual discomfort on your face."

"Is it really showing that badly?"

He smiled and nodded. "But I wasn't asking about this. You've been quiet since the ceremony started. Are you alright?"

Jane blinked at his perceptive question. Had he been observing her the whole time? She felt the heat of his gaze on her face and didn't know how to respond. She could barely articulate her own feelings to herself.

So she nodded. "I'm fine."

It didn't take a rocket scientist to know that she wasn't. Aiden frowned at her and wondered what thought had entered his enigmatic girlfriend's mind. Clearly it was bothering her. He was about to say something else when a large hand clapped him on the shoulder.

"Aiden! Hey!"

A tall blond man with bright blue eyes greeted him from behind. Aiden's face lit up in recognition. "Paul Seederman! How are you, man?"

They hugged each other, clapping backs ecstatically and began to make small talk. Aiden turned to Jane and pressed a hand into the small of her back.

"Paul, allow me to introduce you to my girlfriend, Jane. Jane, this is Paul. We were inseparable on this island as kids."

Jane smiled and shook the friendly man's hand.

"A pleasure to meet you, Jane. Aiden clearly has good taste." She smiled at the compliment. He turned behind him and tapped a petite brunette woman on her shoulder. She turned and to their surprise, carried a small infant in her arms.

"Aiden, Jane, this is my wife, Kate and our little one, Annabelle."

Aiden's eyebrows rose in surprise. "You got married?" He shook Kate's hand and peered over at the baby. "Congratulations! How long have you been married?"

"Five years next June," Kate replied. "Our son, Trevor, is running around the lawn over there."

"You have another one?" Aiden asked, still surprised. Sure enough, the little boy ran headlong into his father's leg and braced himself to be lifted onto his dad's shoulders.

It was a brief look. One that Kate and Paul were too busy to catch. But Jane could see it clear as day. It was the same look she'd worn while watching a complete stranger walk with her family on the steamboat dock. It was the look of someone who witnessed the very thing he wanted for himself.

Envy.

A look of envy flashed in Aiden's eyes as he watched his childhood friend stand beside his wife and two children. He wanted to be in his shoes. He wanted a wife and family of his own. But did he want Jane to be that wife?

Am I even eligible to be it?

Jane felt a heaviness settle in her chest. She extracted her hand from Aiden's. "Excuse me."

He looked at her questioningly. "You okay?"

"Yeah, I'm just going to get some fresh air." He frowned but slowly nodded. She glanced at the happy couple. "It was nice meeting you."

"Likewise," Paul smiled. He turned to Aiden and asked him how things were on Wall Street. They continued to chat but Aiden wouldn't remember most of the conversation. Something was eating at Jane. It was small and she was trying to hide it but he was determined to get to the bottom of it.

Jane walked to the perimeter of the reception hall and grabbed a glass of champagne. She took a sip and instantly felt a pang of pain in her stomach again. Fear rose to the center of her chest. She thought the pain was a one-off thing. Something from the dinner they had eaten last night.

"Hello, Jane." a deep baritone voice said beside her. She looked up and met the cold bright green eyes of JJ Masterson. The pain in her stomach was immediately masked by the rise of discomfort in her chest.

She nodded at him but didn't say anything.

"Now, that's no way to greet me. Aren't you having a good evening?"

I was, she thought. *Until you came lurking about.*

She didn't say anything and continued to nurse her drink. She noticed that her arms had locked across her chest in a protective stance. It was an automatic position whenever she felt uncomfortable. JJ sipped his own drink and looked out on the lawn in front of him.

"How long have you been dating Aiden?" he asked. His tone was casual but the question wasn't.

Jane frowned at him and cut to the chase. "Why are you talking to me?"

His eyes swung to hers with a thirsty, almost predatory expression. "Because you're beautiful."

For the first time, those words did not feel like a compliment. They felt like a curse. If she were ugly, he wouldn't be looking at her, talking to her, or spending time near her. She wished he wouldn't.

"Aiden's your cousin," she said reminded him.

"You're not married to him, are you?"

Unbelievable. But something told Jane that even if she and Aiden *were* married, he would still try to hit on her.

"Excuse me," was all she said. She laid down her drink and turned on her heel, leaving the reception and the people to themselves.

She walked along the sidewalks of the virtually empty town, staying in view and earshot of the party. To her relief, JJ didn't follow her but the party was too crowded to know whether or not he was watching her. The thought sent a shiver down her spine. She was glad they would be leaving soon.

She sat on a quiet bench in the square and looked around the beautiful cluster of colored cottages. *What am I doing?* she thought. There were moments when she felt she understood it all: who she was, her relationship with Aiden, Alexa, their parents. She stroked her gold bangle and smiled. She was pleasantly surprised that she fit in with Carly and Laura. Her interactions with the girls began to dispel her long-held suspicion that she was incapable of gaining or maintaining friendships. It was a theory she'd developed in college when work and school crowded out every social opportunity she had.

At the same time, she was more confused than ever. Two months ago, her life was neatly mapped out in the area of her career, finances, and future goals. She was only twenty-four but she had made a great deal of progress educationally and vocationally. She wanted to continue that momentum and thoughts of her personal life never really surfaced unless she was alone. When they did, she would remind herself of everything she wanted to achieve and stabilize first…before getting serious about someone and making true friends. She'd neglected her personal life in order to serve her professional goals.

Now, her personal life was beginning to bloom while her professional life was becoming unstable. And it scared the hell out of her. She had hope that she would be okay. That the job situation would work out or she would move onto something else if she had to. But her personal life was moving faster than anything she could have anticipated. She was on Martha's Vineyard with her boyfriend and his family, witnessing firsthand the taste of his wealth and a world that couldn't be more different than the one she'd grown up in.

She thought of them in bed that morning. When everything was uncomplicated. When they were silent and just soaked each other in. She wished their whole relationship could consist of that moment – when all that mattered was the two of them and how they felt, in the moment, without the complications of family, money, the future and different pasts.

Everything is up in the air, she realized. Her job. Her education. Her relationship. Her future. But what surprised her most was which category was coming to mean the most to her.

"Hey!" Aiden called. She looked up to find him crossing the lawn, his long legs carrying him to her in five seconds flat. He sat on the bench next to her and pulled her into his side.

"I was wondering where you'd gone off to."

She tucked her nose into his chest, his tantalizing cologne teasing her nostrils.

"I just got some fresh air," she answered.

He looked at her silently for a few moments. She looked back at him, silent as well.

"What's going on?" he asked meaningfully. "Don't try to deny it. I know you've been deep in thought since the minute we arrived."

She shrugged, leaned back, and started looking around. He wondered if it was to avoid his eyes or gather her thoughts. Either way, she finally said what was on her mind.

"I was just thinking about a lot of stuff. My life...where it's going. What *we're* doing."

He frowned. "What are we doing?"

She shrugged again. "I don't know. Having a serious relationship?"

He laughed and nodded. "Yeah. So what's the problem?"

She sighed. "Nothing. I'm just..." she looked at him and saw the patience in his eyes. He really wanted to know what was wrong. "I'm a planner. I plan everything. I like to look down the line hour to hour, day to day, week by week and *know* what I'm doing and why I'm doing it."

He nodded. "I gathered that." She was the most organized, driven person he knew. It was one of the traits he admired about her.

"The thing is…I never really planned my personal life."

He laughed and she frowned at him.

"I'm serious! Aiden!" He saw that she was genuinely starting to get upset at him so he tried his best to stifle his laughter. She continued, "I know that relationships aren't like degrees or jobs or things you can course correct and control at any time. I get that. But I'm not sure how to navigate all of this when things in my career are up in the air too."

He nodded, serious once more. "You're worried. Up until this point, things have gone well because you were able to plan them. Now things seem to be spinning out of your control."

She gasped at his astute summary. "Yes! That's exactly how I feel."

"I get it. I remember when things were up in the air in my career." She knew that he was referring to the collapse on Wall Street. "Everything I'd worked for was at risk. It was a really scary time in my life."

She frowned but said nothing. He looked at her and asked, "What? What are you thinking?"

She shook her head but he insisted, "Tell me. I want to know."

"It's not the same."

"What do you mean?"

"It's not the same," she repeated. "Aiden, if Wall Street never recovered and you lost your career or your livelihood in finance, you still could have bounced back. It's not the same as wondering if you'll have a roof over your head or money to buy food."

A light bulb went off in his head.

"So *this* is what this whole thing's about. You've been uncomfortable here." Why hadn't he seen it before? She wore the same expression she'd worn when she first saw the grandeur of Longbourne. It was the same expression she'd worn when she first had dinner at his parents' place. She felt like she didn't belong. And it triggered a host of other issues that could drive a wedge between them.

"My money bothers you, doesn't it?"

She frowned and he immediately wished he'd worded it differently.

"I mean," he amended. "It makes you uncomfortable to be around affluent people."

She met his eyes and saw nothing but understanding. "I guess. It reminds me of how far I have to go. Not that I'm trying to be rich but I look forward to the day when I'm not always worrying about money or how I'm going to afford something." It felt like that was the story of her whole life.

He nodded. "And being around people who don't think twice about what they spend or what they can afford…how does it make you feel?"

She frowned at his tone. He sounded like his psychiatrist mother. "It depends," she answered honestly. "Some days, I feel jealous. I wish I had it as easy. Sometimes, I feel hopeful – like one day, I'll work myself into a better position. And then other times, I just feel depressed. Like I don't belong. Like my clothes aren't good enough. My hair isn't good enough. The quality of everything I have is under scrutiny because it isn't Dior or Fendi."

"Oh, Jane." Aiden's brows drew together in an unhappy. He pulled her back to him and held her closely. "I don't ever want you to feel like you're not good enough. I had no idea that went through your mind."

She leaned into his chest and spoke against his lapel. "It's not you. It's my own issue."

"Why haven't you told me, though?"

She leaned back. "And have you think I'm some sort of gold digger, pulling your heartstrings to get money?"

He laughed once more. "Jane, no one could ever call you a gold digger. You're the hardest working woman I know. And fiercely independent. Remember how long it took you to tell me about your job situation."

"Don't remind me."

He chuckled then calmed down. "Don't let it get in the way."

"What do you mean?"

"Money. Mine. Yours. Our socioeconomic difference. We have so many other differences between us. Don't let this one do us in."

She knew what he meant. And he was right. They hadn't allowed race to get between them or politics or even personality differences. It would be foolish to let money get in the way.

"Okay," she replied. She looked down at his lips and he leaned in to meet hers.

He leaned back and suddenly said, "I saw JJ talking to you earlier. What did he want?"

She answered bluntly. "To sleep with me."

To her amazement, Aiden's irises changed in color and hue, right before her eyes. They shifted from the light jovial gold to a dark, foreboding copper. So dark, they were almost brown.

"*What?*" he said menacingly. His tone and dark look sent a chill down her spine.

"He was hitting on me," Jane explained. She felt no reason to protect his cousin, especially if it meant lying to Aiden. "I reminded him I was with you and it didn't seem to faze him. I excused myself and came out here."

He was quiet and still for several long moments. Jane watched as various shades of red colored his cheek then disappeared, depending on whatever thought passed through his imperceptible mind. His eyes began to shift back to their natural gold. He stood up and held out a hand to her. They started walking to a group of island taxis.

"He's lucky we're at my grandfather's ceremony," he murmured. "Tomorrow, he won't be." Jane frowned at the threat and looked at him questioningly. He shook his head, pulled out his wallet and continued to walk to the cabs. He paid them the fare, opened the door for her and silently followed when she climbed in.

They were both over the party.

CHAPTER SEVENTEEN

"What's wrong?" he asked.

They were back at the house, in their room, getting ready to relax the rest of the night. Another flash of pain struck Jane unexpectedly and her wince tipped Aiden off. It left as rapidly as it came so Jane shook her head and met his eyes.

"I'm fine."

His frown told her he wasn't buying it but she avoided his look and continued to take off her jewelry. She felt his eyes on the side of her face and turned to meet his probing gaze.

"You're still worried about everything," he said. "Your life. Our relationship. How things will work out."

She was almost afraid to speak but did it anyway. She sighed. "Aiden, I can get past the money and social differences and pretty much every other difference we have but I can't help but wonder if this will work."

The words pierced him. "Why?" he asked in disbelief.

"I've never had a family. Yours is rock solid. I've never been in a committed relationship. You're surrounded by successful marriages."

"So now you're going to let your *past* ruin us?" He was getting upset.

"You said you're serious about us. I don't know if I can give you what you want-"

"*I want you!*" he suddenly exclaimed. He crossed the room, pulled her into his arms and crashed his lips against hers, erasing every objection or argument she could think of in that moment. He pulled back. "*Jane*. Why

190

are you doing this to us?" He scanned her eyes and saw the hope and fear battling within them.

"Jane," he said once more. *I love you.* "I lo…I lo-" She put a hand to his lips.

"Don't. Don't force yourself to say what you don't mean." Tears welled in her eyes and he could see how deeply his hesitation hurt her.

"Jane," he began apologetically. "I *do* mean it." He didn't know why the words wouldn't come out but he wanted them to. More than anything. Still, she shook her head, her tears drying. Part of her was relieved he didn't say it. She saw it in his eyes that morning but he hadn't articulated it then. And for some reason, he couldn't now. She decided she was glad he couldn't. Because if he was able to say it, could she? She looked into his handsome face and knew without a shadow of a doubt that he was it for her. He was the one.

But did that equate to love? It had to be something deeper. Something *more.* Soap opera characters lived on "destiny." She needed something to sink her teeth into.

Aiden tried again. "Jane-"

"Shh." She shook her head. "I don't want to talk or think or reason. I just want to feel better. Can you turn this conversation around and make me feel better?" Her eyes softened. "Please?"

He sighed a deep sigh and nodded before reclaiming her lips. They hadn't reached a resolution. They hadn't defined their expectations. Everything was up in the air like it had been before, if not more so, but neither Jane nor Aiden cared at that point. Hot coals of desire burned in the pit of Jane's stomach as Aiden's full, soft lips worked around her mouth with an expertise only perfected by practice. He nibbled at the edge of her lips and stroked the small of her back with his large powerful hands. He squeezed her waist to his large, hard-muscled frame and demanded entrance into her mouth with his tongue. His clean fresh scent suffused her senses and propelled her deeper into his arms. She felt the solid strength of his back and shoulders as he ravaged her mouth with his own.

She didn't realize they were moving until the back of her legs brushed against the edge of the bed and he fell atop of her on the white satin sheets. His lips migrated to the curve of her neck and she heard his heavy breathing beat against her ear. Her mind narrowed into tunnel mode as she pulled and yanked at his jacket and shirt. She was rewarded with the feel of his warm soft skin covering endless stretches of strong, lean muscle. His hands reached behind and lowered the zipper of her dress. The sound of the zipper chimed in her ear like a reminder. She reached up to turn off the bedside lamp. His hand reached up to stop her.

"Lights off," she panted.

"No," he breathed back. He bent his head to the side of her neck again but this time she pushed him away.

"Lights off," she repeated.

"No," he replied again. There was a determined edge in his voice.

She reached up to turn it off but he held her hand captive.

"Why do you want it off?" he asked, his voice hoarse. His once desire-murky eyes were now focused and clear.

"It doesn't matter why," Jane said defensively. She laid down the law. "If you want to have sex with me, we're doing it with the lights off."

"First of all, we're not just 'having sex.' I'm making love to you. Second of all, you'd better give me a damn good reason for bringing us to this point only to give me an ultimatum about whether or not we're following through. *Why do you want the lights off?*"

His eyes were unyielding and a sense of panic rose in her chest. He saw the shift in her eyes because his own became much softer.

"Hey," he said gently. He cupped her cheek with his hand. "What is it?"

She shook her head and looked away from him. Anger she could handle but when he was extra sensitive and affectionate, Jane felt like her most raw self was exposed to him. She reached up to move his hand but he caught her wrist in his grasp and examined the skin on it. She gasped. She'd forgotten that she removed her bangle and wristwatch earlier. He could see the edge of a scar. She tried to pull her hand back but it was useless trying to move against the steel of his grip.

JANE

He turned her wrist over and lifted the sleeve higher.

"Aiden, don't."

He ignored her and watched as inch by inch, the higher he lifted, lines, circles, discoloration, and scars covered her arm in haphazard patterns. Some were raised, most were flat. Knives, cigarette burns, pinches. He didn't know the story behind all of the scars but he knew they held a world full of pain for her. He felt her hand tremble in his and he finally raised his eyes to her face. Her tears were falling down her cheeks in silent rivulets. The sight of her began to swim and shift behind the tears in *his* eyes. She kept her gaze trained on her arm, still in his hands, refusing to meet his eyes.

"He did this to you?" he asked her softly. She heard the question but didn't answer. He held her wrist with one hand and caressed the scarred skin with the other. She looked at his light golden hands. They were perfect. Smooth, soft, healthy. Completely unmarred. Perfection against disfigurement.

She tried to pull her hand away from his again. He tightened his hand and refused to let go.

"Stop it," he said. She then felt his hand lift from the scars on her wrist to the stubborn set of her chin. He forced her to raise her head and meet his eyes. To her surprise, they were a dark copper again, with tears swimming in them, ready to free fall like hers.

"Who did this to you?" he asked shakily.

"You know who did it," she whispered.

His hand moved from her chin and cupped her cheek. He didn't contort his face into a look of condescending pity but there was sympathy and a deep disturbance at what he saw. She waited for his expression to turn into revulsion. His other hand loosened around her wrist. She quickly pulled it out of his grasp and scrambled off the bed. She felt his gaze follow her as she walked to the drawer and pulled out clothes.

"What are you doing?" he asked.

"Getting dressed. I doubt you're in the mood after what you just saw."

193

He stood up and strode over to her in two seconds flat. "How dare you?" he asked.

She steeled her eyes and looked up at him, a cold expression clashing with his heated one. "Well, I'm sure you're not interested now that you know what I've been hiding."

A look of understanding crossed his face as he recalled the long sleeves, the long pants, virtually all of her covered in one way or another. Her insistence at having the lights off at all times if she wasn't covered.

"The scars are all over," he concluded aloud. She nodded, disappointed at the anticlimactic end of their relationship. She turned to go to the bathroom but immediately felt his arm around her waist.

"Aiden, please."

His mouth descended to her neck. His hand reached up and pulled the clothes out of her hands, dropping them to the floor. He turned her around, ignoring her confused frown. Walking backwards, he lowered himself onto the bed and looked up at her, meeting her eyes.

"Let me see you," he said.

She frowned and scanned his face. His eyes had shifted back to gold and a calmness had taken over his expression. Though upset, he had the look of a man capable of handling anything. It still wasn't clicking for her, though.

"Aiden-"

"Take your clothes off, Jane. Let me see you."

Her heart ricocheted around her chest at his soft but authoritative command. She didn't know what he was doing but somehow knew she was in safe hands. She didn't think he would laugh at her or throw her out. At the same time, she couldn't bear the thought of him looking at her body and rejecting it - even unconsciously - for how it looked.

She shook her head, suddenly paralyzed with fear. "I can't, Aiden. I can't."

Something flickered in his eyes and he reached out a hand, pulling her to him by her hips.

"Then stay still," he said. She felt his hands clamp down around her zipper again and pull. Moments later, she felt the air around her as her dress fell to the ground and she stood in nothing but tights and her lingerie. She closed her eyes as his eyes studied her body. She knew every scar he could see at that point, every inch of damaged skin. Fresh tears welled behind her closed eyes and threatened to spill until she felt his hands, steady at her back, pull her forward, even closer to his body.

She gasped when suddenly, she felt the touch of his lips on her navel. Her ribs, her waist, the curve of her hips. He laid gentle kisses on one piece of exposed flesh after another, running his lips along the outline of every visible scar he could find. She opened her eyes and looked down at his dark blond head, bobbing and weaving back and forth as he sought and found another scar to kiss and caress. His hands moved to her tights and pulled them down insistently. He sank before her on his knees and repeated the action, this time covering the terrain of her long legs with his lips. Her tears of pain and embarrassment transformed into tears of wonder. Wonder at his display of tenderness.

He slowly rose to his full height, once again towering over Jane. He looked down into her teary, awe-filled gaze and slowly kissed her lips. Head still pressed against hers, he leaned back just enough to meet her eyes. His long lashes tickled her own.

"You. Are. Beautiful. Every inch of you is mine."

He captured her lips again and this time, she fully reciprocated.

The rest of their clothes fell to the wayside as they laid on the bed once more and explored each other's bodies in full view of the lights. Jane watched the muscles in his arms flex as he held his weight, caressed her skin, clenched the sheets. She enjoyed the view of his light golden skin as he moved over the terrain of her body.

In the beginning it was perfect. Aiden loved the look of pleasure he brought to her face with every stroke, touch, and kiss. At first, she openly admired his body and allowed him to openly admire hers. But in the middle of their lovemaking, something shifted. He could see it on her face mid-stroke, just like before. Something flickered in her eyes and caused her to shut down. She refused to meet his eyes and instead fixed her gaze on his shoulder or past it. That was, when she kept her eyes open at all. It felt like a nightmare - the most ludicrous of them all. Because as the waves of pleasure rolled in and through his body, Aiden could not fully enjoy the moment. Not as he watched his woman focus on the pleasure and nothing else.

Was he abnormal? Was he strange for wanting her to look at him? Acknowledge him while being joined to his body? For wanting her to meet his eyes and tell him she cared? That she loved him?

Does she love me?

He felt her hands clench and claw at the muscles in his back as her body convulsed with her release. He could tell she was oblivious to the world and he wanted to meet her in the same place but he could not join her. Even as his body released, he was all-too-conscious of the turmoil in his heart. They were having sex - not making love. And he didn't know how to make it the latter. He felt the same way he'd felt days ago, when she left his apartment right after their first time. He felt cheap. Used. Like he was having sex with a client and not his girlfriend.

He rolled off of her, deep in thought as they fought to catch their breaths. He didn't understand it. They'd just had a beautiful moment. She just revealed one of the deepest hurts and insecurities she'd ever had to him. He had reassured her of his love in his actions, if not his words.

Should I have said it? Should I have said "I love you"? He glanced at her, at the beads of sweat pooling around her temple. *Is that what's keeping you from me?*

A coldness washed over him when, instead of curling into his side, she rose from the bed and entered the shower without a word. He listened to her wash off every trace of their union and felt a foreign surge of tears rush to his eyes. He swallowed it back. He wasn't a crier. He was a fixer. The problem was, while he could identify an issue in his relationship, he had no idea how to remedy it. Jane emerged from the bathroom a few minutes later and Aiden wordlessly used it after her. By the time he emerged from his long shower, she had fallen asleep on her side of the bed, her arm extended on his side. He lifted her arm and returned it to her side. Laying down, his back to her, he tried to fall asleep. In time, the sleep came but not before a chilling thought registered. He was in love with a woman who might not be in love with him. And loving her was a risk. Because it could just mean the death of him.

He was upset.

Jane didn't need a crystal ball or pie in the sky to see that something was eating away at Aiden. She sat up in bed, watching him change into his running clothes, tying the laces of his worn Asics.

"Are you okay?" she asked him.

He glanced at her, his eyes guarded. He nodded and returned to his task.

She frowned. If he wasn't even willing to answer her verbally, something was really wrong. *It was last night,* she thought. *I pulled away and he's upset about it.* She didn't blame him. He'd done everything perfectly after finding out about her scars. He'd made her feel safe and desired and sexy. He didn't take advantage of her emotionally but brought healing to a part of her that had desperately needed it.

And what did she do in return?

She shut off. Like a robot. Right in the middle of it. She stopped focusing on him as a person and focused on him as a body, an instrument for her pleasure. He'd wrung out every bit of pleasure from her body that he could but she knew he wanted something more. He wanted the emotional connection. So did she. So why couldn't she stay with him? Why couldn't she connect with him during what was supposed to be their most intimate moment together? It had nothing to do with skill. She'd never met someone who could so easily and consistently manipulate her body into an orgasm. And yet, every time they had sex, her heart went cold. She shut down.

Aiden felt her watching him as she rose from bed. He wasn't interested in appeasing her ego or relieving her concern. The release from last night helped him fall asleep quickly but when he'd woken up, the same troubling thoughts plagued him once more. Was he being oversensitive? Irrational?

Even effeminate for wanting an emotional connection during sex? He felt like he was thinking like a girl. Somehow, in the area of sex, Jane was the stereotypical detached male and he was the clingy woman who wanted more. He'd never felt like that in a relationship. And he hated it.

He wanted to get away from her.

Jane saw his body stiffen at her approach. He really was angry and she didn't know how to navigate his silence. So she resorted to the only thing she could think of: blunt honesty.

"You're mad at me." It wasn't a question.

He kept his eyes trained on his shoes as he tucked the bright laces inside. He didn't answer her. When he finished that task, he moved to go to the door.

"What, are you going to give me the silent treatment? Like a child? That's mature of you."

He paused at the door but didn't look at her. "I have nothing to say."

"That's bullshit," she answered. She felt fear grip at her sides and fought it with her words. "Just tell me what you're thinking now. How you're feeling."

"Like you did last night?" he asked.

So it was about last night.

"I shut down on you," she said. He turned slowly. His eyes finally met hers, surprised at her admission. And in that moment, she saw just how much she'd hurt him by her behavior. Her feet moved on their own accord, closing the space between them. Eyes fixed on his, she cupped his cheek with her hand.

"I'm sorry," she said sincerely.

Aiden couldn't put his finger on it. But something in her tone, the regret reflected in her eyes, the tender touch of her hand…it broke him. He felt a fresh surge of tears and he looked away, embarrassed. Her hand turned his cheek back to her.

"Jane-"

"Shh." She closed her eyes and leaned her head against his chest. "I'm sorry. I'm sorry. I'm so, *so* sorry."

She kept repeating it as she wrapped her other hand around his shoulder, tucking her face into the curve of his neck. A feeling of relief washed over her when his arms circled her small waist. They stood there, at the entrance of their room and held each other wordlessly.

After a few moments, Aiden felt strong enough to pull back slightly. He watched her eyes flicker open. "What happened?" he asked.

Her breath hitched at his simple question. "I don't know," she answered honestly. "I don't know. You were perfect last night. You did everything right. You made me feel safe-"

"So why did you shut down? Was it something I did in the middle-?"

She shook her head. "No."

"Am I a bad partner? Is there something you want me to do differently?"

"God, no! Aiden, you're fantastic in bed. I've never had such pleasure…" She looked away, uncharacteristically bashful. While he was happy to hear he brought her pleasure, he still wanted to get to the bottom of things. He brought them over to the bed and sat down side by side.

"I'm not just some guy, Jane." Aiden began quietly. He met her eyes and saw her nod. "I'm your boyfriend. I'm serious about you. I care about you more than I've ever cared about another woman."

She gasped at the candid declaration.

"We cannot move forward until you trust me. It's up to you."

He stood up and left.

Aiden ran to get his mind off things. Jane took photos to clear her mind. She got dressed, grabbed her camera and headed straight outside, choosing to skip breakfast that morning in favor of getting some early bird shots. The land was beautiful. Quiet. And peaceful in the morning. She didn't know where everyone was but she wasn't about to investigate.

She approached a bench overlooking the water and began to shoot. She experimented with different filters, zoomed in and out several times and shot to her heart's content. While she loved her camera, she wished she had a different one that morning. She wished she owned a camera that could capture beauty with the same precision her very eyes could.

"Bad lighting?"

Jane jumped at the sound of his voice. It took her brain a second to register that she recognized it. She turned as Michael approached the bench with his Canon EOS 5D nestled in his hands. She eyed the camera enviously before smiling into his gray-blue eyes.

"Bad angle," she replied. He took a seat next to her and tried a few shots himself before making some adjustments to his filter.

"I didn't know you shoot," he said lightly, eyes still on his camera.

"Just a hobby."

"Same here," he replied. "When did you start?"

She shrugged. "About four years ago. I took a basic photography class in college and it stuck."

He suddenly smiled and Jane nearly gasped at the brilliance of it. She then realized that she'd never seen such an open expression of joy on his face before. He was a very reserved man.

"I fell in love with it the same way. Photography 101 in 1972."

"Wow," Jane murmured. "You must be a professional by now."

He shrugged nonchalantly. "Some of my stuff has been published but I still do it all for fun."

She smiled at his humility. He didn't care how good he was, he just enjoyed it. She could relate to that. He pointed to another bench several yards away.

"I think that might be a better angle."

She nodded and they moved. When they settled down, they took a few more shots in comfortable silence and Jane appreciated the moment for what it was. Of all his siblings, Michael was the quietest. He wasn't a pushover, she could tell, but he didn't feel the need to fight for his parents' or anyone else's attention. When he did speak, others listened. He commanded that respect.

"How are you enjoying your stay?" he asked as he raised the camera to his eye.

"It's beautiful here," she answered.

He continued to shoot and spoke again. "How about the people?"

She shrugged, fiddling with the lens cap of her Canon. "Everyone's been nice. Well, mostly everyone. I really appreciate the invitation."

He lowered the camera from his eyes and gave her a small smile. "I'm glad you came."

It was a simple statement delivered from a quiet man. But those four words made Jane feel four inches taller. Despite everything that was going on with her and Aiden, his parents still liked her. Their kindness warmed her heart. They continued to shoot next to each other for a few minutes. Michael surprised her when he asked to switch cameras. He shot on hers and showed her how to better manipulate her lens to get more out of her shots. She enjoyed the superiority of his camera and smiled as he noted her natural talent.

By the time they walked down the path, back to the house, they met Aiden stretching at the entrance, sweat shining from his pores.

"Morning, son." Michael greeted him.

"Hi, Dad."

Michael glanced between the two of them and headed inside. Jane stood to the side as he wrapped up his stretching. He wondered what she was going to say now. Already in a better mood, he didn't want to re-hash it all again. Jane could see the slight trepidation on his face when he finished. Before he could speak, she strode up to him and pulled him into her arms, sweat and all, planting a full and tender kiss on his lips.

He reciprocated, hesitantly at first and then with confidence. By the time she pulled back, he was slightly out of breath again. He scanned her face.

"What was that?" he asked.

She looked at his collar bone before meeting his gaze again.

"I'm going to try," she said. "I like what we have and I want to give it a chance. I'm going to try." She didn't know what she expected to see when she said that but her heart soared at his look of elation. He leaned into her and stole another kiss.

"Thank you," he said, his voice a deep rumble. "I..."

He almost said it. He almost admitted that he loved her. But something held him back *again*. "I...I'm so happy you made that decision," he finished lamely. Heat poured into his cheeks but she didn't notice as she took his hand and walked back into the house with him.

CHAPTER EIGHTEEN

They went back into town that day and it was very different from the day before. With less historical sites to explore, Aiden and Jane spent more time in several stores, browsing just to browse. Jane laughed as Aiden looked around and gave his unsolicited opinion about almost every item for sale. There seemed to be an obsession with something called "Black Dog" on the island and one store sold goods exclusively with that label in mind.

Her favorite store naturally ended up being the bookstore. She and Aiden briefly split while he poured over the business section and she explored some classic literature. She realized she had all the greats and was looking at more contemporary writers when an idea struck her. Looking around to pinpoint his location, Jane made a selection and quickly made her purchase. She stuck the item in her purse without him noticing and reveled in the child-like sensation of being a spy.

"You ready?" he asked when he'd had his fill. She nodded and accepted his hand. She looked down at their joined hands, enjoying the feel of his strong grasp and the sight of their different skin tones: golden white and dark brown. She found it beautiful. To her surprise, she watched him raise her hand to his lips and plant a romantic kiss on the back of it. She smiled into his playful gold eyes and followed his lead to a small, busy restaurant.

"Masterson," Aiden told the hostess inside. They were led to a private area of the restaurant. Several tables were lined up to accommodate their large party. The rest of the family was already there but Alexa had managed to save them both seats.

"Thanks, Lex." Jane smiled at her. She winked in response.

Several dishes had already been ordered and delivered. Aiden and Jane put their orders in and were surprised to see them come back so quickly.

"Grandpa's friends with the owner," Alexa explained.

"No wonder," Aiden surmised. Jane smiled at the remark and leaned into his shoulder. He grinned back at her and dug into his food.

As much as he enjoyed it, his appetite began to wane as he noticed the strange behavior of his aunts and uncles. Though trying to hide it, they were watching Jane carefully. The conversation continued to swirl around them but their eyes would land on her every few seconds. Some had wary expressions; others looked at her with pity. He glanced at his cousins and saw that all except Riley were staring at her plate. But even Riley glanced at her from time to time. He frowned, a sense of foreboding washing over him. His eyes clashed with Titus and he knew his uncle was aware of the situation. He tried to ask him with a look.

What did you do?

His uncle shook his head, a bemused expression on his face. Whatever Aiden had shared with him, he hadn't gone out and shared it with others. So why was everyone being so weird?

Jane felt their eyes on her as she slowly chewed her food. Her salad was tiny once more and she cut her lettuce into smaller pieces before bringing it to her mouth. She suddenly wished she'd taken her medicine before walking into the restaurant because that action would be under their scrutiny as well. They were talking about things like the weather or items they'd purchased during the stay but she could feel the heat of their gazes and she knew Aiden could too. He wasn't eating. She glanced at him and saw his grim expression.

"What happened?" she asked. He knew what she meant. Why was everyone lasering in on her?

He looked down at her and gave her a tight smile. "They're just being weird. Not used to seeing a new face."

She knew he was trying to make her feel better but the fact that he didn't know the source of their staring made her feel even more uncomfortable. She also noticed JJ's constant gaze as she tried to eat her meal in peace. His leering had transformed into something just as bad: a look of smug satisfaction.

What does he *have to be happy about?* she wondered.

"Jane, did you enjoy your stay here?" he asked clear across the table. Aiden frowned at his cousin, still remembering his actions the previous night.

Jane nodded and said pleasantly enough, "I did. Thank you."

"Any favorite parts of the trip?" he asked.

"She said she enjoyed it," Aiden snapped. "Do you really need the details?"

The other conversations continued but some quieted down at the sound of his agitated tone.

"Why wouldn't I want the details? I'm sure this must be night and day from what she's used to."

A sense of dread washed over Aiden at his words and the nasty smirking grin on his cousin's smug face. "Drop it, JJ." Aiden warned.

The conversations died altogether.

A malicious frown crossed JJ's face. "What if I don't want to, *Little* Cousin? I think it might be amusing to hear Jane's take on the difference between Martha's Vineyard and the Bronx."

Jane frowned in concern. He spoke like he knew something sinister about her past, like he knew more to her story than the fact that she used to live in an inner city. She felt the eyes of Michael's siblings, nieces and nephews on her face but she kept her eyes on JJ. The flat green eyes glinted with malice, jealousy, and downright bitterness.

All because I turned you down? she wondered. What a pathetic spoiled brat.

Mr. Masterson seemed to have the same sentiment as he looked at his older grandson with barely veiled disdain. He glanced at Aiden before telling JJ, "If you have something to say, say it now and stop being so passive aggressive."

Aiden opened his mouth to defend her when she laid a gentle hand on his wrist. He looked down at her and found her shaking her head, her eyes calm. She didn't mean to contradict the patriarch, but she didn't want to be the cause of a scene either.

"Can we just go home? I don't want to entertain him."

He scanned her eyes and nodded in agreement. They stood up, much to *Nonna's* disappointment.

"You not going!" she cried, her thick accent coated in disbelief.

Ava looked at the pair in concern.

Michael frowned. "Aiden, stay. Don't let him ruin the lunch for you."

Nonna narrowed her eyes at JJ and rattled off her disapproval in Italian. JJ's ears instantly burned red at his grandmother's loud reprimand.

Aiden and Jane ignored his family's protests and walked out into the fresh air. He pulled her into his arms and kissed the top of her head. "Are you okay?"

She nodded. "I'm fine. Thanks for standing up for me."

He smiled. "Of course. Every time I look at him, I want to plant my fist in the side of his jaw."

She frowned. "You're still upset about what he did last night?"

He looked at her in disbelief. "Jane. You're *my* woman. My cousin had the nerve to approach and hit on someone he *knew* was my woman. Of course, I'm upset with him! I'm furious with him."

She saw his amber gold eyes transform into a fiery dark copper. Though he'd chosen not to confront his cousin and ruin the family trip, she knew he could change his mind at any moment. She searched for a way to calm him down.

"Hey," she said, pulling his forehead against hers. She laid a gentle kiss on his lips. "I'm yours. There's no competition. He couldn't even *try*. Okay?"

He leaned in and kissed her once more but they were interrupted by the sound of obnoxious clapping behind them. Aiden rose to his full height as JJ continued to mock them outside. He must have come out on his own. The rest of the family was inside.

"Aww, look at the two love birds."

Aiden frowned at him and shook his head in disgust. He realized there wouldn't be a fight. There wasn't a man in front of him to fight. Alexa and the twins appeared at the door.

"Dude," Aiden said. "*Grow up!*"

JJ's eyes darkened menacingly. "'Grow up'? I'm older than you."

"You don't act like it," Alexa remarked.

"Shut up, Alexa!" he snapped.

"Don't talk to my sister that way," Aiden warned. "Leave her out of this and stay away from Jane. Just leave us alone and go back to spending your daddy's money."

"Nice!" Carly applauded the insult.

Aiden turned to walk away but felt Jane tense at his side. "Aiden!"

He turned right in time to see his cousin lunge at him with a raised fist. He ducked the blow and delivered one of his own clear across his cousin's nose. The twins screamed at the sudden fight. Alexa ducked back in to get help.

"Ahh! Shit!" JJ reeled back, holding his bloody nose. Moments later, the rest of the family poured out and assessed the situation.

"What the hell is going on here?" James IV asked in disbelief.

"Nothing," Aiden panted. "This jerk tried to prove a point and I proved mine."

He turned to Jane and scanned her up and down. "You okay?"

She nodded quickly. He liked the look of admiration in her eyes. He'd have to play the white knight more often. He turned to his dad. "Can we borrow your car home? We really want to get away from him."

Before his father could speak, JJ interjected himself once more, cupping his nose the whole time.

"Don't worry about me, man. You can have her—"

"JJ—"

"Why would I want to go out with some emotional nut who's been in several foster homes and can't even eat because her stomach's too messed up?"

Alexa gasped. It was all Jane could hear as the blood rushed to her ears.

JJ continued, "At least Alexa acts like a normal woman." He gestured at Jane. "This one has emotional baggage that could fill the state dump."

Aiden rushed to punch him once more but this time Michael and Titus stepped in, holding the two back.

"He's not worth it, son!" Michael told him. But Aiden wasn't listening.

"Who told you?" he yelled over his father's shoulder.

JJ laughed. "Everyone here knows courtesy of Uncle Titus and your dear mommy. Aren't you the one who aired all her dirty laundry to them? They've been talking about it ever since."

Titus, who'd been protecting JJ from Aiden, turned around and socked his nephew in the eye.

"Titus!" Jacob Sr. Cried.

"Sorry, Jake." Titus said. "But your son is a nightmare. Anything Ava and I discussed, we did it where we didn't think there'd be prying ears. Clearly we were wrong and this son of a bitch decided to spread the info to the rest of the family."

Hot blinding humiliation filled Jane's gut as she finally understood. *That* was what the looks were for. With the exception of Alexa and Michael, every person there had watched her eat with strange glances.

"Is this true?" Michael asked Ava hotly. "Were you talking about her behind her back all this time?"

Ava looked at Jane with a panicked expression. "I was just trying to help. We thought-"

"Who cares what you thought?" Alexa cut her off coldly. "You had no business snooping into her past like that. And now everyone knows!"

Jane saw Alexa's angry eyes and knew that, like her father, she had no idea what her mother and uncle were up to. But a second wave of horror washed over her as she continued to put the pieces of the puzzle together.

There was only one person besides Alexa who knew about Jane's stomach problems.

There was only one way that information could have filtered into JJ's ears. Jane's eyes shifted to Aiden and saw all of his guilt laid before her like a filleted fish. He approached her with careful steps, fear pulsing in his eyes.

"Jane-"

She shook her head quickly, tears blinding her view. His image began to shift and tilt as the tears gathered in overwhelming portions. Aiden's heart plummeted at the sight. He'd only seen her cry once before and it had never been because of him. He'd hurt her - hurt her worse than he ever could have fathomed and all he wanted to do was cloak her: away from the watchful eyes of his relatives and the poisonous words of his cousin.

He tried again. "Jane-"

"Get away from her," a sharp voice pierced him. Suddenly Alexa came to Jane's side and wrapped a protective arm around her. He'd never seen his sister so angry before. She dipped her head and whispered to Jane.

"Let's get out of here." Jane followed the younger girl wordlessly as she led them across the street to a waiting cab. It was probably reserved by another family member but no one objected as Alexa paid the man and took the two of them back to the property alone.

Jane couldn't take anything in and she sensed that neither could Alexa. Between the two of them, though, Alexa had the more alert mind. She had the wherewithal to thank the driver and ask him to wait for them. She unlocked the door and immediately made calls to what sounded like the Steamship Authority. They were getting out of there that night. Jane operated on autopilot and began to pack. She ignored his scent, ignored the knick knacks that were exclusively his. She pulled out the item from the bookstore and laid it on his pillow.

She pulled her bags together and checked under the desk, bed, and surrounding furniture for anything forgotten. There was a constant buzzing. She realized it was her phone. She pulled it out and saw one of fifteen missed calls. She turned it off and walked downstairs. Alexa was waiting for her.

"Ready?" she asked gently. Her eyes were soft and kind but she didn't say anything else. She knew it wasn't the time to talk. Jane nodded and joined her. They crossed the threshold and quickly loaded their bags into the car. A black SUV rushed onto the property and the door opened before it could properly stop.

"Jane!" Aiden cried, jumping out.

Jane quickly climbed into the cab and locked her door. The driver, at Alexa's insistence, refused to unlock it.

"Jane." His voice was muffled through the window. "I'm sorry. Please, let me talk to you."

He watched as she stared straight ahead, as if unable to register anything he was saying.

"Alexa, let us talk to her." Ava pleaded with her daughter. Alexa stood with her back to the door, shielding Jane on her side. "This whole thing is a misunderst-"

"Save it, Mom." Alexa quickly climbed in and ordered the driver to go. Aiden and Ava jumped back as the cab sped out of the large estate driveway. Whether reconciliation was possible or not, it wasn't going to happen on that island.

CHAPTER NINETEEN

It was surreal. Jane had gone to Martha's Vineyard with the hope that the trip would clear her mind and get it off her troubles at work. Instead, it created an explosion of trouble in her personal life. The only good thing that came of it was a new appreciation for Alexa.

Her friend had made all the arrangements: ordered the tickets, got them food for the journey, and hired a private car service to take them all the way back to the city by nightfall. They were emotionally and physically exhausted by the time they arrived that night. It was a small comfort to be back home. They both had class the next morning and wordlessly began to settle in for the night. Jane hooked her phone to its charger and changed into her pajamas. She was putting her empty suitcase away when she heard Alexa's light knock. Her friend wordlessly sat on the bed and looked up at her, all of her regret in her eyes.

"I'm so sorry."

"Alexa-"

"That will *never* happen to you again. I promise you."

Jane closed her eyes and kept the tears at bay. "I can't, Alexa. I can't."

She couldn't talk about it or she would break down and she couldn't break down yet. When she opened her eyes, she met Alexa's hazel gaze and her friend nodded silently.

"I understand." She stood up and gave her a brief hug. "You used to protect me. Now let me protect you."

She nodded and watched Alexa leave.

She went back into her bathroom and brushed her teeth.

"We can't move forward unless you trust me."

The words shot across her memory like an arrow to her chest. She could still see his smile, feel his hands around her waist, his lips kissing every scar on her body. Little did she know he would open up a new wound. It was worse than any one she could recall in recent history. She was used to strangers hurting her. Caretakers not taking care of her. But she thought she'd protected herself from future attacks. She hadn't counted on betrayal. She could vividly recall the look of regret in his eyes and the emotion that accompanied it: guilt. Guilt for sharing her secrets with someone else. Guilt for talking about her behind her back. Guilt for sharing information that she'd only *just* trusted him with.

That's what you get for opening up, she chided herself. She knew better. She *knew* better than to trust someone with her heart. Her secrets. Alexa was the only person who'd ever truly kept her confidence. Maybe that was why she thought Aiden would too.

No. She chose to trust him because he'd given her the impression that she could. She chose to trust him because she liked him, cared for him, wanted to be with him. She chose to trust him because she thought he might love her. The tears were welling again and she felt powerless to stop them. Suddenly, she felt another flash of pain in her stomach. She put her free hand over her abs and stopped brushing. The pain began to fade but it was slower this time around. She didn't need it to happen again. She made a mental note to see a doctor. She quickly finished brushing her teeth and packed her satchel for the next day's class. She turned the sheets over and climbed into bed. Right as her tired mind began to fade into sleep, she was summoned back to consciousness by the agitated voices at the door.

She could hear Alexa's voice, hard as nails, speak. "You are not going anywhere near her tonight."

"You can't keep me from her, Alexa." Jane's heart pounded at the sound of his voice.

"You want to bet?" Alexa challenged him.

"*Please*," he answered. "I know you're angry but this is between me and her. Let her kick me out if she wants."

"No! This became *my* business the minute you decided to betray her trust. I introduced her to you and you hurt her! You'll get to talk to her eventually, but it won't be tonight. She's probably already in bed."

She heard shuffling at the door, followed by Alexa's irate voice.

"Try it again. You try to get past me one more time and I *will* call the cops on your ass for trespassing."

Jane swallowed in surprise. She'd never heard Alexa so pissed - pissed to the point that she would curse. She couldn't decipher what was said next but Alexa must have gotten her way because moments later, she heard the door shut and no other voices spoke. She closed her eyes and welcomed the reprieve of sleep.

"Lex, you home?" Jane called into the apartment. It was a sunny winter afternoon and the bright weather almost lifted her mood since the events three days earlier.

Almost.

She shut the apartment door and scanned the room for any unwanted faces. She'd successfully avoided any and all contact with Aiden, Ava or Michael. Though she wasn't actively avoiding Michael, she wasn't eager to see anyone from Alexa's family after everything that had happened. So far, Alexa had been the perfect accomplice, warning her when one of her relatives wanted to stop by or claiming that she wasn't home if they dropped by unexpectedly. Jane wondered if her Christian friend felt guilty for lying in those moments but apparently she felt it more important to protect her than be honest to the family she was still angry with.

Jane settled her satchel on one of the barstools and flipped through her mail. She opened one of the envelopes and nodded at the notice. It was a letter from the University of Cambridge, confirming receipt of her application. She was glad she hadn't canceled it for a relationship that didn't last. She'd followed her instincts in this area and would hopefully be rewarded for it.

Now if only I could follow my instincts in my personal life.

"Jane, is that you?" Alexa called from upstairs.

"Yeah!" she yelled back. "And you're crazy late in responding!"

She heard her friend laugh lightheartedly. "Come up! I'm in my bathroom."

She found Alexa curling her hair in her spacious master-sized bathroom. She put down the iron hot device and hugged her. "How was school?"

Jane smirked at the motherly question. She shrugged and sat on the toilet, watching as Alexa resumed burning her hair. "Fine. Nothing out of the ordinary."

"Did President Schneider get back to you?"

Jane shook her head. She was surprised by the woman's lack of professionalism. Though she was a busy university professor, most would at least have their secretary acknowledge receipt of the email and reply accordingly.

Am I too young to even get an email back? she thought bitterly.

"Don't worry," Alexa said cheerfully. "It'll work out. It will all work out."

It was a trite answer that neither knew for sure was true but it comforted Jane all the same.

To her surprise, Alexa walked over to the medicine cabinet, pulled out a small bottle, and carefully emptied out two blue tablets into the palm of her hand. She watched as she popped the pills in her mouth and quickly downed them with a sip of bottled water. Jane waited, watching her with pointed eyes. Alexa shrugged.

"Fluoxetine. My doctor prescribed them about two years ago."

Jane recognized the name.

"Depression?" she asked.

Alexa nodded.

Jane cocked her head and stared at her. She never would have guessed Alexa had a sad day in her life much less needed pills to keep her from offing herself. Alexa grew uncomfortable under Jane's scrutiny. She tucked some dark brown strands behind her ears and pulled out a straight section to curl.

"It's not *that* strange," she said quietly. "People take medicine for chemical imbalances all the time."

"Yeah, but I thought you had *Jesus*. Isn't He your magic medicine?"

Jane regretted the words as soon as they came out of her mouth. Though they were funny to her in theory, it wasn't at all funny how hurt Alexa looked at the comment.

"I'm sorry," she said immediately. "I didn't mean to insult your faith."

Alexa smiled weakly. "I don't pretend to be the best Christian or have the greatest faith out there but I do believe Jesus was a part of my recovery."

"How so?"

"When people think of God helping others, they often think that He only does it by performing miracles and doing jaw-dropping interventions. And He does that sometimes, of course…but most of the time, God helps others in small, almost unnoticeable ways. A lot of times, He helps us in practical, everyday, ways and we give the credit to other people when He was the one who orchestrated it all along."

Jane watched Alexa as she spoke. Her eyes brightened as she opened up about how she understood God and Jane could tell it was *this* understanding of Him that made her enjoy that relationship so much. And in a way, Jane felt her peace.

"When my friend referred me to Dr. Hull, I finally met someone who diagnosed my depression, referred me to a decent therapist, and prescribed me the medication I needed to pull out of that deep, dark hole that was my mind. I could give all the credit to the medicine, or the therapist or Dr. Hull or even my friend. But I know that at the root of it all, it was God pulling the pieces, the conversations, and the help together for me. He did it and He deserves the praise."

Thoughts assailed Jane's mind as Alexa finished her statement. Jane believed in God and even believed in Jesus but she couldn't identify with the personal relationship Alexa professed to have with Him. And it wasn't because of anger. Maybe in her teens, she had been angry at God for not placing her in a better family or at least away from the lunatics who were supposed to take care of her. She remembered reading several articles about "the problem of evil" and why bad things happened to good people - why God allowed these things to happen. That started a whole series of her engaging in theological research to understand what the church and many Christian intellectuals had to say about evil, sin, Satan and his role in the world. And she believed it.

Because even though she had suffered through abuses no one in this world should have to suffer through, hadn't others? Hadn't Christ Himself suffered? She'd been slapped and molested and beaten and starved but hadn't He been flogged, tortured, and forced to suffocate to death on a cross? She never could quite understand atheists and agnostics who had the nerve to say that God didn't exist because of all the bad things that happened in the world. She always thought the presence of evil *was* evidence for the existence of God – i.e. good guy versus bad guy, heaven and hell, and eternal consequences for things that happened on earth. She certainly didn't have a problem imagining that *man* going to hell one day. And she wasn't the type of person to wallow in blame and self-pity anyway. What she *did* have a problem with was blindly trusting and loving *anyone* ever again.

And that included God.

Aiden's face came to mind and Jane blinked the image away. Alexa must have read her mind because his name was soon on her lips.

"Have you talked to Aiden yet?" she asked.

"You know I haven't," Jane answered.

Alexa sighed. "I know I'm supposed to stay mad at them-"

"I never asked you to."

"I know. I'm disappointed with them but…" Her face softened. "I wish we could all just make up."

"Alexa, they're your family." Jane said seriously. "I don't want you to have strife with them because of me."

"But you're my family too."

Jane smiled at the sentiment. Her friend still viewed her like an older sister.

"Your family loves you," she continued. "By all means, make up with them and move on. I just would rather keep my distance."

Alexa nodded. "I understand. I wish it were different. But I understand." She paused. "Are you still going to watch me sing this Sunday? They're planning on going and I can't un-invite them."

Jane felt a tight feeling close around her throat. She wanted to say no but knew it would really disappoint Alexa. Besides, she wanted to see her friend sing and check out the church that meant so much to her.

"Of course, I'll go." she replied. She had between then and Sunday to figure out how to avoid her family. Alexa smiled happily and started to chat about her classes. Jane started flipping through the remainder of her mail, nodding and murmuring at the appropriate times to Lexi's chatter. She frowned at a nondescript letter. It was from the state of New York with an emblem of a city department. Tearing the letter open, Alexa's voice faded to the background as Jane read the words of the brief notice.

It took Alexa a few unanswered questions before she noticed the shell-shocked look on Jane's face. "Jane?" she asked. She glanced at the loosely-held paper in her hands. "What is it? What happened?"

Jane handed her the paper and slowly stood up. "My biological mother died. They buried her last month."

She felt Alexa's arms attempt to wrap her in a hug but she didn't return the gesture. She could barely see as she walked out of the bathroom and over to her room. Her mind didn't know what to do. Shore up tears? Get upset? Work its way into some type of relief?

Jane shook her head, though no one could see. She wasn't going to cry or get upset or seek comfort. As far as she was concerned, there was nothing and no one worth crying for.

He was at his parent's place. He was beginning to get sick of the lavish golden interior of his childhood home. It used to comfort him but now it only reminded him of his standing with Jane. The only people who could stand him outside of work were his parents.

What a life.

They were huddled around the island of the luxury kitchen, talking but not saying much. Aiden studied the grains and lines of his mother's granite counter top. When he raised his eyes, he found her watching him.

He frowned. "What?"

Ava smiled, her blue eyes sad. "I'm sorry."

His dad rubbed her shoulders gently. They'd made up before they even got back to the harbor.

"Mom, you've said it a thousand times," Aiden sighed.

"And I still mean it."

"So do I," he replied. "I forgive you. Please let it go."

He knew she regretted putting him in a compromising position. He didn't even know if his information helped Uncle Titus find what he was looking for. He no longer cared. What was the point of knowing more about his girlfriend if she refused to be his girlfriend moving forward? He thought of the happier moments they shared on the island. Feeling her rest against him in the car, holding her on the boat, sharing their love of history in the old town. He still remembered the ringing guilt he felt when he found the fourth edition *Historical Sites and Stories of Edgartown* guidebook on his pillow. She'd left it for him before leaving alone. She must have bought it as a gift when he wasn't looking and *that* was the way she ended up giving it to him: instead of a token to strengthen their bond, it was a farewell gift of sorts. His stomach burned with anxiety and regret.

"I screwed up," he said more to himself than his parents. He couldn't imagine everything she felt when she found out. Humiliation, her privacy breached, betrayal, hurt, anger…they probably all swirled together in a nauseating melting pot and he only saw a glimpse of it in her tear-filled eyes.

"She's still not taking your calls?" his mom asked.

He shook his head. "And she's never there when I stop by. At least according to Alexa." His sister wouldn't lie to him about that, would she? Her anger had cooled off already.

"You'll just have to keep trying," his dad said.

Aiden felt a buzzing in his pocket. He immediately reached in to answer his phone.

"Alexa?" he said.

"Yeah, it's me." She began to rattle off into almost incoherent sentences, something she only did when she was very worried. Aiden asked her to slow down and repeat herself slowly. He didn't know what he looked like but it couldn't be good because by the time he hung up, his parents' eyes were glued to his face with deeply concerned looks.

"What is it?" his mom asked. "What happened?"

"Is Alexa okay?" his father chimed in.

Aiden slowly nodded, the news sinking into his own mind. He tested the words on his lips. "Jane's mother died. She got the notice today." He heard his mother gasp but barely registered the sound. He started to gather his things.

"Where are you going?" his father asked.

"I need to go to her."

His mother frowned. "Will she let you?"

They both knew the answer to that. "I have to try."

"Aiden," his mother warned gently. "It might upset her more. Maybe I should go first. I'm trained-"

His father shook his head. "She doesn't want to see either of you and that sentiment is probably amplified by her grief."

They couldn't argue with his logic. Why would she want to see the people she'd been avoiding for nearly a week?

"I'll go," his father said to their surprise.

"Okay…it looks like we have everything we need," Dr. Bartels concluded, scanning her chart for any missed steps. A tall man with thinning brown hair, he looked at her thoughtfully over his glasses.

"Once the x-rays come in, I'll take a look and see what's going on with your small intestine. The urine sample should also tell us if there is a particular vitamin deficiency in your system."

"What does that mean?" Jane asked. She'd called out of work that morning and headed directly to his office, managing to get a same day appointment when she mentioned her severe stomach pains. Though not in pain that very moment, her gastroenterologist insisted on getting the tests done.

"If there's a noticeable lack of a particular vitamin in your body in spite of your diet, that would indicate that a part of your small intestine has shut down due to abnormal cell death. We call this necrosis of the intestinal tissue. At least part of it. Depending on which part, we may be able to remove it and supplement that vitamin externally."

"Through pills, you mean?"

"Exactly."

She nodded. Though many others would feel a level of fear or apprehension about what the test results would reveal, Jane wasn't nervous or scared. Rather, she felt relieved. Of all the things going haywire in her life, she took comfort in knowing there was a definitive answer to the health problem she was facing now. Much of her gastroparesis was a headache primarily because it involved treating the symptoms, not curing the condition. There was no cure. But a small part of her hoped that whatever treatment they came up with for *this* issue, it could help her not only recover from her stomach aches, but improve her chronic condition.

After the doctor, she spent most of the afternoon circling Central Park and taking various photographs. It didn't feel the same without him.

Stop it, she chided herself. He wasn't in the picture anymore and she needed to move on. She fiddled with her camera and adjusted the aperture. She lifted her camera to shoot again and was immediately drawn to a subject. It was a mother, in her early thirties, stooping down to help her toddler tie her shoes. The little girl's rosy cheeks bounced up in a contagious grin as she held her mother's shoulder for stability, her tiny dimpled hand resting against it. The mother looked up and met her daughter's eyes. They grinned at each other like they had a special secret.

Jane couldn't look anymore.

She did it. She couldn't believe she did it. Despite her best intentions, she'd ended up at the quiet, nondescript grave yard in Brooklyn. She had no idea how her mother's body ended up at the Episcopalian church cemetery and quite frankly, she couldn't care less.

Then why are you here? She asked herself. Why was she there? What was she thinking? Images assaulted her mind as she remembered the woman's cruelty. She could still see her dark eyes, glinting with hatred. Anger. Resentment. Such fierce vitriol, Jane used to wonder what she had done to hurt her. Why was her very existence such an affront to her? Her mother was beautiful once. Jane knew because she'd seen an old picture of her in her grandmother's house on the fire mantle. She could still remember the tears that welled in the old woman's eyes whenever she looked at the photograph for too long. She no doubt remembered her daughter then - before drugs, rebellion, and a series of miserable choices turned her into the monster she became.

How did she die? The notice said liver failure. *What caused the liver failure?* Probably the excess of liquor she ravaged her body with on a day-to-day basis. Jane would never know if she'd recovered or turned her life around or started a new family in the past twenty years. She probably hadn't - considering she was buried in a plot clearly meant for the abandoned.

Jane nearly jumped out of her skin when she heard someone approach her nearby. She turned to see who it was and almost jumped again. Michael sat down on the bench next to her. She turned back toward the grave. He observed the fierce glare she gave the unremarkable headstone.

"You didn't like her, did you?"

She realized then that Aiden hadn't shared everything about her. Michael didn't know about her mother.

She shook her head. "No."

"Was she as bad as your foster parents?"

"Worse."

Michael remained silent for several long moments. She didn't know what he was doing there so she asked.

"Alexa told me you might be here."

"You were looking for me?" she asked.

"Yes."

"Why?"

He didn't answer.

"How did Alexa know where you could find me?"

"She told me she left the notice on the kitchen counter. I looked up the address."

They were both silent. Jane realized he wasn't afraid of unfilled space. She appreciated that.

"I'm sorry," he finally said. "You deserved so much better."

Jane looked up at him, surprised to find tears springing to her eyes. She quickly looked back at the cemetery and swallowed them back. He gave her the time to do it before slowly wrapping an arm around her shoulder. He paused when she stiffened, but eventually she relaxed and he kept his steadying arm there.

Finally, her bearings together, Jane quietly said, "Thank you."

A gentle squeeze to her shoulder.

"Anytime."

There wasn't a grand goodbye or declaration of any sort but when Jane and Michael left the grave, Jane knew with every fiber of her being that she had finally closed that chapter of her life. The woman who gave birth to her had no place in her mind or her heart. She could finally let her go.

She felt a rush of relief to see a private car waiting in front of the church. She climbed in before Michael and he gave the driver the address to her and Alexa's apartment.

"Why did you come?" she asked again.

He turned his gray-blue eyes to her and finally answered. "To apologize for what my wife, brother, and imbecilic nephew did. I didn't know about what was going on. If I had, I would have stopped it."

She nodded. She knew he wouldn't have allowed Ava and his brother to gossip about her.

"I know you're very upset with them - my son especially for betraying your trust. But I hope after the anger cools down, that you'll try and give him another chance."

She frowned. "Why?"

"Because he cares for you. Deeply. I've never seen him this way with a woman. You don't have to trust him right away, Jane. But I hope you'll hear him out."

She didn't answer right away and he didn't seem to expect an answer either. They rode the rest of the journey in companionable silence and she only spoke when they reached her building.

"Does Aiden know you've come to talk to me?"

Michael nodded.

"He...if he comes, I won't shut the door on him. That's all I can promise."

Michael smiled and nodded once more. He knew it was more than enough.

CHAPTER TWENTY

Jane knew it was him the minute he knocked on the door. His knock had the distinct sound of a man unafraid and ready to bulldoze over any problem. She wondered if he would bulldoze over her.

Aiden didn't know what to expect when Jane opened the door. He was almost relieved to see what he did. She stood there with a blank expression on her face - one of the many times he couldn't read her thoughts or discern her feelings.

"Hi," he said nervously. "I talked to Dad. Is it okay if I come in?"

She stood back wordlessly and let him enter the dimly lit apartment.

"Alexa isn't home?"

She shook her head. He followed her into the living room and waited for her to turn and face him. When she did, he stumbled over his words.

"Thank you for the gift." He immediately winced at the stupid opening. She shrugged and looked away.

"Jane." She turned back and met his clear gold eyes. His regret was written across the irises. "I'm sorry. I'm so sorry for what I did." He shook his head. "There's no excuse for my behavior. I never should have betrayed your trust like that…"

His words tapered off as he saw her do something he never expected her to do. She sniffled. He watched in horror as tears streamed down her face uncontrollably and choked sobs pushed past her clamped lips. He crossed the space to touch her.

"Oh, Jane."

"No!" she sobbed out, shaking her head vehemently. She tried to move around him but his large body blocked her escape. He pulled her stiff frame into his arms and held her close to his chest. It was like the needle to a full balloon. His embrace broke the watershed of hurt, pain, and stuffed emotions that needed to get out.

"I'm sorry. I'm so sorry…" He said the words over and over and over until it was all they could hear, long after she cried her last tear. He smoothed the hair back from her forehead and kissed it while she continued to sniffle.

She raised her head and met his eyes, her own red and swollen.

"I'm sorry," he said once more and she nodded slightly, finally accepting his apology. He leaned his forehead against hers and just breathed. He almost cried in relief at the feel of her hands wrapping around his back. Nudging her cheek with his nose, Aiden angled his head, and found her lips. He could taste the salt of her tears on his tongue. He didn't care. He wanted nothing more than to reconnect with her. He reached up, pressed closer, and deepened the kiss, tightening his arms around her. Their hands quickly moved, pulling, pushing, tearing off the barriers between them.

It was the same as all the other times at all the other places: his apartment, Martha's Vineyard. Just when he thought he'd seen the most vulnerable side to her, Aiden once again saw the wall she erected as he made love to her in the middle of the living room. When she closed her eyes, he wanted to demand more from her. But he knew he couldn't. He didn't have a leg to stand on or a right to demand *anything* from her after what he'd done. So as the pleasure coursed through his body and erupted through hers, he said nothing. He watched and pleased her and tried to catch his breath when it was over. He pulled her into his side and held her secure in both arms. Her eyes were focused on her hand, lying on his chest.

"Do you forgive me?" he asked quietly. She glanced up at him and immediately wished she hadn't. He was hurt, no doubt by her lack of response - again. But she didn't have any answers for him and wasn't in the mood to placate him or analyze her behavior. Not when she could barely keep her head on straight.

He asked again. "Do you forgive me, Jane?"

Eyes focused on her hand, she nodded.

He couldn't tell if she was being sincere or not. Not when she had such a distant look in her eyes. He kissed her forehead and pulled her tighter against him still.

"Jane...Jane, I lo..." the words wouldn't get past his lips. They wouldn't escape his tongue. He wanted to tell her with every fiber of his being but he couldn't form the words, much less speak them. *Why?* he raged in his mind. A startling answer hit him. *She might reject me.*

She might reject him. She might not accept his love, much less reciprocate it - especially with the way things were now. He looked down to see what she was thinking but it was as if she hadn't heard him say anything. She pulled herself out of his arms and sat up, looking around.

"Alexa will be back soon. We should get dressed."

Jane had no problems finding the city church two days later. Alexa had given her clear instructions prior to leaving early. With a rehearsal set before service, her friend had to be there earlier than even the pastor. To Jane's surprise, she arrived at the same time Aiden and his parents did. She paused outside of the church, a few feet away from them and so did they, watching her as if to gage how receptive she would be.

Aiden chided himself and quickly closed the distance between the two of them. He pulled her into his arms and kissed the side of her head.

"Hey," he said. "How are you?"

She felt slightly stiff in his arms and he tried not to let it sting him. Though they'd made love two days prior, their communication had been limited to texts and brief phone calls. She'd told him she wasn't in the mood to see anyone as she processed her mother's untimely death. He'd learned the woman was only forty-two when she died. Another rippled of regret washed through him. If he'd kept his mouth shut to his uncle, he'd be on firmer footing with her and would have been able to push her to talk more, open up more, receive more comfort - all of which she clearly needed. But something was broken between them. And they were just beginning to glue it back together.

He noticed she wasn't quite meeting his eyes. He tipped her chin and forced her to.

"Hey," he said. "I've missed you. Do you miss me at all? Even just a little?"

She frowned. "Of course I do," she replied almost angrily. What kind of question was that?

"It's just...I haven't seen you in two days-"

"I told you-"

"I know you did but I still miss you and I can't help but wonder if you're still punishing me."

Was she punishing him? Jane asked herself in all honesty and realized that maybe she was. Part of her distance also had to do with ease. She didn't feel quite so vulnerable when he wasn't around. She didn't ache all over, half from hurt, half from desire. He elicited feelings in her that were too strong to ignore and too complex to decipher.

"I miss you," he repeated. "I will never do anything like that to jeopardize what we have again. Please. Let us move forward." He dipped his head and kissed her softly. "Please?"

He held her face in his hands and scanned her eyes for her response. They softened just the slightest and her body relaxed. "I want to try," she said, nodding. "I'll try."

He kissed her again, his eyes shining. "Thank you."

Ava and Michael approached the pair. Jane noticed the bouquet of flowers in Michael's hand. She guessed they were for Lexi. She gave Michael a slight smile but he and Aiden looked between the two women, anxious to see what would happen. Jane looked at Ava and nearly gasped at what she saw. There were silent tears welling in the older woman's eyes as she surveyed Jane. She made a hesitant move but quickly pulled Jane into a long, fierce hug.

"I'm so sorry," she said emotionally. "I'm so sorry. Please forgive me. I was just trying to-"

"I forgive you."

Ava pulled back and looked at her in surprise. So did Aiden. He peered down at Jane and saw that she was in fact sincere. She gave Ava a slight smile. It wasn't the warmest but it wasn't void of emotion like it usually was whenever she accepted one of his apologies. She was actually letting it go and not holding it against his mother. Half of him felt jubilant about it, the other half jealous.

Why does she *get instant forgiveness but I'm still in the dog house?*

He realized the reason as soon as he wondered it: they'd both hurt her. But *he* was the one who betrayed her trust. He was the one closest to her and his betrayal therefore hurt her more. Hot shame prickled his neck as his jealousy fell to the wayside. He decided that both his and his mother's exchange with Jane were good starts to church service.

"Shall we go in?" he asked the group. Michael and Ava walked ahead of them, entering the tall, stately building. Aiden didn't know why but he'd expected the interior to look something like the Catholic cathedrals he'd seen in movies - with rows of pews and an intimidating alter in the front. He hadn't been to church in years and only went for weddings and funerals now days. The interior of Alexa's church was unlike anything he'd ever seen before. There was low, ambient lighting. A band stood at the front stage with a simple cross hanging behind them. Instead of pews, there were rows of comfortable chairs and people seemed to sit wherever they wanted. He almost felt overdressed in his suit and tie. Most of the people in attendance wore khakis or jeans.

"Welcome to Redeemer Church," a friendly black woman greeted them. She was wearing a shirt with the church name so he assumed she was an usher of some sort. She asked his parents if they had any preferences for their seat and they told her they did. He and Jane followed his parents into the row they chose, in the middle, closer to the front so they could see Alexa perform. Within minutes, the service started, the lights dimmed a little further and the music began to play.

Jane looked around and watched the people in the audience cheer as a young man sang the first song. It was slow and reflective and peaceful. She didn't go to church but in that moment, she actually wondered why. She watched the people on the fringe. Those who gladly scooted over to accommodate late attendees, greeting them with hugs and cheerful smiles. She watched those absorbed in worship, their hands raised and their eyes closed, the conviction of their beliefs apparent on their faces. She also saw peace there.

Three songs played that neither Aiden nor Jane recognized. The words appeared on a projector by the stage but the pair stood silently, respectfully and waited for Alexa to appear. She did on the fourth song. Walking on stage, she began to sing a song entitled "Waiting Here For You."

Aiden listened as his baby sister sang from the bottom of her heart. A repeated refrain was "Hallelujah" and he could see the joy on her face to sing it out loud. Her sweet voice carried the melody of the song perfectly across the sanctuary. At the bridge of the song, she closed her eyes and lifted her hands and her head. It was as if the audience didn't exist anymore. She sang and praised directly to the God she believed in, so fervently, tears came to her eyes. The song began to taper down and so did her voice. The fervor didn't go away but it was eclipsed by a look of complete peace on her face. And in that moment, Aiden wanted what she had. What would it feel like to have such peace? He knew it wasn't from an absence of problems but from something deeper, something that circumstances couldn't determine or alter.

Peace.

And his little sister had it. The thought stayed with him as he and his family cheered her on and took their seats for the rest of the service. It looked like they were starting with announcements and administrative matters. Not conscious of his actions, Aiden reached out and held Jane's hand. She looked at him in surprise and he met her eyes. She too looked deeply affected by Alexa's performance.

"That was good, wasn't it?" he asked. She nodded wordlessly.

"That was *beautiful*," his mother amended. He glanced at her and saw her dab at the corner of her eyes with her husband's handkerchief. Michael nodded in agreement, a reflective look on his face.

Seconds later, Alexa found the group and they whispered their praises to her. Michael passed her the bouquet and kissed her cheek. "You were phenomenal, sweetheart!"

"Thank you!" she whispered with a large smile. "You didn't have to do this. I'm just glad you came!"

"So are we!" her mother exclaimed. "Your voice is such a gift."

"I concur," Jane said. Alexa squeezed Jane to her side and winked at Aiden before taking a seat next to her. The sermon was about to begin.

"Good morning." A middle-aged man with thick black hair greeted the congregation. Aiden was surprised to hear the congregants greet him back. In all the churches he'd gone to before, the audience always remained silent. He watched as the pastor, who introduced himself as Pastor Jonathan Teller, opened his spiel with a few anecdotes and jokes, comments about the worship, and even a brief acknowledgment of Alexa's powerful singing. He watched his sister blush in uncharacteristic embarrassment and smiled. She deserved the acknowledgment.

"If you have your Bibles, turn to Matthew 5:27-30. It reads: 'You have heard that it was said, 'You shall not commit adultery.' But I tell you that anyone who looks at a woman lustfully has already committed adultery with her in his heart. If your right eye causes you to stumble, gouge it out and throw it away. It is better for you to lose one part of your body than for your whole body to be thrown into hell. And if your right hand causes you to stumble, cut it off and throw it away. It is better for you to lose one part of your body than for your whole body to go into hell.'" The pastor closed the book and looked up at the audience.

"So today, we're going to talk about love versus lust," he said bluntly. Aiden's parents gasped next to him and Aiden felt himself turning red. Of all the services he could have gone to, *this* was the one in which they would talk about sex while he was sitting right next to his parents.

God help me, he thought.

"When you first hear that passage, you might have a negative reaction to it."

Aiden did.

"It would be very natural to say, 'Oh! See? There's that negative view of sex Christians are known for!'" The audience laughed. "We have historically gotten a bad rap for false guilt and shame when it comes to sex - much of which is a misunderstanding. The Christian ethic for sex, though *very* different than what the world maintains, is nevertheless one of the most attractive aspects of Christianity."

Oh, really? Aiden cocked his head to the side in curiosity.

Pastor Teller continued. "During the ministry of Christ, He spent a lot of time teaching about the various areas of life. Love and sex happen to be one of those areas. Today we are going to talk about the integrity of sex. In the passage, Jesus clearly accepts the Old Testament biblical ethic of sex - we have to understand it in order to build off of that idea. So what was the Old Testament sex ethic? That sex is a gift from God reserved for those in a covenant relationship. What's a covenant relationship? Marriage. Meaning, no sex outside of marriage."

Jane shifted in her seat. She could feel more than see Aiden stiffen.

"Some of you are thinking, 'I thought this was supposed to be a positive message about the Christian ethic of sex.'" The audience chuckled. "It is - I promise! Just bear with me a moment. Let's take a look at covenant relationships. Covenant relationships are far more loving and intimate than a merely legal relationship. At the same time, they are far more binding and enduring than a merely emotional relationship. It's more loving *because it's legal.* How can that be? Well, let's consider a consumer relationship."

"When you as a consumer are dealing with a vendor, you have a relationship with them as long as they meet your needs. But you're always looking for an upgrade. There's an unspoken understanding between you and your grocer that if you find another grocer with fresher produce and lower prices, you're out of there. You're just out of there!" Jane couldn't help but chuckle along with the crowd. "The understanding is 'I will be with you as long as you meet my needs. You adjust to me, or I'll find somebody else who can.' A covenant relationship is the opposite. A covenant relationship says, 'I will adjust to you because I've made a promise and our relationship is more important than my needs.'"

It was as if a world of revelation opened up for Jane. The concept of such a relationship was a breath of fresh air because she'd never experienced it before.

"If you're in a consumer relationship, there is no rest to just be yourself. You are constantly performing. You have to perform or they're out. Now listen," he paused. "I know this is countercultural. I *know* this is difficult to process. And I know it might even offend some of you - that is, if I haven't offended you already. I'm going to say it anyway." The congregation chuckled. "Covenant relationships are better than consumer relationships and if I were you, I would ask which one I'm currently in."

Jane felt the hair stand on the back of her neck. Was that what she was doing to Aiden? What were they? Consumers or covenanters? Aiden felt a burning in his chest as the pastor spoke. He couldn't look at Jane to see how she was reacting. He didn't even know what was going on in him.

"In a covenant, which is marriage, you don't have to spin or sell, promote or hide who you really are. There is a zone of safety because when both of you are committed to the covenant, you both have the space to be who you are and be loved just as you are without fear of abandonment. I'm not pitching a Cinderella marriage - by *any* means. Christians do get divorced. But could it be that they never really understood the concept of a godly marriage to begin with?"

Aiden quirked a brow at that. Christians not getting what their religion taught?

"When you get married, things will inevitably get ugly. There will be days when you look at your spouse and realize, 'I honestly don't like you right now. I don't *feel* any sort of affection towards you.' And yet you know and they know that neither of you are going anywhere. Because your commitment to the relationship supersedes your immediate, fleeting needs. You can finally get rid of the façades. You can finally let him or her know about your insecurities. You finally have a place where you can stop marketing, selling, and spinning. You finally have a safe place to be *you* because the man or woman you love isn't going anywhere. Which is precisely what a loving God wants for *all* of His children. When two people give and pour into each other, they serve one another but they are also *being* served."

"Ironically, when you are committed to a person in spite of your feelings, *deeper* feelings grow. A prime example of this is the relationship between parents and children. Parents, wouldn't you agree with me, that when you have kids, you give a heck of a lot and get very little back?" Aiden glanced at his parents and saw them nod. "But isn't it amazing how even when your children act less than lovable, you love them anyway? There is a commitment and loyalty to them that far surpasses your feelings. You are *invested* in them and will always love them, no matter how annoying, sick, unattractive, mean, ungrateful, you-name-it, they are. What would this look like in a marriage?"

The idea of it was breathtaking to Jane. She'd never had parents before - least of all parents to love her unconditionally. And yet she knew that such a love existed. She saw it in the way the Mastersons interacted with their kids. To have that in marriage? It struck a chord in her that she couldn't ignore.

"What does this have to do with sex?" Pastor Teller continued. "Everything. Because according to Scripture, sex is not a consumer good but a covenant good. It isn't meant to keep someone in a relationship but is meant to be a visible symbol of the invisible commitment that has taken place between a man and a woman before God. Meaning, when I, in marriage, make myself *physically* naked and vulnerable, it is a sign of what I've done with my *whole life.*"

Boom. It was like a lightning rod. Both Aiden *and* Jane sat up in their seats, the reality of their relationship filleted before them like gourmet fish.

"Sex is meant to be a sign of what you've done with your whole life and that is why sex outside of marriage, from a Christian worldview, lacks integrity. You're asking someone to do with their body what you're not doing with your life. 'Let's be physically vulnerable with each other but not emotionally transparent. Let's make love but not say we love each other.'"

Aiden's face burned.

"'Let's share our bodies but not share our hearts, home, money and lives as husband and wife.' It's not a buffet. You can't isolate one type of union from all the other unions that were meant to go with it. That is a lack of integrity."

Aiden felt what could only be described as hot coals stacking in the center of his belly. He could feel Jane's eyes on him but couldn't bring himself to look at her. Blood rushed to his ears as the words the pastor spoke sunk deep into his conscience. Had he gotten it wrong? Was his entire paradigm and understanding of sex incorrect? And if it was, what did that mean for him and the woman sitting next to him? The woman he was sure he loved? An anger so foreign, so unwarranted began to rise in the pit of his stomach. He hated how he felt in that moment. Dirty. Guilty. Like someone had shined the light on his problems and pointed out that he was the cause of them. He thought back to every moment he touched Jane, made love to her. According to the man on stage, it hadn't been an act of love but selfish lust. And what of Jane? What did she think? Could that be the reason why she never emotionally responded to him in bed? Was he seeking a connection he couldn't have - that he'd tried to gain prematurely?

"In marriage," Pastor Teller continued. "Sex is a covenant renewal ceremony. You are giving yourselves to each other, over and over, reminding the other person that you are in it no matter *what* you feel. It's incredibly deepening, rewarding, solidifying, and nurturing. You're saying, 'I belong completely and exclusively to you and I'm acting it out. I'm giving you my body as a token of how I've given you my life.'"

Jane nodded, enraptured by the picture he was drawing.

"I can already see some of you stewing in your seats. You probably feel like I'm playing the judge and the executioner right now and I *know* I have offended some of you. Please hear me say that if you've done sex any other way, I *am not* condemning you for it. God is by no means a fan of pre-marital sex but He loves *all people* - including the ones who are having it."

She felt a rush of relief at his words. Tears threatened to well but she kept them at bay.

He continued, "All I'm saying is that God has something infinitely better, deeper, and far more rewarding than what society - and even your personal instinct - has been selling you. Give covenant relationships a chance."

He backed up his thesis by listing articles, psychiatrists, and secular sources that all pointed to the newly discovered phenomenon that couples who lived together prior to marriage were more likely to divorce than those who didn't. Jane listened as he laid out his argument in calm succinct statements, often inflected with humor and very much colored with gentleness. She saw the redness in Aiden's face and the stiff set of his jaw. He looked angry but she couldn't understand why. For the first time in a long time, she felt as though she was hearing the truth and it was being told, like Pastor Teller said, not to condemn her, but to look out for her.

She was glad she came.

They walked out of the service and were met with the bright, shining winter sun. The bright view did nothing to assuage Aiden of his foul mood. He felt Jane's eyes on him but he still couldn't look at her. He knew instinctively that the sermon hadn't bothered her nearly as much as it did him.

Alexa looked at her guests and nervously asked, "What did you think of it?"

Her gaze drifted to her brother and she blinked at the aggravated expression he wore.

"It was lovely, dear." Ava kissed her cheek. "Thank you again for inviting us. We know how important this is to you."

Jane and his parents continued to complement her on her performance and the atmosphere of the church. Aiden kept silent, refusing to meet his sister's probing eyes. She knew something was wrong and he wasn't about to pretend that there wasn't.

"That pastor was pretty good," Michael said off-handedly. Aiden frowned at his father.

"You *liked* what he had to say?" he asked in disbelief.

Michael shrugged. "I didn't agree with all of it but I thought he had some valid points."

"Like what?"

Ava and Michael peered at their son and saw the agitation in his face.

"You didn't like *any* of it?" his father turned the question on him.

"No," Aiden said firmly. His eyes flickered to his sister. "Is this why you invited us this Sunday? To get blasted with some old fashioned, Victorian view of sex? Should I order a pistol and start learning how to duel, too?"

"Aiden!" his mother chided him. But he wasn't listening. He was furious with the pastor, the sermon, how it made him feel, and with Alexa for setting him up like that.

"Aiden," Alexa said, clearly concerned. "I'm sorry if it offended you-"

"*'If?'*" he gave a mirthless laugh.

"I didn't know that's what he would preach-"

"You didn't?" he asked dubiously. "For some reason, I doubt that."

He saw the surprise and hurt flash in her eyes at his suggestion that she was lying. He felt a small pang of guilt for that, and the rest of his behavior, but he was too angry to back down now.

"Do you know why I never go to church?" he said. He could see her trying to brace herself for his words. "It's because of the religious drivel that comes out of church leaders' mouths-"

"Aiden-" his father tried to stop him but he was on a roll.

"—Christians are some of the most prejudiced, hateful, homophobic, bigoted idiots-"

"Stop it, Aiden!" Jane interrupted, her tone uncompromising.

He stopped. Her voice was the only one that could have ceased his onslaught and she stopped it dead in its tracks.

Jane spoke again. "You may not have liked what the pastor had to say but that gives you no right to generalize an entire religion and the people who follow it. In doing so, you are just as prejudiced and bigoted as you accuse them of being."

Aiden felt an unspeakable shame as the truth of her words hit home.

"I'm not religious myself," she continued. "But I wasn't offended by what he had to say. Like your dad said, he had some pretty good points. And even if he didn't, that gives you no right to *attack* Alexa on what is supposed to be her big day."

He closed his eyes and felt his anger taper off. In its place, rose the strong thread of guilt that threatened to strangle him. He took one look at his little sister's face and felt horrible. There were tears shining in her hazel eyes and the hurt was written all over her face. He realized then that in his rant about Christians, he not only insulted her religion, he'd insulted her personally - her identity, everything she stood for. He'd wounded her very deeply.

He didn't know what to say. Though he regretted saying what he did, he was still pissed about the sermon. "Well, since I've messed up the morning-"

His parents immediately protested but he ignored them.

"I'm going to take a walk and clear my head. Sorry I ruined everything."

Jane watched him walk away and almost rolled her eyes. She knew it wasn't that serious but he was being melodramatic and his parents weren't exactly helping by feeding into it. She looked at Alexa, whose tears had since fallen.

"You okay?"

Alexa nodded tremulously and more tears spilled over. Jane was about to hug her when suddenly Ava's arms wrapped around her daughter's slender frame. "Don't mind him," her mother encouraged her. "He'll come around."

Jane agreed that he would but she also knew his words had cut deep - whether they made up or not, Alexa would always remember his opinion of her religion and people like her. She listened as Alexa's parents convinced her to let them treat her to lunch. They turned, about to invite Jane when she shook her head and pointed at the barely-visible Aiden.

"I'm going to talk to him."

They nodded, thanked her for coming, and took their daughter towards the waiting car.

As Jane jogged towards Aiden's retreating back, her phone buzzed in her pocket.

"Hello?" she panted.

"Jane, this is Robert." Dr. Geissner? He never called her on the weekends. "I hope I'm not disturbing you. I just wanted to ask you to meet with me directly after your first class tomorrow. It's important."

Jane immediately felt a sense of worry creep into her chest. She tried to ask over the phone what it was about but he wouldn't give her any hints. They settled on an exact time to meet before she hung up. It could be good news or bad news but Jane was guessing it was the latter. Shoving her concerns aside, she focused on the problem immediately before her. She jogged a few more yards, and finally caught up to him.

He slowed down his stride but didn't turn to face her, keeping his eyes straight ahead. She circled in front of him and forced him to stop. When he finally met her eyes, he was relieved to see confusion, not anger, in them.

"What was that?" she asked.

He sighed and looked away. "I don't know."

"Why did you get so mad at her?"

"I'm not mad at her. I was mad about-"

"The sermon," she said.

"Yes, the sermon."

"But *why?*"

Why? he thought. *Why aren't you mad? Don't you feel a sliver of what I feel right now?*

"What did you think of it?" he asked instead.

She shrugged. "It made sense. I've never had someone break it down to me like that but when I look at my own life, yeah, it made sense."

"So every relationship you've ever had, *including ours*, has been a 'consumer relationship'?"

She opened her mouth to reply when he followed up with, "Is this why you pull back from me whenever we have sex?"

She blinked in surprise. He watched her struggle to answer and it dawned on him that she really didn't know why she behaved the way she did in bed. It worried him but comforted him at the same time. He closed the space between them and cupped her cheeks in his hands.

"I just want us to be okay," he whispered, his forehead touching hers.

She reached up and held his back. "We will be," she replied.

We have to be, she thought.

CHAPTER TWENTY-ONE

"I'm sorry to say I have bad news."

Jane typically liked Dr. Geissner for his forthrightness but on this day, she wished he'd aim for more tact in his delivery. A feeling of dread washed over her and she tried to brace herself for his next words.

There was nothing for her to hold on to.

"President Schneider's policy has been approved by the board of trustees. In accordance with the new policy, the previous tenure track and all professors on it have been reset. Those who were not chosen for tenure will no longer occupy positions as full-time members of faculty after this December. I regret to tell you that you were not chosen for tenure."

No shit, Sherlock. What twenty-four-year-old receives tenure? And without a PhD? It was unheard of.

Geissner continued, "Come this December, we will have to let you go as a full-time member of faculty. You'll be invited to interview for a position as an adjunct professor for the spring until the new full-time faculty policy can be initiated."

Meaning starting over on their new, ageist tenure-track. Like hell she would. Despite the bad signs, premonitions, and warnings about the negative change, Jane could still feel the waves of shock and disappointment try to consume her and pull her under their paralyzing current. She'd foolishly held out hope that the policy wouldn't pass or some amendment would occur that would allow her to keep her position. Despair tried to pull her under but she resisted it. She needed to know the full scope of her firing so she could start to make plans. She willed her emotions to suspend themselves until she was alone.

Ignoring Geissner's sympathetic look, she simply asked, "Is there a severance?"

He looked surprised at her lack of reaction. If only he knew what she was actually feeling and thinking inside.

"Yes," he said. "Staring January 1st, you'll have three months of severance pay and the full benefits of your insurance."

"Including surgery?" she asked. He frowned at the question and she immediately regretted asking it.

"It will be the exact same type of insurance you currently have as an employed professor, until it runs out in April."

She nodded, her mind so far away that she nearly missed his next words.

"I really am sorry about this, Jane. You were one of our finest professors on staff. I truly didn't think President Schneider's proposal would gain such ground. It has cost us an extraordinary asset in you."

She nodded, numbly thanking him. She couldn't remember if she shook his hand or not as she made her way out of the office. All of the shock she'd forced to stay at bay consumed her as she blindly took the subway home. She was grateful that she didn't have any other classes or appointments that day. He probably asked for her to meet him at that time intentionally, so she would have the space to process it all without further obligations.

The only problem was, she wasn't processing it.

Alexa opened the door and immediately blinked in surprise. Aiden felt another pang of guilt at the thought that she was surprised to see him. She wordlessly stepped back and allowed him in. Before she could speak, he said what was on his mind.

"I'm sorry."

She looked at him silently and all he could see was how deeply he'd hurt her. Her hazel eyes grew teary and her delicate little chin began to quiver.

"I've never blown up at you like that and I promise you I never will again. It wasn't your fault the pastor said what he did and I was an idiot for accusing you of knowing what he would say ahead of time. I was just upset and it was easier for me to lash out at you in the moment. Lex, I'm so sorr-"

He didn't get to finish his sentence because his sister crossed the room and quickly enveloped him in her thin arms. He stooped down to receive her hug and held her tightly against his chest.

"I love you," he whispered in her ear.

"I love you, too." she whispered back, her voice still shaky. She pulled back and met his eyes. "Apology accepted. I know you were just upset."

They both shook off the tears and headed into the kitchen. Aiden took a seat at the bar while Alexa pulled out some goods to make a smoothie. He watched her silently for a few moments before finally breaking the ice.

"Do you believe everything he said that morning?"

She looked at him cautiously, as though gauging to see how he would react to her answer. He hated that she was wary of talking to him but willed himself to be quiet and wear an open expression. It assured her that he really wouldn't snap anymore.

She slowly nodded. "I do."

"Can I ask you why?"

She loaded the banana, spinach, and strawberries into the Magic Bullet. "Why what?"

"Why do you believe in abstinence before marriage? Not that I'm complaining, mind you."

She smiled at his big brother stance. She poured some orange juice into the container and met his eyes.

"I believe that sex isn't just an act. It's a sacred union that bonds two humans together. Physically and spiritually. When a man and woman choose to engage in it before taking vows, I believe it's a misuse of the gift God has given them."

"So in your opinion, sex is a gift from God exclusively for married couples because..."

"Because when a man and woman have made the commitment to marry, it is for life and sex is a privilege that allows them to reconnect on a regular basis in good times and bad. It's like the super glue that keeps them together when life gets tough - or even when it doesn't. It's powerful and we treat it too cavalierly now days. At least, that's *my* opinion."

Aiden thought of the numerous women he'd been intimate with. He realized with a sinking feeling that he couldn't even recall some of their faces and yet he'd shared his body with them in the most intimate way a person could. He would never say it to her, but he could resonate just a little bit with what she was saying.

"What about committed couples who don't marry?" he asked. "Why is it a sin if they've made a commitment to each other?"

She shrugged. "There's a difference between a commitment and a vow. It's like comparing a simple handshake to a signed affidavit. When you make a deal at your firm, do you ever just accept someone's word?"

"Of course not," he replied.

"Then why would you do it when committing your life to someone?" She paused, looking around. "I'm struggling to describe it to you but a vow, made under God, is more solemn and sincere than any emotion-driven commitment one could make. People commit to being together all the time and break up when things get rough."

"AKA divorce," Aiden pointed out.

"True," she replied. "Something that God abhors."

She sighed. "People today are too cavalier about sex and too cavalier about commitments. They haven't the faintest idea what marriage means because it's marriage without God."

"What does he have to do with marriage?" Aiden asked, genuinely trying to understand.

"Everything." Alexa replied. "He created marriage. He designed it. The book of Genesis literally opens with the world's first wedding - between Adam and Eve. God was the officiate. If he's truly at the head of any marriage and both people hold themselves accountable to *Him* as well as each other, they cannot fail."

She spoke with such conviction in her tone, such assurance in her eyes, that Aiden couldn't help but feel a surge of hope well inside his heart. Could she be right? Was God somehow the answer or key to a successful relationship? He'd always thought of it as a game of luck. His parents were lucky to stay married, his Uncle Jake and Aunt Celia weren't.

"Mom and Dad have a great marriage," he said quietly. "And they don't believe, Lex."

She nodded. "Mom and Dad are two extraordinarily selfless people. They practice the virtues of the Bible without even knowing it."

She has an answer for everything, he realized. She watched him as he chewed over their discussion. Finally, she asked, "Does this have anything to do with Jane?"

"Of course it does."

She waited for him to elaborate. He felt a blush rise to his cheeks.

"Uh-uh, don't get all bashful on me now, Aiden. Why are you all of a sudden curious about *my* beliefs regarding sex?"

He met her eyes and could find no judgment in them. He chose his words carefully and spoke. "Jane…shuts down whenever we…you know." His face reddened. He couldn't believe he was sharing this with his *sister*. But her eyes were kind so he continued. "She's not all the way there during it and she completely pulls away after."

Alexa nodded her head, like it was no surprise at all.

He frowned at her. "What?"

"You really don't get it?" she asked, an eyebrow raised.

"No, enlighten me, will you?" he answered sarcastically. She ignored it.

"I hate to break it to you, but you are now like every other guy she's been with."

The words smacked him across the face.

Alexa continued. "You're her first serious relationship, right? Which means every guy she's been with before basically used her body. It was nothing. Meaningless. She meets you and the minute you do it, you're like everybody else. You no longer stand out. Maybe if you were married, she could reason that you were different because you're her husband. But she can't say that. She has no idea if you'll stick around for much longer or if you'll run off like every other guy. Maybe that's why she didn't get angry during the sermon. She listened, Aiden."

Alexa turned on the blender and finally made her drink.

As the machine whirred and hummed, the thoughts and feelings that rose within him were too numerous to sort out at once. Alexa turned off the blender and took a sip of her drink. Before Aiden could even organize his thoughts, much less voice them, the front door opened and in walked Jane.

"Hey, girl." Alexa greeted. "How was school?"

Aiden looked at Jane and frowned. She was wearing a strange expression; shell-shocked at something that had happened.

"You okay?" he asked her.

She looked between the two of them, still dazed.

"I lost my job," she said quietly. The calmness in her voice juxtaposed the worry in her eyes.

"What?" Alexa exclaimed.

Aiden's heart sank. He got up from his stool and pulled her into his arms, noting how wooden and stiff she felt. Jane could barely register his arms around her. She inhaled his fresh mountaineer scent and it comforted her in some small way. The minute he pulled away, Alexa pulled her into her lithe but strong arms as well.

"Don't worry about rent," she said. "You're family."

Jane shook her head, for the first time registering things clearly. "I pay my own way."

Something about those words snapped her out of her trance-like state. Annoyed that she'd allowed herself to go into it in the first place, Jane resolved herself to move forward and take the next step. And the next step was finding a new job.

Aiden watched in disbelief as she walked around him and his sister, perched herself on the kitchen barstool and pulled out her laptop from her satchel. She fired up her computer and the minute the Internet became available, opened the pages of several job search engines.

"You're looking for a job *now*?" Alexa asked incredulously.

Jane looked at them and shrugged. "Well, it's not going to fly itself to me, is it? The sooner I start applying to places, the better."

Alexa shot Aiden a disbelieving look. He frowned at Jane in concern while she typed away at her laptop, ignoring the two of them and focusing on the task at hand.

She felt his large hand touch her shoulder. "Can we talk for a minute?"

She frowned at him but he was already walking up the stairs to her room. She followed him and entered the room.

"What is it?" she asked once they had privacy.

"Why are you doing this right now?" he asked.

She rolled her eyes. "*That's* what you've summoned me for?"

He bristled at her condescending tone. "Jane, I'm not one of your students."

"And I won't have any students much longer, Aiden. Not unless I find another job and fast."

"What is the rush?"

She looked at him as if he'd grown horns on his head. "Are you serious?"

It suddenly occurred to her that he was. For her, finding a new job was a matter of survival - life and death. No job equaled no money and no money equaled poverty. Poverty led to abuse, despair, the kind of life she'd clawed her way out of. There was no way *in hell* she was about to return to it.

He saw the fear flicker in her eyes but he didn't understand it at first.

What is she so afraid of? he wondered. Suddenly, he remembered her words at the park…at the reception…

"…I look forward to the day when I'm not always worrying about money or how I'm going to afford something."

It was like a light bulb went off and he understood; and in his understanding, he felt a hint of shame for not getting it sooner. For not remembering. To him, losing a job didn't matter. He was a Masterson. He came from one of the richest families in New York society. That family would be there to catch him - if not the money he'd already saved and accrued from a very lucrative career. For her, she had no such safety net - never did. He couldn't imagine what it was like to be responsible for her own needs and provision from the time she'd turned eighteen. She was twenty-four-years-old and though beautiful, he could see the traces of stress in her brown eyes. Her eyes, in fact, were much older than the rest of her body. She'd grown up far too soon.

She sighed and echoed what he thought. "You wouldn't get it. I don't have a family to turn to. I paid off my loans and barely have enough saved for six months. I *need* to find a new job and stat. I don't have anything to fall back on."

"Oh, sweetheart." He shook his head and cupped her cheek. "You're wrong," he whispered intently. "*So* wrong. You have us now. You have *me*."

They held each other's gaze for several taut seconds. He leaned down and captured her mouth. Once again, she inhaled the heady scent of his cologne and surrendered to the feel of his full soft lips. He broke the kiss and pulled her fully into his arms. His hands rubbed her back and she felt safe in the comfort of his warmth. For just a second, she allowed herself to believe; believe just briefly that she could turn to Aiden and his family for help. She wanted to check that heavy cloak of constant independence at the door and *lean* on somebody for a change.

He's just a boyfriend a voice reminded her. She then remembered: she didn't know how long they would last. She didn't know how long she could count on him. There was no permanence - in her job or her relationship. So she closed her eyes and pretended to accept what he offered. But inside, the burden was still on her shoulders.

"How's the search going?" Alexa asked. She walked in to find Jane perched on her favorite place in the apartment: the kitchen barstool. Come to think of it, it was everyone's favorite area of the apartment. Jane smiled at Alexa, absentmindedly.

She shrugged. "Okay, I guess."

Ten days had passed since Jane was made aware of her position's upcoming termination. She'd worked on applications around the clock. If she wasn't lecturing or fulfilling the responsibilities of her transient job, she was busy searching for its replacement. So far, she'd landed two calls of interest, one phone interview that didn't pan out, and thirty rejections. Alexa once asked how many applications she was sending out. Jane had cryptically answered "until I get a job." Her friend would have toppled over if she admitted to applying to more than ninety positions in such a short amount of time. She would have applied to more - if it wasn't for the necessity of sleep. But sleeping didn't come easily, not when the timer on her livelihood was ticking.

She was going to be jobless by the end of the year and she had no idea if she would get into any of the schools she applied to. She couldn't afford to be complacent.

Alexa reached into the fridge and grabbed a pear. She rinsed it and chomped into it, speaking around her bites.

"You know, several students submitted their petition to the accreditation board for review. They're pissed that you're the only one leaving. They're pissed that you're leaving at all."

Jane nodded, already aware of her students' and co-workers' support. When the policy and consequences of it became campus-wide knowledge, almost all of her students expressed their support for her, to her *and* to Dr. Geissner. Several carried their complaints all the way to the dean of students and some vowed to pester President Schneider herself if the decision wasn't reversed. Jane knew it was a long shot. She was one of only two professors leaving their full time station - and she was the only one under thirty departing. Maybe if she had her PhD, she'd have a leg to stand on but she didn't think she did. It was a lightly-veiled ageist change that she could probably sue over and get a decent settlement. But she also knew better than to become the lawsuit-happy professor no one wanted to hire.

The gesture of her UNY compatriots was sweet and touching but it was time to move on.

"Have you registered for classes yet?" she asked, eager to change the subject.

Alexa shook her head. "Not for another week. I already know I want some sail-through classes. My senior thesis will take up enough of my time. I can't wait to be done."

Jane was sure she couldn't - especially if she had a full-year European tour awaiting her.

"You leave for France when?"

"Beginning of July. I should be back in time to start grad school, assuming I get in."

Jane nodded, reminded once more of her constant state of transition. Even if she managed to find a new job, relatively close to her apartment, she didn't know if she would be able to stay in the apartment after Alexa left.

What is going on? she thought, suddenly disturbed. There were so many changes and uncertainties in her life, it was chafing at her very psyche. Why couldn't things just stabilize? Why couldn't life just get normal?

Why can't it get good? *For longer than a few moments or weeks?*

Her thoughts shifted to Aiden and how she felt around him when she did allow him around. She would be the first to admit that she was keeping him at bay as she searched for a new source of income. There was an unspoken tension developing between them as he tried to assure her of his willingness to support her and she tried to maintain her financial and emotional independence. She refused to become a beneficiary of his charity.

But could it be called charity?

When a man offered to support his girlfriend in her time of need, wasn't he just a man looking out for his woman? Jane couldn't pinpoint exactly what was happening between them now but she could say without a doubt things hadn't been the same since their trip to Martha's Vineyard. Nothing was making sense to her, despite her best efforts to make it so. She felt like she was in the middle of the ocean without a current or tide to carry her to land.

I can't do this much longer, she thought.

She needed land to appear and soon.

CHAPTER TWENTY-TWO

"Hey, Mom." Aiden greeted his mother with a peck on the cheek. He sat opposite her at the trendy little restaurant two blocks from her Upper East Side apartment.

"Hi, sweetie. How was work?"

He shrugged and gave a noncommittal grunt. Work was the last thing on his mind and the primary irritant of his life. What was once something he enjoyed to the point of distraction was now a distraction in and of itself. He shifted in his seat and avoided his mother's probing gaze. Growing up, she could always tell if he was upset or bothered in the slightest. Sometimes it was comforting, other times invasive.

He finally met her eyes and shrugged again. "What's up?"

She smiled at his use of the youthful phrase. "Not much. How's Jane doing?"

He groaned inwardly. His mother wanted to draw out the conversation and, as much as he loved her, he wanted to get to the point. He also didn't want to discuss the specifics of Jane's situation. Not only did it feel like talking about her behind her back - something he would never do again - it also reminded him of the change he'd witnessed in her. He was planning on seeing her later that night and would be lucky to get her full attention. Ever since receiving her notice, she'd been laser focused on finding a new job. Anything else, including his company, was a distraction to that cause.

Things had gotten better between them but he didn't know if it was because she truly forgave him for betraying her trust earlier or if it was because she was too distracted with her job situation to hold it against him any longer. He'd sensed a shift in her demeanor after the church service they'd gone to. She seemed more reflective about many things but he didn't know if that was a good sign for their relationship or not. He sighed. He never had to play the guessing game so often in his life. He was in love with a walking enigma and wondered if she'd ever fully make herself known. Was the pastor right? Would he have to get a wedding ring in order for that to happen? He met his mother's perceptive blue eyes and tried to veil his thoughts.

"She's okay," he answered vaguely. "You sounded like you had something to tell me earlier."

She rolled her eyes at his obvious desire to jump to the chase. But this time, she appeased him. She reached into her large designer tote and pulled out a manila folder. He frowned at the unknown documents that laid inside.

"What is it?" he asked.

"I don't know," she said. "Well, not exactly. Your Uncle Titus did more digging after we left and was able to track down Jane's records."

"Records?"

"Her background, social worker notes, therapy evaluations, and anything else that paints the picture of her life before she left the system."

"How is that possible? Or legal? Isn't all that information protected?"

His mother nodded. "It is. Which is why it was nearly impossible to track her down when your father and I tried to find her as a minor. A normal P.I. couldn't get this amount of info - only someone who works in the system."

Meaning his uncle.

A spike of curiosity struck Aiden as he stared at the folder. It held a world of information, clarity, and the keys to understanding the woman who had come to mean everything to him. His fingers were itching to open the file and read. But he immediately fought the urge.

"No," he quickly said before he lost his nerve. His mother looked at him questioningly.

"Are you sure?"

He nodded. "I won't ask you to read it or not-"

"I won't without you."

He nodded again. "Good. I can't do it, Mom. I can't betray her trust again."

He met his mother's gaze unwaveringly this time and she nodded her understanding. Her hands folded over the file again, tucking it back into her tote and away from their curious eyes.

"Hello?"

"Hi, is this Professor Jane Daugherty?" a man asked on the other line.

Jane sat up on the couch and said, "Yes, this is she."

"Hi Jane, this is Dr. Noah Patson with Cornell University."

Jane nearly gasped into the phone. She immediately bolted up off of the couch and raced to find a pen and paper. She could see Alexa frowning at her behavior from her peripheral vision but she couldn't explain it just then.

Noah continued, "I'm calling because we received your resume for a place within our English department. I was quite impressed with your credentials - and at such a young age. I would like to arrange a time to meet with you for an interview."

By the time Jane hung up the phone, she was grinning from ear to ear.

"What?" Alexa asked, bouncing on her feet.

"An interview. With Cornell!"

"Ahh!!" Alexa squealed, catapulting herself into Jane's arms. "I *told* you it would work out! When do you see them?"

"See who?" a deep baritone voice asked. The girls turned in time to see Aiden walk through the unlocked door.

"Jane has an interview!" Alexa announced happily.

He broke out into a wide smile and pulled Jane into a hug. "That's awesome! With who?"

"Cornell!" Alexa blurted.

Jane turned to her roommate, her arms still around Aiden. "Can I *please* answer some of the questions?"

Alexa rolled her eyes and ignored her. "When is the interview?" she asked.

"Tomorrow. He seemed really eager to see me." She could hardly believe it. Applying had been a shot in the dark, especially considering the fact that they'd rejected her application the first time she tried to teach two years ago. She was far too inexperienced and young back then. Now, it sounded like she had a chance.

Aiden tightened his arms around her waist and kissed her forehead. For the first time in a while, Jane felt hopeful. Like it could all be okay and things could really turn around - not only in her career but also her relationship. She felt her boyfriend pull back slightly and looked up to meet his bright gold eyes.

"I guess you'll want to prepare for the interview?" he asked, though she could see the slight disappointment on his handsome face.

She nodded. "I'm sorry. It came out of nowhere and-"

He shook his head. "Don't apologize. You got something we've all been crossing our fingers for."

"Praying for!" Alexa called from upstairs.

He rolled his eyes and pulled her towards the couch. "Mind if I sit with you a little before you start prepping?"

She smiled at him. "Of course not. I missed you today."

He was surprised by her admission and it showed on his face. She turned away from his probing gaze and sat beside him. He closed his eyes and rolled his neck from side to side.

She frowned. "Rough day?"

"You could say that."

His eyes snapped open when, through his shirt, he felt her slender fingers roll and knead into the muscles of his shoulders. Her thumbs rubbed along the back of his neck and he closed his eyes again, relaxing into the surprisingly strong strokes of her soft hands.

"Ah...thank you," he said with a smile of absolute ecstasy. She continued for several minutes before finally planting a kiss on his uplifted forehead. His eyes flickered open and he fixed her with a look of sheer desire. They stood still for a couple moments, transfixed in each other's gaze before Jane finally broke the connection and circled the couch to sit back down beside him.

"You want to continue working full time, right?" he asked.

She nodded, wondering where this was going.

"What about your PhD?"

She smiled. "If I get into Columbia, I can work on it while working full time."

"You're sure you're up for that?"

She frowned at the doubt in his voice. "I've never had it any other way," she said sharper than she had intended.

"Sorry," he immediately said. "I didn't mean to question your ability or work ethic. I just don't want you to get overwhelmed."

"I can handle it."

He nodded. "Do you want to live here after Lexi leaves for Europe?"

She sighed. "I don't know. I don't even know where I'll be going to school or if I'll have a job in the city anymore."

"Do you-"

"What's with the twenty-one questions, Aiden? I feel like you're interrogating me."

He paused at her outburst and held her dark brown eyes.

"I want to know where I fit."

Her frown deepened. "What do you mean?"

"I want to know where I fit. I know you. You plan everything - or at least try to. If you have a ten year plan in your mind, am I on it?"

"Do you want to be?"

This time, he frowned. "What's that supposed to mean?"

"I mean, you're pushing me to declare something for our future together. Some sort of next step. I don't see you taking those steps."

Aiden felt the heat rush to his face at her blunt words. She was right - he wasn't taking the lead. He was acting like a girlfriend waiting for an engagement ring when he was the one supposed to proffer it.

"You told me you wanted to take it slow," he reminded her.

"I also told you 'no' the first time you asked me out. That didn't stop you then."

He opened his mouth to speak again but she held up a hand. "Can we just...can we not talk about this right now? Even if one of us wanted to take a next step, my life is a shaky mess right now and nothing is certain."

As in, stop pushing her for more. That's what Aiden got out of her words and it filled him with a frustration that made him want to pull his hair out. Why couldn't they just communicate? Say what was truly on their hearts and stop delaying the conversation until later? Aiden wanted to be patient with her. He wanted to be back in her good graces. But he was beginning to wonder how long he would have to prove himself. How long would it have to be about *her* needs and *her* wants and *her* doubts? Didn't she realize that she was putting them *both* on pause by keeping things stagnant? Did she even care how *he* felt about the whole thing?

Is she even worth it? The thought struck him unexpectedly like a fist to his jaw. He couldn't believe he just thought such a thing. His eyes raked over her slender form, cocooned into the corner of the couch. She smiled at him and his heart doubled over. She was so smart. Hard working. Funny. And beautiful. So beautiful, he ached to touch her again.

They were going through a rough patch - made rough by his stupidity, her issues at work, and their inability to communicate clearly with one another.

We'll get through this, he coached himself. They would. They just had to weather the storm and he needed to keep calm. He returned her smile and leaned in to give her a slow kiss. When she moaned against his lips, he felt sure once more.

She was worth it. Completely worth it to him.

Dr. Noah Patson leaned back in his chair and smiled at Jane. She smiled back, surprised at how relaxed he'd made her feel. He was young - a lot younger than Geissner, in his mid-thirties, and had a charming personality to match his bright green eyes and close-cut brown hair. He wasn't gorgeous, like Aiden, but attractive in a "confident nerd" sense. She felt much more comfortable calling him by his first name than she had Dr. Geissner.

The interview was over. It had gone as smoothly as she could hope for and she was surprised to learn that Dr. Geissner had given Paston a glowing recommendation on her behalf.

"I'm gonna be honest with you," Noah said. "I was ready to offer you the job before you walked in the door but…"

Jane's heart began to race at his words. She felt beads of sweat break out in her palms.

"I was ready to offer you a job before you walked in but…"

You're too young.

You've only taught two types of classes.

We can only take you on as an adjunct.

"The interview is a formality we have to do under school policy." He stood up and stretched his hand. "Congratulations. You passed with flying colors."

Jane couldn't remember what she said as she shook his hand. The relief that flooded her brain closely followed by the elation of getting the job was too much to handle. All she could make out was that she had a week to decide and give her final answer.

As she walked out of the building and headed to the closest subway, she dialed the first number that came to mind. "Aiden!" she exclaimed. "I got the job!"

She laughed and pulled the phone back from her ear, Aiden's whoops of jubilation carrying over the noise of the busy street. She felt like squealing herself. For the first time in weeks, she finally had some control in her life.

It felt different. Leaving her office at UNY, knowing she had another one waiting for her at Cornell. Jane hadn't told anyone about her offer at the prestigious university yet. The only people who knew were the Mastersons. She spent the day on an invisible buzz and smiled frequently at the secret she refused to share with what would be her former academic family. The more she taught, the more she graded, the longer she walked down the marble hallways of the school she was once ready to commit her adult life to, the more Jane realized she was ready to say goodbye.

She would miss the school, her students, her colleagues, even her bewildered supervisor. But she would not miss its new president or the board that was behind dismissing her so casually. The UNY they were leading was not the UNY she'd signed up for nor the UNY wanted to be a part of.

As Jane left Burney West, knowing in a few short weeks, she would leave for the last time, she felt a sense of peace and settling at the departure. It didn't happen the way she'd wanted it to but she was no longer upset about leaving. She left the gate of the campus and started walking to the metro when her phone rang.

"Hello?"

"Hello, Daaahling!" Alexa's voice masqueraded as the funny Pixar character, Edna Mode. Jane burst out laughing at the unexpected greeting. One of the things she loved about Alexa was her spontaneity.

"Dear Lord, what did they drop in *your* kool aid?"

"Hey!" her friend replied in mock offense. "I assure you I haven't been drugged *yet*. I just wanted to make sure you'll be back in time for dinner."

Ava and Michael had insisted on throwing a celebratory dinner at her place in honor of her landing the job.

"Yeah, I'm on my way now. But wouldn't it make more sense to have a dinner celebrating the job I *choose*?"

"You're not going to say yes to them?" Alexa asked.

Jane sighed. It's not that she planned on saying no - she just hadn't gotten back to Noah yet. It was a big decision. She knew she couldn't bounce around to too many universities before committing to tenure with one - and Noah had made it clear that she would be on the immediate tenure track if she joined them, possibly right after earning her PhD.

Do you hear yourself? she suddenly thought. She was questioning if a tenured position at Cornell University was a good move for her professorial career; if joining the faculty of an Ivy League institution at twenty-four-years-old would help her. She realized what a complete idiot she was being.

"I should have said yes the minute he offered it," she said, more to herself than Alexa.

"I would agree," Alexa said quietly.

"Okay, I got to go. I'm going to call him now."

"Great, then we'll *really* have something to celebrate! Talk to you later. Love you!"

"Love you, too." Jane replied, happy that it practically fell out of her mouth without hesitation. She wondered if she would ever say the same to Aiden. Shaking her head of the thought, she found Noah's number and dialed.

"Hello?"

"Hi, Noah, this is Jane Daugherty."

"Jane!" his voice brightened several notches. "How are you?"

"I'm good, thank you. I'm great actually, after your offer."

Her mouth was poised to say she accepted when he laughed over the line. "Absolutely. I know Michael saw it as a personal favor to take you on, but I really think our university will be lucky to have you."

Jane's heart stopped. "What?"

There was a silence on the other end. Clearly he'd made a slip.

"Hello?" Jane asked.

"I…I'm sorry, Jane. I wasn't supposed to-"

"Michael? Michael Masterson? Is he who you're referring to?"

She heard him sigh on the other line. "You really are a great candidate for this school. Cornell used to have the ageist policies UNY seems to be adopting but things have changed since I came on board three years ago. Michael knew that as well and thought this might be a good fit for you."

"Why did you agree to help him?"

He hesitated before saying, "Michael Masterson is an alumnus and huge patron of the university. He gave a particularly generous donation to the English Department four years ago and the proceeds are *still* benefiting our students."

She nodded, though she knew he couldn't see her.

"So, he asked you to consider my resume, give me an interview, and make it seem like I had earned the job."

"You *did* earn the job," he corrected her. "I know this isn't exactly the way you might have liked it to happen but people land positions through their connections all the time. That doesn't make you less qualified in any, way, shape or form. And despite this bit of news, I really hope you'll join our team."

Jane felt the prickle of hot tears well behind her eyes. Just seconds ago, she was about to commit to the institution. Now, despite its prestige and value and income, she wanted nothing to do with it. Not when she hadn't earned it.

"I appreciate the offer," she said, swallowing the lump in her throat. "But I'm afraid I'll have to decline."

She hung up and made her way home, a hollowness growing with every step.

CHAPTER TWENTY-THREE

"Hey! There she is - the new Cornell English professor!" Aiden's voice hit her ears before her eyes processed the scene in front of her. The whole clan stood around the kitchen island, a box in the middle of the counter.

Ava and Alexa held up the box and happily yelled, "Surprise!"

Inside, was a beautiful Cornell University sweatshirt, with the well-known Carnelian red and white school colors. Dinner was on the table and everything was set to celebrate her career victory. Two emotions competed for Jane's allegiance: regret and disappointment. Regret that the reason for the celebration was no longer in effect. Disappointment in Michael Masterson for his deception. Next to Alexa, he was the one member of the Masterson family Jane had grown to trust unquestioningly. And yet, he had gone behind her back and manipulated something that meant so much to her. Aiden, though hurtful in his lack of discretion, had never made calls or arranged her interviews. He never meddled in her career, though he'd offered to help. The one thing she'd had complete control over and unwavering success in, Michael had chosen to sully.

She didn't even want to look him in the eye. But she willed herself to. Aiden was the first to notice something was wrong. He looked at Jane and felt a sense of trepidation at her blank, cold stare. He realized that she wasn't looking at him or his mother and sister but her focus was solely on his father.

Jane watched as Michael's warm gray-blue eyes darkened in concern. He frowned at her questioningly before realization dawned on him. Ava and Alexa quieted down, finally registering the tension.

"How big?" she asked quietly.

"Jane-" Michael started.

"How big was the donation that bought me the job? It must have been huge if after four years, the English Department is still willing to take your staff recommendations."

Aiden's heart dropped. He looked at his father.

"Dad, is this true?" When his father closed his eyes and broke contact with Jane's, he knew it was.

"Dad, how could you?" Alexa asked, her voice breaking.

Ava was simply speechless.

Michael opened his eyes and met Jane's disappointed look again. He shook his head, his regret clearly visible on his face. "Jane, I'm sorry. I was only trying to help."

I was only trying to help. It was the same thing Ava had said when she pulled the stunt that gave the whole Masterson family private information about her.

She nodded stiffly, a cold feeling overtaking her bones. She weighed her options. She could rail into him and tell him everything she was wrestling with. That while she understood that he meant well, his actions could have cost her, her academic integrity; she wished he would have at least asked her before calling in a favor; she wasn't angry at him so much as hurt and embarrassed; and now she was enormously disappointed about a counterfeit offer that she couldn't take Or she could remain silent and think things through before she said something she regretted. Because in that moment, she really didn't have the words to communicate her feelings - not when her emotions were so jumbled.

It was better not to engage. She reached into her satchel and grabbed her wallet and keys.

"You may want to call Noah Patson and smooth things over. I turned the position down when I realized it was bought. Maybe he'll give you a refund for inadequate service."

"Jane," Alexa called.

"I'm going for a walk," she said over her shoulder, exiting the apartment like the place was on fire.

Jane powered down the stairwell, too frenetic to wait for the elevator. The cold air was a welcome relief from the choking heat of that apartment. She had no plans for where she would go but she hoped a walk would clear her head.

That got shot to hell the minute she heard Aiden call out behind her. "Jane!"

She turned and saw him running out of the lobby. He looked upset, but she couldn't imagine why. He approached her and waited for her to speak.

"Did you know?" she asked him.

"Of course not. I had no idea." She felt a surge of relief fill her...until he said, "But even if I did, I wouldn't have told you."

"*What?*" she asked incredulously.

"It's a job," he said. "This is the answer to what you've been stressing about for weeks and you decide to throw it away because it came in a package you weren't expecting?" He looked at her incredulously, like she was unreasonable. "Do you know how many professors would kill to work at an Ivy League institution?"

His words pierced her tender spot and drew her ire. "I *earn* my place in the world, Aiden. Everything I've gotten in life, I've worked my ass off for. My career will not be handed to me on a golden spoon by a privileged business magnate looking to use me as his latest charity case."

"Don't you *dare* say that about my father!" he roared at her. He looked so livid she almost took a step back but she held her ground. She would never allow a man to intimidate her again.

Ever.

"Don't talk to me like that," she said.

He looked contrite - but only slightly. "I'm sorry. But my father is not the man you just painted him as, regardless of his actions in this matter."

She nodded. "I'm sorry I characterized him like that," she acknowledged. "But I'm not sorry for the general idea. My career is *my* career. My livelihood is *my* livelihood. I understand that he wanted to help but he had *no right* to interfere."

He frowned at her, shaking his head. "He wasn't trying to control you or your career. You act like he was trying to pull strings like a puppet master. He was giving you the chance you deserve. A chance you keep missing out on because people overlook you due to your age. You're allowing your pride to ruin your future and it isn't just affecting your work."

She frowned at that, knowing he was alluding to the issues in their relationship.

"Aiden, I get that he is your dad and I hear everything you're telling me, but how would you feel if you got your broker license because of a few calls Daddy made?"

Aiden's face crumpled in an ugly frown. "Oh, that is so out of line, Jane."

She frowned, surprised by his response. "Is it? I know how hard you worked to get where you are and I know it was from your blood, sweat, and tears - not his!"

He shook his head. "You're not going to win on that argument. Yes, I didn't accept his help to start my career. But you know what? I accepted his money to pay for my education. He paid every single dime to get me through school so that I could focus on my grades without distraction."

"Well, lucky you." she said sarcastically. She didn't like the sound of her voice just then, or the jealousy that radiated from it. But she also didn't like the reminder that Aiden had been raised with a golden spoon in *his* mouth.

No wonder he can't understand.

Her smarmy answer hit the final nail in the coffin for Aiden. He almost felt ashamed for admitting what his father had done for him and that sense of false shame pushed him over the edge. He was sick of it. Sick of fighting her. Sick of examining himself. Sick of fighting for a relationship she seemed so determined to let go of.

"For God's sake, Jane. Grow up!" he exclaimed, exasperated.

"Grow up?" She glared at him. "Why are you attacking me? I didn't lash out at your dad or you. I came out here to get some air and try to calm down-"

"Because you're angry at a really nice gesture my father made."

"You *still* don't get it, do you?" she reacted. "It may not matter to you how I get work but it matters to me. Cronyism may be standard in politics or even finances but in academia, it lacks integrity and I earn my livelihood as a professor."

"But you won't much longer if you keep rejecting the opportunities given to you."

She cringed at the reminder of her precarious work situation. "Is it a crime to want to *earn* my way in the world? I've had to work my own way since I was a kid. I don't expect you to understand that-"

He blinked at that and lifted an eyebrow. "Oh, is that what this is about? The fact that I come from a loving, stable home with two parents who care about me? Are you really trying to make me feel guilty for the childhood I had?"

"You're not hearing me right," she said, panic rising. They'd never had a fight this bad. "You're twisting my words around-"

"No, I think I'm hearing you pretty clearly."

"Why won't you listen to me?" she asked, her frustration broiling over. "I'm sick of miscommunicating with you-"

"Yeah? Well you know what I'm sick of? I'm sick of your martyr bullshit!"

She gasped but he ignored the shocked hurt on her face.

"*Everybody* goes through things, Jane. Some more than others. But you wear your struggles on your sleeve like a fucking flag." She winced at his language. He never cursed at her. "JJ was right: Alexa had some hard knocks but she-"

"Alexa was never raped!" she screeched at him.

Silence.

He stared at her, his breath completely gone as if he'd been sucker punched.

"Wh...what?"

"Alexa was never raped," she repeated quietly.

"What do you mean?" He looked at her with new eyes, realizing that he didn't *really* know the extent of what she'd suffered as a child. He tried to step closer to her.

"Jane-"

She shook her head. She wouldn't elaborate on her past or expose Alexa's current issues to him. Clearly, he wasn't capable of handling anything she had to deal with.

I'm sick of your martyr bullshit! The words burned at her core and pierced her heart. No one had ever said anything so dismissive, so hurtful about her past to her before.

Aiden's anger was gone. The minute she'd said the word "raped," it had vanished. And in its place was a deep, overwhelming sense of shame for the way he'd spoken to her only moments ago.

"Jane-"

He tried to close the distance but she immediately moved out of reach. She turned to the street, raised a hand and hailed a cab.

"Jane, wait." He grabbed her arm but she yanked it violently out of his grasp, opening the door.

"Screw you, Aiden. We're done."

She climbed in the cab without a backward glance and rode off into the night.

Aiden opened the door to the apartment numbly. His parents and sister were still congregated around the island. Their conversation ceased the minute they saw him. Aiden looked at his mother.

"I want to see the files."

"What happened?" Alexa asked. "Where's Jane?"

Aiden ignored her and repeated to his mother, "I want to see the files."

Ava frowned, deeply concerned. "I don't have them on me," she said.

"I don't care. Get them. Please."

The urgency in his eyes and voice made her frown but she didn't say anything else. He watched her make a call to a courier service, then to their apartment, giving one of the staff permission to retrieve the file.

"Do not look inside," she said in no uncertain terms.

"Aiden," Alexa said, *her* voice urgent now. "Where is Jane? What happened?"

"She's not here, all right, Alexa?" he snapped. He strode over to the couch and sunk his head in his hands. He could still see the hurt on her face when he said what he did. He heard Alexa on her phone, trying to call her. They all looked up when they heard a ringing in the apartment. Alexa, phone in hand, walked over to Jane's satchel and pulled out her ringing cell.

She hung up. "Great. Just great."

She turned to her parents and the spoke for several minutes. He had no idea what they were saying. He couldn't concentrate on their words.

Screw you, Aiden. We're done.

People said things in anger all the time. He'd said something atrocious himself and he hadn't meant it - not really. But he knew the minute she said it, that she meant it. Because she hadn't said it in anger - but in pain. She really was done. He really had lost her. It was one of those surreal moments where he would give anything to turn back time. Rewind and stop himself from following her or get a hold of his temper so he didn't explode like he had. He'd lost her. And he had no one to blame but himself.

A knock on the door.

Aiden strode over to the door faster than anyone else could. The courier stood with the file. He didn't even register the guy's face. Just grabbed the file, handed him a twenty dollar bill, and turned back into the apartment with a mumbled thanks. He flipped it open and started to pull out papers.

"What are those?" Alexa asked. "What's in it?"

"Jane's records," their mother said quietly.

Alexa frowned at her and she explained.

"Uncle Titus retrieved them."

"And you're going to look at it behind her back?" she asked incredulously.

"Aiden," his father said. "I know you're upset but are you sure you want to find out like this?"

"Yes," he replied firmly.

"Aiden, I don't think Jane would-"

"Jane isn't here, Alexa," he said, turning his blazing eyes on her. "She just broke up with me and I want to know what's been tearing us apart this entire time."

"What?" she asked. The shock of that news reverberated around the room as Aiden continued reading the contents inside. There were charts and notes, some typed, others handwritten.

"Aiden, what did you say to her?" his mother asked calmly.

He shrugged, his nonchalant demeanor belying the deep ache in his heart. He kept his eyes fixed on the document and spoke, "Only the most hurtful things I could have said to her. I told her she was letting her pride get in the way and that she was acting like a martyr. I told her to grow up and..." he started choking over his words. "And I told her that everybody goes through things."

"Oh, Aiden." Ava said softly.

He could sense his sister dying to say something but to her credit, she kept quiet. He focused on a document labeled "Notes" from what appeared to be a state therapist. It listed Jane's age at the time as 17-years-old. He realized it was a time line the therapist reconstructed based off of what Jane disclosed to her - as well as the information she retrieved from the system. This document told her story in the most condensed way possible:

Female infant: born Jane Doe - unwanted by mother, father unknown. Turned over to social services at 4-years-old after nurse reported apparent malnutrition in the child. Was reportedly denied food frequently enough to disrupt her digestive and immune system. Hospitalized for eight weeks after the removal. Mother arrested and charged with child abuse and neglect. Child placed with maternal grandmother after release.

Age 8: Received excellent care at grandmother's for four years. Removed from the estate when grandmother died.

Age 10: Stayed with aunts and distant relatives for two years before returned to the system.

He cringed at the words. They made her sound like some package that needed to be returned to the store. He realized that was how she'd been treated almost all of her childhood - like an unwanted *thing* to be dealt with. He continued to read.

Age 10: Transferred to the foster home of a Thomas Cane Smith, age 39 of Morris Heights - Bronx. Initially ignored and minimally cared for. Viewed as a nuisance paycheck source.

Age 12: Touching began.

Aiden's heart stopped at those words. "Touching began." What did that mean?

Age 13: Molested on a daily basis and commanded to perform sexual acts including fellatio on Smith, age 42.

Aiden felt a level of bile rise to his throat.

Foster father was brutally violent. Had severe mood swings that depended on the level of drugs he consumed. Often struck the victim as well as other children in the home. Burned the victim with cigarettes for his amusement.

Aiden thought back to the scars throughout her body.

Age 14-16: Repeatedly raped. Went unreported until a new resident informed a social worker in passing what he heard and saw. Teenager questioned, abuse confirmed, evidence found. She was transferred immediately to another home. Smith, age 45, was charged and convicted of four counts of sexual assault of a minor, eight counts of child abuse and neglect. Sentenced to eighteen years in prison. Wife, Jennifer Smith, age 42, was charged with child neglect and failure to report the abuse. Sentenced to six years in prison.

Aiden closed the file, his hands shaking. His stomach roiled at the content of what he read.

"Aiden? Honey?" his mother asked cautiously. He looked at her and heard her gasp at the look in his eyes. "What is it?" she asked. "What did it say?"

He shook his head and slowly handed it to her. He watched her read the same document, her eyes immediately filling with tears. Aiden looked at Alexa. She was watching them with a wary expression, sitting on the stool as if transfixed.

"You have *no idea* what she really protected you from," he said.

Ava passed the file to her husband and like his son and wife before him, he too was shocked by what he read. So shocked, he had to sit down on one of the stools next to his daughter. Ava looked at Alexa.

"Are you going to read it?" she asked.

"I'm scared," Alexa replied. "I have a guess about what it says."

"He never did anything in front of you? He never touched you, right?"

Alexa shook her head adamantly. "She was always there, looking out for me. He liked to hit things…and people. If he was about to hit me, she would do something to distract him or get him mad at her. I told you, she protected me."

Aiden shook his head. "That wasn't the only way she protected you, Alexa."

His sister took a deep breath and snatched the file out of her father's hand. She read it slowly while her mother braced a hand on her slight shoulder. They could see her start to shake all over.

"Oh my God," her voice broke. *"Oh my God."*

Aiden stood. "I have to find her."

He had to apologize. He had to make it right and take back everything he'd said to her. He hadn't known. He'd had no idea what she'd been through - not even the slightest.

I'm sick of your martyr bullshit! That's what he'd said to her and he had to take it back.

Alexa shook her head. "Aiden, don't."

He looked at her sharply. "What do you mean 'don't'?"

She looked at him, her eyes red-rimmed and teary. "She won't listen to you. Wherever she is, we'll be lucky if she listens to any of us." Her hazel eyes lasered in on his. Her next words felt like a sentencing. "You hurt her. You hurt her where she never thought she'd get hurt again. There's no way she's going to give you another chance."

CHANGE

CHAPTER TWENTY-FOUR

Three Weeks Later

Aiden took heavy steps down the hall to his sister's door. Each step felt heavier and heavier as images of him and Jane walking, talking, laughing, and kissing in various parts of the hall haunted him like a ghost. He knew it wasn't possible but he could still smell her perfume - body spray, as she would correct him - in the air, an intoxicating blend of black raspberry and vanilla.

His sister was right.

Jane never returned to the apartment that night. He later learned that she used the money she had on her and reserved a hotel room somewhere else. The next day, she returned with her two week notice. Alexa told him she'd done everything in her power to convince her to stay but they both knew it was useless. When Jane set her mind on something, she kept at it like a rabid dog. She gave Alexa two weeks' notice and moved out in one. With no forwarding address, Alexa only knew she was back in Harlem.

He knocked on the door and seconds later, his sister opened it.

"Hey," she said softly. He could barely stand to look her in the eye. He loved her but she had a way of looking at him - like he was a broken animal limping about. Maybe he was.

He sure felt like it.

He walked in and headed to the living room, choosing an armchair near the fireplace. It was the only furniture on which he hadn't cuddled with her. He wished they weren't having dinner there. His parents were supposed to arrive soon but he already wanted to leave. He looked up and saw Alexa's eyes raking over him.

"You've lost weight," she said.

He didn't say anything.

Another knock on the door. Alexa answered it and their parents came flooding in. His mother looked around for him and immediately crossed the room to greet him. He stood and hugged her.

"Hi, Mom."

He let go but she held on for a few extra seconds, like she was trying to pour as much love into him as she could. She finally let go and he greeted his dad.

"Hi, son." They shook hands and Aiden saw the feeling he'd grown accustomed to seeing in his dad's eyes: guilt.

The dinner was a somber one. His family ate and conversed around him. They tried to ask him questions about work, his running…he barely answered. They were worried about him. He could tell. They thought he couldn't see the looks they gave each other but he saw them. He didn't have it in him to convince them he was okay. He'd never felt so empty, so listless before.

"Aiden," He looked up when his mother took his hand. "How are you?"

It was a stupid question - one they already knew the answer to. But in clinical psychiatry, you weren't supposed to assume how a person was doing. You were supposed to ask - so she did.

He looked at his sister. "How is she doing?"

His mother sighed.

"She seems to be doing okay," Alexa answered. "I invited her to meet up. Hopefully she'll say yes."

"Is she working again?" Ava asked.

Alexa shook her head. "As far as I know, she's still searching. She's also waiting to hear back from the schools she applied to. She didn't tell me much."

Michael nodded. "And she probably won't. Not after what I did."

"Honey…" his wife started.

"No, it's true. If I hadn't pulled those strings, she'd be sitting at the table with us now. I'm so sorry, Aiden."

Aiden sighed. "Once again, there's nothing to apologize to me for."

"But if I hadn't-"

"Jane left because of what *I* said." he said firmly. The table quieted. "Nothing else."

No one had dessert.

As their parents bid them farewell, Alexa touched Aiden's arm.

"Will you stay here a little?" she asked.

He nodded and put his jacket back on the rack. Aiden went to the sofa and sat on his side. He could still see *her* curled up on the other end, her long legs folding into a ball. He almost smiled at the memory. How could someone so tall and statuesque look so tiny and cute? Alexa sat in the spot.

He re-focused his eyes on hers and saw that look again. The caring, nurturing look of someone who wanted to help but had no idea how.

"Aiden."

He looked away. She touched his arm and he looked back at her.

"I miss her, too."

He shook his head. "Not like I do."

To his horror, tears started to flood his eyes and he looked away. He was breaking the record. He'd gone for five straight days without crying and even then, he always did it in private. In his apartment or in the shower, where he could pretend the tears were just droplets of water from the tap. He'd never allowed himself to break in front of anyone, much less his baby sister.

She wrapped her arms around his shoulders and it only intensified the pain.

"Alexa, please-" his voice broke.

"Shh." Her arms tightened around him and the only sound that could come out of him next were sobs. The tears streamed past his eyes, down his cheeks and onto his clothes. He felt embarrassed. How could one woman transform him into such a crier? He pinched the bridge of his nose but it did nothing to stop the tears. His sister held him, moving with each wracking sob that shook his body. They were ugly sounds, emitted from the deepest parts of him. A loss he couldn't adapt to - no matter how hard he tried.

"I love her," he managed to say past his sobs.

"I know. I know you do."

She rocked him past the waves of grief until he could breathe again, until the room became clear once more. He reached into his pocket and cleaned his face with his handkerchief. He felt his sister's arms still around him, her hand stroking the back of his head, her cheek laid against his shoulder. Her silky hair smelled like fresh shampoo and it comforted him.

"Thank you," he whispered, drained.

"I love you," she said.

"Don't," he said, frowning. "I love you, too, but if you say that again, I'll lose it."

And he'd lost it enough.

She nodded. "Okay."

They were both silent for a few minutes. He sighed and spoke again.

"You don't get it. Things were falling apart before they actually did." He thought of the trip to Martha's Vineyard, the time they made love in this very room, their conversation after the sermon, her fierce independence in the midst of her job crisis. There were so many pitfalls they had chosen to ignore. It was only a matter of time before they got trapped in one of them. He couldn't help but wonder what would have happened if he'd been more selfless - if she'd been selfless too. Teller's words pierced him once more but this time he was listening.

"In a covenant relationship, you don't have to spin or sell, promote or hide who you really are. There is a zone of safety because when both of you are committed to the covenant, you both have the space to be who you are and be loved just as you are without fear of abandonment."

He'd missed the mark on so many things. So had she. But she wasn't willing to repair it. No matter how many calls he made, how many texts he sent, how many emails, begging her to hear him out, she kept the stone wall erected. There was no getting in. He'd considered hiring a P.I. to find her place but knew that would only make things worse. She would consider it a personal violation. He never wanted to inflict that on her. He was respecting her choice, but it still hurt. Deeply. He leaned back into the seat, Alexa's arms falling from around him.

"I can't do this anymore."

She frowned, clearly panicked. "Yes, you can."

He shook his head, knowing he had worried her. "I'm not going to off myself, Lexi. I meant...I can't live like this anymore. Go to work, be miserable, eat, be miserable, try to run, still miserable. There has to be more to life than just existing."

"There is," she said softly.

"I don't want to be proselytized, Alexa."

She shook her head. "I wasn't trying to. I was just going to suggest..." she hesitated and he looked at her.

"What?"

"Maybe looking outside of yourself will help you live with yourself."

He waited.

"I do community service with a group on Saturdays. You should come and check it out. There's something really fulfilling about helping others. If anything, it might take your mind off of Jane—"

He winced at the name.

"—for a while."

He sighed. "I don't know, Lex."

"Think about it," she said gently. "This Saturday, we're serving in Morris Heights."

He frowned. "Why does that name sound familiar?"

"Because that's where Jane and I lived. It was on the therapist notes in the file."

He didn't know if that's why she mentioned where they were going. If she somehow knew he'd want to be wherever she'd lived. That it would somehow make him feel closer to her or understand her better. Whether she knew it or not, it worked.

"I'm in."

Aiden had seen shows of inner city places and what people commonly called "the projects" but for some reason, it never fully registered that people *lived* in such environments. Day in and day out, surrounded by filth, graffiti, noise, and crime. He'd gone to the volunteer meeting the previous night at Redeemer Church. There, the leaders reminded volunteers, and warned new ones, that Morris Heights was one of the poorest communities in America and had been for decades. The community was predominately African American and Hispanic with one of the highest concentrations of public housing.

The leader of the volunteer crew was a guy named David Corey, a black man in his late forties.

"When we go there," he said. "Be mindful to treat these people like *people*, not charity cases." Aiden started at that; it reminded him of something Jane would say. That she didn't want to be someone else's charity. She didn't like receiving handouts. He wondered just how much her years in that community shaped her mindset about money, assistance, and her ability to provide for herself.

They left in two vans mid-morning. Alexa sat next to him and promptly fell asleep. Aiden couldn't follow suit; he leaned against the window and watched, wondering what awaited him. His heart dropped as the landscape and scenery deteriorated right before his eyes. He could not believe that things were so different in the same *city*, much less the same state. Brick buildings consumed the district, with graffiti caking almost every available surface. The sidewalks and streets held a sea of cans, bottles, rags, and trash. Caked with dirt, it was the sort of place a person would be reluctant to pick up something they had dropped, for fear of picking up an unwanted disease. He couldn't believe his sister had lived there. He couldn't believe Jane once walked these streets.

The van was making several turns, getting closer to their destination. Alexa woke up and looked around.

"You ready?" she asked. He looked down at her and was surprised to see the excitement in her eyes.

"This doesn't trigger anything for you?" he asked.

She shook her head. "It feels like a different lifetime since I lived here. I'm happy I'm in a position to help now."

Instead of receiving help.

By the time they arrived, two police cars were stationed with officers ready to assist and guard their resources. Sirens were already blaring in the near distance. No doubt, a shooting or altercation of some sort. David Corey immediately split them into teams, proving at once why he was an effective leader. Their jobs were pretty straightforward: they were to help the community by cleaning up and giving food. Two teams, stocked with gloves, trash bags, and masks started picking up trash along several blocks. Three teams, stocked with sandwiches, drinks, and canned goods, set up tables and began distributing food.

He and Alexa were assigned to one of the food teams. He set up a chart and made note of inventory, previous beneficiaries, and the supplies the church brought in order to assist the people. Within minutes, a long line curved from their booth to the end of the block and around. He and his sister had no time to talk as they wrote down the people's names, their most important needs, and located the food to distribute to them.

A short heavy set woman approached the table with a lanky boy. "Do y'all have tutoring today?"

Alexa smiled at the woman. "I'm sorry, ma'am. I'm afraid our tutoring team isn't here today. We will have it next week. Would you like me to place your son's name on the list?"

She recorded the boy's name and his subject before the two left.

"I didn't know you offered tutoring," he said.

She nodded, reaching back to grab a bag of food. "We do it at least twice a month, though we would like to do it more often. Unfortunately, most of the tutors are good at English and Reading while a lot of the students need help in Math."

A little light bulb went off in his head. He'd always excelled in that subject and even liked to do problems for fun. "I think I can help in that department," he said, handing another bag of food to the woman before him.

The hours flew by like seconds as Aiden greeted and served the residents of Morris Heights. He was relieved to see that his sister was right: helping others filled him with such a counterintuitive joy and satisfaction. Coming from privilege, he felt an overwhelming gratitude for all that he had compared to the lack that he saw. He didn't have to worry about where he was going to live or what he was going to eat or how he would see a doctor if he got sick. It was always a given that he could be safe, healthy, and free to do and buy whatever he wanted. He marveled at the freedom he had and the comfort he lived in - all because he had more money.

This is what she was talking about, he realized. He shook the thought away. He couldn't think about her now.

The cleaning teams managed to finish their areas pretty quickly and joined the food teams to offer assistance. Some helped with the organization and distribution of the food but he was surprised to see that others went out into the lines and struck up conversations with the people waiting. He watched as volunteers held complete strangers' hands and bowed their heads. They were praying. Others gave people long hugs and smiles of encouragement. Some played with the antsy children in line. He realized that those people were serving too, not just the community's physical needs but their emotional and mental ones, as well.

Aiden glanced at his sister and watched her beam at an elderly man with missing teeth. Though imperfect, he had to admit that she practiced what she preached as a Christian. She didn't just talk about God or pray to him, she did what he would do and helped others around her. Wasn't that what Christ did? Heal and feed and help people?

Alexa glanced at him and smiled. "What?"

He shook his head. Once again, he found himself curious.

"Tell me about your religion," he said unceremoniously. It had been several hours since they returned from the volunteer trip. Aiden had accepted Alexa's invitation to dinner at her place. He sat at the kitchen bar and watched her cook.

"First of all," Alexa said. "It's not my 'religion.' My faith is not a religion to me but a way of life."

"What's the difference?" he asked. She grabbed two plates from the cabinet and dished their food - a tasty Bertolli pasta dinner. Sitting down next to him, she bowed her head and said a quick prayer before digging in alongside him.

"Religion is empty," she said around her food. "People go to churches, mosques, and synagogues all the time. They can pray and behave certain ways and follow a bunch of rules and *still* miss out on knowing God. You said it yourself."

He quirked a brow at her.

"That religion often leads to wars and violence and condemnation. Judgmental, hateful people try to use it as a reason for their deplorable behavior. If any of those people *really* knew God, they wouldn't act like that."

He saw her conviction and could see the validity of her claims.

"So what's the difference?" he asked, before popping a forkful of piping hot chicken in his mouth.

"A relationship," she answered. "It's that simple. My faith has brought me a relationship with God and I know Him intimately."

"So why Christianity in particular?" he asked. "Why not just worship God whoever he is without a particular..." he struggled for the word since "religion" wasn't her favorite. "...faith? Why does Jesus have to be involved?"

"Do you think all roads lead to heaven?"

"I don't know," he answered honestly. "I've never really thought of heaven or hell."

He took a sip of his water and watched her process his words.

"So you've never ever thought about where you would go if you died?" she asked in disbelief. "If that van we were in overturned and killed you instantly, you would be prepared to die?"

The question sent a chill through him and forced him to examine his beliefs. The more he thought about it, the more he realized that he *did* have *some* beliefs about life after death. He did believe the soul went on.

"What about you?" he asked, eager to shift the focus. "Is that what made you decide to become a Christian?"

She nodded. "It was simple for me. I've always believed the soul goes somewhere after the body dies. I just didn't know where. In college, I studied all the major religions but there was something about Christianity. It rang true for me."

"Why?" he asked.

"Because I always believed in the God of Judaism and *that* faith dates back to the days when the majority of civilizations worshiped multiple gods and did whatever they wanted while doing so. The God of Judaism has always been unique, setting the standard for righteousness. Just look at the ten commandments. I always believed there was just one - and the Jewish account of the earth, its creation and God's intention for the people in it just made sense. So the next question for me was if Christ was legit or not."

He smiled at the way she said it.

She continued, "That's when a friend of mine loaned me her Bible. She told me to read John and gave me a commentary that explained the Greek translation of it. I realized then that it was an either/or type of thing. Either I accepted everything that Jesus said about himself or I rejected him like many Jewish people have historically."

"Why did you accept him?"

"The evidence was there. There are historical, firsthand accounts of people who encountered him after he rose from the dead - his disciples as well as five-hundred other witnesses. There are prophecies throughout the Old Testament that he fulfilled in the New Testament. The more I studied secular scholars' theories about his life and ministry and compared it with theologians' answers, the more I sided with the account already written in the Bible."

She explained that she was also convinced by the deaths of the martyrs. The food was delicious but paled in comparison to the words she was saying. Aiden wondered why he had never stopped to ask her about her faith before. He realized with embarrassment that he had dismissed it as irrelevant. How could he have called something so significant to her useless?

"Unlike other religions that call for strife, warfare, and the death of infidels, the apostles and disciples of Christ served others until the day they were persecuted to death. So many religions are founded on visions that one person had and people just take his word for it but this is different. The disciples and apostles were willing to be tortured and even die for what *they'd witnessed* with their own eyes - but not harm others like radically religious people do - which tells me what they saw was real. It didn't all click, though, until I took the plunge and chose to believe."

He frowned "What do you mean?"

"I mean, you never really know if something is true until you try it for yourself. It's like ice cream. You would never know that cake batter was the best flavor unless you ate it yourself."

He smiled and nodded.

"So I 'tried' Jesus for myself. I put down all the books and notes, and scholarly debates and I prayed. I asked Christ to be my savior and it was…" she paused, her eyes glowing. "Aiden, I never felt such a flow of peace and joy and truth in my life. There's nothing like it." She shook her head and he could see the tears welling in her eyes. It reminded him of that Sunday, when he watched her sing on stage. The peace she had on her face, the joy that wasn't rooted in how her life was going.

She shook her head and cleared her throat. "Those are all added benefits. Icing on the cake, if you will. I chose to become a Christian not because of the peace it gave me but because it's the truth. People think religion is meant for personal happiness or fulfillment or whatever. And yes, that can happen but there's no point in believing something if it isn't the truth. *This* is the truth. *He* is the truth"

She said it with such conviction, such confidence and joy, that all Aiden could do was nod and look at his empty plate, her words ringing in his head. He stood up and saw anxiety rush to her eyes.

"I'm sorry," she said. "Was that too much? I sometimes forget how reticent people are to talk about faith."

He shook his head and frowned. "No, I was just putting this away. Besides, I was the one who asked you, not the other way around."

He wondered at the level of anxiety he just saw in her eyes. He thought he and his parents were pretty tolerant of her religion - her *beliefs* - they didn't tease her about it too much, did they?

Maybe we shouldn't be teasing her at all.

He put the plate in the sink and filled it with water. Turning back to her, he asked, "Do you have one I could borrow?"

"One what?" she asked. Understanding quickly dawned on her face and she jumped off the stool, rushing up to her room. Seconds later, she re-emerged with a small, pocket sized Bible. She handed it to him with a smile.

"Start with John," she said.

"Thanks. When do you need it back by?"

She shook her head. "It's yours."

Aiden didn't know if it was the exhaustion of volunteering, the tasty pasta his sister made, or the riveting conversation they had while eating, but that night was the first night he slept soundly in weeks. Bible open on his chest, he dozed off to the words of John and had a dream…

He was on a beach, with a woman in his arms. He could hear the waves clapping against the shore and children laughing in the distance. But he couldn't see anything beyond his hand - and the hand he was holding in his. His long white fingers twisted a solid gold ring on her commitment finger - a wedding band. His finger had a solid, thicker band too.

Beep! The alarm snapped him out of his dream and into reality. Stretching in his bed, Aiden swiped a hand across his face. Instantly, the dream came back to him. He could remember it in vivid detail. He got up and started to get dressed for his run.

It was just a dream, he thought. *People get them all the time.*

But while he wanted to dismiss it - shake it off - he couldn't. Running down the sidewalk towards the park, he remembered with startling clarity a detail that hadn't seemed important at the time. The hand he'd been holding in his dream wasn't white like his own.

It was black. The woman he'd been holding was black.

CHAPTER TWENTY-FIVE

February 1st

"Congratulations!"

As soon as Jane read the word, she felt a rush of relief flood her senses. She'd gotten in. She had permission to attend the University of Cambridge. She was still moving forward. She could still start a new life, in a new land with a clean start.

Aiden's face flashed in her mind.

She quickly blinked it away and ignored the throb in her heart. She continued to read the letter and felt that same heart soar at the words written.

> *Dear Miss Daugherty,*
>
> *Congratulations! We are pleased to offer you admission into the University of Cambridge for your PhD in American Literature. We are also pleased to inform you that you have been selected as a recipient of the Cambridge International Scholarship...*

She gasped. The scholarship was only given to a handful of overseas students. It covered the full cost of her education for all three years and included a generous stipend for her to live on. Hundreds, if not thousands, had applied and she'd been selected. There was nothing holding her back.

"Ahh!" Jane squealed and allowed herself to jump up and down in her tiny Harlem apartment. It was slightly bigger than her last studio but a far cry from the luxury she'd almost grown accustomed to in Tribeca.

Once again, Aiden's face flashed in her mind but she squeezed her eyes shut and willed the image to go away. She continued reading the letter as even more good news appeared.

> *You indicated on your application your interest in teaching to supplement your income. While the stipend should be enough to cover your expenses, we are pleased to offer you a teaching fellowship that carries an additional salary and a full teaching load...*

Jane almost pinched herself.

Am I dreaming? she thought. She had to be. Everything she wanted and hoped for in her career was just delivered to her in a large university envelope. She could finally earn her PhD free of charge, move to Europe - which would allow her to travel and visit several countries she'd always dreamed of visiting while there, save a little money, and teach at one of the oldest institutions in the English speaking world. Cornell would have been impressive on her resume but *Cambridge*? The second-oldest university in the English speaking world? *That* was prestige.

Along with her excitement, Jane felt a rush of relief to read the good news. She'd been living *very* frugally while searching for a job non-stop. She hadn't known if the money from her severance check would last her until she got the next job. Now, she could relax. She had more than enough saved to cover her until she started grad school - in Cambridge or Columbia - she hadn't received the notification from the latter yet. But she was relieved that regardless of whether Columbia accepted her or not, she knew without a shadow of a doubt that she was going *somewhere*. She could finally make plans and stop living in the no man's land of uncertainty.

So why was there a lingering sadness in her?

Once more, she saw *him*. His dark blond hair, his strong chiseled jaw, his full pink lips, and his vivid amber gold eyes. She could *hear* his voice, the rumble of his baritone laughter. She could even recall his scent. The masculine cologne that always teased her senses and muddled her concentration.

When will it end? she thought. *When will* he *go away?*

She tossed the acceptance letter on the kitchen counter and sat on her convertible sofa. She hadn't seen or spoken to him in two months. She kept in touch with Alexa via email but ignored the emails and calls of her parents. She'd made a promise to herself that she wasn't going to cut ties with her best friend again - just because things blew up with the girl's family. She could still remember the look on Alexa's face as she tearfully begged her to stay. She'd refused, thanking her for everything but insisting she was done.

Alexa didn't push after that.

Her hand reached into her pocket as if on its own accord. Her slender fingers dialed the buttons and entered the passcode. Pressing "speaker," she listened to the recording yet again.

There was a reason why she could remember his voice so well.

"Jane," his voice was raspy. *"It's me. Please call me back. I know you're angry. You have every right to be but I* need *to speak to you. I need to make this right. There's so much I need to tell you but I can't do it over the phone. Please. Call me. Day or night. I'm here. I miss you. I..."* she knew what he wanted to say but couldn't. *"Please call me back."*

The automated voice came on. "To save this message, press nine. To-"

Jane pressed nine and stuffed the phone back into her pocket. She allowed herself to feel the wound. If she touched her chest, she couldn't see any marks or cuts or blood. But underneath, she hurt. It was a hurt so palpable, she could almost touch it. Most days, she ignored the memories, shoved them in a vault and refused to look at them. She went into robot mode so that she could survive. She hoped with grad school and a new environment and moving forward, that things would get better. Easier. She would forget him once and for all and move on. He probably already had.

But then there were these moments.

When she allowed herself to feel. When she allowed herself to remember. And she dwelled in the pain the way a passing driver absorbs an accident scene. Mercilessly. Pointlessly. Curiously.

"I'm sick of your martyr bullshit!"

It was the lifeline that pulled her out of the sea of nostalgia. She replayed the words he said to her over and over and over again. Until she grew numb. Until she grew self-righteous. Until she could forget almost every good thing about Aiden Masterson and her relationship with him.

Almost.

Her phone rang and she pulled it back out.

"Hello?"

"Hi, is this Jane Daugherty?"

"Yes, this is she."

"This is Alice from Penner Hill Hospital. I'm just calling to confirm your 5:00 check in this afternoon for your surgery tomorrow morning."

"Yes, I'm on my way." She glanced at her watch. The taxi would be there any minute.

"Excellent," the nurse replied. "Did you have any questions before coming in?"

"No," she glanced at her suitcase by the door. "I'm all packed and ready to go."

After hanging up, she looked at the phone, lost in thought. Her doctor had called shortly after she took her tests. Confirmed that part of her small intestine had shut down - the part closest to the colon. Her blood results also confirmed it - she lacked a startling amount of vitamin K, the vitamin needed to assist blood clotting. With her insurance set to expire at the end of her severance late March, she knew she had to get the surgery now.

She re-focused her attention on her phone when a notification showed a new email. She opened it and saw a new message from Alexa.

Hey Jane!

How have you been? I know we spoke a few days ago but I wanted to check in and see how you're doing. I guess I'm not used to not seeing you everyday - even after all this time. I graduate in a few months and am super stoked. UNY isn't the same without you.

No one here is.

I know it's been rough for you since you and Aiden...you know. But I wanted to know if you and I could meet up soon? Hang out and catch up? I really miss you and I really want to know how things are going. Please shoot me an email or better yet give me a call. Unless you've changed your cell, we should be able to chat.

I love you, Jane.

Your "little one,"
Alexa

She smiled at the letter. She could almost hear Alexa saying the words in her sweet, gentle tone. She hadn't mentioned the surgery to her so she had no idea that meeting up wouldn't happen for quite some time.

Someone knocked on the door.

She glanced at her watch and got up, grabbed her bag and wheeled her suitcase. She opened the door and greeted the cab driver, taking one last look at the apartment she wouldn't see again until at least a week later. She loved Alexa and she missed her. But she could only focus on one thing at a time. And right now, her surgery was paramount on her mind.

Email would just have to suffice.

Aiden felt restless. He'd been serving with Redeemer every weekend for five weeks but still couldn't shake the unsettled emptiness he felt inside. It had abated, sure, but it never disappeared.

He walked along the dilapidated sidewalk of Morris Heights, picking up trash with gloved hands. He could have sworn a team cleaned the very same spot last weekend and once again, it was covered with trash. If it weren't for the children who had to live there, Aiden wasn't sure he would continue to volunteer. The adults there, regardless of the aid they received, didn't seem to take pride in their neighborhood or hold each other accountable to make it better.

They weren't serving food that day.

David said it was a cleanup day. "Cleaning the streets and the hearts."

Aiden had no idea what the hell that meant until they arrived. The team could split up into street cleaners or prayer teams. Annoyed, Aiden had chosen the former. His sister was busy praying with an older woman several yards away. His annoyance rose higher when his team completed their task with nearly an hour to spare. To his chagrin, his teammates quickly dispersed into the street, either finding new people to pray for or joining the prayer team members in the middle of their prayers.

Aiden felt heat rush to his face. He didn't want to pray. He flushed again, realizing he didn't really know *how*. He'd read about Jesus doing it in the book of John but he wasn't Jesus. He'd seen Alexa do it and he could recall his *Nonna* on her knees but he'd never tried it for himself, alone, and didn't feel the least bit qualified to pray for or in front of others.

This wouldn't be an issue if I volunteered with a secular organization, he thought. But he quickly dispelled it. He loved what Redeemer did and he didn't want to stop contributing. He glanced at his watch once more, found an empty, relatively clean stop, and sat in front of a townhouse, a few feet away from all the prayer action going on. A few minutes passed while he just watched.

"Hey, Aiden." David emerged from the townhouse behind him, gave Aiden a light pat on the shoulder and moved to sit next to him on the stoop.

"Hi, David." Aiden shifted to make room.

"You doing okay?" he asked casually. Aiden nodded and looked around. When his eyes swept back to David, he found him staring at him.

"What?" Aiden asked. He wasn't going to try and force him to join the prayer team, was he? David must have read his apprehensive expression because he smiled and shook his head.

"You know something? I've had it on my mind to talk to you for a few weeks now."

Aiden frowned. "Really?" When David nodded, he asked, "Why?"

The older man looked ahead and said in measured tones, "At first, I was just curious. You're consistent, always on time, and do excellent work. But you keep your distance, never pray, and rarely chat with anyone besides your sister."

Aiden flushed. "Is this some sort of reprimand?"

David looked surprised. "Reprimand? No, not at all! I'm grateful you're here. We all are at Redeemer. This isn't a paid job and yet you treat it like it is. We really appreciate that. I just wanted to know you better. Ask if there's anything pressing on your heart?"

Aiden looked at him, his frown deepening. How did he know something was bothering him? Did he walk around looking depressed all the time? What did the rest of the crew think about him?

"Hey." Aiden re-focused his attention on David and saw the other man's warm brown eyes soften. "No one's judging you here. We all have our 'stuff.' I just want to help you with yours. If I can."

Aiden looked away. "I don't think you can."

"Try me."

Two words. Two simple words that he should have been able to dismiss but couldn't. They were like keys that opened the watershed of Aiden's crap: his doubts, his worries, his disappointments, and his pain.

His mess.

In disjointed, rambling sentences, Aiden spilled it all to a silent David: his dissatisfaction with Wall Street, his loneliness when not with family, and the disaster that was his relationship with Jane. He *still* couldn't say her name aloud.

He felt hot salty tears spill down his cheeks as he admitted the real reason he volunteered. "It's this or drive myself crazy thinking about *her*."

He swiped at the tears and accepted David's comforting hand on his shoulder. He'd never been so transparent, or emotional, with another man. It felt good - cathartic - to talk to a friend, which, after everything he shared, David now was - whether he wanted to be or not.

"Thank you for trusting me with that," David said quietly.

Aiden nodded, a strange hollow feeling taking over. He felt empty but for the first time, it was good. Like he'd poured out all of the junk that had been weighing him down.

"Can I be honest with you?" David asked.

"Haven't I been honest with you?"

The two chuckled.

"Touché. It seems to me you've been searching for something your entire life. Meaning. Purpose. The reason to live."

Fresh tears stung Aiden's eyes as he looked at David in amazement. His heart started to race at the words the man spoke. David repeated, "You've been searching for meaning. We all do." He gestured to the area they were in. "Some people think they'll find it in the streets. Sex, drugs, money, power. Some think they'll find it in more respectable things like prestige or a successful career." He gestured at Aiden and Aiden nodded, remembering his early days at the firm. The way the partners *still* hungered for deals like starving animals.

"Some people spend their whole lives chasing these *things* to bring them life. Deep inside, you'll always know-"

"There has to be more than this," Aiden whispered, haunted.

"Exactly!" David exclaimed. "There has to be more than this because there *is* more than this."

More than this earth. More than this life. More than these *things*.

"We are all creatures who worship creation when the creator is here all along."

"God." Aiden said. It wasn't a question.

David nodded. "God."

Aiden looked at David and nodded wordlessly, a new wave of *something* - excitement, anticipation, curiosity - *something* washing over him. He felt a strong tug in his heart. It was the urgent feeling he felt when he needed to catch a train and was running late. He didn't want to be left standing on the platform. Suddenly, he remembered the words he read in the Bible section called "John." They were the only words his sister had underlined before giving it to him:

"'For God so loved the world that he gave his only begotten son so that whosoever believes in him shall not perish but have eternal life." Aiden didn't realize he'd said it aloud until David nodded and clapped his shoulder. He looked into the older man's eyes. "I want to," he said. "How do I do it?"

David smiled. "Pray with me."

Hand steady on Aiden's shoulder, David bowed his head and led them in a simple prayer. At first it was repetition, with Aiden repeating David's words, but then it changed…it shifted and Aiden found himself speaking of his own accord, words flowing from his heart that he hadn't even known were trapped inside.

"God, I need you. I need you," his voice broke. "I need you."

He repeated the phrase again and again with David's encouragement. A rush of peace so deep and strong enveloped and consumed him.

I'm free, he thought. For the first time, all of his running, all of his spinning, his efforts to make meaning of his life stopped. Finally, he could breathe. Aiden opened his eyes to find his sister crossing over to him. She stretched out her arms, her smile brilliant.

She knew.

Somehow she knew the decision he had made. He met her eyes and saw joyful tears spilling from them. She shook her head in wonder. He could hardly believe it himself. He'd gotten off of the van an ambivalent wanderer. He was getting on the van a changed man.

He was a Christian.

"You should join a church. And try to get baptized soon." Alexa told him. They were sitting in their favorite diner and grill, eating burgers and celebrating the day. So much had changed since the last time they'd eaten there.

"Baptism doesn't save you, though, right?" he asked.

She shook her head adamantly. "No. You were saved the minute you accepted Christ into your heart. Didn't you feel it?"

He nodded, smiling. He could still feel God's presence in and around him, the way embers stuck around long after the fire died. They'd spent much of their lunch talking about what he could expect as a new believer. They discussed the Holy Spirit and the role He'd play in Aiden's spiritual growth.

"You'll hear him a lot now - if you listen closely and pray regularly."

"Like a voice?" he asked.

"Not exactly. More like thoughts, impressions…you'll know because it's not what you'd normally think to yourself. It sounds different from *you*."

Aiden nodded, noting how much their roles shifted when it came to matters of spirituality. He'd always been the big brother leading Alexa along but in this arena, he was the baby and she was the leader. He didn't mind it. He felt a hunger to know more about the new life and commitment he'd made - to get to know God one-on-one more and more. He hadn't known him for thirty years and didn't want to waste time now.

"When are you going to tell Mom and Dad?" Alexa asked. It was the first time in their conversation that his food turned stale in his mouth. Suddenly, the thought of sharing his newfound faith with his parents was a fear-inducing prospect. He frowned at himself.

What is wrong with me? I'm a grown man. It shouldn't matter what I've chosen to believe.

But deep inside, he knew that it did. He loved his parents and was really close to them. How would they treat him knowing he'd become a "holy roller" as his father liked to put it? He immediately remembered all the instances when his mother and father jokingly picked on Alexa for her old fashioned, "religious" lifestyle. Her commitment to modesty, prayer, going to church, doing things that the majority of people didn't value now days. It was not only a damper on his new victory, but a prickling reminder that he too used to behave less-than-respectfully about her faith. He could still remember the ignorant things he'd spewed at her after the service that one Sunday morning.

He met her eyes. "I'm sorry," he said. She quirked a questioning brow. "All those years of teasing you for converting. I didn't realize how hard that had to be for you, especially when Mom and Dad were doing it too."

She smiled and shrugged but her eyes had misted over. "It was hard. To be honest, Mom was the best of all three of you. But it still hurts when no one in your family understands."

He reached across the table and held her hand. "I understand now. It feels like I have this priceless gift and I want to share it with others but others think it's a piece of junk."

She nodded rapidly, her breathing accelerating. "That's *exactly* how it feels! Sometimes I imagine them getting it. Truly getting it. No jokes about religiosity or 'strange beliefs' or attempting to be tolerant - but truly getting it and supporting it." He nodded. "They don't get it yet, Aiden. But we just have to keep praying. I'm so grateful it clicked for you."

He smiled. "Me too."

That night, Aiden's thoughts shifted to Jane and wouldn't go elsewhere. He attempted to read the Bible his sister had given him but the words faded and mashed into each other until it was an incomprehensible mess in his mind. Her face continued to pop up right behind his eyelids. Her dark molasses skin, sharp cheek bones, the arch of her dark eyebrows, the pools of her brown eyes. He missed the silky texture of her skin, the soft cushion of her lips. His hands ached to explore the swell of her curves and he broke out into a sweat remembering the moments he'd wrapped up around her without any barrier. He was a new Christian, yes.

But he was still a man.

Realizing he wasn't going to get anywhere in the book that night, he got ready for bed. His mind drifted to the sermon he heard at Redeemer in what felt like a lifetime ago. He now understood why the pastor's words had upset him so deeply - why it made him feel dirty at the time.

Because I was.

The Lord was convicting him for something he hadn't even known was a sin. And he hadn't appreciated someone telling him it was. Now, he could accept the truth. This time, instead of desire, a fresh wave of regret washed over him as he remembered those moments with Jane - getting the benefits of a married couple without sticking his neck on the line to make her his wife. He wondered how different things would be if he'd gotten saved before they broke up. But then he realized he wouldn't have gotten saved because he wouldn't have volunteered or made the changes that led up to his decision. He started volunteering for the distraction from his break up. He ended up getting so much more.

But why can't I stop thinking about her, Lord? Why is she still on my mind?

He marveled at the immediate prayer. Hours earlier, he'd been paralyzed by fear and ignorance of the practice. Now, he could do it in the middle of getting ready for bed! What a freeing revelation to know that all prayer was, was talking to God - and he could do it anywhere, anytime.

Thank you, Lord.

He folded himself into bed and turned off the light, his mind taking him to a familiar place once more...

He was on a beach, with a woman in his arms. The brown hand he was holding in his had long, beautiful fingers. His long white fingers twisted a solid gold ring on her commitment finger - a wedding band. His finger had a thicker, matching band. His perspective shifted and lifted from the hand he was holding to the horizon of the beach. There was no one on it. The sun was setting and it cast a beautiful glow on the water. He could hear the laughter of children. Seconds later, he saw them: three kids - a little boy and two little girls with sandy blond hair and light brown skin. They looked like they were all under seven. One of the girls scooped up a handful of water and tossed it at her sister. She returned the favor and the kids erupted into a mini water fight, their squeals of delight ringing in his ear.

"Be careful, kids!"

Aiden started at the voice that spoke next to him. It was a familiar sound. He turned his gaze back to the woman in his arms and finally saw her fully. She was wearing a thick warm cardigan and snug denim capris. His eyes landed on her face and his heart soared. Dark molasses skin, high sharp cheek bones, full soft lips, and dark brown eyes. Jane met his gaze and smiled easily.

"What are you thinking, husband?"

Ring! Ring! Ring! Aiden woke up with a start, the sight of the beach fresh in his mind. He glanced at the clock on his nightstand. It was 4:00 in the morning. It took another second for his mind to register the source of what woke him up. His phone continued to buzz on the nightstand. He picked it up.

"Hello?" he said groggily.

"Aiden, it's me." Alexa's voice was urgent. "You need to get to Penner Hill immediately."

His heart stammered. "What? Why? Is it Mom? Dad?"

"It's Jane."

His heart stopped altogether. He could still see her in her soft cardigan, her fingers entwined in his. Alexa was still speaking.

"…there were complications from her surgery."

"*Surgery?*" he asked incredulously.

"Just get here," Alexa said. "I'll explain it all when you do."

He hung up and jumped out of bed.

LOVE

CHAPTER TWENTY-SIX

Black. It was all Jane could see behind her heavy eyelids. But she could hear voices around her. Voices that pulled her out of the heavy sleep her medication had pulled her under. They were familiar voices. So familiar, she knew exactly who was saying what.

"They re-did her stitches and packed it with antibiotics," Alexa said.

"What caused the infection?" Ava asked.

"Infections happen all the time post surgery." Michael's voice. "Her doctor said this one was minor."

What were they doing there? She hadn't told anyone about the surgery. Anyone.

"Lex, can you get the donation receipt from one of the nurses? They should have it ready by now."

Figures.

She heard the door swing close and assumed Alexa had left the room. She didn't know how long it took but eventually the heaviness behind her eyes receded enough for her to open them. The light was harsh against her pupils and initially hurt.

"Ava, she's waking up."

Jane blinked several times. The light receded slightly as Ava and Michael's heads bobbed above hers.

"Hey," Ava said gently. "Welcome back. How are you feeling?"

Jane made a move to sit up but Michael stopped her. He found the remote on her bed and pressed a button to elevate her. It wasn't quite the position she wanted but it was better than laying so flat now that she was awake. She looked between the two adults with a slight frown.

"What are you doing here?" she blurted, her voice scratchy.

Michael looked nervous but Ava's face crumpled into a sharp frown.

"I could ask you the same question," she said fiercely. Jane looked at her in surprise. What was she-?

"How could you go into an operating room without telling *any of us?*" she asked incredulously. She made wild gestures with her hands. "Jane, you could have *died!* You could have had a worse complication. How could you have done this on your own without telling your family?"

Jane started at that sentence. Her heart skipped a beat at the thought that Ava considered her family.

The older woman read her mind. "And don't even try to deny it. You became a part of this family the minute you walked into our apartment six months ago. I don't just have one daughter, I have two." Her blue eyes welled with tears that freely spilled over as she gently pulled Jane into a tight hug.

Jane was speechless. She knew that Ava cared - that she was concerned about her. But she never knew the depth of her love. It warmed her on the inside and made her heart pound. The woman drew back slightly and looked down at Jane. She stroked her cheek, wearing a softer expression this time. Clearly, she was done rebuking her because the next words out of her mouth were, "Do you want some water? Are those pillows comfortable enough? I'm going to get your diet list from Dr. Lister so we can make you some nice dishes. You're still on a liquid diet for now." Jane couldn't get a word in edgewise and was content to watch as Ava fussed over her, fluffing her pillows - which didn't need fluffing, and giving her water that she hadn't asked for.

Finally, Michael, who had been silently observing the whole time, spoke up.

"Ava, let me have a minute alone with her."

Jane didn't know why but she felt a strange curl of anxiety in her stomach. She glanced at Michael and saw him watching her intently. They hadn't spoken to each other since the night she confronted him nearly three months ago. She didn't know what to say to him but apparently he had something to say to her.

Ava looked between the two of them nervously and said, "Okay."

She leaned down and gave Jane a motherly peck on the forehead. "I'll be back in five."

Jane didn't know why but she, a grown woman used to unilateral independence, felt such a comfort in those words. She watched Ava's retreating back go through the door before turning her attention to the man sitting by her bed. He was nervous but there was a determination in his eyes.

She waited.

Aiden shoved a wad of bills into the driver's hand and slammed the door. "Keep the change!" he yelled over his shoulder. He rushed into the hospital and looked around frantically for a familiar face.

"Aiden!" He turned and saw Alexa waving him over. Half-running, he reached her and started shooting questions.

"Where is she? What happened? What type of surgery did she have? Was she in an accident?"

"Shh," his sister put what was supposed to be calming hands on his arms but it only agitated him further. "Calm down, Aiden. She's fine. She had part of her small intestine removed. Something about 'necrosis of the cell tissue'...? Anyway, the surgery went well and she's in recovery."

Relief flooded Aiden but it only calmed him slightly. "You said there were complications. What happened?"

"She got an infection-"

"*An infection?*" he roared. Other visitors turned to look at them.

"Shh!" she repeated. "Infections happen all the time and hers wasn't severe. They gave her some antibiotics and it should be clear in a couple of days."

He ran shaky fingers through his hair and tried to breathe. She was okay. She was going to be okay. As the panic from the early morning phone call began to subside, a deeper feeling welled within him, competing with the gratitude and relief he felt: sadness.

"She didn't say anything," he said shakily. His sister shook her head, hurt also in her eyes. He shook his head in disbelief. "I understand not telling me," he said, though the words stabbed him inside. "But why didn't she tell you? Or Mom?"

Alexa shrugged. "I don't know. She's been here for four days. The infection started yesterday afternoon. I wouldn't have known about it if Fiona hadn't mentioned it."

Aiden frowned. "Fiona? Your old roommate?"

She nodded. "She's a nursing student and happened to see Jane in the ICU. She asked me how Jane was doing because she knew we were friends. She thought I already knew about her surgery-"

"So she violated HIPPA regulations to ask," Aiden said, not sure why he was irritated about it. It was an invasion of Jane's privacy, yes, but if Fiona hadn't said anything, none of them would know about her condition right now.

"Yes, but I promised her we wouldn't say anything. Mom and Dad made a very generous donation to be able to visit and talk to her doctor. They're in there with her now."

"I want to see her," he said, looking past his sister. "Where's her room?"

The elevator suddenly opened and Ava walked out.

"Mom!" She rushed to them and pulled Aiden into a tight hug.

"Where is she?" he asked again. She pulled back and smiled.

"She's on the fourth floor. Room 405." He started to move past them as soon as he heard the number but his mother grabbed his arm before he could leave.

"Wait a few minutes, Aiden. Your father is talking to her."

"She's awake?" Alexa asked excitedly.

Ava nodded. "She just came to. Your father was really eager to clear the air."

He frowned. The last thing he wanted to do was wait. He had to see her *now*. He had to make sure she was okay. He had to…what?

He had to get her back.

"I need to see her," he said. "*Now*."

"Aiden, please."

He opened his mouth to argue but immediately heard—

Honor thy mother.

Seriously? He'd been saved all of twenty-four hours and he was hearing ancient scripture. Alexa had told him he would continue to hear the voice of God if he paid attention to it. So he took a deep breath and decided to listen. He pulled his arm gently out of his mother's hand and turned to Alexa.

"Is there a waiting area on the fourth floor?"

She smiled and nodded. His mother looked surprised at his immediate acquiescence. He wasn't *that* much of a brat, was he? He followed his sister to the elevator and began to brainstorm. He would see her in a few minutes, after his father spoke to her. If he knew anything about her, he knew it would not be a happy reunion and the thought of it wreaked havoc on his nerves. What would he say to her?

What was the right thing to say to the woman you planned to marry one day? The same woman who currently couldn't stand you?

"I owe you an apology," he began. Jane marveled at the way he dove right in - no small talk, no stupid questions. Just a straight to the point opening. Just like his son.

Stop it, she chided herself. Aiden wasn't with his family so clearly he didn't care. She ignored the disturbing thoughts and re-focused her attention on the older replica of him.

Michael looked at his large hands, folded in between his thighs. He looked back up at her and she saw a vulnerability there she'd never seen before.

"You know that I am a wealthy man." She nodded. "You also know that I come from a wealthy family." She nodded again, not knowing where this was going. "Well, when you are born into a family with the net worth my family has, you are taught early on not to trust others - particularly those outside of your family. For years, my family has been prey to people who have tried to take advantage of our resources - via friendship or even marriages."

She remembered that two of his siblings were divorced. He continued.

"Growing up, my siblings and I learned to watch people very closely and let people in very slowly. When I met Ava," he smiled. "She sort of rocked my cynical view of people. She didn't shatter it but she loosened it up a little. I'm not like Ava. I don't extend my arms or my heart unreservedly. I observe people, question their motives and wait for them to earn my trust. It's what my father taught me and his father taught him. Not to be made fools. So all that to say, when I first met you, I was cautious. Reserved."

She nodded, remembering his polite but distant greeting.

"I've watched you over the past few months." He shook his head in wonder. "How independent you are, how you pull yourself up by your bootstraps. Your work ethic and all you've overcome. You don't blame others or expect things from people. Not once did you try to needle your way into the family or take advantage of what we had. In fact, Ava and Alexa always had to convince you to accept their gifts."

She shifted in her seat, wondering what all this had to do with his initial apology.

He must have sensed her restlessness because his next words were, "I know that Ava has always been more outspoken about how she loves you. But I want you to know that it isn't exclusive to her. I love you, too."

He said it so matter-of-factly, so unexpectedly that Jane blinked in surprise.

"Regardless of what happens between you and my son, I want you to know that I consider you to be one of my own. We didn't know about you at the time we adopted Alexa. Had we known, you would have been adopted right alongside her." Tears started to well and she fought to keep them inside. "I'm sorry that my actions hurt you so deeply. Noah later explained to me that there was a potential integrity issue in what we were doing. I had no idea I was compromising you and…I went about it the wrong way. But I want you to know that I was merely doing for you what I would have done for either of my other children. Because we love you. *I* love you."

The tears free fell down her cheeks. Her chin trembled and her heart soared. Michael watched her silently, clearly not expecting her to reply. But she did.

"I love you, too." she tearfully whispered. She met his surprised gray-blue eyes and silently nodded. "I owe you an apology too. I…I know you were trying to help. It was just the *way* you went about it that hurt. I should have told you that instead of shutting you out and overreacting." Her tears began to fall. "I missed you. I…I love you, too…" He rose and pulled her into his arms. She could feel the strength in his embrace, his deep wood cologne comforted her. He was the only other man whose arms she enjoyed being in. The thought ushered Aiden's face to the forefront of her mind again and she pulled back, the fuzzy feelings mitigated a few notches.

Before she could process the sudden shift in her emotions, the door swung open and Alexa strode in.

"I'm sorry but I couldn't wait any longer. I want to see my best friend!" She crossed the room and enveloped Jane in a tight hug, her floral shampoo suffusing Jane's senses.

"Hi," she whispered. Alexa pulled back, tears already spilling.

"Mom said she already gave you a talking-to so I'll refrain."

Jane laughed. "Thanks." She shrugged sheepishly. "I'm sorry."

Alexa nodded. "Don't do it again. Please."

She shook her head. "I won't."

Her friend hugged her again but this time, past her shoulder, Jane noticed the person standing near the door. She almost gasped as her heart dropped to her stomach. Alexa pulled back and said something else but in that moment, Jane could hear nothing as her eyes fastened to his amber gold irises, transfixed by the sight she hadn't seen in months. She saw something shining in his eyes as he slowly crossed the room and reached her bedside.

"I'm sick of your martyr bullshit."

Aiden didn't know what thought crossed her mind in the two seconds it took for him to reach her bed but he knew it wasn't good because her eyes shifted from a look of amazement to a look of antipathy in two seconds flat. He leaned in and pressed a silent kiss to her forehead. His heart doubled over when she recoiled from his touch. He tried to meet her eyes again but she wouldn't look at him, wouldn't talk to him. Wouldn't acknowledge him. He knew then what she was thinking.

She was remembering what he said. She was remembering how he'd hurt her.

"Jane-"

The door swung open again and a tall, thin man with thick gray hair entered the room. Ava walked in behind him. Dressed in a white lab coat, Aiden guessed he was Jane's surgeon. He took one sweeping look across the room and immediately said, "Jane is recovering from an infection. She cannot have this many people in the room with her at once while she's recovering."

It was a clear message: get out.

The family started to move towards the door. Aiden reluctantly followed his parents but paused when he heard Jane say to Alexa, "Please stay. I want to talk to you."

He frowned at that, feeling completely ignored, but he pushed himself to wait. Impatience was what had gotten him into trouble. Patience would win her back.

When the door closed behind him, Dr. Lister turned to Jane and said. "Well, it looks like you're responding to the antibiotics pretty well, Jane. How are you feeling?"

"Sore," she answered. It almost felt like menstrual cramps but deeper. She asked if they could administer more pain medicine to her.

He nodded. "I'll have the nurse come in as soon as I leave. I've looked at your x-rays and your body appears to be handling the procedure very well. The vitamin K we've been administering is also getting absorbed into your system. You should be in the clear as long as you rest, drink plenty of fluids, and follow your diet precisely. Also," he added, his voice growing stern. "Refrain from doing *anything* that can re-open your stitches. You'll need around-the-clock care for one week after your release but you should be back on your feet shortly after that."

She nodded, trying to remember everything he was saying. She smiled when she realized that Alexa was writing down his instructions on a small notepad. Dr. Lister also limited her visitors to two people at a time. When he left the room, the nurse came in and gave her some more medication.

"Mr. and Mrs. Masterson have asked to come in."

Alexa glanced at Jane, who shook her head.

"Not yet," Alexa told the nurse. "Can you please tell them I'll let them know when they can come in?" The nurse agreed and left the room. Alexa turned to Jane.

"So what's up?"

Jane hesitated. "I...I have a question for you."

"Okay..." Alexa waited.

"What are your thoughts on death?"

Her friend immediately frowned. "Why are you talking like that? The doctor just said you'll be fine-"

Jane shook her head. "No, that's not what I meant. I meant... Do you want to know what I thought about before they put me under? I was facing an eight hour long surgery and all I could think about was one thing: 'where will I go if I die?'" Tears rushed to Jane's eyes as she remembered the terrifying thought. Alexa laid a gentle hand over hers. "Lexi, I was *so* scared. I couldn't stop thinking about it and the more I thought about it, the more scared I got. There was no one to talk to about it and I almost called the whole thing off."

Alexa blinked. "Really?"

Jane nodded emphatically. "I kept thinking, 'I don't want to die. I don't want to die. I don't know where I'm going if I do.' I almost told them to stop but by the time I tried to open my mouth, I couldn't. I was already under the anesthesia. I was already fading away. All I could think was 'Please don't let me die. Not yet.'"

Jane felt Alexa's soft thumb swipe away at the tears rolling down her cheek.

"Hey," she said softly. Jane met her gentle gaze. "It's only natural to think about death when you're facing a potentially deadly situation. I'm so sorry you had to go through that alone."

Jane nodded, unable to speak yet.

Alexa continued. "In answer to your question, though, I'm not scared of death," she said boldly. Jane looked at her and frowned.

"Really?"

Alexa nodded soberly. "I don't *want* to die yet. And I would hate to die before I accomplish certain things. But if a bus were to hit me tomorrow, I wouldn't be scared to die. I believe I'm going to heaven," she said. There was no conceit in her tone or boasting in her demeanor. But she said it with complete confidence and assurance.

"What makes you so sure?"

Jane woke up, the heavy feeling of pain killers still fogging her senses. As the fog started to clear, she looked around her quiet room. Her gaze landed on Aiden and couldn't go elsewhere as he watched her with an intensity that made her senses swim once more.

"Hi," he said softly. He gestured to the closed Bible on her nightstand. "I bookmarked where you were."

She frowned and said nothing in reply. Alexa had given it to her and told her she could keep it. "Start in the book of John," she had advised. Was he secretly judging her for reading it? Did he have an opinion on her curiosity? Her frowned deepened. Why did she even care what *he* thought about it?

I'm sick of your martyr bullshit! The words shored up a wellspring of hurt and anger and she looked down at her lap, willing him to go away.

Aiden felt a sense of panic rise in his chest as she glared at the hands in her lap. She clearly didn't want to talk to him - probably didn't want him in the same room.

Lord, help me, he prayed desperately. *Tell me what to say. I'm at a loss and she is* so *angry.*

The words spilled out of his mouth before he even had time to process them.

"I'm sorry, Jane."

She looked at him in surprise. His amber eyes shined with a sincerity she knew was the truth.

"I've wanted to tell you that since the moment I said those words to you outside Lexi's apartment. They were cruel and hurtful, and completely false. I'm so sorry for minimizing your pain and everything you've been through. I'm sorry I didn't try to understand."

His eyes searched hers, hoping for a modicum of softness, some give or willingness for her to forgive him. To his dismay and utter remorse, her eyes hardened and filled with unshed tears. Her chin trembled and he quickly realized that she was not going to let those tears fall if it was the last thing she did. She was literally barricading her heart right in front of him and he was powerless to stop her.

Jane looked away from Aiden and fixed her eyes on the door to her room. She counted to herself. *Five, four, three, two, one.*

Turning back to him, she said monotonously. "I accept your apology."

His heart sank at the tone and lack of emotion in her voice. "I want you to forgive me."

She almost sighed in exasperation but kept it in. Looking back at the door, she answered him in the same flat tone. "I will. I just need time."

Time.

It was the same thing she'd told him when he first asked her out. He wasn't going to get anywhere with her unless he made his full intentions known.

"I want you back," he said. Her eyes snapped to his like a stick snapping against the chalk board. "I want you back. You don't understand..." his voice choked up and he cleared it. "You mean everything to me."

Next to God, she was the most important person in his life.

He watched her process his words. The blank wall rose higher as she took a deep breath and said, "I appreciate the sentiment but I don't want a relationship with you. As friends or anything else."

The words felt like the crack of a whip against his skin. His heart plummeted so sharply that he almost missed her next words.

"We can be cordial when I'm around Alexa and your parents. Hopefully we won't see each other much."

She knew he wasn't listening because he was shaking his head, eyes fixed on her hands. "Jane, this isn't right."

"It's over, Aiden. Let it go."

"You don't understand. I-"

His words died on his lips as he watched her wince in discomfort. She shifted on her bed and her frown only became more severe.

"What is it?" he asked urgently. "Do you need a nurse? Your doctor?"

She shook her head and sighed. "It's fine. I'm just trying to sit up more."

He looked down and realized that her hands were by her side, trying to support her minuscule weight but the trial of the surgery and infection temporarily robbed her of her strength. Aiden immediately went into action. Ignoring her protests, he gently cupped her upper back with one hand and held her around the waist with the other, shifting her further up. Arm still holding her secure, he pressed the button to tilt the automatic bed so that she was completely upright and completely supported.

"The doctor says you'll need around-the-clock assistance," he said around his movements.

What's it to you? she thought viciously.

"I've hired a nurse," she said instead.

"Which agency?"

She frowned. It was none of his business but she couldn't fathom how giving him the information would affect her.

"Dove Care Center," she replied shortly.

He nodded, adjusting and fluffing her pillows behind her. He noted that she didn't relax until he fully released her and it hurt him to know that his mere touch could make her whole body stiffen like rigor mortis.

Jane waited for him to get out of her personal space. She appreciated the gesture but she could have just as easily called a nurse to help her. Having him in such close proximity wreaked havoc on her concentration and her heart. He still wore the signature cologne she'd come to associate with him. His arms felt just as strong as they did the last time he'd held her. He was opening up new wounds in her left and right and didn't even seem to know it. When she realized that he wasn't moving back, she lifted her eyes to meet his waiting gaze. His look was kind. Inviting. And tender. So tender, she could hardly stand to look at him.

"I know you're not ready to trust me," he said softly. "But I'm ready to fight for it." He leaned in, cupped her stiff cheek, and peered into her eyes. "I love you, Jane. I love you."

Her jaw dropped. It was the first time he'd ever uttered those words to her. He'd come so close to saying it time and again but he'd always held back.

Until now.

Jane felt something shatter in the center of *her* chest. She didn't know what it was or why it was happening in response to three little words but she wanted it to stop. Alexa told her she loved her. Ava said it too. Michael had said it only hours ago. So why was she reacting so deeply to this man's use of the phrase?

It's not just a phrase, something deep within her whispered. She swallowed hard and met his eyes. They were openly affectionate. There was no trace of fear. Aiden just told her he loved her and he'd said it without hesitation, with a candor that told her he was sincere.

She looked away. A fear so deep, so alarming, embedded itself in Jane's heart and mind.

No, she thought, *I can't do this. I can't let him in again.*

If she allowed Aiden into her heart again, if she gave him one more chance and he blurted something or said something in his anger, she knew he would break her. He probably wouldn't mean to but he would.

I'm sick of your martyr bullshit! She hung onto those words like a castaway clinging to a raft. She could not afford to let him in again. In a year, maybe two, maybe twenty - he would let her down and hurt her more than anyone had ever hurt her before. He would break her, if she let him - even if he didn't mean to.

I can't let him in again, she resolved. *I won't.*

Aiden frowned as a blank stare covered all of the shifting emotions he just saw battle across her eyes. She stiffened her spine and narrowed her eyes at him. He wondered why she saw him as the enemy.

"Please leave."

They were two words. Said with the calmest of inflections but they hurt him deeper than any cut or bruise ever could. She just did what he'd feared all along. She rejected his love and ignored his declaration. But despite the crushing blow of that moment, a deep peace settled into his heart. He'd just faced his fear and told his future wife that he loved her.

He met her cold eyes and felt nothing but adoration for her.

Patience, Beloved.

It was the tender voice he needed to shore up his endurance, kill his pride, and give the woman he loved another gentle kiss on her forehead. He leaned back slightly, looked down at her and whispered, "I'm not giving up on us. I'll check in on you soon."

Not waiting for her response, or more likely another rebuff, he turned on his heel and left the room.

CHAPTER TWENTY-SEVEN

Six Days Later

"Will your husband be picking you up, Miss Jane?" Sandra, her favorite nurse, asked. She was helping Jane change into her jeans, moving slowly to accommodate her weakened muscles.

"Husband?" Jane frowned. Was she confusing her with another patient?

"Yeah, tall, blond and handsome. The one who calls us every two hours to check on you."

"He's not my husband," Jane quickly replied. "He's not my anything."

The nurse shrugged, clearly not believing her.

"Did he call himself my husband?" Jane asked, wondering why she even cared.

Sandra shook her head. "I just assumed someone who called that often and visited that often had to be married to you or *something*. Only spouses spend that much time checking on a patient."

Jane kept quiet, unsure of how to respond. It was true. In the six days since he'd learned of her surgery - since she kicked him out of her room - Aiden pestered Jane, and the staff at Penner Hill, like a persistent rash. Only, a very handsome, charming rash. Despite her frequent requests to the staff to bar him from entering, he always managed to charm his way into the good graces, and therefore past the security, of the many changing nurses in her wing. He also called several times a day, from work, inquiring about her health. When he called, she always refused to talk to him. When he visited, she usually pretended to be asleep. They both knew she was faking but they would carry on in a sort of standoff - him visiting for several hours and her keeping her eyes closed the whole time - sometimes, she actually fell asleep from her antics.

The handful of times she copped to being awake, she would order him out of her room to no avail. He'd ask her questions about her health, her plans, how she'd been doing since she moved out from Alexa's apartment. She almost never answered and if she did, they were short, one-word responses. She never asked questions of him or tried to engage him in a conversation. And yet, she still managed to learn something about him.

Aiden had changed.

Last year, he would have shut down and given up on visiting her a long time ago. Or he would have pushed her like a bull in a china shop, demanding that she respond to him and stop her stubborn silent treatment. He might have even shaken her "awake" the many times she pretended to sleep. But he did none of those things. He was patient and calm and kind - the *entire* time. There were moments when she could see the disappointment and hurt flash vividly in his eyes at her rejection but they were fleeting, immediately replaced with a look of resolve. Like he was taking his punishment without complaint and wouldn't give up.

He often brought flowers, cards, and other tokens of affection to her, kissing her on the forehead before he left. Whether she was awake or "asleep," he always left with the same words: "I'll be back soon. I love you."

More than his actions, Jane sensed a deep, innate shift in him. His demeanor was completely different. He was still Aiden: smart, charming, confident. But there was a humility behind his confidence - not an arrogance. And he was much more patient, as evidenced by his tolerance of her behavior. He also had this look about him whenever she did bother to look at him: it reminded her of the look Alexa had.

Peace.

What could have happened to make him so different? The more she thought about it, the more confused she got. She banished Aiden and the mystery surrounding him from her mind. She had to focus today. It was time to check out and go home, continue her recovery there. She was expecting her home nurse any minute and she wanted to be ready. Ava and Alexa nearly threw a fit when she refused to have them help her home but she insisted that she wanted to be left alone on transition day and the nursing agency backed her up so the Mastersons promised to call later. Sandra finished helping Jane into her coat. Jane zipped up her suitcase when someone knocked on the door.

A short Latina woman with long brown hair appeared. "Miss Daugherty?" she asked in a thick accent.

Jane smiled. "Hi, please call me Jane."

She shook the woman's hand, who introduced herself as Esther, and allowed her to take over. Within minutes, Jane could tell that Esther was an excellent nurse. She wheeled her out of the hospital and helped her get into a waiting cab. Jane fell asleep on and off but she could rest easy, knowing that Esther was in charge. The minute they arrived home, Esther gave her another dose of medicine and fed her a bland dish of rice and steamed vegetables. She placed a bucket next to the bed in case the food didn't agree with Jane.

"Is there anything else I can get for you, Miss Jane?" she asked. Jane almost rolled her eyes at the woman's insistence with formality.

"Yes, Esther, can you please retrieve my Bible? It's in the outer pocket of my suitcase."

The young woman smiled, as if pleased by her reading selection, and retrieved the book.

"Thank you, Esther. You can go get lunch or take a break right now. I'm only going to read for a little bit then take a nap."

"Are you sure, Miss Jane? You might need to go to the bathroom."

Jane hadn't considered that. "Oh...well, I should be okay for the next hour."

The young nurse shifted hesitantly on her feet.

"Esther, relax. You're doing a wonderful job. I'm so glad the agency sent you."

The young woman smiled gratefully. "I'm glad you decided to keep me despite the change."

Jane frowned. "What do you mean? What change?"

Now Esther frowned. "The price change." Jane's stomach dropped. "I had to raise my rate yesterday when the agency raised their percentage. I thought they told you."

Jane began to shake. "No, they didn't tell me." She swallowed. "How much did you raise it?"

Esther looked nervous. "By...by $150-"

"An *hour*?!" Jane exclaimed, incredulous.

The nurse jumped at her reaction but nodded. Jane was reeling. She didn't know whether to be shocked, outraged, or depressed. Esther was a fantastic nurse but at this new rate, she *could not* afford her.

She sputtered, "Why - why didn't your agency contact me?" She was visibly growing upset.

"Calm down, Miss Jane. I'll call them for you."

Within minutes, Jane was talking to a representative.

"I'm so sorry for the misunderstanding, Miss Daugherty." a professionally repentant female voice said. "We sent written notification of the change via email, mail, and fax but also instructed Nurse Arroyo to call and inform you directly since the change was made so suddenly. We then instructed her that if you agreed to the new increase, she could proceed to escort you home. Do you mean to tell me Nurse Arroyo did not confirm the new price with you?"

Jane glanced at the nurse and calmly said, "No, she did not."

Just minutes ago, she'd been rejoicing at how lucky she was to be assigned Esther. Now, she questioned the woman's motives and her integrity. How could a breach of communication be *that* wide? Someone was lying and Jane didn't think it was the agency.

"I'm so sorry about that," the representative said. "We will certainly speak with Nurse Arroyo about her failure to clearly communicate the change to you. Would you like to continue using her services for your recovery?"

"No, I would not." Jane replied, gaze fixed on the nurse who suddenly couldn't meet *her* eyes.

The representative on the phone once again apologized and offered to waive the charge that had been accrued up to that point. Jane thanked her for the offer and graciously accepted it. She hung up the phone and waited until Esther met her eyes again. When she did, the guilt was written all over the young woman's face.

"Were you *ever* planning on disclosing the new price to me?"

"The agency sent-"

"The agency realized that I probably would not have access to my email, mail or fax machine while recovering in the hospital. You were supposed to inform me of the change but you didn't. *Why?*"

Esther remained silent and Jane knew the answer.

"You were hoping I would be unaware of the change the whole time you treated me so that I would be forced to pay, whether I could afford it or not."

Red circles dotted her cheeks as she avoided Jane's eyes.

"Do you realize how *evil* that is?" Jane asked. She was shaking again. She still held the Bible in her hand and her fingers itched to pick it up and chuck it right at the woman's head. Instead, she sighed.

"You're fired. Your agency will talk to you about this later."

The young woman opened her mouth as if to say something but closed it again. There was nothing she could say to defend herself or her actions.

"I'm sorry, Miss Jane," was all she said before seeing herself out of the apartment.

Jane sighed and pulled at the ends of her tightly coiled hair. It sprung back to her head as soon as she let go and she repeated the action.

Great, she thought. *A new nervous tick.*

She put the Bible aside and pulled out her phone. She didn't want to use Dove Care anymore but finding a nursing agency comparable to the original price she'd found proved next to impossible. Frustrated, after an hour of clicking on dead ends, Jane tossed the phone aside.

I'll do it myself, she thought. She ignored the spike of fear that came with her new resolve. The doctor had said around-the-clock assistance and she wasn't following his orders. But she reasoned that as long as she was careful, took it slow, and ate what he told her to, she could recover safely without the hassle and added expense of a professional.

Ava and Alexa's faces came to mind. But so did Aiden's so she shook her head. She would do this on her own.

I'll be fine, she coached herself. *I'll be fine.*

She was not fine.

In less than twenty four hours, Jane realized what a foolish error she'd made in foregoing a nurse. She'd slept away most of the night and the next morning but when she woke up in severe pain, she realized that she missed two dosages of her pain medicine. The pain was paralyzing and she couldn't fathom getting off of the bed to try and find the bottle. She had no idea where Esther had put it. Besides, she couldn't take the medicine without food. She realized that she'd also missed several small meals since the last time she was awake. Had a nurse been there, she would have woken Jane up and forced her to eat before falling back asleep.

And when it came to food, she realized she had sorely underestimated her ability to make herself anything when she could barely sit up in bed. She didn't have much energy and the pain was too distracting to hold herself upright long enough to prepare an entire meal. Besides, what was it she was allowed to eat? And how much?

She couldn't remember - not in her foggy, pain-riddled brain.

What she did know was that the lack of food was making her even more tired. And the fatigue was only adding to her pain. She was also starting to feel nauseous and she didn't know exactly why.

Something else the nurse could have figured out.

Late in the afternoon, she felt the urge to use the bathroom but tried to hold it. She didn't know if she could make it across to the bathroom, even though it was less than three yards away. Minutes later, though, she had no choice but to try as she felt a strong *push* from her bladder and her throat at the same time. The latter was what concerned her the most. She sat up and tried to still her dizzying mind. Holding on to various furniture, she managed to stand and slowly walk to the bathroom. She made it just in time to throw open the toilet seat, fall on her knees before the bowl, and lean forward, heaving every last bit of food from her stomach. It wasn't much.

The vomiting made her head pound and before she knew it, she couldn't sit up anymore. She fell to the side of the bowl and felt her face hit the soft cushion of her bathroom mat. To her horror and complete embarrassment, she lost control of her bladder and felt a warm trickle between her legs. Her strength was gone. Much as she wanted, she had no energy or ability to put herself on the seat in time, or clean up the mess her body just made. Chin trembling, the only thing she could do was close her eyes as the hot tears trickled past her lids, across her nose and onto the carpeted mat below.

She was all alone.

She didn't know how much time had passed but Jane woke up to the sound of heavy footsteps nearing the bathroom door. She felt panic rise in her chest. No one had the keys to her place except the super and those weren't his footsteps she was hearing. She commanded her arms to move so she could lift herself up, but devoid of strength or energy, her body remained still. Her tears re-emerged and coated the bridge of her nose. She closed her eyes, waiting for the inevitable from whoever was there to hurt her.

Seconds later, she felt him. Two strong hands turned her onto her back and her heart shattered in relief at the sight.

"Oh my God," Aiden cried. "Oh my God, how long have you been like this?"

He continued to speak but she didn't hear him. She felt his strong arms lift her up and hug her close to his chest. He kissed her forehead and she once again heard his words.

"It's okay. I'm here. It's okay…"

Aiden wasted no time in taking care of her. He mentally arranged her needs in lists, deciding which matters took top priority. Her body slack against him, Aiden turned on the bathtub and filled it with soap. He undressed her and gently eased her into the warm bath, cleaning her as thoroughly as he could. Once dried and dressed, he brought her back to bed, found her exit forms and read the clear instructions written for her care. He ordered soup and rice from a restaurant and spoon-fed it to her the minute it arrived. He gave her medicine then pressed a cool compress to her forehead. She had cooled down slightly after the bath he'd given her but she was still running a fever and he was determined to get it down.

Jane dipped in and out of sleep, often waking whenever Aiden prodded her to eat or take something he offered her. She felt the continual strokes of the cool wet clothe against her head and cheeks. Her pain began to float away as the medicine kicked in. While she rested, she heard him pace around her studio apartment. She could hear snippets of him on the phone: talking to her doctor, then his work, then Alexa and his parents.

"No, Mom, I'll do it. I already called out of work. I'm off for a week. You can visit but not yet. Not until I get her settled. Listen, I've got to go. The bathroom is a mess and I want to clean it while she's sleeping."

He hung up and walked to her. Her eyes were too heavy to open but she smelled his fresh, mountain-scented cologne. The wash cloth was reapplied to her face, cooler than before. Next, she felt his lips, soft and full, press against her forehead.

"I'm here," he whispered. "I love you."

Those were the last words she could remember that night before she fell asleep for good.

The sunlight flooded into the studio the next morning, waking Jane up in gentle waves. She felt so much stronger than she had before. Strong enough to sit up on her own and look around. Her eyes quickly found him.

He *had* been there. It wasn't a dream.

He was lying on the floor next to her bed, using his suit jacket as a pillow. His hand resting on his stomach, one leg folded up, he actually looked comfortable lying there. His five o'clock shadow was becoming a beard and despite the messy, rumpled clothes, he looked beautiful sleeping there.

As if aware that he had an audience, Aiden stirred from his sleep and stretched himself awake. He looked up and was greeted with the most welcome sight he'd seen in months: her beautiful dark eyes. Neither said anything but just looked, drinking in the sight of the other. He scanned her face. She looked much better than she had yesterday. Her skin wasn't as blanched and sweaty and her eyes were fully alert. He silently stood up and approached her. Laying a hand against her forehead, he said, "Good, your fever broke. How did you sleep?"

She just stared at him, as though astonished that he was there. He never really explained how he got in or why he even came.

"Do you need to use the bathroom?" he asked. He watched her turn away from him, as if embarrassed by the question. Rolling his eyes, he stifled a yawn and lifted her in his arms.

"What are you-?"

"If you don't answer my questions, I'll assume the answer is yes. I gave you a lot of water and juice yesterday so you must need to pee."

"That's none of your business!"

"I'm making it my business." He hauled her into the bathroom and set her down gently on the toilet. She noticed the smell of bleach in the room. He'd cleaned the tub and the floor sometime between the previous night and that morning.

Why is he going through all this trouble? What does he want with me?

Any other day, she wouldn't have been able to go with him standing there, watching her. But he *had* given her a lot of fluids so she used the toilet, despite having an audience. He made a move to help her when she finished going but she glared at him.

"I can clean myself."

He stepped back wordlessly and only moved to help her again when she tried to stand up and wash her hands. She looked forward to the day when using the restroom wouldn't be such a daunting task. She was grateful for the bath she'd had - he'd given her - the night before. She felt clean and refreshed for the first time in days. He moved to carry her back to her bed but she shook her head.

"I should try walking."

He nodded in agreement. "Okay."

He extended his hand to her insistently, indicating that it was the only way he was going to allow her to try. She found herself leaning on his arm heavily as she moved slowly to the bed. It was only nine feet away but felt like a mile by the time she reached it and sat down heavily.

Aiden tucked her back in, stacking pillows behind her back to keep her upright. He went into the kitchen and started fiddling around. Minutes later, he came out with hot oatmeal, toast, and some water on a tray. Setting the tray before her, he asked, "Are you strong enough to feed yourself or do you need help?"

He realized belatedly that it was a horrible way to word the question - especially to Jane. She frowned and started to eat wordlessly, though her hands shook slightly as she brought the food to her mouth.

As long as she's eating, he thought. He noticed that she hadn't thanked him for anything he'd done last night or that morning but he didn't expect her to. He was grateful she was allowing him to take over and help her. Had she been any stronger, she would have refused him completely.

Someone knocked on the door. He saw her start at the sound and frowned. Was she always this jumpy living here? He then remembered they were in Harlem. It was smart to be jumpy there. He glanced at his watch. 9:00 AM sharp. Right on time.

He opened the door and greeted him.

"Mr. Masterson," a tall muscular man shook his hand. He was in a driver's uniform, the hat still on, and he looked around the apartment hall, clearly not used to being in such a different neighborhood.

"Hi Renner," Aiden said. "I looked around and unfortunately most of the items are unpacked already." He felt Jane's eyes on his back and could imagine the quizzical expression she was wearing on her pretty face.

Jane watched in surprise as he pulled her largest suitcase out of the closet and passed it to the stranger at the door.

"What are you doing?" she asked, affronted. He couldn't just hand her suitcase to someone like that!

Aiden ignored her and gave the man what looked like a wad of cash. "We're not ready yet. Give us another half hour and we'll be down there." The stranger nodded, took the cash - and the suitcase - downstairs with him.

Aiden closed the door and walked back in, ready to face her wrath.

"What the *hell* was that?" she blazed. "Why did you give him my suitcase? That cost me more than fifty bucks!"

"And I'm sure the clothes in there are worth more," he murmured. She stopped in her ranting and stared at him.

"What do you mean?"

"I mean, the clothes, books, and items I packed in there last night far exceed the value of the suitcase I packed them in."

She stared at him, the question pasted on her face. He shrugged and looked back at her.

"Well, I'm not leaving you here," he said. "And since you refuse to hire a new nurse after the one you fired-"

"How did you know about that?"

"I called the agency to check on you. Imagine my surprise when they told me you fired her the previous day and had yet to replace her with another nurse from their agency. I thought maybe you'd chosen one from a different agency." He almost thought she fired that nurse just to spite him after giving him the name of one agency and then not using it after all. But he dismissed the thought - she wasn't that nonsensical. "I called your cell several times but no answer. So then I found your apartment-"

"How did you do that?"

He rolled his eyes. "I hired a P.I. Did an address search for *fifty bucks* and I came the minute I had it."

"How did you get inside? The door was locked." She specifically remembered Esther locking the door.

"I'm getting there, hold on." he said with a smile. He scratched the corner of his ear and grinned at her, making her nervous. Whenever he did that in the past, it meant he was testing the waters. "I paid off the super to let me in."

"What?" she exclaimed and he winced. He should have known it was useless hoping she wouldn't overreact to that bit of information. Then again, was she really overreacting? He even remembered how shocked he was when the super accepted his money. If he hadn't been so relieved to get to her, he would have knocked the guy's teeth out for allowing a complete stranger to pay him off and let him in. He'd known then and there that he didn't want Jane living in that apartment anymore - while she was recovering and even after she was well.

He pointed at the oatmeal growing cold in her lap. "Finish your food. We have to leave soon."

She stuck the food in her mouth but spoke around it, frowning. "I'm not going anywhere with you."

"Yes, you are." He shrugged on his wrinkled suit jacket and checked his pockets. Wallet and phone intact.

"No, I'm not. Thanks for the help." His eyebrows hitched up in surprise and she knew why. She wasn't too proud to thank him. He'd probably saved her life. But she wasn't about to let him take over. "I can take care of myself now. I have the energy to do it."

He nearly laughed. "That is a lie straight from the pit of hell." She frowned at his use of words. "You could barely walk from the bathroom to your bed. You need around-the-clock care, Jane, and that's why I'm here. That's why you're coming with me."

"I'm not following."

You wouldn't, would you? he thought sarcastically.

"*I'm* going to take care of you. You won't hire another nurse? Fine. I'll nurse you back to health myself."

"Don't be ridiculous."

She saw the irritation flash on his face but his voice remained calm. "I'm not. I'm taking you home and I'm going to take care of you."

She saw the determination in his eyes and it scared her. "Go away."

"No." It was one word. One simple word but it drew the line in the sand. Up until this point, every time she told him to leave or rejected his advances, he quietly accepted the rebuff and promised to return later. Now, he was taking charge. Refusing to back down when she all but commanded him to.

He took her half-eaten bowl of oatmeal and frowned at her. "Finish your toast. Renner is waiting."

"I'm not going anywhere with you, Aiden."

"So you keep telling me." But he moved about like she hadn't said a word. He cleaned the dishes and stacked them neatly, tidied the small studio and made sure everything was shut off. He went to her small suitcase and pulled a sweater from it, wrapping it around her. She shrugged it off and he put it back on silently. She soon realized it was futile to struggle against his arms and waste the small energy she'd regained so she finally allowed him to put the clothing on. When he pulled her out of bed and put on her jacket, she started to huff and puff like a petulant toddler.

"This is trespassing," she said angrily. She watched him open his mouth to say something biting, no doubt. But then the strangest thing happened. He paused, bit his lip, and actually seemed to *think* about his response before speaking again.

He finally leveled his gold eyes at her and calmly said, "Call the cops, then."

They left two minutes later.

CHAPTER TWENTY-EIGHT

"Here, let me help you."

"No."

He reached up to grab her elbow but she yanked it out of his grasp. She continued to hobble into the bathroom, hand clutching her side.

"You can't do it alone. The doctor specifically said to assist you when you go."

"I'm perfectly capable of pissing on my own," she retorted, her tone snappish.

He sighed heavily and refrained from retorting, *you weren't capable two days ago.* Why was it *always* the bathroom? Every time she had to go or take a bath or brush her teeth, it was a perpetual struggle of her pride against his assistance. In the twenty four hours since he moved her into his apartment, Jane had been a nightmare patient. The stronger she grew, the more difficult she became, insisting that she could do tasks on her own that were still beyond her strength. She would get out of bed without notifying him, try to cook when *he* had the approved food list. Every conversation they had was laced with poisonous barbs she darted at him for trying to be kind to her. He'd never seen her behave so nastily to anyone. It was as if she was determined to repel him - or at the very least make him regret his decision to care for her like this.

But he didn't regret it. It was difficult but it was fulfilling. She would never know, that despite her nasty attitude and mean spirited demeanor, he found great joy in taking care of her and watching her recover. He was a very new Christian, but he realized that this experience was a great practice of loving her even when she was less than lovable. And in taking care of her and loving her despite her behavior, he got to experience firsthand what that pastor was talking about. A deeper, richer, more lasting love grew in his heart for her. In such a short span of time, he had changed. Two months ago, he would have cursed her out and left her to fend for herself. Or at the very best, he would have hired a nurse to deal with her nonsense. But he wasn't about to now. He looked at her and wondered how a woman so annoying could still take his breath away with her beauty. Beautiful or not, she was being stubborn and obstinate just for the sake of it and it was starting to wear thin on Aiden's nerves.

"Jane, please. Just let me help you."

He approached her again, this time finding her bent near the toilet, clutching the sink counter for support. He knew he was only seeing the tip of the iceberg that was her discomfort. She was trying her best to hide her weakness.

Jane lifted the seat, turned and paused.

"Get out," she said unceremoniously.

Aiden frowned.

"Get out," she repeated.

"Why?"

"Because I have to pee."

He frowned in confusion before understanding dawned on him. She was attempting modesty! She didn't want him to see her take off her pants to do the deed. After everything they'd done, *now* was the time she wanted to be modest.

He didn't buy it.

"No. You wouldn't be showing me anything I haven't seen before and the only reason you all of a sudden care is because you're too prideful to let me help you."

"Aiden-"

"Jane, I've had enough." he said shortly and she knew he meant it. "Stop fighting me so you can pee. I'll take you back to bed and we can both get a modicum of rest." It was still early in the morning.

Without another word of warning, Aiden reached down to her sweatpants, quickly pulled the drawstring, slid both her pants and her underwear down and, reaching up to her biceps, gently pushed her down onto the toilet, making sure her hips hit the seat without incident.

"Aiden!" Jane cried in outrage, her face trying to decide between shock and anger.

"I thought you had to pee."

"Get out. Please."

"Jane-"

"I can't go with someone just standing here, watching me."

He rolled his eyes but this time acquiesced. Standing just outside the door, he listened to her urinate. The minute the sound stopped, he came back in and found her cleaning herself. When she was done, he helped her up so she could wash her hands.

"When can I do this on my own again?" He knew she was asking in all sincerity. There wasn't the typical acerbic tone in her voice.

"I don't know," he said gently. "Give it another day or so and you should feel strong enough to do it on your own." He settled her back in bed and watched her shift to a more comfortable position. "We got back here in record time," he noted to encourage her. "You're moving a lot quicker than before."

She nodded. "It's just a matter of endurance. I can move quickly but I should be able to stand longer."

He nodded too. "We'll practice that. Today. We'll have you stand and walk around a bit."

"Okay," she whispered. He smiled, marveling at the first peaceful conversation they'd had in ages. He was also surprised that she was allowing him to help. He knew if he had suggested the exercise earlier, she would have turned him down outright.

Jane could feel his eyes on her but didn't say anything else. She was tired, already drifting back to sleep. In the land between consciousness and slumber, she felt him lean over her once more. He kissed her forehead like he always did. Sometimes she felt the imprint of his lips when he was nowhere in sight, he did it so often.

She felt his kiss and heard him whisper, "I love you. Get well soon."

She didn't know how long she slept but she woke up to the sound of voices in the living room. Sitting up slowly, wincing slightly at the stitches still in her skin, Jane listened closely to the sounds.

A man whose voice she didn't recognize said, "We brought you some chicken, rice, vegetables, salad…they're all pretty basic. She should be able to eat them, right?"

Aiden's voice, "Yeah, this will be great. Thank you so much, David."

"Of course. We also brought some cleaning supplies."

"Oh, you don't have to. I hire someone every other week."

"Is she coming this week?" a female voice asked. "I doubt your patient wants to live in this mess all day."

"Aiden, let them!" Jane was surprised to hear Alexa's voice. "You shouldn't wait another week before cleaning this dump up." Jane smiled. Leave it to his little sister to lovingly insult him. She could almost see Aiden roll his eyes.

"Fine, fine. But I'm helping you." The conversation descended into a small argument as the strangers insisted on Aiden taking a break while they served him. A few seconds later, Jane heard light footsteps approach the door. It opened before she could brace herself and in walked Alexa.

"Jane!" she exclaimed. Alexa hugged her gingerly. "Oh, I've missed you." She pulled back and scanned Jane's figure. "How are you feeling? Aiden says you've been weak."

"I'm getting better," she said defensively. She was thin as a rail but had gained more weight since leaving the hospital.

"Good. Have you seen Mom or Dad yet?"

Jane shook her head. "They said they'll visit tomorrow."

"Mom's thrilled Aiden's taking care of you. Though she initially worried he wasn't up for it."

Jane shrugged begrudgingly. "He hasn't killed me yet. Though, I would have loved to have your mom help me."

Alexa was silent for a long moment. Jane looked at her and frowned. "What?"

"You're punishing him."

Jane's frown deepened. "Who?"

"Aiden."

She opened her mouth to protest but Alexa cut her off.

"Don't lie to me. He hasn't said anything but I can see it all over his face. You haven't been the easiest patient, have you?"

"Did he at least tell you *how* he moved me here?"

"Yes, he did." Alexa replied. "He had to when he told me that he decided to take time off and care for you himself since you *fired* the nurse you promised us all would take care of you."

"She changed her price at the last minute and didn't inform me."

Alexa's eyebrows shot up in surprise.

"I was wondering why you fired her. I knew there had to be a good reason." She frowned suddenly. "But you still didn't hire someone new. So why would you begrudge him taking care of you? Clearly, you need it."

Jane felt the familiar wave of shame and guilt wash over her. She truly had been horrible to Aiden - especially if his sister could see it after one look at him. He'd been patient with her, often biting his lip to keep from saying whatever snarky response came to mind when she acted like a brat. And she could admit to herself that she acted like a brat more often than not.

"I don't want to let him back in," she said quietly, more to herself than to Alexa. But Alexa heard her.

"Why, Jane? He loves you." Jane looked at her sharply but Alexa shrugged. "What? It's true. His face lights up when someone even mentions your name. He's *never* taken this much time off - even during Christmas -

to spend time with family. But he loves you enough to single-handedly take care of you."

Jane felt shame and regret burn hot in her chest.

"I'm not asking you to fall in love with him again," Alexa finished. "But could you ease up on him? He's doing the best he can."

Jane nodded silently, grateful for the gentle way Alexa managed to put her in her place.

"Do you want to meet some of my friends?" she asked Jane.

Jane quickly shook her head. "I don't look so hot. But would you tell them I said thank you. For the food and for cleaning? That was really generous of them."

Alexa smiled. "They really love Aiden."

Jane frowned. "How do they know him?"

"When Aiden started volunteering with Redeemer." Jane remembered that was Alexa's church name. So, he'd become a volunteer. Had he become something else as well? Once again, Jane found herself wondering what the root of his change was.

Alexa was still talking. "Last week, David's wife lost her job. Aiden contributed heavily to their assistance fund and filled their fridge for the next month. That's what we do. When one of us struggles, the other lends a hand and gives their resources."

"Sounds like the church in Acts," Jane observed. She watched Alexa blink in surprise.

"You've been reading it," she said, clearly pleased.

Jane shrugged. She didn't want to get her friend's hopes up but she had been reading the small pocket Bible she gave her in the hospital. If anything, it helped her while away the time. She'd moved from John to the other gospels before finishing the rest of the New Testament. The last book, Revelations, confused the hell out of her but she figured she could research it later. Now, she was in the Old Testament and found the numerous stories in there entertaining. Who needed Rhett Butler and Scarlett O'Hara when they could read about the treacherous relationship of Samson and Delilah?

That night, Aiden settled Jane back into bed. They'd spent the past two hours walking around his small apartment, helping her regain strength as she practiced moving about. She even managed to take a couple turns around the apartment without holding his hand. Aiden would never forget the bright smile of victory that lit her face when she'd made it.

The apartment, newly cleaned and organized, also seemed to lift her mood. He knew she liked clean spaces, that messes made her feel hemmed in. He vowed to keep it clean as long as she was there.

Easing into bed, Jane looked at him and asked, "Today's the fourteenth, right?"

He nodded and smiled. "Happy Valentine's Day."

She groaned and he laughed, fluffing the pillows behind her head. Neither of them mentioned how awkward it was to be there, on Valentine's Day, doing something completely void of romance when only months ago, they'd been on that same bed together, making love. Jane saw Aiden blush and knew he was thinking about the intimate moments they'd shared in the past. She could still feel his hands on certain parts of her body and his cologne only made the memories more vivid. He wrapped the sheets around her securely and started to pull back. She grabbed his arm and he paused. Looking down at her, he met her eyes questioningly.

"I'm sorry," she said. He frowned, not getting it. "I'm sorry I've been a bitch-"

"Don't," he cut her off. "Don't ever refer to yourself that way. You may have been mea-"

"*May have?*"

"Okay, you *have* been mean. And difficult. But how you've behaved does not alter my opinion of who you are. Don't ever let me hear you say that about yourself again." He pierced her with his gaze, his gold eyes unflinching. She nodded and watched his face soften.

"I'm sorry," she repeated.

He smiled. "I already forgave you. Thanks, though."

She smiled back and nodded. "Thank *you*. You're going through all this trouble to take care of me. I...I do appreciate it. I'll try not to make it hard from now on."

"I'd appreciate that." They laughed. "Can I ask why you made it hard to begin with?"

She quieted down and a chilling look entered her eyes. He waited.

"I don't...I don't like to be around you," she said. "It...it makes things *harder* for me." The words struck his heart and hurt him more than he liked. But they also gave him hope. Hope that she could love him again. For a brief moment, he saw the veil lift from her eyes and every piece of hurt, pain, and distrust flashed before his sight.

"It doesn't have to be hard, Jane."

"Yes, it does."

Her eyes hardened - not to the mean, nasty person she'd personified for the past day and a half - but to the cold, unfeeling, unaffected woman who shielded herself completely from him. Jane watched as he sighed in disappointment. She knew he wanted more but she didn't care. She repeated his most hurtful words to herself like a dying mantra and her resolve thickened the more she meditated on them.

"Goodnight." She turned to her side, back facing him, effectively dismissing him from her presence for the night.

"Goodnight." He rubbed her back before reaching and turning off the light. She closed her eyes as he shut the door. He wanted her to give him a chance, to let him touch her heart and build something new but he'd better stop now while he was ahead. Because she would never give him access to her heart. Not again.

CHAPTER TWENTY-NINE

Two Days Later

"Well, Jane, I'm happy to report that you're improving really well. *Despite* the stunt you pulled early on in your recovery."

Jane felt heat pour into her face and was glad her skin was dark enough to hide her embarrassment. Aiden had made no promises about telling others the stupid decision she made to try and look after herself. She was only glad he didn't go into detail about the state he'd found her in. As a matter of fact, he never even mentioned it to her. She hadn't thought they could be any more intimate than they had been when involved but there was something really deep about a man who could clean up her vomit and urine and still profess to want her.

She shifted in her seat.

Dr. Lister continued, reading from the chart in his hand. "Your body is responding really well to the vitamin K tablets and your blood count looks healthy. How do you feel?"

She nodded. "Stronger. My diet is still really bland but I don't feel nauseous all the time or bloated. I've noticed that my appetite has increased."

Lister's smile grew exponentially at that news. "Excellent!" he glanced at the chart. "That sounds like an improvement from your general condition before the necrosis."

She nodded, smiling as well. Lister looked at Aiden.

"Is there anything you've noticed about her recovery in particular?"

She glanced at Aiden and found his gaze already on her. She blinked in surprise and he smiled, perusing her face before turning back to him. "She's managing the pain much better. We've reduced her medicine to half its dosage over the past day or so. She's also moving about a lot easier. I wanted to make sure we haven't disrupted her stitches, though."

Dr. Lister nodded. "Let's have a look."

Aiden moved to the side as the doctor lifted her shirt and examined the healing cut across her abdomen. Despite the sterile medical environment and the fact that he had no business feeling what he felt, Aiden could not help but feel a spike of pleasure catching a glimpse of her sloping stomach. Outside of the scar forming, her smooth brown skin stretched tantalizingly over the flesh of her torso. Aiden looked away and cleared his throat. When he looked back at her, he saw Jane's brows quirk questioningly at his response.

*Jesus, Jesus, Jesus...*he repeated to himself in a sing-song mantra. He didn't want to dishonor her physically or mentally. He'd dishonored her enough in the past.

"The stitches are healing nicely," Lister said. At this rate, we'll be able to remove them sooner than I thought. Make sure you check it frequently, though. We do not want another infection creeping up on us."

Aiden blinked. "That's still a possibility?" he asked.

Jane frowned at him. He looked more concerned about the thought of it than she felt.

What is wrong *with him?*

Dr. Lister smiled reassuringly, "It's a very slim possibility. I highly doubt it will happen but better safe than sorry."

Aiden nodded, slightly calmed. He suddenly remembered something else he'd been meaning to ask.

"Dr. Lister, as she moves from the bland diet to a more permanent one, what are some other foods she can start to eat?" Jane's already-present frown deepened at his question. He was taking the caretaker role above and beyond the call of duty. How was it his concern what she ate *post* bland diet? She would be out of his hair by the time that happened.

"Oh, I'll give her a list of foods when that time comes," Lister replied.

"Are you familiar with the paleo diet?" Aiden asked.

"Yes…" the doctor drawled. His tone indicated that he wasn't fond of it.

"What's that?" Jane asked. Aiden turned to her and explained.

"It's similar to a Mediterranean diet, consisting mostly of fruits, veggies, and protein. You try to cut out grain, dairy, and sugar but can basically eat anything else."

Jane nodded slowly. It sounded healthy enough. Why was Dr. Lister wary of it?

"I just wonder," Aiden continued. "If that diet might help her as her stomach adjusts to larger portions and more diverse choices."

Dr. Lister sighed, "I'm hesitant to endorse a diet that cuts out entire food groups. However, in Jane's case, the lack of gluten and dairy *could* be beneficial to her gut's response. Sugar is never recommended so eliminating that always has my approval. Just take it one food at a time. Maybe try a new one a week and see how your body responds, Jane. Make note of it and take it from there."

Jane nodded, suddenly glad that Aiden had asked. But she still wondered about his curiosity. His concern. The amount of research it sounded like he poured into the diet before bringing her to the appointment. He acted like he had a vested role in her overall well being and not just her getting back on her feet.

He loves you.

She gasped at the voice she heard. Aiden looked at her sharply. Dr. Lister frowned.

"What?" Aiden asked. "Are you okay?"

She quickly nodded. "Yeah, I'm fine. Sorry - random thought popped up."

Only it wasn't her thought. And she didn't know what to make of it.

Several hours later, Aiden knocked on the door. Jane sat up in the bed and straightened the sheets around her.

"Come in," she called. She saw his eyes light up the minute they landed on her and it made her ache inside.

"Just checking on you," he said. "Did you get some rest?"

She nodded, placing a bookmark in the book.

"Oh, I'm sorry. I didn't mean to interrupt."

She waved it off. "I was getting a little tired anyway. Don't worry about it."

He crossed the room and sat on the side of the bed, noting how she shifted. It was a slight movement but it hurt knowing she was still trying to create distance between them. Their interactions were much more pleasant since the day she apologized to him, but they were polite. They hadn't *really* talked about their relationship and he was growing anxious about it.

He glanced at the Bible she bookmarked. "What book are you in?"

"2 Corinthians," she said. "I read it already but remembered it always helps to read a text twice if you want to understand it." She shrugged. "Basic English teacher principle."

He grinned and nodded. "The letters to the Corinthians are one of my favorites. Is it the first or second one that has the love chapter?"

Her eyes lit up and she picked up the book again, flipping its pages. She scanned it quickly while he watched her openly. She pointed to it and said, "The first letter. Chapter thirteen. It's really beautiful - no wonder non-believers even reference it."

He nodded. "It rings true." *It's everything I feel for you.* If only she could see it. "You're moving through the text pretty quickly. Already reading it a second time."

She smiled. "You forget - reading is my thing. And I find it all fascinating - especially learning about the early church."

"The history of Christendom." They grinned at each other, realizing they had a new history topic to discuss.

"The church they had back then was so different than the church we see today. I was doing a little research and apparently the early churches were much more intimate. They pooled much, if not all of their resources, and relied on each other to get through periods of famine or lack." She thought about how refreshing it had to be - knowing that no matter what happened in your personal situation, you didn't have to worry - because you could rely on your "family" for support.

Isn't that what the Mastersons offered me?

She tried to figure out why this early church looked so appealing to her when she resisted the aid of a family right in front of her.

They're not rooted in Christ.

There it was again. That foreign voice that liked to answer her probing thoughts. But again, the answer rang true. The kindness of the Mastersons was limited, and sometimes even tainted, by their issues, mistakes, lies, and misguided notions. Everything the early church did was governed, according to them, by a sovereign God. And the people there were held accountable to each other *by* each other and by their leaders. There wasn't room for abuse, dishonesty or strife - not for long.

"I wish churches were like that."

"But they are," Aiden argued.

She quirked a brow at him.

"They are," he insisted. "They're not as common, especially in an individualistic society like ours but they exist. Look at the people from Redeemer who came bearing food and the willingness to clean this place. They don't just do that every now and then. They do it all the time - taking care of their brothers and sisters in Christ."

Oh my God, she thought silently.

She knew it from the way he spoke, the way he defended the modern church. The way his eyes lit up as he mentioned *brothers* and *sisters*. Even his personal study of the Bible.

"You converted," she said quietly. Aiden straightened and held her eyes. Though nervous, he didn't deny it.

"My last foster parents were Christians." Aiden blinked in surprise. He didn't know where she was going or if she would expound but he kept silent, hoping she would.

"They were really nice people. Dirt poor. But kind. They…got me the help I needed after…" she trailed off and he nodded, nothing but gentleness in his eyes.

"I didn't tell anyone when it first happened. Not even Alexa knew. She knew that he did things to me but she was too afraid to ask and I never told her." Aiden nodded, knowing his sister was much weaker then. Much more vulnerable - still a child herself.

"I didn't want it to happen to her so I tried my best to distract him," she said in a small voice. She looked away from Aiden and stared at the view beyond the windows, her eyes haunted.

"He never got tired of me. Sometimes he'd go on for hours." Aiden closed his eyes, pure revulsion washing over him at the thought. A rage unlike anything he'd ever felt coursed through his veins. He never wanted to kill a complete stranger so badly.

This isn't about you. The gentle rebuke shocked him back to attention. He was right - this wasn't about Aiden or his feelings or his reaction. This was about her. He opened his eyes and continued to listen, wondering if the haunted look in her eyes would ever fade away.

"It wasn't until some kid who'd only been there a couple of weeks blurted it out to a social worker. They asked me if it was true and I said yes. They took one sheet from his room and had all the evidence they needed."

They were silent for a moment. Aiden fought the nausea in his stomach and watched as she processed memories he could never imagine or see.

He gently asked, "Why did you keep silent? Did he scare you into it?"

She shook her head and frowned. She opened her mouth then closed it again. She did it several more times but he waited, wondering what was so heavy it was taking everything in her to say it aloud.

"I…I came," she finally said. He frowned in confusion as she met his eyes. "I came. Every time we did it. He would tell me I really wanted it because I had an…orgasm each and every time." Understanding filled him along with the sorrow of what she endured. He couldn't imagine the confusion and shame she must have felt. She confirmed it.

"I didn't know what to think. He was my first." Aiden closed his eyes again, pain racking through his chest. "I didn't know any better. I thought he was right. If I turned him in, how would I explain coming? It wasn't until I had therapy that the psychiatrist explained that it sometimes happens. It's the body's way of protecting itself. It happens in a minority of rape victims and I was a part of that minority."

He nodded. They were silent for a few moments. Jane wondered if he knew that tears were falling silently down his cheeks. She didn't want to admit it but it touched her to know that her pain somehow affected him.

A question came to his mind but he hesitated.

"What?" she said. "Ask. I'm not made out of glass."

"I know you're not. When we..." he paused. "When we...you know...you seemed to enjoy it."

"Sex?"

He nodded.

"I do," she said boldly. He blushed but smiled. "Sex doesn't bother me. Relationships do."

His smile disappeared. She continued to speak, and he grew even more sober. "People can't be trusted. Not intimately, as far as I'm concerned." She said it with such conviction it burned him to his core. He reached out and held her hand.

"Jane-"

No, she thought. *Block him out.*

"I'm sick of your martyr bullshit!" She commanded the words to her memory but to her horror, they wouldn't stick. Not when the same man who had spoken them was sitting before her, holding her hand with tears falling from his eyes on her behalf.

She started to pull her hand out of his. He held on tighter.

"Aiden." She frowned.

"Thank you for sharing this with me."

"Let me go."

"I was wrong for what I said that night."

She pulled harder but he held tighter, rubbing the back of her hand. "You're not a martyr."

"Aiden…"

"You're the most remarkable woman I've ever met. I love you."

"Aiden, stop-"

"No, I'm not done," he said firmly. "I also owe you an apology for the way I behaved before we broke up."

The words "broke up" tore at both of them unexpectedly. Jane stopped pulling and listened, curious about what he was going to say. He took a deep, steadying breath and met her eyes.

"I did not respect you when we were together. I did not honor you as a woman. I did not honor your body and for that, I owe you an apology."

Tears welled in her eyes. He was most *definitely* a Christian. His words shocked her and opened up something in her that she couldn't even begin to understand. Everything they'd done while together had been consensual and mutual but his apology for it made her not only feel convicted for her role in their relationship but respected by the man before her. She started to tremble violently and couldn't control the tears that spilled over.

He looked at her tenderly. "Jane-"

She violently yanked her hand out of his.

"Stop it, Aiden." she said fiercely. "Stop it. Stop trying. Stop apologizing. Just…stop it!"

"No."

"Let it go. Let *me* go."

"No," he repeated.

"*Why?*"

"*Because I love you!*" he cried desperately.

Silence filled the room as she held his eyes and said nothing in response.

"You don't believe me?" he challenged her.

She remained silent.

"I love you," he said once more. "Whether you want me to or not, I do."

He stood up and kissed her forehead, leaving the room to allow her more rest. After a conversation like that, she'd never felt more exhausted.

CHAPTER THIRTY

The next morning, Jane woke up early. She didn't know why but it was a pleasant surprise to discover that she was literally getting stronger with each passing day. Dr. Lister always said the recovery time would only be about a week but it was a complete turnover from how she felt the first two days after checking out of the hospital. Jane swung her legs over the edge of her bed and easily stood up. She walked down the hall to the bathroom, touching the walls to guide her way.

She was surprised to see light filtering from the living room. Had he left the light on for her to see? Or was he up already? Curiosity took over as Jane bypassed the bathroom and peeked in the living room. Sure enough, Aiden was sitting up on the couch, slumped over, elbows on his knees and eyes closed as he prayed. His hands were covering his face but she saw him rock back and forth in his seat just slightly. Suddenly, his hands came down and she got a clear view of his face, his eyes still closed. His eyebrows were drawn together in such earnest, Jane almost felt like someone intruding on a private moment.

Aren't you? she thought to herself. *He's praying. It's kind of an intimate thing.*

And yet she couldn't take her eyes off him. His beautiful face was twisted in a type of sweet agony as he petitioned God hard for something. Suddenly, his expression changed. Every bit of tension, worry, and taut anxiety eased from his face. In its place, a breathtaking smile took over as he grinned, eyes still closed, at something unseen. Someone unseen. She was captivated by the sight.

For the first time, she began to wonder if she was doing the right thing - keeping him out. He was clearly a different man than the one she'd known. It was as if his conversion took the best parts of Aiden, polished the dirt off him, and allowed him to fully shine.

I can do the same for you. The voice shocked her. Jane violently rubbed her eyes and shook her head, turning back to go to the bathroom. She was so rocked by the unexpected voice, she didn't notice that Aiden had caught her right before she turned to go. Aiden looked at her retreating back and sighed. He had no idea how long she'd been standing there and he didn't know if he liked the idea of her watching him pray.

Little did she know she was the object of his prayers.

He'd spent the past hour praying for her, her understanding of God, and the future he felt God calling them to as a couple. He could see God's hand all over her staying with him: allowing him to nurse her and help her recover, spend more time with her, and patiently woo her back. He was beginning to realize that it really *would* take an act of God for her to give him another chance. She no longer believed in relationships.

Did I damage her that badly? he wondered. An even more disturbing thought followed. *What if she's willing to give someone else a chance?* The thought induced such a sharp panic in Aiden, he had to brace himself to catch his breath. Immediately, he felt a calming wave fill him and he once again saw the image of him on the beach, holding Jane and watching their children play. He smiled, grateful for the divine reminder. Why would God move them forward and show him so much only to turn her over to someone else? Aiden shook his head at his own idiocy.

Jane was his. Whether she knew it yet or not.

His prayer required a lot of patience, as he got very few answers and very few visible changes yet. But he was grateful for clarification on one thing. He turned on his computer and began to type the first draft of what would change his life for years to come.

Half an hour later, Aiden shut his laptop and stretched. He felt even more at peace about his decision than before. Standing up, he decided to check on Jane. They no longer had bathroom arguments since she could now go by herself without assistance but he still wanted to make sure she was okay. He went into the bedroom and found the bed empty. Looking around, he called out to her.

"Jane?"

No answer.

He looked around some more, willing himself to stay calm, even as images of her unconscious on the floor assailed his mind. He began to look around the rest of the apartment before realizing there was one place he hadn't checked. He went back into the room and looked through the terrace windows. Relief flooded him when he found her standing there, in only her tank top and bottoms, fiddling with her camera settings.

Jane heard the terrace door open behind her. She braced herself to fight him on this. She wasn't ready to go in yet but she knew he could see her leaning heavily on the railing in front of her. She was determined to get the shot, though. The sun was rising at the perfect place, its warm orange rays glistening over the water and the window panes of the other buildings. It was magnificent. She felt him step up closely behind her and, despite the weather, a sweat broke out on the back of her neck at his nearness.

"Can I hold you?" he asked, his baritone voice a low rumble.

She nodded yes. She wouldn't admit it aloud, but she needed him to hold her so she could take the shot. If he could support her weight, she could use both hands to wield the camera. She didn't know how she would have gotten the shot if he hadn't come. His arms circled tightly around her and her heart stopped for just a moment. The embrace felt so familiar, so warm, it was as if her body had missed the feel of his strong arms enfolding her.

Aiden leaned forward and sunk his nose into the nape of her neck, his lips trailing the junction of her neck and shoulder. He couldn't help it. The minute he felt her waist encircled in his arms, he pulled her tighter against him, enjoying what he knew would be a brief reunion of physical contact. He hadn't held her - really held her - in three months. He didn't count carrying her in the bathroom when she'd been ill. She'd had no say then. But this time, she was willingly allowing him to invade her personal space. It was somehow more intimate than making love to her.

He closed his eyes and enjoyed the silkiness of her dark brown skin against his cheek. He heard her clicking away and smiled at her determination to remain focused.

"Why do you like photography so much?" he asked. Jane almost sighed. He had no idea how difficult it was for her to get a good shot when he held her like that. She hadn't realized that giving him permission to support her weight would equate to him nuzzling her neck and whispering against her ear. It caused something deep within her to ache. She pulled the camera down and adjusted the filter. Pulled it up to her face and shot again.

"Why?" he asked again.

"Because it reminds me that beauty exists. That it's not all bad." She turned slightly and found him looking at her, his vivid amber eyes glowing against the sun. She resisted the urge to take a photo of him. Instead, she showed him the shot she just took.

"It's beautiful," he said.

"I love sunrises. They always signify something new and something beautiful. The darkness fading away." They watched the sun silently. She wasn't taking any more shots but Aiden kept his arms fastened around her. She could feel the strong, steady heartbeat behind his tightly muscled chest.

"That's what I want for you," he said suddenly. She frowned. "I want you to see the sun."

She met his eyes and saw nothing but tenderness in them.

Instantly, she knew what he meant.

I want you to see the sun.

I want you to see the beauty of life.

I want you to see the hope and joy it has for you.

I want you to have that hope and joy...with me.

Minutes later, they returned to the room. Aiden hovered but allowed Jane to climb into the bed on her own. She'd forgotten how quickly she could tire. In a few days, she wouldn't need around-the-clock care but she would still need to take it easy before she was one-hundred percent again. She leaned heavily against the headboard and flipped through some of the shots. Smiling at what she knew would be her favorite one, Jane turned off the camera and put it aside. She looked up to find him watching her. He looked at her so intently she remembered she wasn't wearing makeup or a sleeved shirt. She suddenly felt self-conscious.

"Don't," he said. "Your skin is literally glowing with the sun on you." He looked at her in wonder. "You're stunning." She was astonished that he could sense her discomfort and discern the cause of it. She also noticed that he wasn't charming her. He didn't touch his ear with his hand or smile flirtatiously. He looked her right in the eye and said it candidly, genuinely saying what he thought.

When she didn't say anything in response, Aiden frowned and glanced down at his bare feet. He met her mysterious dark eyes and added, "I hope one day you'll forgive me."

She frowned. Did he think she was still mad at him?

"Aiden, I do forgive you. I'm sorry for not stating it but after everything you've done for me, how can I possibly hold that night against you?"

"Aren't you?" he asked.

"No, I'm not," she insisted. "I forgive you but I'm choosing not to forget. When a person shows you who they are, you believe them. How do you think I've survived?"

Her words sent a chill down his spine. He found it surreal to look at her with the glowing sun across her face, knowing the horror she once endured.

Another thought occurred to him. "You don't want a family?"

"I used to. In fact, I wanted one like yours." *I wanted one* with *you.* "But I don't anymore. If it's any consolation, it would have been with you."

He bristled. "Well, it's not a consolation - it's torture."

They were both silent.

"Jane." She looked at him. "What would it take for you to give me another chance?"

She smiled sadly and shook her head. "You'd have to be a completely new person, someone I'd never met for me to give love another shot. And even then, I couldn't give that new person a chance because the only person I'd ever want is you."

His heart shattered into a thousand pieces at the revelation. At the same time, he felt it soar in hope. "Jane-"

She shook her head and looked away. "I'm hurting us both and confusing myself. Can you please leave? I'm really tired."

He opened his mouth to say something but then closed it. He bit his lip - hard - before releasing it and leaning into her. He gently kissed her forehead, a habit she'd grown used to, and quietly said, "Okay. Get some rest. I love you."

Leaving the room, Aiden realized that it no longer stung him when she said nothing in reply. His love for her wasn't dependent on her reciprocation or lack thereof.

She was his. And he would act accordingly.

February 18th

Aiden watched while Jane packed the last of her things in her large suitcase. After a week of 24-hour care, she'd gotten the clear from Dr. Lister to continue recovery on her own. Jane felt his eyes on her but avoided his gaze as she dug in her bag for the straps to secure her luggage. The sun was high in the sky since it was mid-morning and the light flooded the beautiful spacious room. But despite the bright environment, her heart was subdued. Somber. He'd dragged her to his apartment kicking and screaming and she was leaving it with a heavy heart. She would miss this place.

You're going to miss this place *or you're going to miss* him? her thoughts nailed her.

"Why won't you move back in with Alexa?" he asked. She glanced at him and saw the same sadness in his eyes. He was the only one who would openly admit to wanting her to stay.

Jane shook her head. "I'm already settled in my place and signed a lease. Besides," she reasoned. "Alexa will be out of the apartment in less than six months. She has all of Europe waiting for her after she graduates." Jane didn't want to influence her friend to stay or delay her journey. For all she knew, she might be joining her in Europe soon. The thought was the only thing that lifted her mood slightly. Knowing that there was a possibility she could maintain her friendship with Lex.

Aiden sighed, knowing he wasn't going to win the argument. He reached into his pocket and held out a tiny envelope to her. She frowned at it questioningly.

"Your keys," he said. "I got the locks changed and threatened the super."

"You *threatened* the super?" she asked incredulously.

"Yes, I did." he said nonchalantly. "I told him if he ever gave out your key or allowed someone into your apartment *ever* again, I would not hesitate to call the police and report him to the state association of landlords."

She marveled at his fierce look of protection. She cautiously took the keys from him.

"Thank you."

He smiled tightly then turned to the dresser behind him. Opening a drawer, he pulled out another wrapped item - this one, a much larger box. He held it out to her and she frowned.

"What's this?"

"The Christmas gift I never got to give you." Her stomach dropped at the words. It felt as if she was opening a gift from a man she used to know. The old Aiden who purchased this gift for her wasn't the new Aiden standing before her. But the new Aiden seemed intent on giving it to her anyway, so she tore the wrapper open and nearly dropped the box when she saw what it held.

"Oh my God!" she gasped. He immediately smiled. "Oh my God," she repeated.

In her hands, she held a brand new Canon EOS 5D Mark III. The same camera Michael owned. She scanned his eyes in wonder.

"How did you-?"

"My dad. He said this was the best and you'd probably really like it. Do you?"

She could barely catch her breath. Her heart was still pounding in her ears. "Do I like it? Is the sky blue? Of course I like it. I love it! Thank you. *Thank you!*"

He laughed. "You're welcome."

As he watched her start to tear into the box, a child-like giddiness behind her every move, Aiden knew that he wanted to bring her that joy every day for the rest of his life. *I will,* he vowed to himself. *I will.*

Jane held the camera in her hands and enjoyed the new weight of it, the feel of its geography under her fingers. She'd held one before, courtesy of Michael, but she could barely wrap her mind around the fact that she was now holding *her own*. Beyond the haze of her excitement and surprise, Jane realized that she'd gotten it wrong. Aiden had changed but much of who he was today was always there before. The fact that he'd purchased the camera for her for Christmas, before they'd broken up; and had the forethought to ask his father because he knew she loved photography, told her something about his character and his feelings for her even before things blew up. He'd observed her. He'd done the research, and he'd spent a lot of time, and a hell of a lot of money to make her smile. She felt a tinge of regret for breaking up with him when she did. How had he felt when he saw the wrapped gift he wouldn't get to give her during the holidays?

Who breaks up with their boyfriend right before the holidays too? She cringed but shrugged it off. It was too late to rewind things and she wasn't sure if she would. Clearly everything that had gone down between them brought about the transformation she saw in him. She also noted that he *had* kept the camera for all those months - despite her actions prior to him finally giving it to her.

He'd held out hope. Hope that he would see her again.

He'd been right.

"Yoo-hoo?" a familiar voice called and knocked on the bedroom door. Alexa's pretty head popped in followed by the rest of her trim, tall figure. She'd all but forced Jane and Aiden to allow *her* to escort Jane home. Aiden watched his sister help Jane stuff the new camera into the suitcase.

"You need to get new luggage," Alexa said. "Especially if you're going to Cambridge this fall."

Aiden's heart stopped. "What?"

Jane felt apprehension rise at the look in his face. She never mentioned it to him but she had told Alexa via text.

"You didn't know?" Alexa said. "Jane got into the University of Cambridge! She's still waiting on Columbia but she's definitely getting her doctorate!"

Jane watched Aiden's golden eyes as the happy news fought with the horror that she might be leaving the country. She could also see the hurt that she'd neglected to say anything for the entire week he'd been caring for her. He was visibly upset but to her amazement, and admiration, he bit his full bottom lip once more. It was a new habit of his that allowed him to refrain from saying the first thing that popped into his head. Instead he took a deep breath, raised his worried eyes to her and managed to rasp out, "Congratulations. You've worked really hard and you deserve this."

It was the most selfless, loving thing he'd done for her and she knew it. He didn't push her to stay or guilt her about her decisions. He swallowed his pride, his plans, and his feelings to tell her that he knew how much this victory meant to her. It warmed and hurt her heart all at the same time. Alexa looked between the two of them.

"I'm gonna take this to the car," she said. They barely heard her as she lugged the suitcase out of the apartment.

Jane looked at him in wonder. "Thank you."

For the camera. For caring for her. For congratulating her. For *loving* her.

Aiden closed the space between them and touched her cheek with his large hand. She could feel the strength behind his long fingers but they caressed her skin so tenderly.

"Aiden-"

"Shh." He leaned down and placed his head against her forehead. He inclined his head and right before his lips met hers, he stopped. He opened his eyes and saw hers closed. Seconds passed before she opened her eyes again and saw a bright hope in his. He smiled at her and she smiled back, though she didn't know why.

"Thank you," she said again, fighting against the storm raging inside her chest.

"Anytime," he calmly replied, his meaning clear. Before she could respond, he pulled her into his arms and held her in a warm, strong hug. Jane couldn't help herself - her limbs moved on their own accord. He felt like shouting out in joy when he felt her arms wrap around his back in return, her hands splayed across his lean muscles. For a moment, the polite façade disappeared, and in its place, a man and a woman deeply flawed held each other.

Jane gasped against his shoulder as tears rushed to her eyes.

Oh God, she thought. *Oh my God.* A rush of joy and despair assailed her at the same time as the realization sunk into her chest. *No, no, no!* she screamed inside but it was to no avail. For the first time since meeting him, she allowed herself to admit what she'd always known deep inside.

I love you, she thought. *I love you, too.*

Aiden felt her hands tighten around his back. He could hear her breathing hitch and in that moment, he *knew* from the base of his skull to the soles of his feet. He knew. Her eyes were finally opened. *She loves me too.*

Jane pulled back first. Aiden watched her shore up her independence, like a pendant to her chest. She could barely look at him.

"I've got to go."

Be patient. The reminder was the only thing that kept him from asking her what he already knew to be true.

He nodded silently and allowed her to leave. He didn't ask when he would see her again. Common sense would have told him to but something deeper kept him. As he watched her walk down the hall and out of his apartment, Aiden kept the panic and sadness at bay. He knew he would see her again, though he wasn't sure when.

It didn't matter when, he realized, smiling.

She loves me, he thought.

She was his.

CHAPTER THIRTY-ONE

March 1st.

What if I see him? It was the only worrisome thought that crossed Jane's mind as she entered Redeemer Church. Alexa had invited her a few days ago, telling her she wouldn't want to miss it. Unlike Aiden, she hadn't minded it the last time so she decided to come. Besides, she had a thank you card she wanted Alexa to pass on to her church friends for helping her during her recovery.

"Jane!" She turned around in the sanctuary and was surprised to see Ava and Michael waving her down. Going over to their row, she greeted them both with easy hugs.

"What are you doing here?" she asked. She hoped it didn't sound rude but they were *not* churchgoing folks. Did they convert too and she just didn't know it?

Michael answered, "Well, it looks like both of our kids have found religion."

"Aiden's baptism," Ava explained.

Jane's heart skipped a beat. Not only was she *going* to see him, she was going to see him make public his spiritual decision. Alexa had invited her to be a part of that.

"Hey everyone!" Alexa entered the row and greeted her guests.

Speak of the devil.

Jane turned to her and quietly said, "You didn't tell me this was Aiden's baptism ceremony."

Alexa shrugged. "I didn't? Oh, well now you know. How are you feeling?"

Jane wanted to hit her. It was clear from her mischievous grin that she'd planned to lure Jane to the service all along, telling her it would be a special morning but not telling her *why* it would be. Jane opened her mouth to confront her but the band started playing and everyone started standing.

Once again, an atmosphere of peace surrounded the room. Alexa's parents stood respectfully silent during the worship and tried to sing along to a couple of the old hymns that were sung, but for the most part remained disengaged. Alexa, on the other hand, had both hands raised, eyes closed, and was belting it out to God. She looked so beautiful and the joy on her face was captivating to Jane. It reminded her of the joy she saw on Aiden's face the morning she saw him praying.

I want that, she realized. *I want to know how that feels.*

After worship, a young Asian woman in her twenties appeared and greeted the congregation. "Welcome to Redeemer Church. We're so glad you could be here with us this morning. If you take a look at your bulletin, a lot of you will see that today is Baptism Sunday. We do this on the first Sunday of every month to welcome new believers into the body of Christ." She turned to the elevated area of the stage a few yards behind her and Jane realized that, just below the large cross affixed to the wall, there was a built-in tub. The sanctuary was clearly designed for public baptisms. She smiled.

This is awesome.

"Pastor Teller is already in the water and our new believers are ready to be baptized so let's support them accordingly and pray." She bowed her head and gave a quick prayer of thanks for those about to be baptized and their life changing decisions. Jane realized that it was a much more personal prayer since she knew one of the people about to be submerged in the water.

As each person answered Pastor Teller's question and got submerged, Jane could tell who their family was because they almost always managed to cheer over the general crowd. It dawned on her that it was a celebration, not a quiet ceremony. And if the Christian theology was correct, Aiden had much to celebrate in his decision - so did those who loved him.

That would include you, a small voice reminded her. Her heart quickened when Aiden finally appeared and joined Pastor Teller in the water. A worker passed the pastor the mic and he spoke into it while grasping Aiden's shoulder.

"Aiden Masterson, do you believe that Jesus Christ is God, the son of God, and died and rose again for your sins?"

"I do," Aiden said without hesitation.

"Do you confess him to be your Lord and Savior?"

"I do," he said with the same confidence.

"Then by the power of the Holy Spirit," he placed the mic aside and grabbed a firm hold of Aiden, his voice yelling out the rest of his words. "I baptize you in the name of the Father, the Son, and the Holy Spirit." He helped Aiden sink back into the water and pulled him out the minute he was fully submerged. The crowd roared and Alexa and her parents' ruckus gave some serious competition in the Loudest Family Award; but even as Jane cheered, she focused - on Aiden: his face, his joy, and the unlikely decision that he'd made while they were apart. Between the two of them, she sensed that he was on a better track.

The ceremony soon ended and Aiden sat in a row with the other new believers, dried and changed, while Pastor Teller gave his sermon.

"I recognize," he began. "That a lot of you are only here to see your loved one get baptized. Many of you do not believe yourselves or if you *do* believe, you haven't made a decision to commit on the level that you just witnessed this morning." Jane felt like he was talking directly to her. "My sermon today is about trusting others."

Jane shifted in her seat, for the first time feeling a hint of discomfort.

"We live in a very individualistic society. America, over the generations, has shifted to a dog-eat-dog, 'you're on your own' kind of country. Some claim that this has always been the case since the war that called for our...*independence.*" The audience chuckled a little. "But I would like to argue that this is a relatively new phenomenon and it is increasingly disturbing. In colonial times, people were far more engaged in the lives, businesses - personal and professional - of the people in their community." Jane nodded silently, knowing this to be true. "Everyone knew about Sarah missing school or Johnny catching a cold. They knew if the Baileys needed extra loaves of bread or if Johanna Wilson would be able to sew that dress in time. Much of their entertainment focused on social events and gatherings. They didn't have TVs or movies. They had theater and town hall meetings - but even then, it was a community event and everyone was talking to everyone else." The pastor paused. "You see, in community, you are *known*, and you are accounted for. The only way to foster true community is to trust the people you are building it with."

Jane glanced at Ava and saw her hand curled lovingly in her husband's palm. They were both looking at the pastor with serious interest and she wondered what they were thinking. The pastor continued to explain how community crumbled over the years, particularly after the Industrial Revolution, and progressively over the decades leading to today.

"Now," he reasoned. "We don't really *see* each other. Let's be honest. We live in a city with several *million* other people and rarely will we engage with a fraction of the people in this town - even if we see them over and over again on the subway, in our apartment building, at work. Opportunity isn't the issue. Attitude is."

"Some of you," he got right into it. "Have trust issues. Maybe you were bullied as a child or you placed your trust in someone you thought was a friend and they turned around and betrayed you. Some of you have experienced more traumatic breaches of trust - abuse, molestation, the robbing of your innocence from the person who should have been caring for you."

Jane began to shake. She felt as if a hot light were on her and she wanted to escape. She felt a hand suddenly encircle hers and she looked to find Alexa holding it, rubbing the back of it with her thumb. The gesture was comforting and soothed her enough to stay put.

"Some of you have had things happen to you that have seriously wounded your soul. Some of you have made the vow, and maybe even did it the minute you first got hurt that you would *never* trust others again." Jane inhaled sharply. She felt as if she'd been found out. "Some of you told yourselves that in order to go on, in order to make life good again, in order to pick yourselves up by your bootstraps and overcome all the crap you've had to endure, you were going to learn your lesson and never allow anyone to get close again. Let me tell you why that doesn't work." Jane's hand gripped Alexa's tightly.

"You were made for community." He repeated it again, "You were made for community. You were made to have a trusting relationship with God and with others because that is how God designed you. Want to know who lived out community and trust in the universe first? God. The Father, Son, and Holy Spirit - one God, three persons, all hanging out together before the foundation of the earth. There was an intimate communion there and since we are made in the image of God, we too, have that wiring for community and fellowship."

Jane thought about all the years she'd been alone. She'd gone through college without friends and much of her young career was defined by being polite and tolerating others - not befriending them. She could remember the stinging sense of loneliness that almost always propelled her to think that life could be better. And it did get better, when Alexa and her family came into hers. The joy of that renewed friendship made Jane realize she really couldn't do it on her own. This thing called life.

"If you are holding back on trusting others in order to protect yourself from getting hurt, I want to tell you right now that you are hurting yourself far more than anyone could ever hurt you." Jane frowned at the strong assertion. "Let me tell you why. When you try to inoculate yourself from the pain, you end up inoculating yourself from the love and you need the love to *thrive*. You have to be willing to realize that people hurt people - good *or* bad, it's just what we do. I mean, think about how *Jesus* got hurt relationally - one of his disciples turned him in to his death! The ultimate betrayal! All of his other disciples scattered and one of them, Peter, denied him three times. You think that didn't hurt him to his core? People hurt people. Some do it more than others, some do it more egregiously than others but part of having relationships involves getting hurt, getting past it, and moving on for the prize of a healthy, loving relationship. But the pain will come. If you don't have battle scars, you didn't fight the good fight. So how do we do it? In order to trust others, you start with trusting God."

Trusting God. Jane's heart began to pound, knowing her life would never be the same after what she was about to hear.

"Failure to trust others renders your life empty. Failure to trust God shatters your life completely. 2 Samuel 7:28, Psalm 9:10, Psalm 56:3, Proverbs 3:5-6, Daniel 6:23, John 14:1. These are just a handful of verses that point to the necessity of trusting in God. Why? Because He'll give you everything you want and you'll feel happy all the time if you do? *No!* Let me tell you something right now. Trusting God is hard, hard, *hard,* hard work. But you either do it or you don't. If you do it, He will always come through. If you don't, He owes you no promises and you can worry yourself into an early grave."

Jane nodded in understanding and marveled at the timing of the message. If she had heard this last year or even a month ago, she would have ignored it completely. So much of her life had revolved around making it on her own and needing no one. But contrary to what she thought would bring her happiness and peace, the lack of community and trust left her empty at best, and depressed at worse. She was aware of the fact that the past six months had pushed her into a space of increasing trust, even as those she trusted, broke that trust again and again. With the exception of Alexa, all of the Mastersons had betrayed her at some point...and yet they apologized and sought to make amends. And their relationship was stronger. She loved them *more.*

So why have I given everyone a second chance except him? And why couldn't she relay her trust to God? She believed He existed. She believed in His Son. She didn't struggle with doubt about the Bible.

You're holding it against me. Jane sighed again but rather than run away, she decided to engage the voice.

What am I holding against you?

"Some of you are thinking, 'Okay Pastor Teller, this all sounds good and dandy, but why should I trust a God who allowed me to get abused?'" It felt like someone had poured a bucket of water over Jane. "Some of you are thinking, 'If he's such a trustworthy God, why would he endorse everything that happened to me?' Let me give you the short answer, though there are a plethora of books written on the problem of evil and the trustworthiness of God. Short answer on God endorsing your pain? He didn't." Jane's heart pounded faster. "God does not delight in the suffering of his children. He does not rejoice in the pain and sorrow that accompanies this world. He did not tell that abuser to do what he did."

I know that, Jane thought. *But He allowed it.* She realized that *that* was what she was holding against Him. Not the abuse itself but the fact that He'd allowed it. How could she trust a God who would let her go through that horror?

"God almost *never* short changes or circumvents the free will of another human being, even if it results in the suffering of another person. But He can and *does* heal the broken, comfort the wounded, and set about protecting those who turn into Him for protection - many times before they even know He does."

Like a watershed, Jane suddenly saw images flash before her mind: the social worker showing up at her door, the kid who reported what he'd heard, the transfer to a new home, the therapy sessions, her education and job, renewing her relationship with Alexa - having it in the first place. *Aiden.* One by one, she could see all the blessings in her life against the backdrop of a very difficult setting and she could actually understand what he was saying. While God had allowed those things to happen to her, He'd given her enough strength and resources to get *through* the ring of fire - then He provided her with the people and resources she needed to heal from her burns.

I want you to be completely healed.

Tears rushed to Jane's eyes. She squeezed Alexa's hand - hard. So hard that the girl turned to her in concern.

"Jane?" she whispered. But Jane wasn't looking at her. She wasn't looking at the pastor either. Eyes fixed ahead, she finally said the words she hadn't been able to bring herself to say for years.

"I believe."

Alexa looked at her and hesitantly asked, "What do you mean?"

Jane gasped in wonder and repeated, mostly to herself. "I believe." She looked at her friend and explained. "I get it. I believe."

Understanding registered in Alexa's eyes and she immediately perked up with joy.

"Really?" she gasped.

Jane nodded fervently. "I want to be His. Help me."

Across the room, neither woman noticed Aiden watching them. Tears sprang to his eyes as he watched his sister bow her head with Jane and pray. He *knew*. Somehow he knew in the center of his being what they were praying about.

She believed.

Thank you, Lord. Thank you.

She didn't stay for the end of service. In fact, she left right before communion but it didn't matter. Because not only was she closer to being his, she now belonged to the One who mattered most. That night, he had the same dream of Jane that he'd had for several weeks now: married, three kids, on the beach with the sun setting. But there were two differences: he saw greater detail as to where they were and he woke up with something else to smile about. When his eyes opened, his smile dimmed just slightly. He woke up to the Lord telling him one - albeit annoying - word.

Wait.

One Month Later

It still felt strange walking down the hall of what was once her apartment building. She still missed the place but after a couple visits, it didn't sting so much knowing that she lived in Harlem while her best friend lived in this palatial building. Jane arrived at the door and gave a firm bur friendly knock.

To her surprise, Aiden opened it.

She gasped. He smiled.

"Hi," he said. His eyes devoured her like a starving man looking at bread. He hadn't seen her since the day she prayed with Alexa.

Jane blinked in surprise and tried to get her bearings. "Hi." She stepped inside the apartment and watched him close the door.

"How have you been?" he asked.

She nodded. "I'm doing well."

She was fully recovered. Not only did the surgery stop the pain, it improved her condition. Her stomach digested food in double the time it used to. It was still slower than average but not to a debilitating or risky degree.

She glanced at her watch. "Out of the office early?"

He smiled. "You could say that."

She wondered at his mysterious reply.

"Alexa will be back soon," he told her. "She went out to get you some ice cream."

Jane laughed. "I told her it was fine."

He shook his head. "No, no, no - 'fine' isn't fine for her. She had cake batter but she remembered that you liked butter pecan."

Jane cocked her head at him. "And who reminded her?"

He gave a devilish little smile but said nothing in return. She held his gaze and smiled as well. Memories of their first date rushed back to them and the smiles faded slowly. Jane looked away and in that second, Aiden let all of his longing pour out into his eyes as he watched her. He covered it up and re-started the conversation.

"Congratulations."

She frowned at him.

"On your baptism," he reminded her.

"Oh! Thank you! And thank you so much for the editing software. Your parents told me it was your idea."

He smiled and nodded. "You're welcome. I'm only sorry I couldn't make it." He'd had something to attend to out of state that day. "New software to go with your new camera. Maybe I'll buy you a new computer and make it a trifecta."

She rolled her eyes. "Please don't. You've done enough."

They laughed at that. But the laughter soon died and they were right back where they started. Looking at each other, taking the other in. There was a new charge and energy between them - so palpable, they could almost taste it. Aiden realized it was the new reality of their relationship. They were no longer just former lovers. They were new people.

Jane waited while Aiden's gaze raked over her face before landing on her eyes.

"You're different," was all he said.

"I know," she whispered back. She was surprised that he could see it - but then, so could Alexa. Ever since giving her life to Christ and taking the leap, she now knew the peace and joy Alexa and her brother had. The broken pieces of her life were starting to make sense and the ones that didn't, she could live with because she had a greater joy to look to. She also felt an enormous relief of pressure. Trusting God came with the underestimated benefit of knowing that it wasn't all on her to figure out life - that when she gave it to Him, it became His responsibility and she was the participant in following Him. She never would have thought she'd sign up for that.

But it worked.

She smiled at the thought. Of how much she'd changed. How her whole worldview had changed. Shifting her thoughts, she noticed that Aiden was still standing there, looking at her.

"What?" she asked again.

"I miss you," he said.

She looked away. "Aiden-"

"You don't think I'm serious?" he asked.

"I find it difficult to believe," she replied. She met his eyes again. "I owe you an apology. Another one, I mean." He smiled, confused. "You're right,

I have changed. And looking back on who I was, I wonder what you ever saw in me-"

He shook his head. "Don't."

"No, I mean it. Aiden, I made you miserable. I made both of us miserable. Sure, I wasn't saved, but I was such a tough nut to crack. Why would you ever want to be with someone like me-?"

He crossed the room and touched a finger to her lip, silencing her. She looked up at him and for a second, he let it all rush to the forefront of his eyes. His hope, his longing, his sadness, his loneliness, his joy...even his desire. He laid it all out and it all equated to one thing for her: a deep, abiding love.

"I miss you, Jane." His baritone voice was husky.

They held each other's gaze for several taut seconds, growing closer and closer until he bent his head and captured her lips. A feeling of complete elation flooded Jane's heart while an overwhelming pleasure flooded her body. She gave herself into his kiss and allowed her mouth to explore his full, soft lips - lips she hadn't touched in nearly six months.

Aiden's body buzzed with the sensation of her in his arms. He somehow felt stronger, physically and emotionally, as he held her waist tightly, her hands gripping his shoulders. He reached up and cupped the side of her neck, tilting his neck to deepen the kiss. He kissed her until she couldn't stand straight, until she was leaning completely on him. He supported his weight and hers and kissed her still.

Finally, Jane pulled back, gasping for air. If a man could make love to a woman solely through a kiss, he just did it. She couldn't even look him in the eye as she took her weight off of him and stood on her own. Her eyes were fixed on the floor until she felt his finger lift her chin to meet his gaze.

There was nothing but tenderness, affection, and joy.

"You love me," he said. She gasped at his frank assessment. How did he know?

He smiled as her lips trembled and she struggled to respond. His heart soared when she didn't bother to deny it. She merely looked at him and kept quiet, clearly wondering how he would respond.

"I've been waiting for you," he said. "I've kept my distance because your relationship with Him is more important than your relationship with me." She knew exactly who he was referring to. "But it won't be long before I stop hearing 'Wait' whenever I pray."

She shivered, amazed to know that he prayed about them. That the Lord was speaking to him about her. She finally understood the source of his patience. She also remembered the verse that defined love as *being* patient.

Suddenly, the door opened behind them and they both turned to see Alexa spill in, grocery bags in hand.

"Hey!" she said. She strode over to the counter and dumped the items on top. "Jane, are you ready to-?" She stopped suddenly, looking between the two of them. "Oh my, I just interrupted something big, didn't I?"

Aiden gave Jane one last look before crossing the room and kissing his sister's forehead. "See you later, Shark Bait. Love you."

"Love you, too." she replied. Jane watched him leave the apartment without a word of goodbye to her. *He doesn't see it as goodbye,* she realized.

Her gaze shifted to Alexa, who was watching her closely. She knew her friend wanted her to spill but she was grateful for her restraint. She was still trying to process it herself. She'd *kissed* him. She shook her head to clear it and re-focused on Alexa. Her friend quietly served them both bowls of ice cream and Jane again rejoiced that she could have a larger helping than ever before. Her stomach, since the surgery and since utilizing the paleo diet, was better than it had ever been. She only used her medicine when necessary and it hadn't been necessary for over a month. They moved over to the living room couch and ate, curled up on opposite ends.

"Ready for graduation?" Jane asked.

Lexi nodded. "Ready for grad school?"

Jane shrugged. "I would be if I could turn in my final answer."

"You have until when?"

"June."

"Oh," Alexa nodded. "You still have time. Though, I wonder what you're waiting for."

Jane looked at her. "What do you mean?"

"You've been telling me since before you received admission that you were drawn to Cambridge. You talk about it twice as much as Columbia. And now you're telling me you're not sure."

"You're right," Jane quickly conceded. "I suppose I'm being full of it. The more I pray about it, the more I feel drawn to going." The thought of moving to Cambridge filled her with joy and despair at the same time. If she left, she would embark on a new life. But that life would be without Aiden. No question about it.

As if reading her mind, Alexa asked, "Is grad school the *only* thing you've been praying about?"

Jane met her eyes and said, "I know what - *who* - you're talking about. But I can't. I...I'm scared."

Lexi nodded, put down her bowl of ice cream and gestured for Jane to do the same. When she did, Alexa grabbed both of her hands and bowed her head. "Dear Lord..."

Jane smiled at her friend before closing her eyes. She'd never been one for delaying something.

"...you know how much I want them to be together," she said. "But I ask that you would make it clear to Jane what *you* want for her life and for her relationships - whether she has a future with Aiden or not - please make it clear to her. Please give her a sign so that she knows without a shadow of a doubt."

She was on a beach, with a man holding her in his arms. She leaned against his chest and felt the solid strength of his arms and chest. He held her hand - his long white fingers twisting a solid gold ring on her commitment finger - a wedding band. His finger had a solid, thicker band too. Her perspective shifted and lifted from her hand to the horizon. They were on a beach. There was no one on it. The sun was setting and it cast a beautiful glow on the water. She turned, hearing the laughter of children. Seconds later, she saw them: three kids - a little boy and two little girls with curly sandy blond hair and light brown skin. They looked like they were all under seven. One of the girls scooped up a handful of water and tossed it at her sister. She returned the favor and the kids erupted into a mini water fight, their squeals of delight ringing in her ear. She could just see them descending into a fight in a few seconds.

"Be careful, kids!" she yelled.

She leaned back into the solid chest supporting her and looked up. Jane gasped at the face staring back at her. Dark blond hair, golden tan skin, strong sharp jaw, and slight five o'clock shadow. Golden irises that glowed against the setting sun. Jane looked into Aiden's eyes and saw a look of complete adoration in them. She smiled easily and asked, "What are you thinking, husband?"

The hand that was holding hers shifted and she looked down. He placed his palm, above hers, on the peak of her swollen belly. "I'm thinking we'd better have another boy or our son will be far too outnumbered."

Jane jolted up in bed, a heavy sweat on her chest. She gasped and then cried as the vivid images stayed permanently planted in her mind's eye.

"Oh my God," she sobbed to no one in particular. Hands shaking, she reached to her nightstand and pulled out her cell phone. She could barely see the screen past her tears as she texted him.

Can we please meet this morning?

She tried to regulate her breathing, telling herself he wouldn't respond until later in the morning. It was only 4AM. To her surprise, her phone buzzed a few seconds later.

Tonight, he had replied. She was about to call and insist it be earlier but she stopped herself when she saw his follow up text: *Meet me at Alexa's tonight at seven. Trust me.*

She sighed and nodded to no one again. As she turned back into bed and tried to fall back asleep, she had no way of knowing that half an hour down town, near the edge of the peninsula, Aiden was in bed, smiling widely to no one but himself. He knew with a deep *knowing* that the charge had been lifted. "Wait" was no longer his instruction. He tapped on his phone and texted Alexa.

I need your help.

CHAPTER THIRTY-TWO

Jane walked into the lobby of the Tribeca apartment and could feel her heartbeat match the clicks of her heels against the marble floor. Her nerves were frayed as she tugged on the sleeves of her sweater in anxiety.

Finally.

After sixteen hours and forty-two minutes, she was finally going to see him. She'd spent the day pacing holes into her living room floor, chewing her nail beds raw, and wiping the dark brown skin on her cheeks red as she worried and wondered how he would respond to what she had to say. The nerves were still there, in full throttle, but so was the excitement as she made her way to the elevators.

To her surprise, Ava and Alexa stepped out of the one she was about to enter.

"Jane, hi!"

If it was possible for mother and daughter to wear the same expression, those two were. They both looked excited and over-the-moon about something and it piqued Jane's curiosity.

Ava gave Jane a quick bear hug and allowed her daughter to do the same. Jane noticed Lexi bouncing on the balls of her feet.

"Is something going on?" Jane asked. Alexa bit her lip, making Jane frown, but shook her head, her long waves jumping around her face. Jane frowned. Ava glanced at her daughter before reaching out a hand and holding the elevator door that was about to close.

"You're going up, right?" she asked quickly, as though pressed for time.

"Um, yeah. Is everything okay?" she asked. They were acting strangely.

"Everything's fine, sweetheart." Ava said, breaking out into a brilliant smile. She always looked happy but this time her face literally glowed about *something*. Jane felt her hand push her gently into the elevator. She saw Alexa bounce on her feet just a little bit higher but could barely get a word out as the doors closed.

"Bye, dear!" Ava said, waving excitedly.

"We'll see you soon," Alexa added in a strangled voice. Jane frowned at their behavior before shrugging it off. She had other things to worry about.

She leaned against the elevator wall and breathed.

Lord, please let him accept me, was all she could think.

The elevator ride was the longest she'd ever had. She stepped out on shaky legs but forced herself to stiffen her spine.

Why am I acting like this? she wondered as she all but ran down to Alexa's door. She shouldn't have been so nervous after everything they'd been through. She knew him. He knew her. She loved him. And he loved her - something he hadn't been afraid to tell her just yesterday.

For goodness sake, he'd *kissed* her just yesterday!

And yet her heart still raced as she knocked on the door.

No one answered. She knocked again and waited.

Still no answer.

"Aiden?" she called out, knocking once more. Instinct took over and she tried the handle. The door opened and Jane peeked inside before stepping in.

"Aiden?"

She barely made it across the threshold before all the remaining air in her lungs rushed out as an astonished gasp. The apartment had been transformed. She barely recognized the place she once called home. None of the lights were on. Candles illuminated the entire space in an ambient glow. The New York skyline in the windows lit whatever the candles couldn't. Hanging from the ceiling of the kitchen and living room were photos: life-sized, gallery-worthy photos of Jane, Aiden, and his family. She recognized the image of their pit stop at the gas station, Jane and Aiden on the bench in Oaks Bluff. There was even a photo of Jane by herself, on the dock, laughing at something unseen and Jane remembered - it must have been the moment she saw the "perfect" family become like every other family right before her eyes.

Aiden saw her eye the photo he spontaneously took of her so long ago. He'd never imagined using it for this very moment. She was transfixed by the scenery around her and he knew the minute she stepped in, that all of their hard work, planning, printing, and decorating during the day, was worth it. Well worth it.

He stepped out from behind one of the portraits and immediately caught her eye.

Jane looked into his beautiful gold eyes and saw nothing but gentle warmth. She opened her mouth to speak but nothing came out so she looked around again then back at him.

"Let me explain," he said cautiously, approaching her. They laughed but tears were rapidly rendering her speechless.

"The minute you texted me," he said. "I knew what He showed you."

Jane waited.

"We're on a beach-"

She gasped.

"I'm twirling a wedding band on your finger and three kids - two girls and one boy - are running and playing near the water while the sun sets. You warn them to be careful before pulling my hand to your belly, pregnant with our fourth child."

Her tears fell carelessly down her cheeks. He stepped closer to her. "Do you want to know how many times I've had that dream? Three times."

Her mouth dropped.

"Do you want to know when I first saw you in that dream?"

She nodded wordlessly.

"Eight weeks ago. Hours after I accepted Christ. The same morning Alexa called and told me you were in the hospital." Jane felt a shiver go down her spine at the words. She had no idea all of this had happened on his end. Aiden closed the distance completely and peered down into her dark wet eyes.

"Do you know what I'm about to ask you?" She shook her head, still not saying a word.

He answered, "What I've been prepared to ask you since that very night."

He bent down on one knee and the tears really started to fall. Jane's heart soared at the sight of him before her and she could see, even through her own tears, that his beautiful gold eyes were filling too. He flipped open a tiny velvet box and inside stood a sparkling, princess cut solitaire. It was noticeable but not flashy, with glittering diamonds, encased in white gold.

"Jane Daugherty, you are everything I have ever wanted in a woman, a friend, and a lover. Second to God, you are the most important, most essential part of my life. I have never loved another like I love you. Will you do me the honor of becoming Jane Masterson? Will you do me the honor of becoming my wife?"

He reached out and put a steadying hand on her waist as her cries rocked her slender body. He waited for her to respond, soaking in the beauty of the woman before him. His hand moved from her waist and traveled up to her cheek. Using the pad of his thumb, he wiped away some of the tears. She met his eyes and immediately a floodgate of peace washed over him. It soon became elation as she nodded and said the words he yearned to hear.

"Yes. A thousand times, yes."

His tears fell as he slid the ring onto her commitment finger. She shook her head and marveled at the perfect fit. He stood and pulled her tightly into his arms. For a moment, they just held each other; her nose resting against the sweater on his chest, inhaling his cologne. She felt his large hand reach down and cup her cheek. Caressing her face, he lifted her lips to meet his and they kissed. Softly, gently, chastely. The sweetest kiss they'd ever shared - because it was full of promises for things to come.

May 3rd - Edgartown, Massachusetts

It was hard to believe that she once left this island hurt, embarrassed, and - in her mind - alone. But as Jane stood in front of the mirror in her room at the town Bed and Breakfast, she knew this day would redeem her last trip to Martha's Vineyard. Ava, Alexa, the twins and the other Masterson women squawked around her, pulling at her train, adjusting the lace on her dress, fixing her veil. Her makeup was done and orders were given not to cry in front of her. She wasn't going to have it done again. Every now and then, she saw Alexa pause and look at her, clearly wanting to have an emotional heart to heart but then she met Jane's eyes and smiled, moving on to some other task.

Her maid of honor had so much to do.

As they drove in the beautiful, old fashioned town car, several people stepped out of their shops and watched the wedding procession go down the street to South Summer, where the Federated Church awaited. It was a happy blur to Jane as she was literally carried away to her future with the man she loved. She wondered when she would see this place again. When grad school started up and she and Aiden got caught up in the hustle and bustle of life, would they stop and take their kids to the island?

Surely, they would be able to since they were staying in New York.

For the first time, Jane faced a wide open future and didn't mind it one bit. She had an idea of where things were going but held that idea with very loose hands. It was all in God's hands and she would be content - with Him and with Aiden.

They arrived at the picturesque white-steepled church and made their way in. Everyone around her seemed manic, frenetic, or just downright giddy. She felt peace and joy. Her heart was as bright as the sun shining above them that morning. It was as if God was blessing their union by blessing the weather under which they'd have it. When it finally came time to enter the church, Jane glanced at the memorial of pastor names. She smiled, rejoicing in the fact that she was among good company. The men listed on that board were not just historical religious figures, but brothers in

Christ with a life mission she now shared - to serve God above all else. She turned from the board and smiled at Michael, who waited with an outstretched arm, tears visible in his gray-blue eyes.

"Ready, Dad?" she asked. His tears fell over and he nodded.

"You look breathtaking."

Breathtaking. It was the first word Aiden used to compliment her when he'd made his intentions known. And it was fitting that as she walked down the aisle and saw him raise both hands to his mouth in wonder, she knew he was thinking the same word once more. Silent tears fell as he looked at her, speechless. She truly was his breathtaking bride.

Her heart soared in gratitude at the gift of the man who stood before her. When she reached his side, she took his hand and they turned to Pastor Teller before them, ready to become one.

Four Hours Later

"Yay!!!"

Aiden felt the friendly pelting of rice as he and his lovely bride exited their reception and climbed into their waiting car. Cheers roared in their ears as all of his family, except an absent JJ, wished them farewell on their wedding night.

"Godetevi la vostra moglie!" Nonna yelled out to Aiden. Jane saw him blush vividly while the family members who understood *Nonna* laughed in visible shock.

"What did she say?" she asked as the car drove off.

The blush grew redder across his cheeks but he answered, "'Enjoy your wife.'"

She laughed at the quip and seemed completely unbothered by it but for Aiden, it triggered a fresh wave of anxiety that he'd managed to keep at bay during the entire celebration. The hour was quickly coming when they would stand before each other as man and wife and consummate their vows. How would she react?

Will she respond to me this time? Or will she shut me out again?

The thought of giving himself to her properly this time only to have her respond the same way when they were in sin was terrifying to Aiden. He'd work through it with her, of course, but just once, he wanted it to be the way God intended it to be from the start. He was her Adam and she was his Eve. And in their Garden, he wanted to experience the wonder, joy, and complete openness of being vulnerable to his wife.

When they reached their hotel room, Aiden carried Jane across the threshold and kicked the door shut. She looked up at her husband as he set her down gently. He was nervous. She could tell by the way he bit his lip and chewed on it - the same way he was chewing over something in his mind. She was about to ask him what was wrong when she saw his eyes land on the bed, something flickering in his gaze. She knew immediately what concerned him.

"Hey," she said, laying a hand against his cheek. His worried eyes shifted back to her. He looked so vulnerable, almost like a boy, and it softened her heart all the more. He was scared. Not to make love to her but to feel rejected all over again.

She wouldn't let that happen.

"You have me," she said, piercing his eyes with her own. She reached behind her and undid the ties of her dress. Aiden watched, breathlessly, as his wife disrobed right in front of him. She looked at him and nodded, clearly asking him to do the same. In seconds, they stood before each other, man and wife, completely nude.

She smiled at him in assurance and repeated, "You have me." Her hands reached out to his and placed them on her body. "All of me."

He closed the remaining space between them and quickly covered her lips with his own. His kiss was soft and thorough. It quickly accelerated from tender to fiery, his bruising lips only assuaged by his expert tongue. She attempted to catch her breath as he caught her up in his arms and carried her onto the massive bed awaiting them. He covered the terrain of her body with his hands and lips and she responded in turn, caressing, stroking, loving every inch of smooth skin covering his taut muscles.

His hand slid down to her tailbone, just above her rear, and he found her sacrum, a spot that always put her on edge. Jane gasped loudly as Aiden's fingertips pushed and rubbed the dimpled curve of her tailbone, an erogenous zone he knew would turn her on. His lips met hers again and his tongue began to explore every crevice of her mouth. He felt her hands caress the wide expanse of his shoulders, his back. Her hips undulated beneath him and he knew what she was wordlessly asking him for. He braced himself on his left forearm and reached down her body with his right hand. Feeling her readiness, he paused as his nerves once again assailed him with memories. Memories of all the times he'd given her his body but she refused him her heart.

Jane felt him falter and opened her eyes to meet his. He was looking at her with an intensity that only increased her pleasure and her desire to join with him. She also saw the fear in his eyes and was determined to destroy it once and for all. Aiden looked at her in wonder as she smiled up at him and gasped without hesitation, "I love you. I'm yours."

It was all he needed to hear. Rocking his hips forward, he joined the two of them as man and wife and allowed the tidal wave of sensation to take over. He enjoyed every inch of her and she did the same. Moving in the familiar rhythm, Jane closed her eyes and held onto his back, lifting her knees to give him greater access. She braced herself against his shoulders as he led and commanded their movement. She could hear the headboard creak against the wall and felt the budding tension build as they both climbed towards the precipice of ultimate pleasure as man and wife. She got swept away with him and he rejoiced in the woman he was joined to. He saw the pleasure claim her senses and yet she was present with him the whole way through, opening her eyes every now and then to check on him, to explore his body, to assess his pleasure. She looked up at him with such love, such open adoration, that when she finally reached her limit, he was able to dive into the pool of bliss with her - nothing held them back.

Crashing into the sheets beneath them, they gasped aloud and fought to catch their breaths.

"That was..." Aiden trailed off.

Jane nodded. "I know."

Pre-marital sex had been pleasurable. But marital sex was miraculous.

Jane curled up beside her husband and enjoyed the afterglow of their consummation. Her body buzzed with the throbbing sensation of their lovemaking.

"I love you," he whispered.

"And I love you," she replied freely. It still made his heart soar to hear the words on her lips. She stretched alongside him and he felt himself begin to stir again.

"Jane," he said warningly. Though, he didn't need to warn her. He knew they'd be back at it like rabbits in a few minutes. She smiled up at him mischievously and he grinned in reply.

Yep, they'd be back at it soon.

"We're covenanters," Jane observed.

He laughed. "Covenanters who were former consumers."

"*Were* being the operative word. We have our whole lives to do it right this time," she murmured against him.

"Yep," he murmured, pulling her closer. "Our whole lives together."

The thought alone made him smile.

"Remind me to send my notice to Columbia," she told him.

He frowned at the non sequitur. "Columbia? Why?"

She looked at him in disbelief, though enjoying the rumpled look of his sex-mussed hair. She gestured between the two of them.

"Obviously, I'm staying here."

Aiden looked at her for a few moments before getting up. He walked across the room to his suitcase and Jane whistled at the view of him in all his glory. She saw him blush slightly and smiled. He came back to bed with a piece of paper and passed it to her.

"What is it?" she asked. She looked down and started to read before gasping.

"My resignation letter," he confirmed.

She looked at the date. "Two months ago?"

He nodded. He'd resigned from the brokerage firm two months earlier, having written the first draft while she was still recovering in his apartment. "The meeting I had? During your baptism? It was to close off my remaining accounts."

Jane looked at him, confused. "Why? You don't want to practice anymore?"

He shook his head. "I was in it for the wrong reasons. Don't worry, we have more than enough to live on comfortably for years," he assured her. *For life* was more accurate. "I would still like to work in finance but for a ministry. In the U.K."

She gaped at him. "What are you saying?"

He climbed into bed beside her and made himself comfortable. Pulling her to him by the waist, he finally said, "The last time I had *our* dream, I saw a sign on the beach clearly labeled 'Frinton-on-Sea.'"

She looked at him and frowned. "So?"

"So…Frinton-on-Sea is an actual beach in Essex, just south of Cambridge; you know, the town that houses the University of Cambridge? I think you might want to send *them* your notice."

Pulling an Alexa, Jane squealed in delight and threw her arms around her husband. They kissed and kissed until the end of her and the beginning of him couldn't be determined. Joining once again as lovers, Aiden groaned in her ear, "I love my life."

She smiled at the words.

"Me too, baby." she replied breathlessly. "Me too."

The End.

Author's Note

Dear Reader:

I want to thank you for taking the time to read *Jane*. It is my hope that you were able to empathize with Jane (one of my toughest characters), but even if you weren't, I hope you were able to enjoy the journey she and Aiden took together.

As stated on the copyright page, the academic world referenced in the book is entirely fictitious and has nothing to do with the real workings of various universities, including the real universities mentioned. I also want to note that I am well aware that foster care and the social workers in it work very hard to support the well-being of children. Jane's circumstance was not a commentary on the system but merely a tool to convey her pain and the source of her flawed character.

The sermon featured in chapter twenty was heavily inspired by a sermon entitled "Love and Lust" by Dr. Timothy Keller of Redeemer Presbyterian Church. Some quotes were taken verbatim but many were summarized or created entirely by me. The general message is the same but the delivery was different and I am in no way associated with Dr. Keller or his church. If you are interested in hearing the sermon yourself, you can find it on iTunes or on the church website at www.redeemer.com.

I want to thank you for having an open mind and taking the time to escape into this work, regardless of your spiritual background. If I could rank the number one critique I often get as a writer, it is for my references to Christ in a novel that is available on the secular market. Certainly, some may find spiritual references offensive – especially if they are not ambiguous but I am a believer and I am a writer; I will check neither aspects of my identity at the storytelling door. I believe I have the right to express them in the public forum like any other author, without being hemmed in to the Christian fiction niche.

If you enjoyed the story, **please take the time to write a review and let me and other readers know what you thought of the book.** Unless you're J.K. Rowling, the royalties from a book don't mean nearly as much as the feedback of the person who took the time to read it. I do read the reviews and it warms my heart to see the encouragement! Please also stay in touch. Join my Facebook page to stay in the loop (www.facebook.com/authormichelleonuorah). If you want to be notified of new releases, go to http://tinyletter.com/mnomedia Please also feel free to explore my other work via my Amazon page or my website: www.mnomedia.com.

Also, if you are a non-believer and are curious to learn more about Christ, please feel free to visit my website or contact me directly. I am more than willing to share ☺

Sincerely,
Michelle

The MNO Media Challenge

Stories are powerful. If you liked this novel and think that others would benefit from reading it, regardless of their background, please consider the MNO Media Challenge by:

1.) Writing a review on Amazon, Goodreads, and Barnes & Noble.
2.) Recommending it to people in your inner circle – family and friends.
3.) Purchasing copies of this book and other MNO Media titles as a gift for others.

Stories can impact lives and with your help, a bigger impact can be made. Thanks!

Remember Me

CHAPTER ONE
Prologue

January 1st

"Ahh - get it! Get it, Caleb!"

The little boy with butterscotch skin quickly shot his rifle at the Terminator advancing towards his mother's video game character. He smiled up at his mom and watched in awe as she shot several other terminators in quick succession, all with a look of sheer excitement on her face.

"Take that, you evil monster! Ooh, a grenade!" Kristen aimed her remote at the gaming weapon and loaded up for the journey ahead. As she and her son played the Terminator Salvation video game, everyone else at Chuck-E-Cheese disappeared to them. They had laser focus on the screen in front of them, not even realizing their game had attracted the attention of several kids as well as parents.

Mark smiled as Kristen shot exuberantly at the screen. His wife always did have a way of garnering attention - whether it was at Chuck-E-Cheese or the studio at ABC. His smile dimmed a bit. It was a bitter reminder of her upcoming trip, scheduled only two days after their son's birthday.

She'll be fine, he tried to tell himself. *She's traveled before for special reports. She'll be careful and will return to us in four days. She'll be fine... But did it have to be Afghanistan of all places? Lord, please keep her safe.*

So deep in his thoughts was he that he nearly jumped at the feel of her arms wrapping around his waist.

"You okay?" Kristen asked in concern. He looked down at her and smiled.

"Yeah, I'm fine."

Kristen knew he was lying. She could tell when he was worried even when he tried his best to hide it. And she knew it was because of her upcoming trip. There were numerous things she loved about her job as a reporter - traveling used to be one of them. Now, it was becoming a dreaded aspect of her popular news show. She had traveled to all of Western Europe, much of Eastern Europe, India, China, South America, several nations in Africa from her ancestors' Nigeria to Tanzania, and even North Korea. She knew it was a rare privilege to say she had visited most of the world; but as she got older and her family grew larger, she knew that it was taking a toll on them all, particularly her husband.

She looked up at him and openly admired his chiseled jaw. Mark was tall, lean, and strikingly attractive. At six feet, four inches, he had a body that could easily bulldoze over anything in its path but he was graceful in all of his movements. He had thick dark brown hair that matched his dark brown eyes and his face was arranged with such symmetry and precision that Kristen often thought *Lord, you did good.*

His brows were creased in a worried frown again.

"Honey-"

"Mom, can we go now?" an impatient teenage voice asked. At fifteen, Jasmine was horrified at the idea of spending part of her holiday at Chuck-E-Cheese. When they'd first adopted her at six-years-old, she couldn't get enough of the place; but she had long since outgrown the center and was beyond done with the screeching children running around in obnoxious circles. Mark and Kristen looked at their eldest and were surprised to see that she had already read through the second novel she brought to the party. It had been three hours since they first arrived and they too were ready to leave.

"It's up to your brother," Mark said. "It's his birthday party."

"He's ready to cash his tickets," Jasmine replied.

"And Kylie?"

"YEAH!!!!"

All three heads whipped over to Kylie's exuberant cry. Worried expressions quickly dissolved into shock as they watched their four-year-old daughter jump up and down in the pile of tickets that flowed freely from the "lottery" machine. Caleb rushed up to them.

"Kylie won! She won ten thousand tickets!"

Kristen surmised, "Yeah, I think she's ready to cash hers out too."

The ride home was a happy one. Mom, Dad, brother and sisters couldn't stop chattering about Kylie's good fortune. The little girl was still grinning from ear to ear as she held tightly to the new Barbie doll her tickets had afforded her. The Barbie house and car were sitting in the trunk. Caleb was admiring the G.I. Joe his sister had been kind enough to get for him. Jasmine was busily recalling the look of horror on the management's faces at the sight of all those tickets…and the merchandise they had had to cough up in return.

"Mom, do you have to go?" Caleb suddenly asked.

Kristen sighed. It was the elephant in the car, and the house, and the party that everyone had tried to ignore. It was getting bigger each day her date of departure drew closer. For some reason this particular location was causing triple the anxiety. She glanced at her husband's profile and saw a muscle tick in his jaw. He kept his eyes on the road. She looked back at her three "babies" scrunched together with saddened expressions.

"We've gone over this, you guys. I'll be back in less than a week."

"But why does it have to be Afghanistan?" Jasmine asked, echoing Mark's earlier thoughts.

"That's where the wa—" she caught herself at Caleb and Kylie's expressions, "—the story takes place. It makes no sense for me to go to a different location if the story isn't happening there."

"I thought the war was ending." Jasmine said, refusing to censor herself for her siblings. Her mother glared at her but answered nonetheless.

"It is - which is why we're going. To give updates on how that's moving along and how the troops that are still there are doing."

She could see the concern etched on every single face in the car.

Kylie's small voice piped up, "Can we pray about this?"

"Again?" Kristen asked.

"Why not?" Jasmine countered. "You can never pray too much."

Kristen caught Mark grinning out of the corner of her eye.

She shrugged. "Touché. All right, let's pray."

She reached out her hands and watched as the kids linked up and bowed their heads. Mark kept his eyes on the road but glanced back at the rear view mirror, listening closely to his wife's prayer. When she finished her thoughts, each child took their turn and asked the Lord to protect their mother. They finished with a resounding "Amen!" and Kristen turned back around in her seat.

"Mom?" Caleb asked softly. She turned to him again. "You promise you'll be back soon?"

She smiled and said, "I promise."

Mark drove with one hand on the wheel and reached over to his wife's lap. He gently squeezed her leg before finding her hand and holding it in his own. She smiled at him and met his eyes. Their children had no idea what had just passed between them but it was the agreement of two lovers who were eager for their kids to go to bed.

Thankfully, they didn't have to wait long. The adrenaline of the win began to wear off and the birthday boy, exhausted from running around Chuck-E-Cheese, was soon ready for bed. Kylie's eyes were already drooping and Jasmine had resolved to get her "beauty sleep."

The minute Kristen securely tucked in their youngest, Mark took hold of her waist and swooped her up in his arms like a hat box. Kristen laughed.

"Wow, someone is eager tonight."

"You have no idea."

Fully satiated, Mark rolled over onto his back and pulled Kristen into his side.

"How long are you going to be gone?" he complained. She chuckled and stroked his chest softly.

"It's only four days. I'll be back before you know it."

CHAPTER TWO
Loss

March 15th – Two Months Later

Somewhere in the land between consciousness and slumber, Mark smiled, eyes closed, as he reached out to her side. He turned over as if to capture her beneath his arm and then woke up with a start at the feel of empty sheets.

He was awake.

The smile disappeared as he opened his eyes to the confirmation of what was not there. On the nightstand next to his wife's side of the bed stood the lone photograph of her in her wedding dress, smiling into the camera with a look of sheer joy. He reached out and pulled the frame to him. He caressed the lines of her cheek, the curve of her eyebrows with the very tips of his large fingers. It had become a sort of ritual to him; a way to comfort himself every time he woke up to the reminder that she wasn't there.

He sat up in bed, his hands still clinging to the frame. He glanced at his own nightstand and grimaced. The cards were stacked neatly in the order received, all from family and friends. He had yet to open the cards from the President, other dignitaries, or any of her fans - most of those were held in storage, waiting for him to retrieve them when he was ready. He looked at her photo again and like clockwork, that horrible day came shooting at him all over again.

The kids were scrambling around the house like that of a crew on a ship. Mark, their captain, issued orders on what chores needed to be done and what chores they could check off as complete.

"Okay, the upstairs bathrooms are done, the living room looks clean, you guys already did your bedrooms, so now we have to tackle the kitchen."

Jasmine groaned. "Oh, that's going to be fun."

"You want it to look nice for Mom, don't you?" Caleb pointed out.

"Let's do it!" Kylie declared with a grin on her chubby cheeks. Mark smiled at his youngest and led the charge.

For the first hour, they ignored the phones. So wrapped up were they in getting the house ready, they completely zoned everything out. But as they stopped to take a break, Mark noticed that the ringing wouldn't stop. He looked at the caller ID as the last call dropped off and saw that the caller had rung three times in a row. He pulled up the log and frowned at several other numbers that had called in repeated succession. Even more disconcerting were the caller names: all of them were from family and friends on both sides; the most frequent call was from the ABC producer in charge of Kristen's reporting special: Lance Carson.

He dialed Lance's number, stepped out onto the deck and pulled the phone up to his ear. Lance answered after the first ring.

"Oh, thank God! Mark, is that you?" a panicked Lance exclaimed.

"Yes, it's me. Lance, are you okay?"

There was a moment of silence on the other end.

"Hello?" Mark repeated, *"Lance, are you okay?"*

"You haven't heard yet," Lance stated in an eerily quiet voice.

Mark's heart dropped. Kristen. He tried to stay calm and kept his voice level.

"Heard what?" he asked. *"What happened?"*

Suddenly, he heard a rapping on the deck door. He turned around to see his and Kristen's friends, Reed Smith and Dierdra Cole, standing just inside the deck. He frowned at them in confusion. Why were they there?

"Lance, hold on."

He quickly reached the door and pulled it open. Almost immediately, he felt Dierdra enclose him in her arms.

"You haven't told the kids yet. Are you okay?" she asked in near tears.

He looked down at her with a perplexed expression. He glanced at Reed and told them both:

"You guys are scaring me. What happened?"

Their mouths dropped at his question. Mark pulled the phone back to his ear.

"What happened, Lance? Just spit it out."

"It's Kristen," he said without preamble. Mark sat back down on the deck step. "There's been an accident with the crew. Some sort of explosion and we've lost contact with the entire team."

If it was possible to feel all the blood escape from one's heart, Mark felt this was the moment it was happening. He heard a slight ringing in his ears and his palms began to sweat. His breathing was uneven, shallow, and he had to close his eyes to regain any semblance of concentration.

Father, no. Please, no. Not Kristen…

"Mark…?" He lifted the phone back to his ear. "Mark, nothing has been confirmed yet. I just wanted to tell you. Please, keep calm. We're going to get to the bottom of this and find out what is going on. Keep the kids away from the TV."

Mark nodded, although he knew Lance couldn't see him.

"I'll be here," he replied quietly. Lance hung up.

He could feel the eyes of both friends on his back. He stood up on shaky legs and turned to face them. Dierdra's tears had long since fallen. Reed looked at his friend helplessly and said:

"The kids are in Jasmine's room. We got them all to watch a movie."

Mark nodded in appreciation and walked past them into the house again, as though in a trance. He went to the living room, pulled the remote and turned to CNN. In bold letters, the headline appeared:

"KRISTEN TYVERSON AND ABC NEWS CREW MISSING IN AFGHANISTAN EXPLOSION."

Kristen's picture along with various reels of her past reports played on the corner of the screen while in the center, above the headline, footage showed the wreckage of the explosion site. Remnants of a large tankard burned on the wide dirt road as several soldiers and civilians scrambled around it. The reporter reappeared on the screen.

"For those of you just joining us, it has been reported that the vehicle carrying ABC World News anchor, Kristen Tyverson, and the film crew along with her, has exploded. Tyverson and six members of ABC news team, escorted by two soldiers, were in the middle of surveying civilian sites. Authorities have not released word on the status of any survivors. Details are unclear as to

whether all members of the team were in the vehicle. Authorities are still trying to tame the flames and explore the wreckage."

The ringing returned to Mark's ears as he sat on the coffee table Kristen had chosen for the living room. He was dimly aware of Reed turning off the TV. He barely felt his friend grasp his shoulder. He could barely make out the words in his friend's prayer.

The rest happened in a blur. The same day Kristen was supposed to return home, authorities spent it digging through the wreckage and confirming the deaths of all those aboard. They did not find her body amongst the remains but made an official announcement presuming the deaths of all those who were a part of the reporting team. Accompanied by Lance Carson, two men - one in a military uniform, the other, a police uniform - offered Mark their condolences and left him the last of her effects. Mark would never forget the looks on his children's faces as he told them the news. Each of them responded differently. Kylie wailed in anguish, her small face crumpled in defeat; Caleb ran to his room and refused to open his door for hours. Jasmine quietly cried her grief. With Reed and Dierdra's help, Mark managed to pull them together and comfort them. A week later, they held a private memorial and funeral for Kristen and watched as ABC organized a public, televised memorial.

Present

Mark shook his head and tried to get the images of that time to disappear. It had been more than two months since her passing and he felt the same way he had the minute he'd received Lance Carson's call. He looked down at her portrait. The thought of her body gone, nonexistent, so completely obliterated by a blast that he didn't even have remains with which to bury...

Just two months ago, he had held her in his arms and made love to her. Just five years ago, he had watched her give birth to their daughter. He sometimes wondered if the authorities had been too quick to presume her dead. When he'd first received the notice, he looked for every possible alternative to her being inside of that tankard, especially when they hadn't found her remains. But they had gently reasoned that an explosion like that could vaporize any individual and that some of the crew remains were as little as twenty percent. At her funeral, they arranged a small grave and buried some of her possessions from the trip.

He picked up a card and tore the envelope open. From a distant relative, it simply read Revelation 21:4.

"...and He shall wipe away every tear from their eyes; and there shall no longer be any death; there shall no longer be any mourning, or crying, or pain; the first things have passed away."

A tear slipped down his cheek. And then another. And another. Something rumbled out of his throat from deep within; a cry of loss, loneliness, and shock. He dropped the card and folded the frame to his chest.

Hunching over, he wept.

March 15th - Afghanistan

She woke up with a start. The nurse in attendance had rudely shoved her awake. As Kristen stared up at the Afghan woman ordering her about in her native tongue, Kristen could do nothing but look at her in bewilderment.

"I'm sorry but I don't understand you."

She knows I can't understand a word she's saying. Why does she insist on bothering me before the translator gets here?

To her relief, the young Arab woman in her twenties strode into the ward and spoke to the nurse in their native language. The nurse gave her instructions, glanced at Kristen in annoyance, and left the cot without hesitation.

"Sorry, I'm late," Alima whispered. "How are you feeling?"

"Sore," Kristen replied. "Stiff. Still a bit weak."

"Your muscles have atrophied. Not severely but enough for you to notice a difference."

"How long have I been out again?"

Alima looked at her chart. "You were brought in on the eighth of January. The man who brought you here said you'd been unconscious for a day. You were in a coma from January eighth until February twenty fifth. It's now the fifteenth of March so you've had about three weeks of consciousness."

Kristen remained silent. Alima watched her closely.

"You still can't remember?"

Kristen shook her head.

"Well, you know your name." Alima pointed out. "That's a start. You know where you're from-"

"I just don't know how I got *here*." Kristen interrupted, disturbed. "I've never been to Afghanistan. The only places I've ever been abroad have been in Western Europe. What was I doing here? Where is my family?"

What year is it? Kristen thought the question but was too afraid to ask. She could read the concern in Alima's eyes and knew her memory loss was no joke but she didn't want to know the full extent of it yet. The last thing she remembered was celebrating her job appointment with her mom. She could still remember the disorientation when she first woke up, surrounded by strange faces, all of Middle Eastern descent. The air around her was hot, an arid heat she had never known before; as if it were two seconds away from emitting flames out of thin air. Her muscles had felt weak, her jaw stiff. Even worse, she couldn't speak the language with which the uniformed doctors and nurses were trying to communicate. For the first two weeks, Kristen survived on gestures, paying close attention to the pantomime of her caretakers as they helped her rehabilitate her stiff, wasting muscles. Both sides had learned rudimentary phrases to make the adjustment slightly easier.

When Alima had finally arrived, Kristen had almost cried for joy. But in that time, her presence there had only deepened the mystery. With no identifying documents or personal effects, the local clinic had no idea what to do with Kristen, short of treating her. The mysterious man who brought her in while she was unconscious had disappeared, leaving no contact information behind and Kristen could remember no such man. Even as Alima worked to get her out of the country, a screening process had to be followed, which included confirming her identity and ensuring she was well enough to travel. Given her atrophy and the physical effects from her injuries, the clinic's main priority was to treat Kristen to the best of their ability. That in and of itself was difficult because the clinic had the setup of a 1940s war hospital, with cots lined up back-to-back and no privacy to be found.

Kristen thought of her mom. Alima had tried to contact her via the number Kristen provided but the line was disconnected, confusing Kristen even more.

I need to go home. She'll help me piece the puzzle together.

"I need to get out of here," Kristen said. Alima looked back down at her charts.

"Alima, I've been here for three weeks doing physical therapy. When can I go home?"

"That's the problem, Kristen. I believe that you are an American citizen. You have the accent and everything but we can't find your passport or any evidence that you belong abroad."

Even worse, they could not find records of a "Kristen Johnson" ever having entered the country.

"Then what is the procedure?" Kristen asked.

"There are several documents that need to be processed. It's easier if you have an organization to leave with...which is why I'm having you transferred."

"What?"

Alima smiled. "Surprise. I found a local Red Cross stationed four miles away. They've agreed to take you. You'll have better treatment and an easier time communicating. You won't have to rely on a translations intern to get by. You can also get the travel clearance you need if they approve you."

Kristen closed her eyes in gratitude. She felt weak and drained and she had only woken up a few minutes ago but she was grateful. Grateful that she could soon get out of there and get to the bottom of everything that had happened.

It felt like months to her but five days later, Kristen found herself entering a new medical ward. This one was much cleaner with more space and advanced equipment. There were a variety of patients, mostly local civilians, who were receiving treatment. For once in over three weeks, Kristen was able to communicate seamlessly with several staff members, all of whom spoke English. She noticed that a couple of them took second glances at her and one even froze in astonishment but quickly recovered their expressions. She shrugged off the reactions as simple placement issues. How often do you see an African American woman walking around in Afghanistan in casual clothing? She knew she stood out.

She waited in a makeshift room drawn of nothing but standing curtains. After nearly an hour had passed, the curtain drew back and in walked a tall man with light brown hair and friendly blue eyes; those eyes became saucers the minute he saw her. His eyes swept over her in shock.

"I can't believe it," he whispered. "You survived. You actually survived."

She frowned at his familiar tone. "You know me?"

He nodded and said with a slight frown, "Reed Smith. Friend of the family."

She frowned at this but didn't argue. She had never met him before but she knew her mom had several friends she hadn't been introduced to yet.

"I'm a Red Cross medic out here for a mission. I honestly didn't believe them when they said you were here. Kristen, everyone had presumed you dead."

"My family thinks I'm dead?" Kristen asked.

"There was a funeral service and everything. How did you survive it?"

"Survive what?"

"The bomb. I'm assuming you were near it when it went off."

"That would explain the coma."

He looked down at her chart and nodded, finally understanding.

"I see you have some memory issues."

She nodded. "I know who I am and where I'm from. I just don't remember how I got here."

Reed nodded. "With an explosion at that close range, it's a miracle you're alive, much less with most of your memory intact. It's normal not to remember the moments leading up to your accident."

His mouth was poised to ask another question when the curtain ripped open and a young medic appeared.

"Excuse me," he told Kristen. He turned to Reed. "You're needed in ward four. Emergency amputation."

Reed immediately stood up. He promised Kristen he would return. Several hours elapsed before he did and by then, they only had time for a brief conversation. He initially wanted to contact her family and alert them of her safety but Kristen, in a burst of spontaneity, begged him not to.

"Are you crazy?" he asked. "Kristen, your family has been mourning your death for months. Don't you want to put them out of their misery?"

Her family consisted of her mother and distant relatives she had only met once in a blue moon. *He must mean my mom and close friends,* she thought. Well, as far as she was concerned, her friends could wait. Her mom, she wanted to surprise. She could only imagine the look on her face when she realized her daughter was actually alive. So she insisted and eventually, Reed complied.

In five days' time, though they barely spoke to each other between his other responsibilities and her physical therapy, Reed managed to arrange for Kristen's travel clearance. They left together in a Red Cross-appointed helicopter, returning to the States without any fanfare or struggle. When they arrived on U.S. soil, Kristen allowed Reed to do all of the paperwork and all of the talking. Landing on a private airfield helped the process immensely.

CHAPTER THREE
Reunited

March 25th

Kristen could hardly contain the excitement coursing through her body. After her ordeal, she was relieved to finally see the familiar surroundings of Atlanta, Georgia. As Reed drove past the city structures and into the suburban part of town, she began to imagine the expression on her mother's face when she realized that she was alive. Sure, she'd probably smack her once she learned of how long Kristen had kept it a surprise and she would probably call her daughter out for being so selfish but Kristen couldn't help but see for herself the shock and relief that would cross her mother's face.

Kristen thought it odd that they were driving into Buckhead – the most affluent part of town. Did he have to make a stop before taking her home? Reed entered a quiet subdivision that she didn't recognize but it wasn't until he pulled up to a large, brick-front house that Kristen voiced her confusion.

"Where are we?"

Reed looked at her, a slight look of confusion crinkling his eyes.

"Your home." Before she could respond, he slid out of the car and opened her door.

"Come on, let's see your family."

They made it half way across the lawn before the door burst open and a tiny, little biracial girl sprinted out of the house and into Reed's arms.

"Uncle Reed!"

"Kylie! How's my little munchkin?" But Kylie had stopped listening. She froze stock still in Reed's arms as she looked over his shoulder. An older biracial girl in her teens crossed the threshold, a look of irritation and worry mingled on her face.

"Kylie, how many times have I told you not to just burst out of the hou-"

She stopped mid-sentence, staring at Kristen, eyes wide. A shorter boy with cafe-au-lait skin appeared beside her.

"Mom?"

Kylie had recovered. She shoved herself out of Reed's arms, landed on her feet and sprinted over to Kristen.

"Mommy!"

The boy and teenage girl quickly followed. They embraced her as if she were life itself. Kristen stood still as the children invaded her space and grabbed at her waist.

Kristen frowned at Reed in confusion and Reed's smile slowly disappeared. Why was she reacting this way? He looked closer at her and the realization slowly started to take shape.

"What's going on out here?" a deep, baritone voice called out. The teen pulled back from Kristen a fraction of an inch and turned to the brown haired, brown-eyed man at the threshold.

"Dad, she's alive. She's alive!"

But he had already registered that. A look of complete astonishment was written on his handsome face as Mark crossed the lawn. He didn't know that his feet were running. He didn't know that Reed stood on the lawn. He could barely register the tears that blurred his vision and ran down his cheeks.

His children parted slightly from their mother's form as he reached her and drew her tightly into his arms - so tightly, she felt as though her ribs were about to break. His hands reached up to cup her face as he bent down and kissed her soundly on the lips. Only when she yanked back, eyes wide, did he and those around him snap out of it.

Kristen looked at the people in front of her in horror before turning her gaze to Reed's.

"Where is my family? *Who are these people?*"

Like the sample?
Find out what happens next by ordering *Remember Me*.
Available Online

Check out these other titles by Michelle N. Onuorah:

Remember Me
Type N
Taking Names
Wanna Be on Top?

Acknowledgements

I want to thank Dr. Victoria Oshodi for undertaking the daunting task of editing this novel. I would also like to thank Karla Henderson and Marcia Walkerdine for serving as my beta readers. All of you were invaluable to the development of this novel.

About the Author

Michelle N. Onuorah is the bestselling author of *Remember Me, Type N, Taking Names, Double Identity*, and *Wanna Be on Top?* Originally from Maryland, Michelle grew up with a love of storytelling. She wrote down some of her stories in a notebook and continued to write for fun. At the tender age of thirteen, she wrote her first book, *Double Identity*, and got it published the next year. For three years, she ran an independent magazine, *MNO*, and served as the main writer and editor-in-chief. In 2009, Michelle won the *Captured Moments Creativity Award* for her poem entitled *Encounter*. Her writing has appeared in *Vestiges Literary Magazine, Avalon Literary Review*, and *Medium.com* among others. Michelle also enjoyed a successful career as a model in her teens, walking down runways during New York Fashion Week. In August of 2013, Michelle broke several of Amazon Kindle's Bestsellers lists for her debut novel, *Type N*. The following year, she enjoyed another bestseller with the well-loved romance, *Remember Me*. A graduate of Biola University, Michelle continues to write and publish under her company, MNO Media, LLC (www.mnomedia.com). You can learn more about Michelle at the website as well as like her page at www.facebook.com/authormichelleonuorah. Those interested in being notified of her new releases can go to www.tinyletter.com/mnomedia.

Big momma 1971 - pressware

Big momma 1971 (empire)

CPSIA information can be obtained at www.ICGtesting.com
Printed in the USA
LVOW07s0826060915

452957LV00012B/725/P

9 780692 373262